JACK HIGGINS

THREE
COMPLETE
NOVELS

ALSO BY JACK HIGGINS

On Dangerous Ground
Thunder Point
Eye of the Storm
The Eagle Has Flown
Cold Harbour
Memories of a Dance-Hall Romeo
A Season in Hell
Night of the Fox
Confessional
Exocet
Touch the Devil
Luciano's Luck
Solo
Day of Judgement
Storm Warning
The Eagle Has Landed
The Run to Morning
Dillinger
To Catch a King
The Valhalla Exchange

JACK HIGGINS

THREE COMPLETE NOVELS

The Last Place God Made

The Savage Day

A Prayer for the Dying

G. P. PUTNAM'S SONS   NEW YORK

G. P. Putnam's Sons
Publishers Since 1838
200 Madison Avenue
New York, NY 10016

Library of Congress Cataloging-in-Publication Data

Higgins, Jack, date.
  [Novels. Selections]
  Three complete novels/Jack Higgins.
    p. cm.
  Contents: The last place God made—The savage day—A prayer
for the dying.
  ISBN 0-399-13992-3
  1. Indians of South America—Brazil—Fiction. 2. Air pilots—
Brazil—Fiction. 3. Violence—Northern Ireland—Fiction.
I. Title.
PR6058.I343A6   1994b   94-9383 CIP
823'.914—dc20

Printed in the United States of America
1   2   3   4   5   6   7   8   9   10

CONTENTS

INTRODUCTION

For many years writing was a part-time occupation for me. I left school at fifteen, and tried a variety of jobs—labourer, truck driver, even circus roustabout. Service in the Royal Horse Guards ended with my returning to a rather unsatisfactory life, again taking on a number of jobs until I finally went to college at twenty-seven, received a double honours degree in social psychology and sociology, and entered the academic world.

I had my first book published when I was thirty, and from then on, under many names, I produced a string of detective stories and thrillers, but always as a spare-time occupation. While I was working training teachers at Leeds University, my book *The Violent Enemy* was filmed. The money from this gave me a breathing space that meant I could manage for three or four years, so I left the university and started my life as a full-time writer.

My mother was a Higgins, and I was brought up by her family in Belfast; as a boy I was plunged headfirst into the Irish Troubles. Although an Orange Protestant, I lived for a while with a Republican Catholic aunt; that explains the accuracy of the backgrounds, both political and religious, in what I think of as my Irish books. The original Jack Higgins, my great-uncle, was an Orange Protestant gunman in his day; I ran from my first bomb at the age of seven. My mother and I came under sniper fire in a tram in Belfast when I was ten, and she still, at eighty-six, proudly tells of how she lay on top of me to protect me.

All this has produced a strange ambivalence in my attitude to the Troubles. I have a foot in both camps: I have sympathised deeply with Roman Catholics, who have been treated very badly. I have been, if you like, a Protestant Nationalist, a Republican by belief. Nothing strange in that. From Wolfe Tone to Charles Parnell, many Protestants have espoused the Republican cause. None of this means that I approve of ruthless brutality or of the bomb that slaughters the innocent, and my books dealing with Ireland have made this point strongly. Take Liam Devlin of *The Eagle Has Landed* fame: poet, scholar, gunman, and proud soldier of the Irish Republican Army, but he makes it very clear that he will have nothing to do with indiscriminate bombing campaigns.

So, to *The Last Place God Made*, the first book in this volume. It was here that I introduced what I call a theme of importance into my work: in this case, the genocide of the Indians of the Brazilian rain forest. The action involves a young English pilot and an American ace, a World War I veteran, flying mail in ancient biplanes along the Amazon River in 1939.

I changed publishers in England with this book. The editorial director of my new publisher told me that I was a good thriller writer, slightly better than average. "Don't let it go to your head," he warned. I wasn't too happy with his attitude, but the publisher had a reputation for selling books, and proved it by pushing me up from three thousand copies to eight thousand.

I was over the moon. I searched for a new idea, the bit between my teeth, and came up with *The Savage Day*, my first thriller set in Ulster during the present Troubles. I put all my family background, all my feeling for Ireland into that book. The publisher was not happy, as the Higgins technique of treating everyone on both sides as a human being gave the impression that I was perhaps being kind to the IRA. The public, however, took the book to heart. It was serialised in newspapers all over the world and has been reprinted numerous times.

In my next book I asked an intriguing question. What if you were a soldier of the IRA, an educated, intelligent man who believed in your cause—until, that is, a bomb intended for British soldiers instead blew up a bus full of schoolgirls? Where would you go? Where could you hide from yourself? So was born *A Prayer for the Dying*, with Martin Fallon on the run from his past and tragically drawn back into violence by gangsters who need his special skills. The book was made into a movie with Mickey Rourke as Fallon, Bob Hoskins as the priest da Costa, and Alan Bates as the gangster Meehan. The film generated enormous controversy. Bob Hoskins told me that in spite of everything he felt they'd made a cult movie. He was right. *A Prayer for the Dying* is now in the repertory of the National Film Theatre in London.

An endpiece: The book that came after was *The Eagle Has Landed*. When the editorial director who had told me that I was a bit better than average asked me what the book was about, I said: "It's 1943, Winston Churchill is spending a quiet weekend in Norfolk, six miles from the sea, and German paratroopers disguised as Poles in the British SAS drop in to seize him." The editorial director was horrified. "What a terrible idea," he said. "Where are your heroes? Your readers won't be able to identify with a bunch of Nazis." I tried to explain that I was writing a new kind of war story. That good men could find themselves fighting for a rotten cause. He simply didn't understand. Eighteen years later, and *The Eagle Has Landed* has been filmed, book-clubbed scores of times, translated into forty-four languages.

The Last Place God Made

And this one for my sister-in-law, Babs Hewitt,
who is absolutely certain it's about time . . .

1

Ceiling Zero

When the port wing began to flap I knew I was in trouble, not that I hadn't been for some little time. Oil pressure mainly plus a disturbing miss in the beat of the old Pratt & Whitney Wasp engine that put me uncomfortably in mind of the rattle in a dying man's throat.

The Vega had been good enough in its day. Typical of that sudden rush of small high-winged, single-engined airliners that appeared in the mid-1920s. Built to carry mail and half a dozen passengers at a hundred or so miles an hour.

The one I was trying to keep in the air at that precise moment in time had been built in 1927 which made it eleven years old. Eleven years of flying mail in every kind of weather. Of inadequate servicing. Of overuse.

She'd been put together again after no fewer than three crash landings and that was only what was officially entered in the log. God alone knows what had been missed out.

Kansas, Mexico, Panama, Peru, sinking a little lower with each move, finding it much more difficult to turn in her best performance, like a good horse being worked to death. Now, she was breaking up around me in the air and there wasn't much I could do about it.

From Iquitos in Peru, the Amazon River twists like a brown snake through two thousand miles of some of the worst jungle in the world, its final destination Belém on the Atlantic coast of Brazil with Manaus at the junction with the Rio Negro, the halfway point and my present destination.

For most of the way, I'd followed the river which at least made for easy navigation, alone with three sacks of mail and a couple of crates of some kind of mining machinery. Six long, hard hours to Tefé and I managed to raise three police posts on the way on my radio although things were quiet as the grave at Tefé itself.

From there, the river drifted away in a great, wide loop and to have followed it would have made the run to Manaus another four hundred miles and the Vega just didn't have that kind of fuel in reserve.

From Tefé, then, I struck out due east across virgin jungle, aiming for the Rio Negro a hundred and fifty miles farther on, where a turn downstream would bring me to Manaus.

It had been a crazy venture from the first, a flight that to my knowledge no one had accomplished at that time and yet at twenty-three, with the sap rising, a man tends to think himself capable of most things and Belém was, after all, two thousand miles closer to England than the point from which I'd started and a passage home at the end of it.

Yet I see now, looking back on it all after so many years, how much in the whole affair was the product of chance, that element quite beyond calculation in a man's affairs.

To start with, my bold plunge across such a wide stretch of virgin jungle was not quite as insane as it might appear. True, any attempt at dead reckoning was ruled out by the simple fact that my drift indicator was not working and the magnetic compass was wholly unreliable, but the Rio Negro did lie a hundred and fifty miles due east of Tefé, that was fact, and I had the

18

sun to guide me in a sky so crystal clear that the horizon seemed to stretch to infinity.

Falling oil pressure was the first of my woes, although I didn't worry too much about that to start with, for the oil pressure gauge, like most of the instruments, frequently didn't work at all and was at best less than reliable.

And then, unbelievably, the horizon broke into a series of jagged peaks almost before my eyes. Something else about which I couldn't really complain, for on the map, that particular section was merely a blank space.

Not that they were the Andes, exactly, but high enough, considering the Vega's general condition, although the altimeter packed in at four thousand feet, so everything after that was guesswork.

The sensible way of doing things would have been to stay far enough from them to be out of harm's way, and then to gain the correct height to cross the range by flying round and round in upward spirals for as long as may be. But I didn't have enough for that, by which I mean fuel, and simply eased back the stick and went in on the run.

I don't suppose there was more than four or five hundred feet in it as I started across the first great shoulder that lifted in a hog's back out of the dark green of the rain forest. Beyond, I faced a scattering of jagged peaks and not too much time for decisions.

I took a chance, aimed for the gap between the two largest and flew on over a landscape so barren that it might have been the moon. I dropped sickeningly in an air pocket, the Vega protesting with every fibre of its being and I eased back the stick again as the ground rose to meet me.

For a while it began to look as if I'd made a bad mistake. The pass through which I was flying narrowed considerably, so that at one point, there seemed every chance of the wing-tips brushing the rock face. And then, quite suddenly, I lifted over a great, fissured ridge with no more than a hundred feet to spare

19

and found myself flying across an enormous valley, mist rising to engulf me like steam from a boiling pot.

Suddenly it was a lot colder, and rain drifted across the windshield in a fine spray, and then the horizon of things crackled with electricity as rain swept in from the east in a great cloud to engulf me.

Violent tropical storms of that type were one of the daily hazards of flying in the area. Frequent and usually short-lived, they could wreak an incredible amount of damage and the particular danger was the lightning associated with them. It was usually best to climb over them, but the Vega was already as high as she was going to go, considering the state she was in, so I really had no other choice than to hang on and hope for the best.

I didn't think of dying. I was too involved in keeping the plane in the air to have time for anything else. The Vega was made of wood. Cantilevered wings and streamlined wooden skin fuselage, manufactured in two halves and glued together like a child's toy and now, the toy was tearing itself to pieces.

Outside, it was almost completely dark and water cascaded in through every strained seam in the fuselage as we rocked in the turbulence. Rain streamed from the wings, lightning flickering at their tips and pieces of fuselage started to flake away.

I felt a kind of exultation more than anything else at the sheer involvement of trying to control that dying plane and actually laughed out loud at one point when a section of the roof went and water cascaded in over my head.

I came out into bright sunlight of the late afternoon and saw the river on the horizon immediately. It had to be the Negro, and I pushed the Vega towards it, ignoring the stench of burning oil, the rattling of the wings.

Pieces were breaking away from the fuselage constantly now and the Vega was losing height steadily. God alone knows what was keeping the engine going. It was really quite extraordinary. Any minute now, and the damn thing might pack up altogether and a crash landing in that impenetrable rain forest below was not something I could reasonably hope to survive.

A voice crackled in my earphone. "Heh, Vega, your wings are flapping so much I thought you were a bird. What's keeping you up?"

He came up from nowhere and levelled out off my port wing, a Hayley monoplane in scarlet and silver trim, no more than four or five years old from the look of it. The voice was American and with a distinctive harshness to it that gave it its own flavour in spite of the static that was trying to drown it.

"Who are you?"

"Neil Mallory," I said. "Iquitos for Belém by way of Manaus."

"Jesus." He laughed harshly. "I thought it was Lindbergh they called the flying fool. Manaus is just on a hundred miles downriver from here. Can you stay afloat that long?"

Another hour at least. I checked the fuel gauge and air-speed indicator and faced the inevitable. "Not a chance. Speed's falling all the time and my tank's nearly dry."

"No use jumping for it in this kind of country," he said. "You'd never be seen again. Can you hold her together for another ten minutes?"

"I can try."

"There's a patch of *campo* ten or fifteen miles downstream. Give you a chance to land that thing if you're good enough."

I didn't reply because the fuselage actually started to tear away in a great strip from the port wing and the wing, as if in pain, moved up and down more frantically than ever.

I was about a thousand feet up as we reached the Negro and turned downstream, drifting gradually and inevitably towards the ground like a falling leaf. There was sweat on my face in spite of the wind rushing in through the holes in the fuselage and my hands were cramped tight on the stick for it was taking all my strength to hold her.

"Easy, kid, easy." That strange, harsh voice crackled through the static. "Not long now. A mile downstream on your left. I'd tell you to start losing height only you're falling like a stone as it is."

21

"I love you too," I said and clamped my teeth hard together and held on as the Vega lurched violently to starboard.

The *campo* blossomed in the jungle a quarter of a mile in front of me, a couple of hundred yards of grassland beside the river. The wind seemed to be in the right direction although in the state the Vega was in, there wasn't much I could have done about it if it hadn't been. I hardly needed to throttle back to reduce airspeed for my approach—the engine had almost stopped anyway—but I got the tail trimmer adjusted and dropped the flaps as I floated in across the tree-tops.

It took all my strength to hold her, stamping on the rudder to pull her back in line as she veered to starboard. It almost worked. I plunged down, with a final burst of power to level out for my landing and the engine chose that precise moment to die on me.

It was like running slap into an invisible wall. The Vega seemed to hang there in the air a hundred feet above the ground for a moment, then swooped.

I left the undercarriage in the branches of the trees at the west end of the *campo*. In fact I think, in the final analysis, that was what saved me for the braking effect on the plane as she barged through the top of the trees was considerable. She simply flopped down on her belly on the *campo* and ploughed forward through the six-foot-high grass, leaving both wings behind her on the way and came to a dead halt perhaps twenty yards from the bank of the river.

I unstrapped my seat belt, kicked open the door, threw out the mail bags and followed them through, just in case. But there was no need and the fact that she hadn't gone up like a torch on impact wasn't luck. It was simply that there wasn't anything left in the tanks to burn.

I sat down very carefully on one of the mail sacks. My hands were trembling slightly—not much, but enough—and my heart was pounding like a trip-hammer. The Hayley swooped low overhead. I waved without looking up, then unzipped my flying jacket and found a tin of Balkan Sobranie cigarettes, last of a carton I'd bought on the black market in Lima the previous month. I don't think anything in life to that moment had ever tasted so good.

After a while, I stood up and turned in time to see the Hayley bank and drop in over the trees on the far side of the *campo*. He made it look easy and it was far from that, for the wreckage of the Vega and the position where its wings had come to rest in its wake left him very little margin for error. There couldn't have been more than a dozen yards between the tip of his port wing and the edge of the trees.

I sat down on one of the mail sacks again, mainly because my legs suddenly felt very weak, and lit another Sobranie. I could hear him ploughing towards me through the long grass, and once he called my name. God knows why I didn't answer. Some kind of shock. I suppose. I simply sat there, the cigarette slack between my lips and stared beyond the wreck of the Vega to the river, taking in every sight and sound in minute detail as if to prove I was alive.

"By God, you can fly, boy. I'll say that for you."

He emerged from the grass and stood looking at me, hands on hips in what I was to learn was an inimitable gesture. He was physically very big indeed and wore a leather top-coat, breeches, knee-length boots, a leather helmet, goggles pushed up high on the forehead and there was a .45 Colt automatic in a holster on his thigh.

I put out my hand and when I spoke, the voice seemed to belong to someone else. "Mallory—Neil Mallory."

"You already told me that—remember?" He grinned. "My name's Hannah—Sam Hannah. Anything worth salvaging in there besides the mail?"

As I discovered later, he was forty-five years of age at that time, but he could have been older or younger if judged on appearance alone for he had one of those curiously ageless faces, tanned to almost the same colour as his leather coat.

He had the rather hard, self-possessed, competent look of a man who had been places and done things, survived against

23

odds on occasions and yet, even from the first, there seemed a flaw in him. He made too perfect a picture standing there in his flying kit, gun on hip, like some R.F.C. pilot waiting to take off on a dawn patrol across the trenches, yet more like a man playing a part than the actuality. And the eyes were wrong—a sort of pale, washed blue that never gave anything away.

I told him about the mining machinery and he climbed inside the Vega to look for himself. He reappeared after a while holding a canvas grip.

"This yours?" I nodded and he threw it down. "Those crates are out of the question. Too heavy for the Hayley anyway. Anything else you want?"

I shook my head and then remembered. "Oh, yes, there's a revolver in the map compartment."

He found it with no difficulty and pushed it across, together with a box of cartridges, a Webley .38 which I shoved away in one of the pockets of my flying jacket.

"Then if you're ready, we'll get out of here." He picked up the three mail sacks with no visible effort. "The Indians in these parts are Jicaros. There were around five thousand of them till last year when some doctor acting for one of the land companies infected them with small pox instead of vaccinating them against it. The survivors have developed the unfortunate habit of skinning alive any white man they can lay hands on."

But such tales had long lost the power to move me for they were commonplace along the Amazon at a time when most settlers or prospectors regarded the Indians as something other than human. Vermin to be ruthlessly stamped out, and any means were looked upon as fair.

I stumbled along behind Hannah who kept up a running conversation, cursing freely as great clouds of grasshoppers and insects of various kinds rose in clouds as we disturbed them.

"What a bloody country. The last place God made. As far as I'm concerned, the Jicaros can have it and welcome."

"Then why stay?" I asked him.

We had reached the Hayley by then, and he heaved the mail

bags inside and turned, a curious glitter in his eyes. "Not from choice, boy, I can tell you that."

He gave me a push up into the cabin. It wasn't as large as the Vega. Seats for four passengers and a freight compartment behind, but everything was in apple-pie order and not just because she wasn't all that old. This was a plane that enjoyed regular, loving care. Something I found faintly surprising because it didn't seem to fit with Hannah.

I strapped myself in beside him and he closed the door. "A hundred and eighty this baby does at full stretch. You'll be wallowing in a hot bath before you know it." He grinned. "All right, tepid, if I know my Manaus plumbing."

Suddenly I was very tired. It was marvellous just to sit there, strapped comfortably into my seat and let someone else do the work and as I've said, he was good. Really good. There wasn't going to be more than a few feet in it as far as those trees were concerned at the far end of the *campo* and yet I hadn't a qualm as he turned the Hayley into the wind and opened the throttle.

He kept her going straight into that green wall, refusing to sacrifice power for height, waiting until the last possible moment, pulling the stick back into his stomach and lifting us up over the tops of the trees with ten feet to spare.

He laughed out loud and slapped the bulkhead with one hand. "You know what's the most important thing in life, Mallory? Luck—and I've got a bucket full of the stuff. I'm going to live to be a hundred and one."

"Good luck to you," I said.

Strange, but he was like a man with drink taken. Not drunk, but unable to stop talking. For the life of me, I can't remember what he said, for gradually my eyes closed and his voice dwindled until it was one with the engine itself and then, that too faded and there was only the quiet darkness.

2

Maria of the Angels

I had hoped to be on my way in a matter of hours, certainly no later than the following day, for in spite of the fact that Manaus was passing through hard times, there was usually a boat of some description or another leaving for the coast most days.

But things went wrong from the beginning. To start with, there was the police, in the person of the *comandante* himself, who insisted on giving me a personal examination regarding the crash, noting my every word in his own hand, which took up a remarkable amount of time.

After signing my statement I had to wait outside his office while he got Hannah's version of the affair. They seemed to be old and close friends from the laughter echoing faintly through the closed door and when they finally emerged, Hannah had an arm round the *comandante*'s shoulder.

"Ah, Senhor Mallory." The *comandante* nodded graciously. "I have spoken to Captain Hannah on this matter and am happy to say that he confirms your story in every detail. You are free to go."

Which was nice of him. He went back into his office.

Hannah said, "That's all right, then." He frowned as if concerned and put a hand on my shoulder. "I've got things to do, but you look like the dead walking. Grab a cab downstairs and get the driver to take you to the Palace Hotel. Ask for Senhor Juca. Tell him I sent you. Five or six hours' sleep and you'll be fine. I'll catch up with you this evening. We'll have something to eat. Hit the high spots together."

"In Manaus?" I said.

"They still have their fair share of sin, if you know where to look." He grinned crookedly. "I'll see you later."

He returned to the *comandante*'s office, opening the door without knocking and I went downstairs and out through the cracked marble pillars at the entrance.

I didn't go to the hotel straight away. Instead, I took one of the horse-drawn cabs that waited at the bottom of the steps and gave the driver the address of the local agent of the mining company for whom I'd contracted to deliver the Vega to Belém.

In its day during the great rubber boom at the end of the nineteenth century, Manaus had been the original hell-hole, millionaires walking the streets ten-a-penny, baroque palaces, an opera house to rival Paris itself. No sin too great, no wickedness too evil. Sodom and Gomorrah rolled into one and set down on the banks of the Negro, a thousand miles up the Amazon.

I had never cared much for the place. There was a suggestion of corruption, a kind of general decay. A feeling that the jungle was gradually creeping back in and that none of us had any right to be there.

I felt restless and ill-at-ease, a reaction to stress, I suppose, and wanted nothing so much as to be on my way, looking back on this place over the sternrail of a riverboat for the last time.

I found the agent in the office of a substantial warehouse on the waterfront. He was tall, cadaverous, with the haunted eyes of a man who knows he has not got long to live and he coughed repeatedly into a large, soiled handkerchief which was already stained with blood.

He gave thanks to Our Lady for my deliverance to the extent

27

of crossing himself and in the same breath pointed out that under the terms of my contract, I only got paid on safe delivery of the Vega to Belém. Which was exactly what I had expected and I left him in a state of near collapse across his desk doing his level best to bring up what was left of his lungs and went outside.

My cab still waited for me, the driver dozing in the heat of the day, his straw sombrero tilted over his eyes. I walked across to the edge of the wharf to see what was going on in the basin which wasn't much, but there was a stern-wheeler up at the next wharf loading green bananas.

I found the captain in a canvas chair under an awning on the bridge and he surfaced for as long as it took to tell me he was leaving at nine the following morning for Belém and that the trip would take six days. If I didn't fancy a hammock on deck with his more impoverished customers, I could have the spare bunk in the mate's cabin with all found for a hundred *cruzeiros*. I assured him I would be there on time and he closed his eyes with complete indifference and returned to more important matters.

I had just over a thousand *cruzeiros* in my wallet, around a hundred and fifty pounds sterling at that time which meant that even allowing for the trip down-river and incidental expenses, I would have ample in hand to buy myself a passage to England from Belém on some cargo boat or other.

I was going home. After two and a half years of the worst that South America could offer, I was on my way, and it felt marvellous, definitely one of life's great moments. All tiredness left me as I turned and hurried back to the cab.

I had expected the worst of the hotel, but the Palace was a pleasant surprise. Certainly it had seen better days, but it had a kind of baroque dignity to it, a faded charm that was very appealing, and Hannah's name had a magic effect on the Senhor Juca he had mentioned, an old, white-haired man in an alpaca jacket who sat behind the desk reading a newspaper.

He took me upstairs personally and ushered me into a room with its own little ironwork terrace overlooking the river. The whole place was a superb example of late Victoriana, caught for all time like a fly in amber from the brass bed to the heavy, mahogany furniture.

An Indian woman in a black bombazine dress appeared with clean sheets and the old man showed me, with some pride, the bathroom next door of which I could have sole use, although regrettably it would be necessary to ring for hot water. I thanked him for his courtesy, but he waved his hands deprecatingly and assured me, with some eloquence, that nothing was too much trouble for a friend of Captain Hannah's.

I thought about that as I undressed. Whatever else you could say about him, Hannah obviously enjoyed considerable standing in Manaus. That was interesting, considering he was a foreigner.

I needed that bath badly, but suddenly, sitting there on the edge of the bed after getting my boots off, I was overwhelmed with tiredness. I climbed between the sheets and was almost instantly asleep.

I surfaced to the mosquito net billowing above me like a pale, white flower in the breeze from the open window. Beyond it a face floated disembodied in the diffused yellow glow of an oil lamp.

Old Juca blinked sad, moist eyes. "Captain Hannah was here earlier, senhor. He asked me to wake you at nine o'clock."

It took its own time in getting through to me. "Nine o'clock?"

"He asks you to meet him, senhor, at *The Little Boat*. He wishes you to dine with him. I have a cab waiting to take you there, senhor. Everything is arranged."

"That's nice of him," I said, but any irony in my voice was obviously lost on him.

"Your bath is waiting, senhor. Hot water is provided."

He put the lamp down carefully on the table. The door closed with a gentle sigh behind him, and the mosquito net fluttered in the eddy like some great moth, then settled again.

Hannah certainly took a lot for granted. I got up, feeling vaguely irritated at the way things were being managed for me and padded across to the open window. Quite suddenly, my whole mood changed for it was pleasantly cool after the heat of the day, the breeze perfumed with flowers. Lights glowed down there on the river and music echoed faintly, the fredo from the sound of it, pulsating through the night, filling me with a vague, irrational excitement.

When I turned back to the room I made another discovery. My canvas grip had been unpacked and my old linen suit had been washed and pressed and hung neatly from the back of a chair waiting for me. There was really nothing I could do, the pressures were too great, so I gave in gracefully, found a towel and went along the corridor to have my bath.

The main rainy season was over. But rainfall always tends to be heavy in the upper Amazon basin area, and sudden, violent downpours are common, especially at night.

I left the hotel to just such a rush of rain and hurried down the steps to the cab waiting for me, escorted by Juca, who insisted on holding an ancient black umbrella over my head. The driver had raised the leather hood, which kept out most of the rain if not all, and drove away at once.

The streets were deserted, washed clean of people by the rain, and from the moment we left the hotel until we reached our destination, I don't think we saw more than half a dozen people, particularly when we moved through the back streets towards the river.

We emerged on the waterfront at a place with a considerable number of houseboats of various kinds. A great many people actually lived on the river this way. We finally came to a halt at the end of the long pier.

"This way, senhor."

The cabby insisted on placing his old oilskin coat about my shoulders and escorted me to the end of the pier, where a lantern hung from a pole above a rack festooned with fishing nets.

An old riverboat was moored out there in the darkness, lights gleaming, laughter and music drifting across the water. He leaned down and lifted a large, wooden trapdoor and the light from the lamp flooded in to reveal a flight of wooden steps. He went down and I followed without hesitation. I had, after all, no reason to expect foul play, and in any event, the Webley .38, which I'd had the forethought to slip into my right-hand coat pocket, was as good an insurance as any.

A kind of boardwalk stretched out through the darkness towards the riverboat, constructed over a series of canoes, and it dipped alarmingly as we moved across.

When we reached the other end the cabby smiled and slapped the hull with the flat of his palm. "*The Little Boat*, senhor. Good appetite in all things, but in food and women most of all."

It was a Brazilian saying and well intended. I reached for my wallet and he raised a hand. "It is not necessary, senhor. The good captain has seen to it all."

Hannah again. I watched him negotiate the swaying catwalk successfully as far as the pier then turned and went up some iron steps which took me to the deck. A giant of a man moved from the shadows beside a lighted doorway, a Negro with a ring in one ear and a heavy, curly beard.

"Senhor?" he said.

"I'm looking for Captain Hannah," I told him. "He's expecting me."

The teeth gleamed in the darkness. *Another friend of Hannah's.* This was really beginning to get monotonous. He didn't say anything, simply opened the door for me and I passed inside.

I suppose it must have been the main saloon in the old days. Now it was crowded with tables, people crammed together like sardines. There was a permanent curtain of smoke that, allied to the subdued lighting, made visibility a problem, but I managed to detect a bar in one corner on the other side of the small, packed dance floor. A five-piece rumba band was banging out a *carioca* and most of the crowd seemed to be singing along with it.

31

I saw Hannah in the thick of it on the floor dancing about as close as it was possible to get to a really beautiful girl by any standards. She was of mixed blood, Negro-European variety was my guess, and wore a dress of scarlet satin that fitted her like a second skin and made her look like the devil's own.

He swung her round, saw me and let out a great cry. "Heh, Mallory, you made it."

He pushed the girl away as if she didn't exist and ploughed through the crowd towards me. Nobody got annoyed even when he put a drink or two over. Mostly they just smiled, and one or two of the men slapped him on the back and called good-naturedly.

He'd been drinking, that much was obvious, and greeted me like a long-lost brother. "What kept you? Christ, but I'm starving. Come on, I've got a table laid on out on the terrace where we can hear ourselves think."

He took me by the elbow and guided me through the crowd to a long, sliding shutter on the far side. As he started to pull it back, the girl in the red satin dress arrived and flung her arms around his neck.

He grabbed her wrists, and she gave a short cry of pain—that strength of his again, I suppose. He no longer looked anything like as genial and somehow, his bad Portuguese made it sound worse.

"Later, angel—later I'll screw you just as much as you damn well want, only now I want a little time with my friend. Okay?"

When he released her she backed away, looked scared if anything, turned and melted into the crowd. I suppose it was about then I noticed that the women vastly outnumbered the men, and commented on the fact.

"What is this, a whorehouse?"

"Only the best in town."

He pulled back the shutter and led the way out to a private section of the deck with a canvas awning from which the rain dripped steadily. A table, laid for two, stood by the rail under a pressure lamp.

He shouted in Portuguese, "Heh, Pedro, let's have some action here." Then he motioned me to one of the seats and produced a bottle of wine from a bucket of water under the table. "You like this stuff—Pouilly-Fuissé? They get it for me special. I used to drink it by the bucketful in the old days in France."

I tried some. It was ice-cold, sharp and fresh and instantly exhilarating. "You were on the Western Front?"

"I sure was. Three years of it. Not many lasted that long, I can tell you."

Which at least explained the Captain bit. I said, "But America didn't come into the war till nineteen-seventeen."

"Oh, that." He leaned back out of the way as a waiter in a white shirt and cummerbund appeared with a tray to serve us. "I flew for the French with the Lafayette Escadrille. Nieuport Scouts, then Spads." He leaned forward to re-fill my glass. "How old are you, Mallory?"

"Twenty-three."

He laughed. "I'd twenty-six kills to my credit when I was your age. Been shot down four times, once by von Richthofen himself."

Strange, but at that stage of things I never doubted him for a second. Stated baldly, what he had said could easily sound like boasting and yet it was his manner which said most and he was casual in the extreme as if these things were really of no account.

We had fish soup, followed by a kind of casserole of chicken stewed in its own blood, which tasted a lot better than it sounds. This was backed up by eggs with olives, fried, as usual, in olive oil. And there was a mountain of rice and tomatoes in vinegar.

Hannah never stopped talking and yet ate and drank enormously with little visible effect except to make him talk more loudly and more rapidly than ever.

"It was a hard school out there, believe me. You had to be good to survive and the longer you lasted, the better your chances."

"That makes sense, I suppose," I said.

"It sure does. You don't need luck up there, kid. You need to know what you're doing. Flying's about the most unnatural thing a man can do."

When the waiter came to clear the table, I thanked him. Hannah said, "That's pretty good Portuguese you speak. Better than mine."

"I spent a year on the lower Amazon when I first came to South America," I told him. "Flying out of Belém for a mining company that had diamond concessions along the Xingu River."

He seemed impressed. "I hear that's rough country. Some of the worst Indians in Brazil."

"Which was why I switched to Peru. Mountain flying may be trickier, but it's a lot more fun than what you're doing."

He said, "You were pretty good out there today. I've been flying for better than twenty years and I can't think of more than half a dozen guys I've known who could have landed that Vega. Where did you learn to fly like that?"

"I had an uncle who was in the R.F.C.," I said. "Died a couple of years back. He used to take me up in a Puss Moth when I was a kid. When I went to University, I joined the Air Squadron which led to a Pilot Officer's commission in the Auxiliary Air Force. That got me plenty of weekend flying."

"Then what?"

"Qualified for a commercial pilot's licence in my spare time, then found pilots were ten-a-penny."

"Except in South America."

"Exactly." I was more than a little tight by then and yet the words seemed to spill out with no difficulty. "All I ever wanted to do was fly. Know what I mean? I was willing to go anywhere."

"You certainly were if you drew the Xingu. What are you going to do now? If you're stuck for a job I might be able to help."

"Flying, you mean?"

He nodded. "I handle the mail and general freight route to Landro which is about two hundred miles up the Negro from here. I also cover the Rio das Mortes under government contract. Lot of diamond prospecting going on up there these days."

"The Rio das Mortes?" I said. "The River of Death? You must be joking. That's worse than the Xingu any day. I've been there. I took some government men to a Mission Station called Santa Helena maybe two years ago. That would be before your time. You know the place?"

"I call there regularly."

"You used a phrase today," I said. "The Last Place God Made. Well, that's the Rio das Mortes, Hannah. During the rainy season it never stops. At other times of the year it just rains all day. They've got flies up there that lay eggs in your eyeballs. Most parts of the Amazon would consider the piranha bad enough because a shoal of them can reduce a man to a skeleton in three minutes flat, but on the Mortes, they have a microscopic item with spines that crawls up your backside given half a chance and it takes a knife to get him out again."

"You don't need to tell me about the damn place," he said. "I've been there. Came in with three Hayleys and high hopes a year ago. All I've got left is the baby you arrived in today. Believe me, when my government contract's up in three months you won't see me for dust."

"What happened to the other two planes?"

"Kaput. Lousy pilots."

"Then why do you need me?"

"Because it takes two planes to keep my schedule going or to put it more exactly, I can't quite do with one. I managed to pick up an old biplane the other day from a planter downriver who's selling up."

"What is it?"

"A Bristol."

He was in the act of filling my glass and I started so much that I spilled most of my wine across the table. "You mean a Brisfit? A Bristol fighter? Christ, they were flying those over twenty years ago on the Western Front."

He nodded. "I should know. Oh, she's old all right, but then

35

she only has to hold together another three months. Do one or two of the easy river trips. If you'd wanted the job, you could have had it, but it doesn't matter. There's a guy in at the weekend who's already been in touch with me. Some Portuguese who's been flying for a mining company in Venezuela that went bust which means I'll get him cheap."

"Well, that's okay, then," I said.

"What are you going to do?"

"Go home—what else."

"What about money? Can you manage?"

"Just about." I patted my wallet. "I won't be taking home any pot of gold, but I'll be back in one piece and that's all that counts. There's a hard time coming from what I read of events in Europe. They're going to need men with my kind of flying experience, the way things are looking."

"The Nazis, you mean?" he nodded. "You could be right. A bunch of bastards, from what I hear. You should meet my maintenance engineer, Mannie Sterne. Now he's a German. Was a professor of engineering at one of their universities or something. They arrested him because he was a Jew. Put him in some kind of hell-hole they call a concentration camp. He was lucky to get out with a whole skin. Came off a freighter right here in Manaus without a penny in his pocket."

"Which was when you met him?"

"Best day's work of my life. Where aero engines are concerned the guy's the original genius." He re-filled my glass. "What kind of stuff were you flying with the R.A.F. then?"

"Wapitis mainly. The Auxiliaries get the oldest aircraft."

"The stuff the regulars don't want?"

"That's right. I've even flown Bristols. There were still one or two around on some stations. And then there was the Mark One Fury. I got about thirty hours in one of those just before I left."

"What's that—a fighter?" I nodded and he sighed and shook his head. "Christ, but I envy you, kid, going back to all that. I used to be Ace-of-Aces, did you know that? Knocked out four

Fokkers in one morning before I went down in flames. That was my last show. Captain Samuel B. Hannah, all of twenty-three and everything but the Congressional Medal of Honour."

"I thought that was Eddie Rickenbacker?" I said. "Ace-of-Aces, I mean."

"I spent the last six months of the war in hospital," he answered.

Those blue eyes stared vacantly into the past, caught for a moment by some ancient hurt, and then he seemed to pull himself back to reality, gave me that crooked grin and raised his glass.

"Happy landings."

The wine had ceased to affect me, or so it seemed, for it went down in a single easy swallow. The final bottle was empty. He called for more, then lurched across to the sliding door and pulled it back.

The music was like a blow in the face, frenetic, exciting, filling the night, mingling with the laughter, voices singing. The girl in the red satin dress moved up the steps to join him. He pulled her into his arms, and she kissed him passionately. I sat there feeling curiously detached as the waiter re-filled my glass and Hannah, surfacing, grinned across at me.

The girl who slid into the opposite seat was part Indian to judge by the eyes that slanted up above high cheekbones. The face itself was calm and remote, framed by dark, shoulder-length hair, and she wore a plain white cotton dress which buttoned down the front.

She helped herself to an empty glass and I reached for the newly opened bottle of wine and filled it for her. Hannah came across, put a hand under her chin and tilted her face. She didn't like that, I could tell by the way her eyes changed.

He said, "You're new around here, aren't you? What's your name?"

"Maria, senhor."

"Maria of the Angels, eh? I like that. You know me?"

"Everyone along the river knows you, senhor."

He patted her cheek. "Good girl. Senhor Mallory is a friend of mine—a good friend. You look after him. I'll see you're all right."

"I would have thought the senhor well able to look after himself."

He laughed harshly. "You may be right, at that." He turned and went back to the girl in the satin dress and took her down to the dance floor.

Maria of the Angels toasted me without a word and sipped a little of her wine. I emptied my glass in return, stood up and went to the rail. My head seemed to swell like a balloon. I tried breathing deeply and leaned out over the rail, letting the rain blow against my face.

I hadn't heard her move, but she was there behind me and when I turned, she put her hands lightly on my shoulders. "You would like to dance, senhor?"

I shook my head. "Too crowded in there."

She turned without a word, crossed to the sliding door and closed it. The music was suddenly muted, yet plain enough a slow, sad samba with something of the night in it.

She came back to the rail and melted into me, one arm sliding behind my neck. Her body started to move against mine, easing me into the rhythm and I was lost, utterly and completely. A name like Maria, and the face of a madonna to go with it perhaps, but the rest of her . . .

I wasn't completely certain of the sequence of things after that. The plain truth was that I was so drunk, I didn't really know what I was doing.

There was a point when I surfaced to find myself on some other part of the deck with her tight in my arms and then she was pulling away from me, telling me this was no good, that there were too many people.

She must have made the obvious suggestion—that we go to her place—because the next thing I recall is being led across that swaying catwalk to the pier.

The rain was falling harder than ever now and when we went up the steps to the pier, we ran into the full force of it. The thin cotton dress was soaked within seconds, clinging to her body, the nipples blossoming on her breasts, filling me with excitement.

I reached out for her, pulling all that ripeness into me, my hands fastening over the firm buttocks. The gap was rising with a vengeance. I kissed her pretty savagely and after a while she pushed me away and patted my face.

"God, but you're beautiful," I said, and leaned back against a stack of packing cases.

She smiled, for the first and only time I could recall in our acquaintance, as if truly delighted at the compliment, a lamp turning on inside her. Then she lifted her right knee into my crotch with all her force.

I was so drunk that I was not immediately conscious of pain, only of being down on the boardwalk, knees up to my chest.

I rolled over on my back, was aware of her on her knees beside me, hands busy in my pockets. Some basic instinct of self-preservation tried to bring me back to life when I saw the wallet in her hands, a knowledge that it contained everything of importance to me, not only material things, but my present future.

As she stood up, I reached for her ankle and got the heel of her shoe squarely in the center of my palm. She kicked out again, sending me rolling towards the edge of the pier.

I was saved from going over by some sort of raised edging and hung there, scrabbling for a hold frantically, no strength in me at all. She started towards me, presumably to finish it off, and then several things seemed to happen at once.

I heard my name, clear through the rain, saw three men halfway across the catwalk, Hannah in the lead. He had that .45 automatic in his hand and a shot echoed flatly through the rain.

Too late, for Maria of the Angels was already long gone into the darkness.

3

The Immelmann Turn

The stern-wheeler left on time the following morning, but without me. At high noon, when she must have been thirty or forty miles downriver, I was sitting outside the *comandante*'s office again for the second time in two days, listening to the voices droning away inside.

After a while, the outside door opened and Hannah came in. He was wearing flying clothes and looked tired, his face unshaven, the eyes hollow from lack of sleep. He'd had a contract run to make at ten o'clock, only a short hop of fifty miles or so downriver for one of the mining companies, but something that couldn't be avoided.

He sat on the edge of the sergeant's desk and lit a cigarette, regarding me anxiously. "How do you feel?"

"About two hundred years old."

"God damn that bitch." He got to his feet and paced restlessly back and forth across the room. "If there was only something I could do." He turned to face me, really looking his age for the first time since I'd known him. "I might as well level with you, kid. Every damn thing I buy round here from fuel to booze is on credit. The Bristol ate up all the ready cash I had. When my government contract is up in another three months, I'm due a reasonable enough bonus, but until then . . ."

"Look, forget about it," I said.

"I took you to the bloody place, didn't I?"

He genuinely felt responsible, I could see that, and couldn't do much about it, a hard thing for a man like him to accept, for his position in other people's eyes, their opinion was important to him.

"I'm free, white and twenty-one, isn't that what you say in the States?" I said. "Anything I got, I asked for, so have a decent cigarette for a change and shut up."

I held out the tin of Balkan Sobranie and the door to the *comandante*'s office opened and the sergeant appeared.

"You will come in now, Senhor Mallory?"

I stood up and walked into the room rather slowly which was understandable under the circumstances. Hannah simply followed me inside without asking anyone's permission.

The *comandante* nodded to him. "Senhor Hannah."

"Maybe there's something I can do," Hannah said.

The *comandante* managed to look as sorrowful as only a Latin can and shook his head. "A bad business, Senhor Mallory. You say there was a thousand *cruzeiros* in the wallet besides your passport?"

I sank into the nearest chair. "Nearer to eleven hundred."

"You could have had her for the night for five, senhor. To carry that kind of money on your person was extremely foolish."

"No sign of her at all, then?" Hannah put in. "Surely to God somebody must know the bitch."

"You know the type, senhor. Working the river, moving from town to town. No one at *The Little Boat* had ever seen her before. She rented a room at a house near the waterfront, but had only been there three days."

"What you're trying to say is that she's well away from Manaus by now and the chances of catching her are remote," I said.

"Exactly, senhor. The truth is always painful. She was three-quarters Indian. She will probably go back to her people for a while. All she has to do is take off her dress. They all look the same." He helped himself to a long black cigar from a box on his desk. "None of which helps you. I am sensible of this. Have you funds that you can draw out?"

"Not a penny."

"So?" He frowned. "The passport is not so difficult. An application to the British Consul in Belém backed by a letter from me should remedy that situation within a week or two, but as the law stands at present, all foreign nationals are required to produce evidence of employment if they do not possess private means."

I knew exactly what he meant. There were public work gangs for people like me.

Hannah moved round to the other end of the room where he could look at me and nodded briefly. He said calmly, "No difficulty there. Senhor Mallory was considering coming to work for me anyway."

"As a pilot?" The *comandante*'s eyes went up and he turned to me. "This is so, senhor?"

"Quite true," I said.

Hannah grinned slightly and the *comandante* looked distinctly relieved. "All is in order, then." He stood up and held out his hand. "If anything of interest does materialise in connection with this unfortunate affair, senhor, I'll know where to find you."

I shook hands—it would have seemed churlish not to—and shuffled outside. I kept right on going and had reached the pillared entrance hall before Hannah caught up with me. I sat down on a marble bench in a patch of sunlight and he stood in front of me looking genuinely uncertain.

"Did I do right, back there?"

I nodded wearily. "I'm obliged to you—really, but what about this Portuguese you were expecting?"

"He loses, that's all." He sat down beside me. "Look, I know you wanted to get home, but it could be worse. You can move in with Mannie at Landro, and have a room at the Palace on me between trips. Your keep and a hundred dollars American a week."

The terms were generous by any standards. I said, "That's fine by me."

"There's just one snag. Like I said, I'm living on credit at the moment. That means I won't have the cash to pay you till I get that government bonus at the end of my contract which means sticking out this last three months with me. Can you face that?"

"I don't have much choice, do I?"

I got up and walked out into the entrance. He said, with what sounded like genuine admiration in his voice, "By God, but you're a cool one, Mallory. Doesn't anything ever throw you?"

"Last night was last night," I told him. "Today's something else again. Do we fly up to Landro this afternoon?"

He stared at me, a slight frown on his face, seemed about to make some sort of comment, then obviously changed his mind.

"We ought to," he said. "There's the fortnightly run to the mission station at Santa Helena to make tomorrow. There's only one thing. The Bristol ought to go, too. I want Mannie to check that engine out as soon as possible. That means both of us will have to fly. Do you feel up to it?"

"That's what I'm getting paid for," I said and shuffled down the steps towards the cab waiting at the bottom.

The airstrip Hannah was using at Manaus at that time wasn't much. A wooden administration hut with a small tower and a row of decrepit hangar sheds backed on to the river, roofed with rusting, corrugated iron. It was a derelict sort of place and the Hayley, the only aircraft on view, looked strangely out of place, its scarlet and silver trim gleaming in the afternoon sun.

It was siesta, so there was no one around. I dropped my canvas grip on the ground beside the Hayley. It was so hot that I took off my flying jacket—and very still except for an occasional roar from a bull-throated howler monkey in the trees at the river's edge.

There was a sudden rumble behind and when I turned, Hannah was pushing back the sliding door on one of the sheds.

"Well, here she is," he said.

The Bristol fighter was one of the really great combat aircraft of the war and it served overseas with the R.A.F. until well into the thirties. As I've said, there were still one or two around on odd stations in England when I was learning to fly and I'd had seven or eight hours in them.

But this one was an original—a veritable museum piece. She had a fuselage which had been patched so many times it was ridiculous and in one place, it was still possible to detect the faded rondel of the R.A.F.

Before I could make any kind of comment, Hannah said, "Don't be put off by the state of the fuselage. She's a lot better than she looks. Structurally as sound as a bell and I don't think there's much wrong with the engine. The guy I bought it from had her for fifteen years and didn't use her all that much. God knows what her history was before that. The log book's missing."

"Have you flown her much?" I asked.

"Just over a hundred miles. She handled well. Didn't give me any kind of trouble at all."

The Bristol was a two-seater. I climbed up on the lower port wing and peered into the pilot's cockpit. It had exactly the right kind of smell—a compound of leather, oil and petrol— something that had never yet failed to excite me, and I reached out to touch the stick in a kind of reluctant admiration. The only modern addition was a radio which must have been fitted when the new law made them mandatory in Brazil.

"It really must be an original. Basket seat and leather cushions. All the comforts of home."

"They were a great plane," Hannah said soberly.

I dropped to the ground. "Didn't I read somewhere that von Richthofen shot down four in one day?"

"There were reasons for that. The pilot had a fixed machine-gun up front—a Vickers. The observer usually carried one or two free-mounting Lewis guns in the rear. At first, they used the usual two-seater technique."

"Which meant the man in the rear cockpit did all the shooting?"

"Exactly, and that was no good. They sustained pretty heavy losses at first until pilots discovered she was so manoeuvrable you could fly her like a single-seater."

"With the fixed machine-gun as the main weapon?"

"That's right. The observer's Lewis just became a useful extra. They used to carry a couple of bombs. Not much—around two hundred and forty pounds—but it means you can take a reasonable pay load. If you look, you'll see the rear cockpit has been extended at some time."

I peered over. "You could get a couple of passengers in there now."

"I suppose so, but it isn't necessary. The Hayley can handle that end of things. Let's get her outside."

We took a wing each and pushed her out into the bright sunshine. In spite of her shabby appearance, she looked strangely menacing and exactly what she was supposed to be—a formidable fighting machine, waiting for something to happen.

I've known people who love horses—any horse—with every fibre of their being, an instinctive response that simply cannot be denied. Aeroplanes have always affected me in exactly the same way and this was an aeroplane and a half in spite of her shabby appearance and comparatively slow speed by modern standards. There was something indefinable here that could not be stated. Of one thing I was certain—it was me she was waiting for.

Hannah said, "You can take the Hayley. I'll follow on in this."

I shook my head. "No, thanks. This is what you hired me to fly."

He looked a little dubious. "You're sure about that?"

I didn't bother to reply, simply went and got my canvas grip and threw it into the rear cockpit. There was a parachute in there, but I didn't bother to get it out, just pulled on my flying jacket, helmet and goggles.

He unfolded a map on the ground and we crouched beside it. The Rio das Mortes branched out of the Negro to the north-east about a hundred and fifty miles farther on. There was a military post called Forte Franco at its mouth; Landro was another fifty miles upstream.

"Stick to the river all the way," Hannah said. "Don't try cutting across the jungle whatever you do. Go down there and you're finished. It's Huna country all the way up the Mortes. They make those Indians you mentioned along the Xingu look like Sunday-school stuff, and there's nothing they like better than getting their hands on a white man."

"Doesn't anyone have any contacts with them?"

"Only the nuns at the medical mission at Santa Helena and it's a miracle they've survived as long as they have. One of the mining companies was having some trouble with them the other year so they called the head men of the various sub-tribes to-gether to talk things over, then machine-gunned them from cover. Killed a couple of dozen, but they botched things up and about eight got away. Since then it's been war. It's all martial law up there. Not that it means anything. The military aren't up to much. A colonel and fifty men with two motor launches at Forte Franco and that's it."

I folded the map and shoved it inside my flying jacket. "From the sound of it, I'd say the Hunas have a point."

He laughed grimly. "You won't find many to sympathise with that statement around Landro, Mallory. They're a bunch of Stone Age savages. Vermin. If you'd seen some of the things they've done . . ."

He walked across to the Hayley, opened the cabin door and climbed inside. When he got out again, he was carrying a shot-gun.

"Have you got that revolver of yours handy?" I nodded and he tossed the shotgun to me and a box of cartridges. "Better take this as well, just in case. Best close-quarters weapon I know; ten-gauge, six-shot automatic. The loads are double-O steel buckshot. I'd use it on myself before I let those bastards get their hands on me."

I held it in my hands for a moment, then put it into the rear cockpit. "Are you flying with me?"

He shook his head. "I've got things to do. I'll follow in half an hour and still beat you there. I'll give a shout on the radio when I pass."

There was a kind of boasting in what he said without need, for the Bristol couldn't hope to compete with the Hayley when it came to speed, but I let it pass.

Instead I said, "Just one thing. As I remember, you need a chain of three men pulling the propeller to start the engine."

"Not with me around."

It was a simple statement of fact made without pride for his strength, as I was soon to see, was remarkable. I stepped up on to the port wing and eased myself into that basket seat with its leather cushions and pushed my feet into the toestraps at either end of the rudder bar.

I made my cockpit checks, gave Hannah a signal and wound that starting magneto while he pulled the propeller over a compression stroke. The engine, a Rolls-Royce Falcon, exploded into life instantly.

The din was terrific, a feature of the engine at low speeds. Hannah moved out of the way and I taxied away from the hangars towards the leeward boundary of the field and turned into the wind.

I pulled down my goggles, checked the sky to make sure I wasn't threatened by anything else coming in to land and opened the throttle. Up came the tail as I pushed the stick forward just a touch, gathering speed. As she yawed to starboard in a slight cross-wind, I applied a little rudder correction. A hundred and fifty yards, a slight backward pressure on the stick and she was airborne.

At two hundred feet, I eased back the throttle to her climbing speed which was all of sixty-five miles an hour, banked steeply at five hundred feet and swooped back across the airfield.

I could see Hannah quite plainly, hands shading his eyes from the sun as he gazed up at me. What happened then was entirely spontaneous, produced by the sheer exhilaration of being at the controls of that magnificent plane as much as by any desire to impress him.

The great German ace Max Immelmann came up with a brilliant ploy that gave him two shots at an enemy in a dogfight for the price of one and without losing height. The famous Immelmann Turn, biblical knowledge for any fighter pilot.

I tried it now, diving in on Hannah, pulled up in a half-loop, rolled out on top and came back over his head at fifty feet.

He didn't move a muscle, simply stood there, shaking a fist at me. I waved back, took the Bristol low over the trees and turned upriver.

You don't need to keep your hands on a Bristol's controls at cruising speed. If you want an easy time of it, all you have to do is adjust the tail plane incidence control and sit back, but that wasn't for me. I was enjoying being in control, being at one with the machine if you like. Someone once said the Bristol was like a thoroughbred hunter with a delicate mouth and a stout heart, and that afternoon over the Negro, I knew exactly what he meant.

On either side, the jungle, gigantic walls of bamboo and liana which even the sun couldn't get through. Below, the river, clouds of scarlet ibis scattering at my approach.

This was flying—how flying was meant to be—and I went down to a couple of hundred feet, remembering that at that height it was possible to get maximum speed out of her. One hundred and twenty-five miles an hour. I sat back, hands steady on the stick, and concentrated on getting to Landro before Hannah.

*   *   *

I almost made it, banking across the army post of Forte Franco at the mouth of the Rio das Mortes an hour and a quarter after leaving Manaus.

I was ten miles upstream, pushing her hard at two hundred feet when a thunderbolt descended. I didn't even know the Hayley was there until he dived on my tail, pulled up in a half-loop, rolled out on top in a perfect Immelmann Turn and roared towards me straight-on. I held the Bristol on course and he pulled up above my head.

"Bang, you're dead." His voice crackled in my earphones. "I was doing Immelmanns for real when you were still breast-feeding, kid. See you in Landro."

He banked away across the jungle where he had told me not to go, and roared into the distance. For a wild moment, I wondered if he might be challenging me to follow, but I resisted the impulse. He'd lost two pilots already on the Mortes. No sense in making it three unless I had to.

I throttled back and continued upriver at a leisurely hundred miles an hour, whistling softly between my teeth.

4

Landro

I came to Landro, dark clouds chasing after me, the horizon closing in—another of those sudden tropical rainstorms in the offing.

It was exactly as I had expected—a clearing in the jungle at the edge of the river. A crumbling jetty, pirogues drawn up on the beach beside it, a church surrounded by a scattering of wooden houses and not much else. In other words, a typical upriver settlement.

The landing strip was at the north end of the place, a stretch of *campo* at least three hundred yards long by a hundred across. There was a windsock on a crude pole, lifting to one side in a slight breeze, and a hangar roofed with corrugated iron. Hannah was down there now with three other men, pushing the Hayley into the hangar. He turned as I came in low across the field and waved.

The Bristol had one characteristic which made a good landing difficult for the novice. The undercarriage included rubber bungees which had a catapulting effect if you landed too fast or too hard, bouncing you back into the air like a rubber ball.

I was damned if I was going to make that kind of mistake in front of Hannah. I turned downwind for my approach. A left-hand turn, I throttled back and adjusted the tail trimmer. I glided down steadily at just on sixty, selected my landing path and turned into the wind at five hundred feet, crossing the end of the field at a hundred and fifty.

Landing speed for a Bristol is forty-five miles an hour and can be made without power if you want to. I closed the throttle, eased back the stick to flatten my glide and floated in, the only sound the wind whispering through the struts.

I moved the stick back gradually to prevent her sinking and stalled into a perfect three-point landing, touching the ground so gently that I hardly felt a thing.

I rolled to a halt close to the hangar and sat there for a while, savouring the silence after the roar of the engine, then I pushed up my goggles and unstrapped myself. Hannah came round on the port side followed by a small, wiry man in overalls that had once been white and were now black with oil and grease.

"I told you he was good, Mannie," Hannah said.

"You did indeed, Sam." His companion smiled up at me.

The liking between us was immediate and mutually recognised. One of those odd occasions when you feel that you've known someone a hell of a long time.

Except for a very slight accent, his English was perfect. As I discovered later, he was fifty at that time and looked ten years older which was hardly surprising for the Nazis had imprisoned him for just over a year. He certainly didn't look like a professor. As I've said, he was small and rather insignificant, untidy, iron-grey hair falling across his forehead, the face brown and wizened. But then there were the eyes, clear grey and incredibly calm, the eyes of a man who had seen the worst life had to offer and still had faith.

"Emmanuel Sterne, Mr. Mallory," he said as I dropped to the ground.

"Neil," I told him and held out my hand.

He smiled then, very briefly and thunder rumbled across the river, the first heavy spots of rain staining the brown earth at my feet.

"Here we go again," Hannah said. "Let's get this thing inside quick. I don't think this is going to be any five-minute shower."

He gave a yell and the other two men arrived on the run. They were simply day labourers who helped out with the heavy work when needed for a pittance. Undernourished, gaunt-looking men in straw hats and ragged shirts.

There were no doors to the hangar. It was really only a roof on posts, but there was plenty of room for the Bristol beside the Hayley. We had barely got it in when the flood descended, rattling on the corrugated-iron roof like a dozen machine-guns. Outside, an impenetrable grey curtain came down between us and the river.

Mannie Sterne was standing looking at the Bristol, hands on hips. "Beautiful," he said. "Really beautiful."

"He's fallen in love again." Hannah took down a couple of old oilskin coats from a hook and threw me one. "I'll take you to the house. You coming, Mannie?"

Mannie was already at the engine cowling with a spanner. He shook his head without looking around. "Later—I'll be along later."

It was as if we had ceased to exist. Hannah shrugged and ducked out into the rain. I got my canvas grip from the observer's cockpit and ran after him.

The house was at the far end of the field, not much more than a wooden hut with a veranda and the usual corrugated-iron roof. It was built on stilts as they all were, mainly because of the dampness from all that heavy rain, but also in an attempt to keep out soldier ants and other examples of jungle wildlife.

He went up the steps to the veranda and he flung open a louvered door and led the way in. The floor was plain wood with one or two Indian rugs here and there. Most of the furniture was bamboo.

"Kitchen through there," he said. "Shower-room next to it.

There's a precipitation tank on the roof, so we don't lack for a generous supply of decent water, it rains so damn much."

"All the comforts of home," I said.

"I would think that something of an overstatement." He jerked his thumb at a door to the left. "That's my room. You can share with Mannie over here."

He opened the door, stood to one side and motioned me through. It was surprisingly large and airy, bamboo shutters open to the veranda. There were three single beds, another of those Indian rugs on the floor, and actually some books on a shelf beside the only bed, which was made up.

I picked one out and Hannah laughed shortly. "As you can see, Mannie likes a good read. Turned Manaus upside down for that little lot."

The book was Kant's *Critique of Pure Reason*. I said, "This must have been like putting his pan in the river for water and coming up with a diamond."

"Don't tell me you go for that kind of stuff, too?" He looked genuinely put out. "God help me, now I do need a drink."

He went back into the living-room. I chose one of the unoccupied beds, made it up with blankets from a cupboard in the corner, then unpacked my grip. When I returned to the other room he was standing on the veranda, a glass in one hand, a bottle of Gordon's gin in the other.

The rain curtain was almost impenetrable, the first few wooden huts on their stilts at the edge of town, the only other sign of life.

"Sometimes when it gets like this, I could go crazy," he said. "It's as if this is all there is. As if I'm never going to get out."

He tried to re-fill his glass, discovered the bottle was empty and threw it out into the rain with a curse. "I need a drink. Come on—if you're not too tired I'll take you up town and show you the sights. An unforgettable experience."

I put on my oilskin coat again and an old straw sombrero I found hanging behind the bedroom door. When I returned to the veranda he asked me if I was still carrying my revolver. As it happened, it was in one of my flying-jacket pockets.

He nodded in satisfaction. "You'll find everybody goes armed here. It's that kind of place."

We plunged out into the rain and moved towards the town. I think it was one of the most depressing sights I have ever seen in my life. A scabrous rash of decaying wooden huts on stilts, streets which had quickly turned into thick, glutinous mud. Filthy, ragged little children, many of them with open sores on their faces, played listlessly under the huts, and on the verandas above, people stared into the rain, gaunt, hopeless, most of them trapped in that living hell for what remained of their wretched lives, no hope on earth of getting out.

The church was more substantial and included a brick and adobe tower. I commented on that and Hannah laughed shortly. "They don't even have a regular priest. Old guy called Father Conté who works with the nuns up at Santa Helena drops in every so often to say a Mass or two, baptise the babies and so on. He'll be coming back with us tomorrow, by the way."

"You want me to go with you?"

"I don't see why not." He shrugged. "It's only a hundred-mile trip. Give you a chance to fly the Hayley. We'll have a passenger. Colonel Alberto from Forte Franco. He'll arrive about ten in the morning by boat."

"What's he do? Some kind of regular inspection?"

"You could say that." Hannah smiled cynically. "The nuns up there are American. Little Sisters of Pity, and very holy ladies indeed. The kind who have a mission. Know what I mean? The government's been trying to get them to move for a year or so now because of the way the Huna have been acting up, only they won't go. Alberto keeps trying, though, I'll say that for him."

In the centre of the town, we came to the only two-storeyed building in the place. The board above the wide veranda said *Hotel*, and two or three locals sat at a table without talking, staring lifelessly into space, rain blowing in on them.

"The guy who runs this place is important enough to be polite to," Hannah observed. "Eugenio Figueiredo. He's the government agent here so you'll be seeing a lot of him. All mail and freight has to be channelled through him for the entire upper Mortes region."

"Are they still keen on the diamond laws as they used to be?" I asked.

"And then some. Diamond prospectors aren't allowed to work on their own up here. They have to belong to an organised group called a *garimpa*, and the bossman holds a licence for all of them. Just to make sure the government gets its cut, everything they find has to be handed over to the local agent who issues a receipt and sends the loot downriver in a sealed bag. The off-off comes later."

"A hell of a temptation to hang on to a few."

"And that draws you a minimum of five years in the penal colony at Machados which could fairly be described as an open grave in a swamp about three hundred miles up the Negro."

He opened the door of the hotel and led the way in. I didn't care for the place from the start. A long, dark room with a bar down one side and a considerable number of tables and chairs. It was the smell that put me off more than anything else, compounded of stale liquor, human sweat and urine in about equal proportions, and there were too many flies about for my liking.

There were only two customers. One with his back against the wall by the door, glass in hand, the same vacant look on his face as I had noticed with the men on the veranda. His companion was sprawled across the table, his straw hat on the floor, a jug overturned, its contents dribbling through the bamboo into a sizeable pool.

"*Cachaça*," Hannah said. "They say it rots the brain, as well as the liver, but it's all these poor bastards can afford." He raised his voice, "Heh, Figueiredo, what about some service."

He unbuttoned his coat and dropped into a basket chair by one of the open shutters. A moment later, I heard a step and a man moved through the bead curtain at the back of the bar.

55

Eugenio Figueiredo wasn't by any means a large man, but he was fat enough for life to be far from comfortable for him in a climate such as that one. The first time I saw him, he was shining with sweat in spite of the palm fan in his right hand which he used vigorously. His shirt clung to his body, the moisture soaking through, and the stink of him was the strongest I have known in a human being.

He was somewhere in his middle years, a minor public official in spite of his responsibilities, too old for change and without the slightest hope of preferment. As much a victim of fate as anyone else in Landro. His amiability was surprising in the circumstances.

"Ah, Captain Hannah."

An Indian woman came through the curtain behind him. He said something to her, then advanced to join us.

Hannah made the introduction casually as he lit a cigarette. Figueiredo extended a moist hand. "At your orders, senhor."

"At yours," I murmured.

The smell was really overpowering, although Hannah didn't appear in any way put out. I sat on the sill by the open shutter, which helped, and Figueiredo sank into a basket chair at the table.

"You are an old Brazilian hand, I think, Senhor Mallory," he observed. "Your Portuguese is too excellent for it to be otherwise."

"Lately I've been in Peru," I said. "But before that, I did a year on the Xingu."

"If you could survive that, you could survive anything."

He crossed himself piously. The Indian woman arrived with a tray which she set down on the table. There was Bourbon, a bottle of some kind of spa water and three glasses.

"You will join me senhors?"

Hannah half-filled a sizeable tumbler and didn't bother with water. I took very little, in fact drank at all only as a matter of courtesy, which, I think, Figueiredo was well aware of.

Hannah swallowed it down and helped himself to more, staring morosely into the rain. "Look at it," he said. "What a bloody place."

It was one of those statements that didn't require any comment. The facts spoke for themselves. A group of men turned out from between two houses and trailed towards the hotel, heads down, in a kind of uniform of rubber poncho and straw sombrero. "Who have we got here?" Hannah demanded.

Figueiredo leaned forward, the fan in his hand ceasing for a moment. It commenced to flutter again. "*Garimpeiros*," he said. "Avila's bunch. Came in last night. Lost two men in a brush with the Huna."

Hannah poured another enormous whisky. "From what I hear of that bastard, he probably shot them himself."

There were five of them, as unsavoury-looking a bunch as I had ever seen. Little to choose between any of them, really. The same gaunt, fleshless faces, the same touch of fever in all the eyes.

Avila was the odd man out. A big man. Almost as large as Hannah, with a small, cruel mouth that was effeminate in its way although that was perhaps suggested more by the pencil-thin moustache which must have taken him considerable pains to cultivate.

He nodded to Figueiredo and Hannah, the eyes pausing fractionally on me, then continued to a table at the far end of the bar, his men trailing after him. When they took off their ponchos it became immediately obvious that they were all armed to the teeth and most of them carried a machete in a leather sheath as well as a holstered revolver.

The Indian woman went to serve them. One of them put a hand up her skirt. She didn't try to resist, simply stood there like some dumb animal while another reached up to fondle her breasts.

"Nice people," Hannah said. Figueiredo seemed completely unperturbed, which was surprising in view of the fact that the woman, as I learned later, was his wife.

She was finally allowed to go for the drinks when Avila intervened. He lit a cigarette, produced a pack of cards and looked across at us. "You would care to join us, gentlemen?" He spoke in quite reasonable English. "A few hands of poker, perhaps?"

They all turned to look at us and there was a short pause. It was as if everyone waited for something to happen and there was a kind of menace in the air.

Hannah emptied his glass and stood up. "Why not? Anything's better than nothing in this hole."

I said, "Not for me. I've got things to do. Another time, perhaps."

Hannah shrugged. "Suit yourself."

He picked up the bottle of bourbon and started towards the other end of the bar. Figueiredo tried to stand up, swaying so alarmingly that I moved forward quickly and took his arm.

He said softly, lips hardly moving, "Give him an hour, then come back for him on some pretence or other. He is not liked here. There could be trouble."

The smile hooked firmly into place, he turned and went towards the others. I moved to the door. As I opened it, Avila called, "Our company is not good enough for you, senhor?"

But I would not be drawn—not then at least, for I think that out of some strange foreknowledge, I knew that enough would come later.

When I ran out of the rain into the shelter of that primitive hangar, I found Mannie Sterne standing on a wooden platform which he had positioned at the front of the Bristol. The engine cowling had been removed, and the engine was completely exposed in the light of a couple of pressure lamps he had hung overhead.

He glanced over his shoulder and smiled. "Back so soon?"

"Hannah took me to the local pub," I said. "I didn't like the atmosphere."

He turned and crouched down, a frown on his face. "What happened?"

I gave him the whole story including Figueiredo's parting words. When I was finished, he sat there for a while, staring out into the rain. There was a sort of sadness on his face. No, more than that—worry. And there was a scar running from his right eye to the corner of his mouth. I'd failed to notice that earlier.

"Poor Sam." He sighed. "So, we do what Figueiredo says. We go and get him in a little while." With an abrupt change in direction, he stood up and tapped the Bristol. "A superb engine, Rolls-Royce. Only the best. The Bristol was one of the greatest all-purpose planes on the Western Front."

"You were there?"

"Oh, not what you are thinking. I wasn't a Richthofen or an Udet in a skin-tight grey uniform with the blue Max at my throat, but I did visit the front-line Jagdstaffels fairly often. When I first started as an engineer, I worked for Fokker."

"And Hannah was on the other side of the line?"

"I suppose so."

He had returned to the engine, examining it carefully with a hand-lamp. "This is really in excellent condition."

I said, "What's wrong with him? Do you know?"

"Sam?" He shrugged. "It's simple enough. He was too good too soon. Ace-of-aces at twenty-three. All the medals in the world—all the adulation." He leaned down for another spanner. "But for such a man, what happens when it is all over?"

I considered the point for a while. "I suppose in a way, the rest of his life would tend to be something of an anti-climax."

"An understatement as far as he is concerned. Twenty years of flying mail, of barnstorming, skydiving to provide a momentary thrill for the mindless at state fairs who hope to see his parachute fail to open, of risking his life in a hundred different ways and at the end, what does he have to show for it?" He swept his arms out in a gesture which took in everything. "This, my friend—this is all he has, and three months from now, when his contract ends, a government bonus of five thousand dollars."

He looked down at me for several seconds, then turned and went back to tinkering with the engine. I didn't know what to say, but he solved the situation for me.

"You know, I'm a great believer in hunches. I go by what I think of people, instantly, in the very first moment. Now you interest me. You are your own man, a rare thing in this day and age. Tell me about yourself."

So I did for he was the easiest man to talk to I'd ever known. He spoke only briefly himself, the odd question thrown in casually now and then, yet at the end of things, he had squeezed me dry.

He said, "A good thing Sam was able to help you when he did, but then I'm also a great believer in fate. A man has to exist in the present moment. Accept what turns up. It's impossible to live any other way. I have a book at the house which you should read. Kant's *Critique of Pure Reason*."

"I already have," I said.

He turned, eyebrows raised in some surprise. "You agree with his general thesis?"

"Not really. I don't think anything in this life is certain enough for fixed rules to apply. You have to take what comes and do the best you can."

"Then Heidegger is your man. I have a book of his which would interest you in which he argues that for authentic living what is necessary is the resolute confrontation of death. Tell me, were you afraid yesterday when you were attempting to land that Vega of yours?"

"Only afterwards." I grinned. "The rest of the time, I was too busy trying to hold the damned thing together."

"You and Heidegger would get on famously."

"And what would he think of Hannah?"

"Not very much, I'm afraid. Sam exists in two worlds only. The past and the future. He has never succeeded in coming to terms with the present. That is his tragedy."

"So what's left for him?"

He turned and looked at me gravely, the spanner in his right hand dripping oil. "I only know one thing with certainty. He should have died in combat at the height of his career like so many others. At the last possible moment of the war. November 1918, for preference."

It was a terrible thing to have to say, and yet he meant it. I knew that. We stood staring at each other, the only sound the rain rushing into the ground. He wiped the oil from his hands with a piece of cotton waste and smiled sadly.

"Now I think we had better go and get him while there is still time."

I could hear the laughter from the hotel long before we got there and it was entirely the wrong sort. I knew then we were in for trouble and so did Mannie. His face beneath the old sou'wester he wore against the rain was very pale.

As we approached the hotel steps I said, "This man, Avila? What's he like?"

He paused in the middle of the street. "There's a story I'm fond of about an old Hassidic rabbi who, having no money around the house, gave one of his wife's rings to a beggar. When he told her what he'd done, she went into hysterics, because the ring was a family heirloom and very valuable. On hearing this, the rabbi ran through the streets looking for the beggar."

"To get his ring back?"

"No, to warn him of its true value in case anyone tried to cheat him when he sold it."

I laughed out loud, puzzled. "What's that got to do with Avila?"

"Nothing much, I suppose." He grinned wryly. "Except that he isn't like that."

We turned into the alley at the side of the hotel and paused again. "You'll find the kitchen door just round the corner as I described," he said. "Straight through to the bar. You can't miss it."

There was another burst of laughter from inside. "They seem to be enjoying themselves."

"I've heard laughter like that before. I didn't like it then and I don't like it now. Good luck," he added briefly, then went round to the front of the hotel.

The kitchen door he had mentioned stood open. Figueiredo's wife was seated on a chair slicing vegetables into a bowl on her knee. I stepped past her, ignoring her look of astonishment, and walked across the kitchen to the opposite door.

There was a short passage with the entrance to the bar at the far end. Figueiredo was standing on this side of the bead curtain peering through, presumably keeping out of the way.

He glanced over his shoulder at my approach. I motioned him to silence and looked through. They were still grouped around the table, Hannah in the chair next to Avila. He was face-down across the table, quite obviously hopelessly drunk. As I watched, Avila pulled him upright by the hair, jerking the head back so that the mouth gaped.

He picked up a jug of *cachaça* and poured in about a pint. "You like that, senhor? The wine of the country, eh?"

Hannah started to choke and Avila released him so that he fell back across the table. The rest of them seemed to find this enormously funny and one of them emptied a glass over the American's head.

There was a sudden silence as Mannie moved into view from the right. In the old sou'wester and yellow oilskin he could easily have looked ridiculous, yet didn't, which was a strange thing. He walked towards the group at the same steady pace and paused.

Avila said, "Go away, there is nothing for you here."

Mannie's face was paler than ever. "Not without Captain Hannah."

Avila's hand came up holding a revolver. He cocked it very deliberately so I produced the automatic shotgun I had been holding under my oilskin coat and shoved Figueriedo out of the way. There was a wooden post on the far side of Avila, one of several set into the floor to help support the plank ceiling. It was the kind of target that even I couldn't miss. I took careful aim and fired. The post disintegrated in the centre, and part of the ceiling sagged.

I have seldom seen men scatter faster than they did. When I stepped through the bead curtain, shotgun ready, they were all flat on the floor, except for Avila, who crouched on one knee beside Hannah, revolver ready.

"I'd put it down if I were you," I told him. "This is a six-shot automatic and I'm using steel ball cartridges."

He placed his gun very carefully on the table and stood back, eyeing me balefully. I went round the end of the bar and handed the shotgun to Mannie. Then I dropped to one knee beside Hannah, heaved him over my shoulder and stood up.

Avila said, "I will remember this, senhors. My turn will come."

I didn't bother to answer, simply turned and walked out. Mannie followed, the shotgun under one arm.

Hannah started to vomit halfway down the street, and by the time we reached the house, there couldn't have been much left in him. We stripped him between us and got him into the shower. That revived him a little, but the truth was that he was saturated with alcohol and partly out of his mind, I think, as we put him to bed.

He thrashed about for a while, hands plucking at himself. As I leaned over him, his eyes opened. He stared up at me, a slight frown on his face, and smiled.

"You new, kid? Just out from England?"

"Something like that." I glanced at Mannie, who made no sign.

"If you last a week you've got a chance." He grabbed me by the front of my flying jacket. "I'll give you a tip. Never cross the line alone under ten thousand feet, that's lesson number one."

"I'll remember that," I said.

"And the sun—watch the sun."

I think he was trying to say more but his head fell to one side and he passed out again.

I said, "He thought he was back on the Western Front."

Mannie nodded. "Always the same. Hopelessly trapped by the past."

He tucked the blankets in around Hannah's shoulders very carefully and I went into the living-room. It had stopped raining and moisture, drawn by the heat, rose from the ground outside like smoke.

It was still cool in the bedroom, and I lay down and stared up at the ceiling, thinking about Sam Hannah, the man who once had had everything and now had nothing. And after a while, I drifted into sleep.

5

The Killing Ground

Forte Franco must have been the sort of posting which to any career officer was equivalent to a sentence of death. A sign that he was finished. That there was no more to come. Because of this I had expected the kind of second-rater one usually found in command of up-river military posts: incapable of realising his own inadequacies and permanently soured by his present misfortunes.

Colonel Alberto was not at all like that. I was helping Mannie get the Hayley ready to go when the launch came into the jetty and he disembarked. He was every inch the soldier, parade-ground smart in a well-tailored drill uniform, shining boots, black polished holster on his right thigh. The face beneath the peaked cap was intelligent and firm, although tinged with yellow as if he'd had jaundice, which was a common enough complaint in the climate.

There were half a dozen soldiers in the boat, but only one accompanied him, a young sergeant as smartly turned out as his colonel, with a briefcase in one hand and a couple of machine-guns slung over one shoulder.

Alberto smiled pleasantly and spoke in quite excellent English. "A fine morning, Senhor Sterne. Is everything ready?"

"Just about," Mannie told him.

"And Captain Hannah?"

"Will be down shortly."

"I see." Alberto turned to me. "And this gentleman?"

"Neil Mallory," I said. "I'm Hannah's new pilot. I'm going up with you, just to get the feel of things."

"Excellent." He shook hands rather formally then glanced at his watch. "I have things to discuss with Figueiredo. I'll be back in half an hour. I'll leave Sergeant Lima here. He'll be going with us."

He moved away, a brisk, competent figure, and the sergeant opened the cabin door and got rid of the machine-guns and the briefcase.

I said to Mannie, "What's his story? He doesn't look the type for up-country work."

"Political influence as far as I understand it," Mannie said. "Said the wrong thing to some government minister or other in front of people. Something like that, anyway."

"He looks a good man to me."

"Oh, he's that, all right. At least as far as the job is concerned, but I've never cared for the professional soldier as a type. They make the end justify the means too often for my liking." He wiped his hands on a rag and stood back. "Well, she's ready as she'll ever be. Better get Hannah."

I found him in the shower, leaning in the corner for support, head turned up into the spray. When he turned it off and stepped out, he tried to smile and only succeeded in looking worse than ever.

"I feel as if they've just dug me up. What happened last night?"

"You got drunk," I said.

"What on—wood alcohol? I haven't felt like this since Prohibition."

He wandered off to his bedroom like a very old man and I went into the kitchen and made some coffee. When it was ready, I took it out on a tray and found him on the veranda dressed for flying.

He wrapped a white scarf around his throat and took one of the mugs. "Smells good enough to drink. I thought you Limeys could only make tea." He sipped a little, eyeing me speculatively. "What really happened last night?"

"Can't you remember anything?"

"I won a little money at poker, that's for sure. More than my share and Avila and his boys weren't too happy. Was there trouble?"

"I suppose you could say that."

"Tell me."

So I did. There was little point in holding anything back for he was certain to hear it for himself one way or the other.

When I was finished, he sat there on the rail holding the mug in both hands, his face very white, those pale eyes of his opaque, lifeless. As I have said, the appearance of things was of primary importance to him. His standing in other men's eyes, the image he portrayed to the world, and these men had treated him like dirt—publicly humiliated him.

He smiled suddenly and unexpectedly, a slow burn as if what I had said had touched a fuse inside. I don't know what it would have done for Avila, but it certainly frightened me. He didn't say another word about the matter, didn't have to and I could only hope Avila would be long gone when we returned.

He emptied what was left of his coffee over the rail and stood up. "Okay, let's get moving. We've got a schedule to keep."

Flying the Hayley was like driving a car after what I'd been used to and the truth is, there wasn't much enjoyment in it. Everything worked to perfection, it was the last word in comfort and engine noise was reduced to a minimum. Hannah was beside me and Colonel Alberto sat in one of the front passenger seats, his sergeant behind to preserve, I suppose, the niceties of military rank.

Hannah opened a Thermos flask, poured coffee into two cups and passed one back. "Still hoping to get the nuns to move on, Colonel?" he asked.

"Not really," Alberto said. "I raise the matter with Father Conté on each visit, usually over the sherry, because it is part of my standing orders from Army Command Headquarters. A meaningless ritual, I fear. The Church has considerable influence in government circles and at the highest possible level. No one is willing to order them to leave. The choice is theirs, and they see themselves as having a plain duty to take God and modern medicine to the Indians."

"In that order?" Hannah said, and laughed for the first time that morning.

"And the Huna?" I said. "What do they think?"

"The Huna, Senhor Mallory, want no one. Did you know what their name means in their own language? The enemy of all men. Anthropologists talk of the noble savage, but there is nothing noble about the Huna. They are probably the cruelest people on earth."

"They were there first," I said.

"That's what they used to say about the Sioux back home," Hannah put in.

"An interesting comparison," Alberto said. "Look at the United States a century ago, and look at her now. Well, this is our frontier, one of the richest undeveloped areas in the world. God alone knows how far we can go in the next fifty years, but one thing is certain—progress is inevitable, and these people stand in the way of that progress."

"So what answer have you got?" I said. "Extermination."

"Not if they can be persuaded to change. The choice is theirs."

"Which gives them no choice at all." I was surprised to hear my own bitterness.

Alberto said, "Figueiredo was telling me you spent a year in the Xingu River country, Senhor Mallory. The Indians in that area have always been particularly troublesome. This was so when you were there?"

I nodded reluctantly.

"Did you ever kill one?"

"All right," I said. "I was at Forte Tomas in November, thirty-six, when they attacked the town and butchered thirty or forty people."

"A bad business," he said. "You must have been with the survivors who took refuge in the church and held them off a week till the military arrived. You must have killed many times during that unfortunate episode."

"Only because they were trying to kill me."

"Exactly."

I could see him in my mirror as he leaned back and took a file from his briefcase, effectively putting an end to the conversation.

Hannah grinned. "I'd say the colonel's made his point."

"Maybe he has," I said, "but it still isn't going to help the Huna."

"But why in the hell would any sensible person want to do that?" He seemed surprised. "They've had their day, Mallory, just like the dinosaurs."

"Doomed to extinction, you mean?"

"Exactly." He groaned and put a hand to his head. "Christ, there's someone walking around inside with hob-nailed boots."

I gave up. Maybe they were right and I was wrong—perhaps the Huna had to go under and there was no other choice. I pushed the thought away from me, eased back the stick and climbed into the sunlight.

The whole trip took no more than forty minutes, mostly in bright sunshine although as we approached our destination we ran into another of those sudden violent rainstorms and I had to go down fast.

Visibility was temporarily so poor that Hannah took over the controls in the final stages, bringing her down to two hundred feet, at which height we could at least see the river. He throttled back and side-slipped neatly into the landing strip, which was a large patch of *campo* on the east bank of the river.

"They don't have a radio, so I usually fly in over the settlement just to let them know I'm here," Hannah told me. "The nuns enjoy it, but this isn't weather to fool about in."

"It is of no consequence," Alberto said calmly. "They will have heard us land. The launch will be here soon."

The mission, as I remembered, was a quarter of a mile upstream on the other side of the river. Alberto told Lima to go and wait the launch's arrival and produced a leather cigar case.

Hannah took one, but I declined and on impulse opened the cabin door and jumped down into the grass. The rain hammered down relentlessly as I went after the sergeant. There was a crude wooden pier constructed of rough-hewn planks extending into the river on piles, perhaps twenty or thirty feet long.

Lima was already at the end. He stood there, gazing out across the river. Suddenly he leaned over the edge of the jetty, dropping to one knee as if looking down at something in the water. As I approached, he stood up, turned to one side and was violently sick.

"What's wrong?" I demanded, then looked over the edge and saw for myself. I took several deep breaths and said, "You'd better get the colonel."

An old canoe was tied up to the jetty and the thing which floated beside it, trapped by the current against the pilings was dressed in the tropical-white robes of a nun. There was still a little flesh on the skeletal face that stared out from the white coif, but not much. A sudden eddy pulled the body away. It rolled over, face-down, and I saw there were at least half a dozen arrows in the back.

Lima climbed up out of the water clutching an identity disc and crucifix on a chain which he'd taken from around the nun's neck. He looked sicker than ever as he handed them to Alberto and stood there shaking and not only from the cold.

Alberto said, "Pull yourself together, for God's sake, and try and remember you're a soldier. You're safe enough here anyway. I've never known them to operate on this side of the river."

If we'd done the sensible thing we'd have climbed back into the Hayley and got the hell out of there. Needless to say, Alberto didn't consider that for a second. He stood at the end of the jetty peering into the rain, a machine-gun cradled in his left arm.

"Don't tell me you're thinking of going across?" Hannah demanded.

"I have no choice. I must find out what the situation is over there. There could be survivors."

"You've got to be joking," Hannah exploded angrily. "Do I have to spell it out for you? It's finally happened, just as everyone knew it would if they didn't get out of there."

Colonel Alberto ignored him and said, without turning round, "I would take it as a favour if you would accompany me, Senhor Mallory. Sergeant Lima can stay here with Senhor Hannah."

Hannah jumped in with both feet, his ego, I suppose, unable to accept the fact of being left behind. "To hell with that for a game of soldiers. If he goes, I go."

I don't know if it was the result Alberto had intended, but he certainly didn't argue. Sergeant Lima was left to hold the fort with his revolver, I took the other machine-gun and Hannah had the automatic shotgun he habitually carried in the Hayley.

There was water in the canoe. It swirled about in the bottom breaking over my feet in little waves as I sat in the stern and paddled. Hannah was in the centre, also paddling and Alberto crouched in the prow, his machine-gun at the ready.

An old log, drifting by, turned into an alligator by flicking his tail and moving lazily out of the way. The jungle was quiet in the rain, the distant cough of a jaguar the only sound. On the far side of the river, sandbanks lifted out of the water, covered with ibis, and as we approached, thousands of them lifted into the rain in a great, red cloud.

The sandbanks appeared and disappeared at intervals for

most of the way, finally rising in a shoal a good two hundred yards long in the centre of the river opposite the mission jetty.

"I landed and took off from there twice last year during the summer, when the river was low," Hannah said.

I suspected he had made the remark for something to say more than anything else for we were drifting in towards the jetty now and the silence was uncanny.

We tied up alongside an old steam launch and climbed up on to the jetty. A couple of wild dogs were fighting over something on the ground at the far end. They cleared off as we approached. When we got close, we saw it was another nun, lying face-down, hands hooked into the dirt.

Flies rose in clouds at our approach and the smell was frightful. Alberto held a handkerchief to his face and dropped to one knee to examine the body. He slid his hand underneath, groped around for a while and finally came up with the identity disc he was seeking on its chain. He stood up and moved away hurriedly to breathe fresh air.

"Back of her skull crushed, probably by a war club."

"How long?" Hannah asked him.

"Two days—three at the most. If there has been a general massacre, then we couldn't be safer. They believe the spirits of those killed violently linger in the vicinity for seven days. There isn't a Huna alive who'd come anywhere near this place."

I don't know whether his words were supposed to reassure, but they certainly didn't do much for me. I slipped the safety catch off the machine-gun and held it at the ready as we went forward.

The mission itself was perhaps a hundred yards from the jetty. One large single-storeyed building that was the medical centre and hospital, four simple bungalows with thatched roofs and a small church on a rise at the edge of the jungle and close to the river, a bell hanging from a frame above the door.

We found two more nuns before we reached the mission, both virtually hacked to pieces, but the most appalling sight was at the edge of the clearing at the end of the medical centre, where we discovered the body of a man suspended by his ankles above the cold ashes of what had been a considerable fire, the flesh peeling from his skull. The smell was nauseating, so bad that I could almost taste it.

Alberto beat the flies away with a stick and took a close look. "Father Conté's servant," he said. "An Indian from downriver. Poor devil, they must have decided he'd earned something special."

Hannah turned on me, his face like the wrath of God. "And you were feeling sorry for the bastards."

Colonel Alberto cut in quickly. "Never mind that now. Your private differences can wait till later. We'll split up to save time, and don't forget I need identity bracelets. Another day in this heat and it will be impossible to recognise anyone."

I took the medical centre, an eerie experience because everything was in perfect order. Beds turned down as if awaiting patients, mosquito nets hooked up neatly. The only unusual thing was the smell, which led me to the small operating theatre, where I found two more nuns, their bodies already decomposing. Like the one at the end of the jetty, they seemed to have been clubbed to death. I managed to find their identity discs without too much trouble and got out.

Alberto was emerging from one of the bungalows. I gave him the discs, and he said, "That makes ten in all; there should be a dozen. And there's no sign of Father Conté."

"All they've done is kill people," I said. "Everything else is in perfect order. It doesn't make sense. I'd have expected them to put a torch to the buildings, just to finish things off."

"They wouldn't dare," he said. "Another superstition. The spirits of those they have killed need somewhere to live."

Hannah moved out of the church and called to us. When we joined him he was shaking with rage. Father Conté lay flat on his back just inside the door, an arrow in his throat. From his position, I'd say he had probably been standing on the porch facing his attackers when hit. His eyes had gone, probably one of the vultures which I had noticed perched on the church roof.

Most terrible thing of all, his cassock had been torn away and his chest hacked open with a machete.

Hannah said, "Now why would they do a thing like that?"

"They admired his courage. They imagine that by eating his heart, they take some of his bravery into themselves."

Which just about finished Hannah off. He looked capable of anything as Alberto said, "There are two nuns missing. We know they're not inside anywhere so we'll split up again and work our way down through the mission in a rough line. They're probably face-down in the grass somewhere."

But they weren't, or at least we couldn't find them. When we gathered again at the jetty, Hannah said, "Maybe they went into the water like the first one we found?"

"All the others were either in their middle years or older," Alberto said. "These two, the two who are missing, are much younger than that. Twenty or twenty-one. No more."

"You think they've been taken alive?" I asked him.

"It could well be. Like many tribes, they like to freshen the blood occasionally. They frequently take in young women, keep them until the baby is born then murder them."

"For God's sake, let's get out of here," Hannah said. "I've had about all I can take." He turned and hurried to the end of the jetty, and boarded the canoe.

There wasn't much more we could do anyway so we joined him and paddled back downstream. The journey was completely uneventful. When we drifted in to the jetty at the edge of the *campo*, Lima was waiting for us looking more nervous than ever.

"Everything all right here?" Alberto demanded.

Lima said anxiously, "I don't know, Colonel." He nodded towards the green curtain of jungle. "You know what it's like. You keep imagining that someone is standing on the other side, watching you."

Forest foxes started to bark in several different directions at once. Alberto said calmly, "I suggest we walk back to the plane quietly and get inside with the minimum of fuss. I think we're being watched."

74

"The foxes?" I said.

"Aren't foxes—not at this time in the morning."

The walk to the plane was an experience in itself and I expected an arrow in the back at any moment. But nothing happened. We all got inside without incident and I took the controls.

I taxied to the end of the *campo*. As I turned into the wind, an Indian emerged from the jungle and stood on the edge of the clearing watching us, face painted for war, magnificent in a head-dress of parrot feathers, a spear in one hand, a six-foot bow in the other.

Hannah picked up one of the machine-guns and reached for the window. Alberto caught his arm. "No, leave it. Our turn will come."

As we moved past, another figure emerged from the forest, then another and another. I don't think I have ever felt happier than when I lifted the Hayley over the trees at the edge of the *campo*, stamped on the rudder and swung north.

There was no landing strip at Forte Franco, for the simple reason that the post had been built on an island strategically situated at the mouth of the Negro about a century before the Wright brothers first left the ground.

We radioed the bad news ahead the moment we were in range, just to get things moving, then put down at Landro. Alberto wasted little time in getting under way. He ordered his men to prepare the launch for a quick departure, then went into Landro with Hannah to see Figueiredo. I was waiting at the jetty with Mannie when the colonel returned. Hannah was not with him.

"What happens now?" I asked.

"There should be a reply to my message from Army Headquarters by the time I reach Forte Franco. I would imagine my instructions will be to proceed upriver at once with my command. All thirty-eight of them. I've a dozen men down with fever at the moment."

"But surely they'll send you reinforcements?" Mannie said.

"Miracles sometimes happen, but not very often, my friend. Even if they did, it would be several weeks before they could arrive. This kind of thing is an old story, as you must know, Senhor Mallory." He looked out across the river to the forest. "In any case, in that kind of country, a regiment would be too little, an army not enough."

"When we landed, you said we'd be safe on that side of the river," I reminded him. "That they never crossed over."

He nodded, his face dark and serious. "A cause for concern, I assure you, if it means they are moving out of their usual territory." The engine of the launch broke into life and he smiled briskly. "I must be on the move. Senhor Hannah stayed at the hotel, by the way. I'm afraid he has taken all this very hard."

He stepped over the rail, one of the soldiers cast off and the launch moved into midstream. We stood watching it go. Alberto waved, then went into the cabin.

I said, "What about Hannah? Do you think there's any point in going for him? If he runs into Avila in the mood he's in . . ."

"Avila and his bunch moved out just before noon." Mannie shook his head. "Best leave him for now. We can put him to bed later."

He turned and walked away. A solitary ibis hovered above the trees on the other side of the river before descending like a splash of blood against the grey sky. An omen, perhaps, of worse things to come?

I shivered involuntarily and went after Mannie.

6

The Scarlet Flower

In the days that followed, the news from upriver wasn't good. Several rubber tappers were killed and a party of diamond prospectors, five in all, died to the last man in an ambush not ten miles above the mission.

Alberto and his men, operating out of Santa Helena, didn't seem to be accomplishing much, which wasn't really surprising. If they kept to the tracks the Huna ambushed them, and if they tried to hack a way through the jungle, their progress was about one mile a day to nowhere.

In a week, he'd lost seven men. Two dead, three wounded and two injured, one by what was supposed to be an accidental cut on the leg with a machete, which sounded more as if it had been self-inflicted to me. I saw the man involved when Hannah, who was flying him out to Manaus, dropped in at Landro to refuel and I can only say that considering his undoubted pain, he seemed remarkably cheerful.

Hannah was making a daily trip to Santa Helena under the circumstances which left me with the Landro–Manaus mail run in the Bristol. The general attitude in Manaus was interesting.

Events upriver might have been taking place on another planet as far as they were concerned, and even in Landro no one seemed particularly excited.

Two things changed that. The first was the arrival of Avila and his bunch—or what was left of them—one evening just before dark. They all seemed to have sustained minor wounds of one sort or another and had lost two men in an ambush on a tributary of the Mortes on the side of the river where the Huna weren't supposed to be.

Even then, people didn't get too worked up. After all, Indians had been killing the odd white up-country for years. It was only when the boat drifted in with the two dead on board that the harsh reality was really brought home.

It was a nasty business. Mannie found them early on Sunday morning when he was taking a walk before breakfast and sent one of the labourers for me. By the time I got there people were already hurrying along to the jetty in twos and threes.

The canoe had grounded on the sandbank above the jetty, pushed by the current. The occupants, as was discovered later from their papers, were rubber tappers and were feathered with more arrows than I would have believed possible.

They had been dead for at least three days and were in the condition you would have expected considering the climate, flies buzzing around in clouds and the usual smell. There was one rather nasty extra. The man in the stern had fallen backwards, one arm trailing in the water, and the piranha had taken the flesh from his bones up to the elbow.

No one was particularly cheerful after that and they clustered in small groups, talking in low voices until Figueiredo arrived and took charge of things. He stood there leaning on his stick, face sombre, the sweat soaking through shirt and linen jacket and watched as half a dozen labourers with handkerchiefs around their faces got the bodies out.

The Huna bows were six feet in length, taller than the men who used them and so powerful that an arrow taken in the chest frequently penetrated the entire body, the head protruding from the back. They were usually tipped with piranha teeth or razor-sharp bamboo.

A labourer pulled one out of one of the corpses and handed it to Figueiredo. He examined it briefly then snapped it in his two hands and threw the pieces away angrily.

"Animals!" he said. "They'll be coming out of the jungle next."

Which started the crowd off nicely. They wanted blood, that much was evident. The Huna were vermin and there was only one way to handle vermin. Extermination. The voices buzzed around me. I listened for a while, then turned, sick to the stomach, and walked away.

I was helping myself to a large Scotch from Hannah's private stock when Mannie came in. "That bad?" he said calmly.

"Everywhere you go, the same story," I said. "It's always the Indians' fault—never the whites'."

He lit one of those foul-smelling Brazilian cigars he favoured and sat on the veranda rail. "You feel pretty strongly about all this. Most people would think that strange in someone who was at Forte Tomas. Who came as close to being butchered by Indians as a man can get."

"If you reduce men to symbols, then killing them is easy," I said. "An abstraction. Kill a Huna and you're not killing an individual—you're killing an Indian. Does that make any kind of sense to you?"

He was obviously deeply moved, and knew in detail what was even then happening to his people. I suppose the plain truth was that I was hitting close to home.

He said, "A profound discovery to make so early in life. May I ask how?"

There was no reason not to speak of it, although the tightness was there in my chest the moment I began, the constricted breathing. An unutterable feeling of having lost something worth having.

"It's simple," I said. "In my first month on the Xingu I met the best man I'm ever likely to see, even if I live to be a hundred. If he'd been a Catholic, they'd have tossed a coin to decide between burning or canonising him."

"Who was he?"

"A Viennese named Karl Buber. He came out here as a young Lutheran pastor to join a mission on the Xingu. He threw it all up in disgust when he discovered the unpalatable fact that the Indians were suffering as much at the hands of the missionaries as at the hand of anyone else."

"What did he do?"

"Set up his own place upriver from Forte Tomas. Dedicated his life to working amongst the Civa, and they could teach the Huna a thing or two, believe me. He even married one. I used to fly him stuff up from Belém without the company knowing. He was the best friend the Civa ever had."

"And they killed him?"

I nodded. "His wife told him her father was desperately wounded and in urgent need of medical attention after the Forte Tomas attack. When Buber got there, they clubbed him to death."

Mannie frowned slightly as if not quite understanding. "You mean his own wife betrayed him?"

"She did it for the tribe," I said. "They admired Buber for his courage and wisdom. They killed him as Father Conté was killed in Santa Helena, that their chiefs might have his brains and heart."

There was genuine horror on his face now. "And you can still think kindly of such people?"

"Karl Buber would have. If he were here now, he'd tell you that the Indian is as much a product of his environment as a jaguar. That he only survives in that green hell out there across the river by being willing to kill instinctually, without a moment's thought, several times a day. Killing is part of his nature."

"Which includes killing his friends?"

"He doesn't have any. He has his blood ties—family and

tribe. Anyone else is outside and on borrowed time. Ripe for the block sooner or later, as Buber discovered."

I poured another whisky. Mannie said, "And what is your personal solution to the problem?"

"There isn't one," I said. "There's too much here worth the having. Diamonds in the rivers, every kind of mineral ever heard of and probably a few we haven't. Now what man worth his salt would let a bunch of Stone Age savages stand between him and a slice of that kind of cake?"

He smiled sadly and put a hand on my shoulder. "A dirty world, my friend."

"And I've had too much to drink considering the time of day."

"Exactly. Go have a shower and I'll make some coffee."

I did as he suggested, sluicing myself in lukewarm water for ten minutes or so. As I was dressing, there was a knock at the door and Figueiredo stuck his head in.

"A bad business." He sank into the nearest chair, mopping his face with a handkerchief. "I've just been on the radio to Santa Helena, giving Alberto the good news."

The military had installed a much more powerful radio transmitter and receiving unit than his in the hangar and had left a young corporal to man it.

"Hannah stayed up there overnight," I said as I pulled on my flying jacket. "Any word from him?"

Figueiredo nodded. "He wants you to join him as soon as possible."

"At Santa Helena?" I shook my head. "You must have got it wrong. I've got the mail run to make to Manaus."

"Cancelled. You're needed on military business which takes precedence."

"Well, that's intriguing," I said. "Any idea what it's all about?"

He shook his head. "Not my business to know. Where military affairs are concerned, I have no jurisdiction at all, and what's more, I like it that way."

Mannie kicked open the door and came in with coffee in two tin cups. "You've heard?" I said.

He nodded. "I'd better get across to the hangar and get the Bristol ready to move."

I stood at the window beside Figueiredo, sipping my coffee, gazing down towards the jetty. A cart came towards us, pulled by a couple of half-starved oxen, a collection of moving bones held together by a bag of skin. The driver kept them going by sticking a six-inch nail on the end of a pole beneath their tails at frequent intervals.

As the cart went by, the smell told us what was inside. Figueiredo turned, an expression of acute distaste on his face. He opened his mouth to speak and the rain came down in a sudden rush, rattling on the corrugated-iron roof, drowning all sound.

We stood there together and watched the cart disappear into the gloom.

It was still raining when I took off, not that I was going to let that put me off. The massacre of Santa Helena had been worse, but the two poor wretches in the canoe had brought a whiff of the open grave with them, a touch of unease, a feeling that something waited out there in the trees across the river. Landro was definitely a place to put behind you on such a morning.

I followed the river all the way and seeing no reason to push hard, especially once I ran out of the rain, took over a good hour getting there, giving myself time to enjoy the flight.

I went in low over Santa Helena itself, just to see how things stood. The mission launch was just leaving the jetty and moving downriver, but the old forty-foot military gunboat was still there. A couple of soldiers moved out of the hospital and waved and Hannah came out of the priest's house. I circled again, then cut across the river and dropped into the airstrip.

There was a permanent guard of ten men with two heavy machine-guns. The sergeant in charge detailed one man to take me up to Santa Helena in a dinghy powered by an outboard motor.

Hannah was waiting at the end of the jetty, smoking a cigarette. "You took your own sweet time about getting here," he commented sourly.

"Nobody told me there was any rush," I said as I scrambled up on to the jetty. "What's it all about anyway?"

"We're going to drop a few Christmas presents into your friends the Huna," he said.

He had a couple of large sacks with him which he handed to the soldier in the boat. He went down the ladder and cast off. "I'll send him back for you. I've got things to do. You'll find Alberto at the priest's house. He'll fill you in."

He sat down in the prow, lighting another of his interminable cigarettes, and shoved his hands into the pockets of his leather coat, looking about as fed-up as it was possible to be.

I was completely mystified by the whole affair and keen for an early explanation, so I turned away and hurried along the jetty. There was a sentry at the land end who looked bored and unhappy, sweat soaking through his drill tunic. There were two more beside a machine-gun in the church porch.

I found Alberto in the priest's house. He was lying on a narrow bed, minus his breeches, his right leg supported across a pillow while his medical corporal swabbed away at a couple of leg ulcers with cotton wool and iodine. Alberto, who looked anything but happy, was obtaining what solace he could from the glass in his left hand and the bottle of brandy in his right.

"Ah, Senhor Mallory," he said. "I would not wish these things on my worst enemy. Like acid, they eat right through to the bone."

"Better than having them on your privates."

He smiled grimly. "A sobering thought. Has Captain Hannah explained things to you?"

"He said something unintelligible about Christmas presents for the Huna, then took off across river. What's it all about?"

"It's simple enough. I've managed to lay hands on a half-breed who's been living with them. He's fixed the position of their main village for me on the map. About forty miles into the bush from here."

"You're going to attack?"

He groaned aloud and moved restlessly under the corporal's hand, sweat beading his forehead. "An impossibility. It would take us at least three weeks to force a way through even if my man agreed to lead us which he would certainly refuse to do under those circumstances. It would be suicide. They'd pick us off one by one."

"What about reinforcements?"

"There aren't any. They're having trouble with the Civa along the Xingu again, and the Jicaro are making things more than difficult along their stretch of the Negro. My orders are to come to some sort of terms with the Huna, then to abandon Santa Helena. I've just sent the mission launch down to Landro with everything on board worth saving."

"And why am I here?"

"I want you to fly to this Huna village with Hannah. Drop in a couple of sackfuls of trade goods of various kinds, as a gesture of goodwill. Then I'll send in this man who's been living with them to try and arrange a meeting for me."

He reached for a clean glass as the sergeant started to bandage his leg, half-filled it with brandy and passed it across to me. I didn't really want it, but took it out of politeness.

He said, "I've been making inquiries about you, Mallory. You were friendly with that madman Buber when you were on the Xingu. Probably know more about Indians than I do. What kind of chance do you think my plan has for working?"

"Not a hope," I said. "If you want the truth, that is."

"I agree entirely." He toasted me, then emptied his glass. "But at least I'll have made the kind of positive step to do something that even Headquarters won't be able to quarrel with."

I tried the brandy which tasted as if someone had made it in the bath. I placed the glass down carefully. "I'll be off, then. Presumably Hannah is straining at the leash."

"He isn't too pleased, I can tell you that." Alberto reached across and picked up my glass. "Safe journey."

I left him there and went out into bright sunlight again. The heat was terrific, dust rising from the dry earth with each step, and the jungle was already beginning to creep in at the back of the hospital, lianas trailing in across the roof from the trees. It didn't take long. People came and went, but the forest endured, covering the scars they left as if they had never existed.

The dinghy was waiting and had me back across at the landing strip in a quarter of an hour. I found Hannah lying in the shade of the Hayley's port wing, studying a map. He was as bad-tempered and morose as ever.

"Well, what do you think?" he demanded impatiently.

"A waste of time."

"Exactly what I told him, but he will have it." He got to his feet. "Have a look at that. I've marked a course although the bloody place probably won't exist when we get there."

"You want me to fly her?"

"That's what I pay you for, isn't it?"

He turned and climbed up into the cabin. Strange, in view of what happened afterwards, but I think it was at that precise moment in time that I started to actively dislike him.

I flew at a thousand feet, and conditions were excellent, the sun so bright that I had to wear dark glasses. Hannah was directly behind me in the front passenger seat beside the rear door. He didn't say a word, simply sat there scanning the jungle below with a pair of binoculars.

Not that it was really necessary. No more than fifteen minutes after leaving the airstrip we passed over a large clearing, and I went down to five hundred and circled it a couple of times.

"Wild banana plantation," Hannah said. "We're dead on course. Must be."

Most forest Indians engaged in a crude form of husbandry

when clearings such as the one below allowed it and it was an infallible sign that we were close to a large village.

I flew on, staying at five hundred feet and almost immediately felt Hannah's hand on my shoulder. "We're here."

The clearing seemed to flower out of the jungle beneath my port wing. It was larger than I had expected, fifty yards in diameter at least, the thatched long huts arranged in a neat circle around a central space with some sort of tribal totem in the centre.

There must have been two hundred people down there, perhaps three, scurrying from the huts like brown ants, faces turned up as I went in across the clearing at three hundred feet. No one ran for the forest for they were familiar enough with aeroplanes, I suppose, to realise we couldn't land. Many of the warriors actually loosed off arrows at us.

"Stupid bastards. Would you look at that now?" Hannah laughed harshly. "Okay, kid, let's get it over with. Take her in at a hundred feet, slow as you like."

I banked to starboard, throttled back and went down across the trees. Hannah had the door open, I was aware of the wind and then the village was directly in front, faces upturned, arrows arching up towards us impotently.

I eased back the stick to climb, glancing over my shoulder in time to see a ball of fire explode in the centre of the crowd closely followed by another.

I saw worse things in the war that was to come, far worse, and yet it haunts me still.

I should have known, I suppose, expected it at least, yet it's easy to be wise after the event. He was laughing like a madman as I took the Hayley round again and went in through the smoke.

There were bodies everywhere, dozens of them, a large central crater and the thatched roofs of several of the long-huts had caught fire.

I glanced over my shoulder. Hannah was leaning out of the open door and laughed out loud again. "How do you like that, you bastards?" he yelled.

I struck out wildly at him backwards with one hand. The Hayley lurched to one side, faltered, then the nose went down. We grabbed at the stick together, pulling her out with no more than three hundred feet in it, and it took the two of us to do it.

I levelled off and started to climb. He took his hands off mine and dropped back into his seat. Neither of us said a word and as I turned back across the clearing for the last time, flames blossomed into a scarlet flower in the clear air.

I was numb, I suppose, from the horror of it all, for the next coherent thing I remember is coming in to land at the airstrip at Santa Helena. I wasn't aware of anything very much except the Bristol at the south end. I went in that way, which gave me the whole of the strip to play with, and rolled to a halt about forty yards from the trees.

I sat there in the silence after cutting the engine, my hands shaking, mouth dry, teeth clenched together in a kind of rictus, aware that Hannah had opened the rear door and had got out. When I opened mine, he was standing below lighting a cigarette in cupped hands.

He looked up and grinned. "It's always rough the first time, kid."

The grin was a mistake. I jumped straight at him and put my fist into it at the same time. We milled around there on the floor for a while, my hands at his throat and in spite of his enormous strength, I didn't do too badly, mainly because surprise was on my side. I was aware of voices shouting, men running and then several different hands grabbed me at once and dragged me off him.

They clammed me hard up against the side of the Hayley, a sergeant holding the barrel of a revolver under my chin. Then Colonel Alberto arrived. He waved the man with the revolver away and looked me straight in the eye.

"It would pain me to have to arrest you, Senhor Mallory, but I will do so if necessary. You will please remember that military law only applies in this area. I am in sole command."

"God damn you!" I said. "Don't you realise what this swine's just done? He's killed at least fifty people, and I helped him do it."

Alberto turned to Hannah and produced a cigarette case from his tunic pocket which he offered to him. "It worked, then?"

"Like a charm," Hannah told him, and took a cigarette.

Alberto actually offered me one. I took it mechanically. "You know?"

"I was in a difficult situation, Senhor Mallory. I needed both of you to do the thing successfully, and it did not seem likely, in view of the sentiments you expressed at our last meeting, that you would give your services willingly."

"You've made me an accessory to murder."

He shook his head and answered gravely, "A military operation from start to finish, and fully authorised by my superiors."

"You lied to me," I said. "About wanting to talk with the Huna."

"Not at all. Only now, having shown that we mean business, that we can hit them hard when we want to, I can talk from a position of strength. You and Captain Hannah may very well prove to have been instrumental in bringing an end to this whole sorry business."

"By butchering poor, bloody savages with high explosives dropped from the air."

They stood around me in a semi-circle, the soldiers, few of them understanding, for we spoke in English.

Hannah was quieter now, his face white and strained. "For God's sake, Mallory, what about the nuns? Look what they did to Father Conté. They ate his heart, Mallory. They cut out his heart and ate it."

My voice seemed to come from outside me; I was someone else inside my head, listening to me talking. Patiently, genuinely wanting him to understand—or so it seemed to me—I said, "And what good does it do to act just as barbarically in return?"

It was Alberto who answered. "You have a strange morality,

Senhor Mallory. For the Huna to rape and butcher the nuns, to roast men over a fire is acceptable. For my men to die in ambush out there in the forest is all part of some game for which you apparently can accept rules."

"Now you're twisting it. Making it something else."

"I don't think so. You would allow us to shoot them in a skirmish in the bush, but to kill them with dynamite from the air is different. . . ."

I couldn't think of anything to say for by then, reaction had set in and I was hopelessly confused.

"A bullet in the belly, an arrow in the back, a stick of dynamite from the air." He shook his head. "There are no rules, Senhor Mallory. This is a dirty business. War has always been thus, and this is war, believe me. . . ."

I turned and walked away from them towards the Bristol. When I reached it, I leaned on the lower port wing for a while, then I took my flying helmet and goggles from one pocket of my leather jacket and put them on.

When I turned, I found Hannah standing watching me. I said, "I'm getting out as soon as I get back. You can find someone else."

He said tonelessly, "We've got a contract, kid, with your signature on the bottom under mine and legally enforceable."

I didn't say anything, simply climbed in and went through the fifteen checks, then I wound the starting magneto. Hannah pulled the propeller over, the engine clattered into life and I started to move forward so quickly that he had to duck under the lower port wing.

His face was very white, I remember that, and his mouth opening and closing as he shouted to me, but his words were drowned by the roar of the Falcon engine and I didn't wait to hear, didn't care if I never clapped eyes on him again.

I was not really aware of having been asleep, only of being shaken awake. I lay there staring up through the mosquito net at the pressure lamp on its hook in the ceiling, moths clustering thickly around it. The hand shook me again, I turned and found Mannie at my side.

"What time is it?" I asked him.

"Just after midnight." He was wearing his yellow oilskin coat and sou'wester and they ran with moisture. "You'll have to help me with Sam, Neil."

It took a moment for it to sink in. I said, "You've got to be joking," and turned over.

He had me half-up by the front of the cotton shirt I was wearing with a grip of surprising strength. "When I left he was just finishing his second bottle of brandy and calling for number three. He'll kill himself unless we help him."

"And you really expect me to give a damn after what he did to me today?"

"Now that's interesting. You said what he did to you, not what he did to those poor bloody savages out there in the bush. Which is most important?"

It almost made my hair stand up on my head in horror at what he was suggesting. I said, "For God's sake, Mannie."

"All right, you want him to die, then?"

I got out of bed and started to dress. I'd gone through the whole sorry story with Mannie as soon as I'd got back. Had to get it off my chest before I went mad. What I was looking for, I think, was the reassurance which would come from finding someone else who was just as horrified as I was myself.

His attitude hadn't been entirely satisfactory, and he'd seemed to see rather more in Colonel Alberto's argument than I was prepared to accept myself. The strange thing was that he seemed worried about Hannah, who had avoided me completely since he'd flown in.

I'd washed my hands of both of them. I'd helped myself to far more of Hannah's Scotch than was good for me, and my head ached from it all as I went up the main street through the rain at Mannie's side.

I could hear music from the hotel as we approached and light filtered out through the shutters in golden bars. There was the sound of a glass breaking and someone called out.

We paused on the veranda and I said, "If he decides to go beserk, he could probably break the two of us in his bare hands. I hope you realise that."

"You're the devil himself for looking on the black side of things." He smiled and put a hand on my arm for a moment. "Now let's have him out of here while there's still hope."

There were two or three people at the far end of the room, Figueiredo behind the bar and Hannah propped up against it in front of him. An old phonograph was playing the *Valse Triste*, Figueiredo's wife standing beside it.

"More, more!" Hannah shouted, pounding on the bar with the flat of his hand as the music started to run down.

She wound the handle vigorously and Hannah reached for the half-empty bottle of brandy and tried to fill the tumbler at his elbow, sending a couple of dirty glasses crashing to the floor at the same moment.

He failed to notice our approach until Mannie reached over and firmly took the bottle from his hand. "Enough is enough, Sam. Now I think we go home."

"Good old Mannie." Hannah patted him on the cheek then turned to empty his glass and saw me. God, he was drunk, his face swollen with the stuff, the hands shaking and the look in his eyes. . . .

He took me by the front of the coat and said wildly, "You think I wanted to do that back there? You think it was easy?"

The man was in hell or so it seemed to me then. Certainly enough to make me feel sorry for him. I pulled free and said gently, "Let's get you to bed then, Sam."

Behind me the door opened, there was a burst of careless laughter, then silence. Hannah's eyes widened and hot rage flared. He brushed me aside and plunged forward and I turned in time to see him give Avila his fist full in the mouth.

"I'll teach you, you bastard," he yelled and pushed Avila back across a table with one hand while he pounded away at him with the other.

Avila's friends were already running into darkness which left Mannie and me. God knows, it took everything we had for I think it was himself Hannah was trying to beat to death there across the table and his strength was incredible.

As we got him out through the door, he turned and grabbed at me again. "You won't leave me, kid, will you? We've got a contract. You gave me your word. It means everything—everything I've got in the world."

I didn't need the look on Mannie's face, but it helped. I said soothingly, "How can I leave, Sam? I've got the mail run to Manaus at nine a.m."

He broke down completely at that, great sobs racking his body as we took him down the steps between us into the rain and started home.

7

Sister of Pity

I didn't see anything of Hannah on the following morning. When I took off for Manaus at nine, he was still dead to the world and Mondays were usually busy so I didn't have time to hang around.

There was not only the mail but a parcel of diamonds from Figueiredo in the usual sealed canvas bag to be handed over to the government agent in Manaus. After that, I had two contract runs downriver for mining companies delivering mail and various bits and pieces.

It added up to a pretty full day and I arrived back at Manaus in the early evening with the intention of spending the night at the Palace, and the prospect of a hot bath, a change of clothes, a decent meal, perhaps even a visit to *The Little Boat*, was more than attractive.

There wasn't much activity at the airstrip when I landed although on some days, you could find two or three planes parked by the hangars, in from down-river or the coast. There were still a couple of mechanics on duty and they helped me get the Bristol under cover for the night, then one of them gave me a lift into town in the company truck, an ancient Crossley tender.

When I entered the hotel, there was no sign of Juca behind the desk. In fact there was no one around at all, so I went through the door on the left into the bar.

There seemed to be no one there either except for a rather romantic, or disreputable-looking figure, depending on your point of view, who stared at me from the full-length mirror at the other end.

I was badly in need of a shave. I wore lace-up knee-length boots, whipcord breeches, and a leather flying jacket open to reveal, in its shoulder holster, the .45 automatic, which Hannah had insisted on giving me in place of the Webley, his theory being that there was no point in carrying a gun that wouldn't either stop a man dead in his tracks or knock him down.

I dropped my canvas grip to the floor, went behind the bar and helped myself to a bottle of cold beer from the ice-box. As I started to pour it into a glass, there was a slight, polite cough.

The woman who had come in through the open french windows from the terrace was a nun in tropical white, a small woman, not much over five feet in height with clear, untroubled eyes, not a wrinkle to be seen on that calm face in spite of her age which must have been fifty at least.

She spoke with the kind of accent that is associated with the New England states, which made sense. As I discovered later, she had been born and raised in the town of Vineyard Haven, Massachusetts, on the island of Martha's Vineyard.

"Mr. Mallory?" she said.

"That's me."

"We've been waiting for you. The *comandante* said you were expected back this evening. I am Sister Maria Teresa of the Little Sisters of Pity."

She had said "We." I looked for another nun, but instead a young woman sauntered in from the terrace, a creature from another world than this, cool, elegant in a white chiffon frock, wide-brimmed straw hat, a blue silk scarf tied around it, the ends fluttering in the slight breeze. She carried an open parasol over one shoulder and stood, a hand on her hip, legs slightly apart, casually insolent as if challenging the world at large.

And there was one other possibility that made her herself alone—a silver bracelet about the right ankle, studded with tiny bells that jingled rather eerily as she walked, a sound that has haunted me for years. I couldn't see much of her face for with the evening sunlight behind her, the rest was in shadow.

Sister Maria Teresa said, "This is Miss Joanna Martin. Her sister served with our mission at Santa Helena."

I knew then, I suppose, what it was all about, but played dumb. "What can I do for you ladies?"

"We want to go upriver as soon as possible."

"To Landro?"

"To start with, then Santa Helena."

The simple directness of that remark was enough to take the breath away. I said, "You've got to be joking."

"Oh no, I assure you, Mr. Mallory. I have complete authority from my order to proceed to Santa Helena to assess the situation and to report on the feasibility of our carrying on there."

"Carrying on?" I said stupidly.

She didn't appear to have heard me. "And then there is the unfortunate business of Sister Anne Josepha and Sister Bernadette whose bodies were never recovered. I understand that in all probability they were taken alive by the Huna."

"That would depend on your definition of living," I said.

"You don't think it's possible?" It was the Martin girl who had spoken, the voice as cool and well-bred as you would have expected from the appearance, no strain there at all.

"Oh, it's possible." I swallowed the impulse to give them the gory details on the kind of life captive women in such a situation could expect and contented myself by adding, "Indians are very much like children and subject to sudden whims. One minute it seems like a good idea to carry off a couple of white women, the next, equally reasonable to beat them to death with an ironwood club."

Sister Maria Teresa closed her eyes momentarily, and Joanna Martin said in the same cool voice, "But you can't be certain of that?"

"Any more than you can be that they're alive."

"Sister Anne Josepha was Miss Martin's younger sister," Maria Teresa said simply.

I'd suspected something like that, but it didn't make it any easier. I said, "I'm sorry, but I know as much about Indians as most people and more than some. You asked me for my opinion and that's what I've given you."

"Will you take us up to Landro with you in the morning?" Sister Maria Teresa said. "I understand from the *comandante* that we could fly from there to Santa Helena in under an hour."

"Have you any idea what it's like up there?" I demanded. "About as bad as any place on this earth could possibly be."

"God will provide," she said simply.

"He must have been taking a day off when the Huna took out Father Counté and the rest of them at Santa Helena," I said brutally.

There was the briefest flash of pain on that calm face and then she smiled beautifully and with all the understanding in the world. "The *comandante* told me you were one of those who found them. It must have been terrible for you."

I said slowly, "Look, Sister, the whole area comes under military jurisdiction."

Joanna Martin came forward to join her, opened the embroidered handbag which hung from her wrist and took out a folded document which she tossed on the bar.

"Our authorisation to travel, counter-signed by the president himself." Enough to bring Alberto's heels together sharply, so much was certain and enough for me.

"All right, have it your own way. If you want to know what it's like to fly two hundred miles over some of the worst jungle in South America in the oldest plane in the territory, be at the airstrip at eight-thirty. As it happens, the rear cockpit's been enlarged to carry cargo, but there's only one seat. One of you will have to sit on the floor."

I swallowed the rest of my beer and moved round the bar. "And now you'll really have to excuse me. It's been a long day."

Sister Maria Teresa nodded. "Of course."

Joanna Martin said nothing, simply picked up my grip and handed it to me, a gesture totally unexpected and quite out of character. My fingers touched hers as I took it, and there was the perfume. God knows what it was, but the effect was electrifying. I had never experienced such direct and immediate excitement from any woman; my stomach went hollow.

And she knew, damn her, I was certain of that, her mouth lifting slightly to one side as if in amusement at men and their perpetual hunger. I turned from that scorn and went out quickly.

There was still no sign of Juca, but when I went up to my usual room, I found him turning down the sheets.

"Your bath is ready, Senhor Mallory," he told me in that strange, melancholy whisper of his. "You wish to eat here afterwards?"

I shook my head. "I think I'll go out. If anyone wants me I'll be at *The Little Boat*."

"The senhor has seen the ladies who were waiting for him downstairs?"

"Yes. Are they staying here?"

He nodded and withdrew and I stripped, pulled on an old robe and went along the corridor to the bathroom. The water was hot enough to bring sweat to my face, and I lay there for half an hour, soaking away the fatigue of the day and thinking about the two women in the bar. Sister Maria Teresa was familiar enough. One of those odd people who live by faith alone and who seem to be able to survive most things, protected by the armour of their own innocence.

Joanna Martin's presence was more difficult to explain. God knows who had advised her to come. Certainly they must have

97

an awful lot of pull between them to get hold of that authorisation with the president's signature on it. Colonel Alberto was not going to be pleased about that.

I went back to my room, towelling my head briskly and started to dress. I'd actually got my trousers on and was pulling a clean linen shirt over my head when a slight noise made me turn quickly, one hand sliding towards the butt of the .45 automatic which lay on the dressing-table in its shoulder harness.

Joanna Martin moved in from the balcony, closing her parasol. "Don't shoot," she said coolly. "I'm all I've got."

I stood looking at her, without saying anything, noticing the face for the first time. Not really beautiful, yet different enough to make her noticeable in any crowd. Auburn hair, obviously regularly attended to by a top hairdresser. Good bones, an up-turned nose that made her look younger than she was, hazel eyes spaced widely apart, curious golden flecks glinting in them.

I wondered how she'd look after a week upriver. I also wondered how that hair would look spread across a pillow. The physical ache was there again, disturbing in its intensity.

"The door was unlocked," she explained. "And the old man said you were in the bath. I thought I'd wait."

I tucked in my shirt and reached for my shoulder harness. For some reason I found difficulty in speaking. That damned perfume, I suppose, the actual physical presence of her.

"Do you really need that thing?" she asked.

"It's a rough town after dark," I said. "Now what can I do for you?"

"Tell me the truth for a start."

She moved back to the balcony. Outside the sky was orange and black, the sun a ball of fire. Standing there, against the light her legs were clearly outlined through the flimsy dress.

I said, "I don't understand."

"Oh, I think you do. You were being polite to Sister Maria Teresa down there in the bar. About my sister and the other girl, I mean. You were letting her down lightly."

"Is that a fact?"

"Don't play games with me, Mr. Mallory. I'm not a child. I want the truth."

"Who in the hell do you think I am?" I demanded. "The butler?"

I'm not sure why I got so angry—possibly because she'd spoken to me as if I were some sort of servant, but there was more to it than that. Probably some weird kind of defence mechanism to stop me from grabbing her.

"All right," I said. "I was asked if it was possible your sister and the other girl were still alive and I said it was. What else do you want to know?"

"Why would they take her. Why not kill her straight away. Even the older nuns were raped before being killed, isn't that so? I've read the report."

"They like to freshen the blood," I said. "It's as simple as that."

I started to turn away, tiring of it suddenly, wanting to be away from her, aware of the strain finally blowing through the surface.

She grabbed me by the shoulder and pulled me round. "I want to know, damn you!" she cried. "All of it."

"All right," I said, and caught her wrists. "It's a pretty complicated ritual. First of all, they're virgins, they undergo a ceremonial defloration in front of everyone using a tribal totem. That's Huna custom with all maidens."

There was horror in those eyes now and she had stopped struggling. "Then for seven nights running, any warrior in the tribe is allowed to go in to them. It's a great honour. Any woman who doesn't become pregnant after that is stoned to death. Those outsiders who do are kept till the baby is born, then buried alive. The reasons for all this are pretty complicated, but if you have an hour to spare sometime, I'll be happy to explain."

She stared up at me, head moving from side to side. Gravely I added, "If I were you, Miss Martin, I'd pray she ended up in the river in the first place."

The rage came up like hot lava and she pulled free of me,

the left hand striking across my face and then the right, helpless, impotent anger and grief mingling together. She stumbled to the door, wrenched it open and ran into the corridor.

I walked to *The Little Boat*—a dangerous thing to do after dark, especially along the waterfront. But such was the rage against life itself that filled me that I think it would have gone hard with any man who had crossed my path that night. I needed a drink and perhaps another, to use one of Hannah's favourite phrases, and a woman certainly: a dangerous mood to be in.

The Little Boat was not particularly busy, but that was only to be expected on a Monday night. The rumba band was playing, but there couldn't have been more than a dozen people on the floor. Lola, Hannah's girl friend from that first night, was there, wearing the same red satin dress. I rather liked her. She was an honest whore, but she was crazy about Hannah and made it obvious, her one weakness.

Knowing that he wouldn't be in that night, she concentrated on me; she knew what she was about. Strange, but it didn't seem to work. I kept thinking of Joanna Martin and when I did that, Lola faded rapidly. The message got through to her after a while and she went off to try her luck elsewhere.

Which at least left me free to drink myself into a stupor if I was so inclined. I went up to that private section of the deck where I had dined with Hannah on that first night, ordered a meal and a bottle of wine to start with, and closed the sliding doors.

My appetite seemed to have gone. I picked at my food, then went and stood at the rail, a bottle of wine in one hand and a glass in the other, and stared out over the river. The reflected lights of the houseboats glowed in the water like candle flames. I was restless and ill at ease, waiting for something—wanting her, I suppose.

Behind me, the sliding doors opened, then closed again. I turned impatiently and found Joanna Martin standing there.

* * *

"Do you think we could start again?" she said.

There was a spare glass on the table. I filled it with wine and held it out to her. "How did you find me?"

"Old Juca at the hotel. He was very kind. Got me a cab with a driver who bore a strong resemblance to King Kong. Gave him strict instructions to deliver me in one piece." She walked to the rail and looked out across the river. "This is nice."

I didn't know what to say, but she took care of it all more than adequately. "I think we got off on the wrong foot, Mr. Mallory. I'd like to try again."

"Neil," I said.

"All right." She smiled. "I'm afraid you've got the wrong impression of me entirely. Joanna Martin's my stage name. Originally I was just plain Joan Kowalski of Grantville, Pennsylvania." Her voice changed completely, dropped into an accent she probably hadn't used in years. "My daddy was a coal miner. What was yours?"

I laughed out loud. "A small-town lawyer—what we call a solicitor in England—at a place called Wells, in Somerset. A lovely old town near the Mendip Hills."

"It sounds marvellous."

"It is, especially now in the autumn. Rooks in the elms by the cathedral. The dank, wet smell of rotting leaves blowing across the river."

For a moment I was almost there. She leaned on the rail. "Grantville was never like that. We had three things worth mentioning, none of which I ever wish to see again. Coal mines, steelworks and smoke. I didn't even look back once when I left."

"And your sister?"

"We were orphaned when she was three and I was eight. The nuns raised me, I guess it became a habit with her."

"And what about you?"

"I'm doing fine. Sing with some of the best bands in the

country. Dorsey, Guy Lombardo, Sammy Kaye." There was a perceptible change in her voice as she said this, a surface brashness as if she was really speaking for an audience. "I've played second lead in two musicals in succession on Broadway."

"All right." I held up both hands defensively. "I'm convinced."

"And you?" She leaned back against the rail. "What about you? Why Brazil?"

So I told her, from the beginning right up until that present moment, including a few items on the way that I don't think I'd ever mentioned to another living soul, such was the effect she had on me.

"So here we are," she said at last when I was finished. "The two of us at the edge of nowhere. It's beautiful, isn't it?"

The moon clouded over, sheet lightning flickered wildly, the rain came with a sudden rush bouncing from the awning above our heads.

"Romantic, isn't it?" I said. "We get this every day of the week at sometime or another. Imagine what it's like in the rainy season." I refilled her glass with wine. "Bougainvilleas, acacias and God knows how many different varieties of poisonous snakes that can kill you in seconds. As for the river, if it isn't the alligators or piranhas, it's water snakes so long they've been known to turn a canoe over and take the occupants down. Almost everything that looks nice is absolutely deadly. You should have tried Hollywood instead. Much safer on Stage Six."

"That comes next month. I've got a screen test with MGM." She smiled, then reached out to touch me, her hand flat against my chest, the smile fading. "I've got to know, Neil. Just to know, one way or the other. Can you understand that?"

"Of course I can." My hand fastened over hers and I was shaking like a kid on his first date. "Would you like to dance?"

She nodded, moving against me and behind us, the sliding door was pulled open. "So this is what you get up to when my back is turned?" Hannah said as he came through.

* * *

He was dressed in flying clothes and badly in need of shave, but he was a romantic enough figure in his leather coat and breeches, a white scarf knotted carelessly about his neck.

He smiled with devastating charm and rushed forward with a sort of boyish eagerness, hands outstretched. "And this will be Miss Joanna Martin. Couldn't very well be anyone else."

He held her hands in his for what seemed to me no good reason. I said, "What in the hell is going on here?"

"You might as well ask, kid." He yelled for the waiter and pulled off his coat. "A lot happened since you left this morning. Alberto got through to me on the radio in the middle of the afternoon. Wanted me to pick him up at Santa Helena and fly him straight down to Manaus. We got in about an hour and a half ago. Met Miss Martin's companion at the hotel. When I left, she and the colonel were having quite an argument."

"What's it all about?"

"That half-breed of Alberto's, the guy who'd lived with the Huna. Well, Alberto put him over the river last evening, and by God, he was back at noon today."

"You mean he'd made contact?"

"Sure had." The waiter arrived at this point with a couple of bottles of Pouilly-Fuissé in a bucket of water. "According to him, all the tribesmen along the river had already heard what had happened to that village we visited and were scared stiff. A delegation of head men have agreed to meet Alberto a couple of miles upriver from the mission day after tomorrow."

"Sounds too good to be true to me," I said, and meant it.

But Joanna Martin didn't think so. She sat down beside him and said eagerly, "Do you think they'll be able to get news of my sister?"

"Certain to." He took one of her hands again. "It's going to be fine. I promise you."

After that, to say that they got on like a house on fire would have been something of an understatement. I sat in the wings, as it were, and watched while they talked a lot, laughed a great deal and finally went down to join the small crowd on the dance floor.

I wasn't the only one who was put out. I caught a flash of scarlet in the half-light, Lola watching from behind a pillar. I knew then what the saying meant by a woman scorned. She looked capable of putting a knife between Hannah's shoulder blades if given half a chance.

I don't know what was said between the two on the floor, but when the band stopped playing, they moved across to the piano and Hannah sat down. As I've said before, he was a fair pianist. He moved straight into a solid, pushing arrangement of "St. Louis Blues," and Joanna Martin took the vocal.

She was good—better than I'd thought she would be. She gave it everything she had, a total dedication, and the crowd loved it. She followed with "Night and Day" and "Begin the Beguine," which was a tremendous hit that autumn and all one seemed to hear from radios everywhere, even on the River Amazon.

But by then I'd had enough. I left them to it, negotiated the catwalk to the jetty and walked morosely back to the hotel in the pouring rain.

I had been in bed for at least an hour, had just begun to drift into sleep when Hannah's voice brought me sharply to my senses. I got out of bed, padded to the door and opened it. He was obviously very drunk, standing with Joanna Martin outside the door of what I presumed must be her room at the end of the corridor.

He was trying to kiss her in that clumsy, uncoordinated way a drunken man has. She obviously didn't need any assistance, because she was laughing about it.

I closed the door, went back beneath the mosquito net and lit a cigarette. I don't know what I was shaking with—rage or thwarted desire, or both, but I lay there smoking furiously and cursing everyone who ever lived—until my door opened and closed again softly. The bolt clicked into place and there was silence.

I sensed her presence there in the darkness even before I smelled the perfume. She said, "Stop sulking. I know you're in there. I can see your cigarette."

"Bitch," I said.

She pulled back the mosquito net, there was the rustle of some garment or other falling to the floor, then she slipped into bed beside me.

"That's nice," she said and added, in the same tone of voice, "Colonel Alberto wants to be off at the crack of dawn. Sister Maria Teresa and I have strict instructions from Hannah to be at the airstrip not later than seven-thirty. He seems to think we'll be safer with him."

"You suit yourself."

"You're a good pilot, Neil Mallory, according to Hannah, the best he's ever known." Her lips brushed my cheek. "But you don't know much about women."

I wasn't going to argue with her, not then, with the kind of need burning inside that could not be borne for long. As I pulled her to me, I felt the nipples blossom on her breasts, cool against my bare skin.

The excitement she aroused in me, the awareness, was quite extraordinary. But there was more to it than that. I lay there holding her, waiting for some sort of sign that might come or might not—the whole world waited. And in that timeless moment, I knew, out of some strange foreknowledge, that whatever happened during the rest of my life, I'd never know anything better than this. That whatever followed would always have the savour of anti-climax, just like Hannah.

She kissed me, hard, mouth opening, and as lightning flickered across the sky and it started to rain again, the whole world came alive.

8

The Tree of Life

I awakened to sunlight streaming through the window, the mosquito net fluttering in the slight breeze. I was quite alone, at least as far as the bed went, but when I pushed myself up on one elbow I discovered Juca on the other side of the net placing a tray on the table.

"Breakfast, Senhor Mallory."

"What time is it?"

He consulted a large, silver pocket watch gravely. "Eight o'clock exactly, senhor. The senhorita told me you wished to be awakened at this time."

"I see—and when was this?"

"About an hour ago, senhor, when she was leaving for the airstrip with the good Sister. Will that be all, senhor?"

I nodded and he withdrew. I poured myself a coffee and went to the window. They'd be well on the way to Landro by now. Strange the sense of personal loss, and yet, in a way, it was almost as if I was prepared for it. I didn't feel like any breakfast after that, but dressed quickly, had another cup of coffee and went about my business.

There were several calls to make before going out to the

airstrip so I caught a cab in front of the hotel. First of all there was the mail, then some dynamo parts for one of the mining agents at Landro and Figueiredo had asked me to pick up a case of imported London gin.

It was close to half past nine when I finally arrived at the airstrip. A de Havilland Rapide was parked by the tower and seemed to be taking up all the ground staff's attention. The Bristol was still under cover. I opened the doors and the cab driver followed me in with the crate of gin.

Joanna Martin was sitting in the pilot's cockpit reading a book. She looked up and smiled brightly. "What kept you?"

I couldn't think what to say for a moment, so great was my astonishment. I was only certain of one thing—that I had never been so pleased to see anyone. She knew it, I think, for the face softened for a moment.

"What happened?" I said.

"I decided to fly with you, that's all. I thought it would be more fun."

"And what did Hannah have to say to that?"

"Oh, he wasn't too pleased." She pushed herself up out of the cockpit, swung her legs over the edge and dropped into my arms. "On the other hand, he did have rather a bad hangover."

The cab driver had returned with the mail sack, which he dropped on the ground beside the case of gin. He waited, mouth open in admiration, and I paid him and sent him on his way.

The moment we were alone I kissed her, and it was rather disappointing, nothing like the night before. Her lips now cool and aseptic, she very definitely held me at arm's length.

She patted my cheek. "Hadn't we better get moving?"

I couldn't think of anything that would explain the change, although I suppose, on looking back at it all, I was guilty of simply expecting too much, still young enough to believe that if you loved someone they were certain to love you back.

Anyway, I loaded the freight behind the seat in the observer's cockpit and found her an old leather flying coat and helmet we kept for passengers. Three ground staff turned up about then, having seen us arrive, and we got the Bristol outside.

I helped Joanna into the observer's cockpit and strapped her in. "It's essential you keep your goggles on," I warned. "You'll find a hell of a lot of insects about, especially as we take off and land."

When she pulled the goggles down, she seemed more remote than ever, another person altogether, but that was possibly just my imagination. I climbed into the cockpit, did my checks and wound the starting magneto, while the three mechanics formed a chain and pulled the propeller.

The engine broke into noisy life. I looked over my shoulder to check that she was all right. She didn't smile, simply nodded, so I eased the throttle open, taxied to the end of the runway, turned into the wind and took off feeling, for some unknown reason, thoroughly depressed.

The trip was something of a milk run for me by now, especially on a morning like this with perfect flying conditions. I suppose it must have had some interest for her, although she certainly gave no sign of being particularly excited. In fact we spoke only twice over the voice pipe during the entire trip: once as we turned up the Mortes from the Negro and I pointed out Forte Franco on the island below, and then as we approached Landro and I made preparations to land.

One thing did surprise me, the Hayley parked by the hangar. I had imagined it would be well on the way to Santa Helena by now.

As we rolled to a halt, Mannie came to meet us with a couple of labourers. He grinned up at me. "What kept you? Sam's been like a cat on hot bricks, isn't that what you say?"

"I didn't know he cared," I said and dropped to the ground.

"He doesn't," he replied and elbowed me out of the way as I turned to help Joanna down. "The privilege of age, Miss Martin." He held up his hands.

She liked him, that much was obvious, and her smile was of

that special kind a woman reserves for a man she instantly recognises as good friend or father confessor. No strain, no cut-and-thrust, someone she would never have to surrender to or keep at arm's length.

I made some kind of lame, formal introduction. Mannie said, "Now I understand why Sam's been acting as if he's been struck over the head with a Huna war club." As I took off my flying helmet, he ruffled my hair. "Has the boy here been treating you all right? Did he give you a good flight?"

It was the one and only time I felt angry with him, and it showed, for his smile faded slightly and there was concern in his eyes.

I turned away. Hannah came running across the airstrip rather fast, considering the heat and the fact that he was dressed for flying. When he was about ten yards away, he slowed down as if suddenly realising he was making a fool of himself, and came on at a walk.

He ignored me and said to Joanna Martin, "Satisfied now?"

"Oh, I think you could say that," she said coolly. "Where's Sister Maria Teresa?"

"When I last saw her she was down at the jetty having a look at the mission launch. Had some sort of crazy idea that you and she might sleep on board."

"What's wrong with the local hotel?"

"Just about everything, so I've arranged for you both to move into my place. I'll take you up there now and show you round, then I've got to run Alberto up to Santa Helena."

He picked up her suitcase and I said, "What are the rest of us supposed to do?"

He barely glanced at me. "We can manage in hammocks down here in the hangar for a few nights. Mannie's moved your gear out."

He took her arm and they started to walk away. He paused after a few yards and called over his shoulder, "I'd get that mail up to Figueiredo fast if I were you, kid. He's had the district runners standing by for an hour."

"And that puts you in your place," Mannie said, and started to laugh.

For a moment, the anger flared up in me again, and then, for some unaccountable reason, I found myself laughing with him. "Women," I said.

"Exactly. We have all the trees in the world and an abundance of fruit. All we needed was Eve." He shook his head and picked up the mail sack. "I'll take this up to Figueiredo for you. You go and have a cup of coffee and relax. I can see you've had a hard morning."

He walked away towards town and I got my grip out of the Bristol and went into the hangar. He'd fixed three hammocks on the other side of the radio installation with a wall of packing cases five or six feet high to give some sort of privacy. There was a table and three chairs and a pot of coffee simmered gently on a double-ring oil stove.

I poured some into a tin mug, lit a cigarette and eased myself into one of the hammocks. I couldn't get Joanna Martin out of my mind—the change in her. It didn't seem to make any sense at all, especially in view of the fact that she'd deliberately chosen to travel with me in the Bristol instead of in the Hayley.

My chain of thought was interrupted by Alberto, who appeared in the gap in the end wall of packing cases. "Camping out, I see, Mr. Mallory."

"Hannah isn't here. He took the Martin girl up to the house."

"I am aware of that. It's you I want to see." He found another tin mug and helped himself to coffee. "I've spent most of the morning arguing with Sister Maria Teresa, who insists on her right to proceed to Santa Helena." He shook his head sadly. "God protect me from the good and the innocent."

"A formidable combination," I said. "Are you going to let her go?"

"I don't see how I can prevent it. You've seen the authorisation she and the Martin woman have? Counter-signed by the president himself." He shrugged. "If she decided to start upriver in the mission launch now, this very morning, how could I stop her except by force, and there would be the very devil to pay if I did that."

"So what are you going to do?"

"You've heard my man managed to make contact with the Huna? Well, he's arranged a meeting for me tomorrow at noon in a patch of *campo* near the river about a mile upstream from the mission."

"How many will be there?"

"One chief and five elders. It's a start, no more. A preliminary skirmish. I'm supposed to go on my own except for Pedro, of course, the half-breed who's made the contact for me. What do you think?"

"It should be quite an experience."

"Yes, stimulating to put it mildly. I was wondering whether you might consider coming with me?"

The impudence of the request was breathtaking. I sat up and swung my legs to the floor. "Why me?"

"You know more about Indians than anyone else I know. You could be of considerable assistance in the negotiations."

"How far is it to the river if we have to start running?"

He smiled. "See how you feel about it tomorrow. Hannah will be flying the women in first thing in the morning. You could come with them. I've agreed to let them look over the mission."

"Not that you had any choice in the matter."

"Exactly."

He moved out into the sunlight. Hannah came round the tail of the Hayley, buttoning the strap of his flying helmet, Mannie at his side.

"Okay, Colonel, let's go!" he called. "The sooner I get you there, the sooner I'm back."

"Can't you wait?" I asked.

He hesitated, the cabin door of the Hayley half-open, then turned very slowly. His face had a look on it I'd seen before—on that first night at *The Little Boat*, when he'd got rough with Lola.

111

He moved towards me and paused, no more than a foot in it. "Just watch it, kid, that's all," he said softly.

I told him what to do, in good and concise Anglo-Saxon. I think for a moment there he was within an ace of having a go at me; then Mannie got between us, his face white. It wasn't really necessary, for Hannah turned abruptly, climbed up into the cabin where Alberto was already waiting, and shut the door. A moment later the engine burst into life and he taxied away.

He took off too fast, banking steeply across the river, barely making it over the trees, all good showy stuff and strictly for my benefit, just to make it clear who was boss.

Mannie said softly, "This isn't good, Neil. Not good at all. You know what Sam can be like. How unpredictable he is."

"You make all the allowances for him you want," I said. "But I'm damned if I will. Not any more."

I left him there and walked along the edge of the airstrip towards the house. There was no sign of life when I got there; but the front door was open, so I simply walked into the living-room.

I could hear the shower running, so I lit a cigarette, sat on the window ledge and waited. After a while, the shower stopped. I could hear her singing, and a little later she entered the room dressed in an old robe, a towel tied around her head like a turban.

She stopped singing abruptly, eyebrows raised in surprise. "And what can I do for you? Did you forget something?"

"You can tell me what I've done," I said.

She stood there, looking at me calmly for a long, long moment, then moved to where her handbag lay on a bamboo table, opened it, found herself a cigarette and a small mother-of-pearl lighter.

She blew out in a long column of smoke and said calmly, "Look, Mallory, I don't owe you a thing. All right?"

Even then I couldn't see it and in any case, after that, all I wanted to do was hurt her. I moved to the door and said, "Just one thing. How much do I owe you?"

She laughed in my face and I turned, utterly defeated, stumbled down the veranda steps and hurried away towards the river.

* * *

All right, so I didn't know much about women, but I hadn't deserved this. I wandered along the riverbank, a cigarette smouldering between my lips, and finally found myself at the jetty.

There were several boats there, mainly canoes, and Figueiredo's official launch was tied up next to a boat belonging to one of the big land company agents. The mission launch was at the far end, Sister Maria Teresa in the rear cockpit. I started to turn away, but it was already too late. She called to me by name, and I had no choice but to turn and walk down to the boat.

She smiled as I reached the rail. "A beautiful morning, Mr. Mallory."

"For the moment."

She nodded and said calmly, "Would you have such a thing as a cigarette to spare?"

I was surprised and showed it I suppose as I produced a packet and offered her one. "They're only local, I'm afraid. Black tobacco."

She blew out smoke expertly and smiled. "Don't you approve? Nuns are only human, you know, flesh and blood like anyone else."

"I'm sure you are, Sister." I started to turn away.

She said, "I get the distinct impression that you do not approve of me, Mr. Mallory. If I hadn't called out to you, you wouldn't have stopped to talk. Isn't that so?"

"All right," I said. "I think you're a silly, impractical woman who doesn't know what in the hell she's getting mixed up in."

"I've spent seven years in South America as a medical missionary, Mr. Mallory. Three of them in other parts of Northern Brazil. This kind of country is not entirely unfamiliar to me."

"Which only makes it worse. Your own experience ought to tell you that by coming here at all, you've only made a tricky situation even more difficult for everyone who comes into contact with you."

"Well, it's certainly a point of view," she said good-humouredly. "I've been told that you have a great deal of experience with Indians. That you worked with Karl Buber on the Xingu."

"I knew him."

"A great and good man."

"Who stopped being a missionary when he discovered you were doing the Indians as much harm as anyone else."

She sighed. "Yes, I would agree that the record has been far from perfect, even amongst the various religious organisations involved."

"Far from perfect?" I was well into my stride now, my general anger and frustration at the morning's events finding a convenient channel. "They don't need us, Sister, any of us. The best service we could offer them would be to go away and leave them alone and they certainly don't need your religion. They wear nothing worth speaking about, own nothing, wash themselves twice a day and help each other. Can your Christianity offer them more than that?"

"And kill each other," she said. "You forgot to mention that."

"All right, so they look upon all outsiders as natural enemies. God alone knows, they're usually right."

"They also kill the old," she said. "The disfigured, the mentally deficient. They kill for the sake of killing."

I shook my head. "No, you don't understand, do you? That's the really terrible thing. Death and life are one, part of existence itself in their terms. Waking, sleeping—it's all the same. How can it be bad to die, especially for a warrior? War is the purpose for which he lives."

"I would take them love, Mr. Mallory, is that such a bad thing?"

"What was it one of your greatest Jesuits said? The sword and the iron rod are the best kind of preaching."

"A long, long time ago. As the times change so men change with them." She stood up and straightened her belt. "You accuse me of not really understanding and you may well have a point. Perhaps you could help me on the road to rehabilitation by showing me the sights of Landro."

114

THE LAST PLACE GOD MADE

Defeated for the second time that morning, I resigned myself to my fate and took her hand to help her over the rail.

As we walked along the jetty, she took my arm and said, "Colonel Alberto seems a very capable officer."

"Oh, he's that, all right."

"What is your opinion of this meeting he has arranged tomorrow with one of the Huna chieftains? Is it likely to accomplish much?"

"It all depends what they want to see him for," I said. "Indians are like small children—completely irrational. They can smile with you one minute and mean it—dash out your brains the next on the merest whim."

"So this meeting could prove to be a dangerous undertaking?"

"You could say that. He's asked me to go with him."

"Do you intend to?"

"I can't think of the slightest reason why I should at the moment, can you?"

She didn't get a chance to reply. At that moment her name was called, and we looked up and found Joanna Martin approaching. She was wearing the white chiffon dress again, the same straw hat, and she carried the parasol over one shoulder. She might have stepped straight off a page in *Vogue*. I'd never seen anything more incongruous.

Sister Maria Teresa said, "Mr. Mallory is taking me on a sight-seeing trip, my dear."

"Well, that should take all of ten minutes." Joanna Martin took her other arm, ignoring me completely.

We walked through the mean little streets, hopeless faces peering out of the windows at us, ragged half-starved children playing beneath the houses. An ox had died in a side alley, obviously of some disease or other that had rendered the flesh unfit for human comsumption. It had been left exactly where it had fallen, and had swollen to twice its normal size. The terrible smell managed even to kill the stink from the cesspool a few yards farther on, which had overflowed and now ran in a steady stream down the centre of the street.

Sister Maria Teresa didn't like any of it, nor for that matter did Joanna Martin. I pointed out the steam house, one of those peculiarities of upriver villages where Indians went through regular purification for religious reasons with the help of red-hot stones and lots of cold water, but it didn't help.

We moved out through a couple of streets of shanties, constructed of iron and pieces of packing cases and inhabited mainly by forest Indians who had made the mistake of trying to come to terms with the white man's world.

"Strange," I said, "but in the forest, naked as the day they were born, most of these women look beautiful. Put them in a dress and something inexplicable happens. Beauty goes, pride goes. . . ."

Joanna Martin put a hand out to stay me. "What was that, for God's sake?"

We were past the final line of huts, close to the river and the edge of the jungle. The sound came again, a sharp bitter cry. I led the way forward, then paused.

On the edge of the trees by the river, an Indian woman knelt in front of a tree, arms raised above her head, a tattered calico dress pulled up above her thighs. The man with her was also Indian in spite of his cotton trousers and shirt. He was tying her wrists above her head by lianas to a convenient branch.

The woman cried out again. Sister Maria Teresa took a quick step forward, and I pulled her back. "Whatever happens, you mustn't interfere."

She turned to me and said, "This is one custom with which I am entirely familiar, Mr. Mallory. I will stay here for a while if you don't mind. I may be able to help afterwards, if she'll let me." She smiled. "Amongst other things, I'm a qualified doctor, you see. If you could bring me my bag along from the house at some time, I'd be most grateful."

She went towards the woman and her husband and sat down on the ground a yard or two away. They completely ignored her.

Joanna Martin gripped my arm fiercely. "What is it?"

"She's going to have a child," I said. "She's tied by her wrists with lianas so that the child is born while she is upright. That way he will be stronger and braver than a child born to a woman lying down."

The woman gave another low moan of pain, her husband squatted on the ground beside her.

Joanna Martin said, "But this is ridiculous. They could be here all night."

"Exactly," I said. "And if Sister Maria Teresa insists on behaving like Florence Nightingale, the least we can do is go back to the house and get that bag for her."

On the way back through Landro, a rather unusual incident took place which gave me a glimpse of another side of her character.

As we came abreast of a dilapidated house on the corner of a narrow street, a young Indian girl of perhaps sixteen or seventeen rushed out of the entrance on to the veranda. She wore an old calico dress and was barefoot, obviously frightened to death. She glanced around her hurriedly as if debating which way to run, started down the steps, missed her footing and went sprawling. A moment later Avila rushed out of the house, a whip in one hand. He came down the steps on the run and started to belabour her.

I didn't care for Avila and certainly didn't like what he was doing to the girl, but I'd learned to move cautiously in such cases. This was still a country where most women took the occasional beating as a matter of course.

Joanna Martin was not so prudent, however. She went in like a battleship under full sail and lashed out at him with her handbag. He backed away, a look of bewilderment on his face. I got there as quickly as I could, and grabbed her arm as she was about to strike him again.

"What's she done?" I asked Avila, and pulled the girl up from the ground.

"She's been selling herself round the town while I've been away," he said. "God knows what she might have picked up."

"She's yours?"

He nodded. "A Huna girl. I bought her just over a year ago."

We'd spoken in Portuguese and I turned to give Joanna a translation. "There's nothing to be done. The girl belongs to him."

"What do you mean, belongs to him?"

"He bought her, probably when her parents died. It's common enough upriver and legal."

"Bought her?" First there was incredulity in her eyes, then a kind of white-hot rage. "Well, I'm damn well buying her back," she said. "How much will this big ape take?"

"Actually, he speaks excellent English," I said. "Why not ask him yourself."

She was really angry by then. She scrabbled in her handbag and produced a hundred-*cruzeiro* note, which she thrust at Avila. "Will this do?"

He accepted it with alacrity and bowed politely. "A pleasure to do business with you, senhorita," he said, and made off rapidly up the street in the direction of the hotel.

The girl waited quietly for whatever new blow fate had in store for her, that impassive Indian face giving nothing away. I questioned her in Portuguese, which she seemed to understand reasonably well.

"She's a Huna, all right," I told Joanna. "Her name is Christina and she's sixteen. Her father was a wild rubber tapper. He and the mother died from smallpox three years ago. Some woman took her in, then sold her to Avila last year. What do you intend to do with her?"

"God knows," she said. "A shower wouldn't be a bad idea to start with, but it's more Sister Maria Teresa's department than mine. How much did I pay for her, by the way?"

"About fifty dollars—a hundred *cruzeiros*. Avila can take his pick of girls like her for ten which leaves him ninety for booze."

"My God, what a country," she said, and taking Christina by the hand, started down the street towards the airstrip.

118

I spent the afternoon helping Mannie do an engine check on the Bristol. Hannah arrived back just after six and was in excellent spirits. I lay in my hammock and watched him shave while Mannie prepared the evening meal.

Hannah was humming gaily to himself and looked years younger. When Mannie asked him if he wanted anything to eat, he shook his head and pulled on a clean shirt.

I said, "You're wasting your time, Mannie. His appetite runs to other things tonight."

Hannah grinned. "Why don't you give in, kid? I mean, that's a real woman. She's been there and back and that kind need a man."

He turned his back and went off whistling as I swung my legs to the floor. Mannie grabbed me by the arm. "Let it go, Neil."

I stood up, walked to the edge of the hangar and leaned against a post looking out over the river, taking time to calm down. Funny how easily I got worked up over Hannah these days.

Mannie appeared and pushed a cigarette at me. "You know, Neil, women are funny creatures. Not at all as we imagine them. The biggest mistake we make is to see them as we think they should be. Sometimes the reality is quite different. . . ."

"All right, Mannie, point taken." Great heavy spots of rain darkened the dry earth. I took down an oilskin coat and pulled it on. "I'll go and check on Sister Maria Teresa. I'll see you later."

I'd taken her bag of tricks, an oilskin coat and a pressure lamp up earlier, in case the vigil proved to be a prolonged one. Just as I reached the outer edge of Landro, I met her on the way in. The mother walked beside her, carrying her newly born infant in a blanket; the father followed behind.

"A little girl," Sister Maria Teresa announced, "but they don't seem to mind. I'm going to stay the night with them. Will you let Joanna know for me?"

I accompanied them through the gathering darkness to the

119

shack the couple called home. Then I went back along the street to the hotel.

The rain was really coming down now, in great solid waves. I sat at the bar with Figueiredo for a while, playing draughts and drinking some of that gin I'd brought in for him, waiting for it to stop.

After an hour, I gave up, lit my lamp and plunged down the steps into the rain. The force was really tremendous. It was like being in a small enclosed world, completely alone, and for some reason, I felt exhilarated.

Light streamed through the closed shutters when I went up the steps to the veranda of the house, and a gramophone was playing. I stood there for a moment listening to the murmur of voices, the laughter, then knocked on the door.

Hannah opened it. He was in his shirtsleeves and held a glass of Scotch in one hand. I didn't give him a chance to say anything.

I said, "Sister Maria Teresa's spending the night in Landro with a woman who's just had a baby. She wanted Joanna to know."

He said, "Okay, I'll tell her."

As I turned away Joanna appeared behind him, obviously to see what was going on. It was enough. I said, "Oh, by the way, I'll be flying up to Santa Helena with you in the morning. The mail run will have to wait."

His face altered, became instantly wary. "Who says so?"

"Colonel Alberto. Wants me to take a little walk with him tomorrow to meet some Huna. I'll be seeing you."

I went down into the rain. I think she called my name, though I could not be sure. But when I glanced back over my shoulder, Hannah had moved out onto the veranda and was looking at me.

Some kind of small triumph, I suppose, but one that I suspected I would have to pay dearly for.

9

Drumbeat

I did not sleep particularly well, and the fact that it was three a.m. before Hannah appeared didn't help. I slept only fitfully after that and finally got up at six and went outside.

It was warm and oppressive, unusually so, considering the hour, and the heavy grey clouds promised rain of the sort that would last for most of the day. Not my kind of morning at all, and the prospect of what was to follow had little to commend it.

I wandered along the front of the open hangar and paused beside the Bristol, which stood there with its usual air of expectancy. It came to me suddenly that other men must have stood beside her like this, coughing over the first cigarette of the day as they waited to go out on a dawn patrol, sizing up the weather, waiting to see what the day would bring. It gave me a curious feeling of kinship, which didn't really make any sense.

I turned and found Hannah watching me. That first time we'd met after I'd crash-landed in the Vega, I'd been struck by the ageless quality in his face, but not now. Perhaps it was the morning or more probably, the drink from the previous night,

121

but he looked about a hundred years old. As if he had experienced everything there ever was and no longer had much faith in what was to come.

The tension between us was almost tangible. He said harshly, "Do you intend to go through with this crazy business?"

"I said so, didn't I?"

He exploded angrily. "God damn it, there's no knowing how the Huna might react. If they turn sour, you won't have a prayer."

"I can't say I ever had much faith in it anyway." I started to move past him.

He grabbed my arm and spun me around. "What in the hell are you trying to prove, Mallory?"

I see now, on reflection, that he saw the whole thing as some sort of personal challenge. If I went, then he would have to go or appear less than me, and not only to Joanna Martin. As I have said, he was a man to whom appearances were everything.

He was angry because I had put him in an impossible position; that should have pleased me. Instead I felt as sombre as that grey morning itself.

"Let's just say I'm tired of life, and leave it at that."

And for a moment, he believed me enough to slacken his grip so that I was able to pull free. As I walked back along the edge of the hangar, the first heavy drops of rain pattered against the roof.

The run to Santa Helena was uneventful enough in spite of the bad weather. We didn't get away until much later than had been anticipated because of poor visibility, but from nine o'clock on, there was a perceptible lightening in the sky, although the rain still fell heavily. Hannah decided to chance it.

He asked me to take the control, which suited me in the circumstances, for it not only kept me out of Joanna Martin's way, but also meant that I didn't have to struggle to find the right things to say to Sister Maria Teresa. I left all that to

Hannah, who seemed to do well enough, although for most of the time the conversation behind was unintelligible to me, bound up as I was in my thoughts.

The situation at Santa Helena was no better. The same heavy rain drifting up from the forest again in grey mist because of the heat, but landing was safe enough and I put the Hayley down with hardly a bump.

I had radioed ahead on take-off and had given them an estimated time of arrival. In spite of this I was surprised to find Alberto himself waiting to greet us with the guard detail at the side of the strip.

He came forward to meet us as the Hayley rolled to a halt, and personally handed the two women down from the cabin, greeting them courteously. Beneath the peaked officer's cap his face was serious, and he presented a melancholy figure, adrift in an alien landscape. The caped cavalry greatcoat he wore was obviously an echo of better days.

He led the way back to the small jetty, where the motor launch waited. It presented a formidable appearance. There was a Lewis gun on the roof of the main saloon, another in the prow, each protected by sandbags, and a canvas screen along each side of the boat deck made it possible to move unobserved and also provided some sort of cover against arrows.

An awning had been rigged in the stern against the rain, there was a cane table and canvas chairs and as we approached, an orderly came out of the saloon carrying a tray. He wore white gloves and, as the ladies seated themselves, served coffee from a silver pot in delicate china cups. The rain hammered down, a couple of alligators drifted by. A strange, mad dream standing there by the rail, with only the stench of rotting vegetation rising from the river to give it reality.

Alberto approached and offered me a cigarette. "In regard to our conversation yesterday, Senhor Mallory. Have you come to any decision?"

"A hell of a morning for a walk in the forest," I said, peering

out under the awning. "On the other hand, it could be interesting."

He smiled slightly, hesitated, as if about to say something,
obviously thought better of it and turned away, leaving me at
the rail on my own. To say that I instantly regretted my words
was certainly not so, and yet I had voluntarily committed myself
to a situation of grave danger, which made no kind of sense at
all. Now why was that?

A couple of soldiers were already casting off, and the launch
eased away from the jetty. Alberto accepted a cup of coffee from
the orderly and said, "There won't be time to drop you at Santa
Helena at the moment. The Huna have changed our meeting-
place to the site of an older rubber plantation, a ruined *fazenda*
about five miles upriver from here and a mile inland. The ap-
pointed hour is still the same however, noon, so we shall barely
make the rendezvous on time as it is. Under the circumstances,
I'm afraid you'll all have to come along for the ride."

"May I ask what your plans are, Colonel?" Sister Maria Teresa inquired.

"Simplicity itself, Sister." He smiled wearily. "I go to talk
peace with the Huna as my superiors, who are at present sitting
on their backsides a good thousand miles from here behind
their desks, insist."

"You don't approve?"

"Let us say I am less than sanguine as to the result. A delegation, one chief and five elders, has agreed to meet me on their
terms, which means I go alone except for my interpreter and
very definitely unarmed. The one change in the arrangement
so far is that Senhor Mallory, who knows more about Indians
than any man I know, has agreed to accompany me."

Joanna Martin went very still, her coffee cup raised halfway
to her mouth. She turned and looked at me fixedly, a slight
frown on her face.

Sister Maria Teresa said, "A long walk, Mr. Mallory."

Hannah was good and angry, glared at me, eyes wild, then
at Joanna Martin. He didn't like what he was going to say, but

he got it out, I'll say that for him. "You can count me in too, Colonel."

"Don't be stupid," I cut in. "Who in the hell would be left to fly the women out in the Hayley if anything went wrong?"

There was no arguing with that, and he knew it. He turned away angrily and Sister Maria Teresa said, "It has been my experience in the past, Colonel, that Indians do not look upon any group containing a woman as a threat to them. Wouldn't you agree, Mr. Mallory?"

Alberto glanced quickly at me, aware instantly, as I was myself, of what was in her mind. I said, "Yes, that's true up to a point. They certainly don't take women to war themselves, but I wouldn't count on it."

"A risk I am prepared to take," she said simply.

There was a short silence. Alberto shook his head. "An impossibility, Sister. You must see that."

There are times when the naiveté of the truly good can be wholly infuriating. She said, with that disarming smile of hers, "I am as much for peace as you, Colonel, but I also have a special interest here, remember. The fate of Sister Anne Josepha and her friend."

"I would have thought the church had martyrs in plenty, Sister," he replied.

Joanna Martin stood up. "That sounds to me like another way of saying you don't really expect to come back. Am I right?"

"Se Deus quiser, senhorita."

If God wills. Joanna Martin turned to me, white faced. "You must be mad. What are you trying to prove?"

"You want to know if your sister's alive, don't you?" I asked.

She went into the saloon, banging the door behind her. Sister Maria Teresa said patiently, "Am I to take it that you refuse to allow me to accompany you, Colonel?"

"Under no circumstances, Sister." He saluted her gravely. "A thousand regrets, but I am in command here and must do as I see fit."

"In spite of my authorisation?"

125

"Sister, the Pope himself could not make me take you with us today."

I think it was only then that she really and truly appreciated the danger of the entire undertaking. She sighed heavily. "I did not understand before. I think I do now. You are brave men, both of you."

"I do my duty only, Sister," he said, "but I thank you."

She turned to me. "Duty in your case also, Mr. Mallory?"

"You know what they say, Sister." I shrugged. "I go because it's there."

But there were darker reasons than that—I knew it, and so did she, for it showed in her eyes. I thought she might say something—a personal word, perhaps. Instead she turned and followed Joanna into the saloon.

Hannah threw his cigarette over the rail in a violent gesture. "You're dead men walking. A dozen arrows apiece waiting for each of you up there."

"Perhaps." Alberto turned to me. "The stipulation is that we go unarmed. What do you think?"

"As good a way of committing suicide as any?"

"You don't trust them?"

"Can you trust the wind?" I shook my head. "As I've said before, whatever they do will be entirely as the mood takes them. If they decide to kill us instead of talking, it won't be out of any conscious malice, but simply because it suddenly strikes them as a better idea than the last one they had."

"I see. Tell me, what was Karl Buber's attitude regarding guns?"

"He was never without one prominently displayed, if that's what you mean. Forest Indians fear guns more than anything else I can think of. It doesn't mean they won't attack you if you're armed, but they'll think twice. They still think it's some sort of big magic."

"And yet they demand that we go unarmed." He sighed. "An unhealthy sign, I'm afraid."

"I agree. On the other hand, what the eye doesn't see . . ."

"The same thought had occurred to me, I must confess. That

oilskin coat of yours, for example, is certainly large enough to conceal a multitude of sins."

He was suddenly considerably more cheerful at the prospect, I suppose, of finding himself with a fighting chance again.

"I'll see to the necessary preparations," he said. "We'll go over things in detail closer to the time."

He went along the deck to the wheelhouse, leaving me alone with Hannah. His face was white, eyes glaring. For a moment I thought he might take a punch at me. He didn't get the chance because Joanna chose that precise moment to appear from the saloon.

I could have sworn from her eyes that she had been crying, although that didn't seem possible, but there was fresh powder on her face and the wide mouth had been smeared with vivid orange lipstick.

She spoke to Hannah without looking at him. "Would you kindly get to hell out of here, Sam? I'd like a private word with Galahad here."

Hannah glanced first at her, then at me, and went without argument—some indication of the measure of control she had over him by then, I suppose.

She moved in close enough to make her presence felt. "Are you doing this for me?"

"Not really," I said. "I just like having a good time."

She slapped me across the face hard enough to turn my head sideways. "Damn you, Mallory," she cried. "I don't owe you a thing."

She did the last thing I would have expected. Flung her arm about my neck and fastened that wide mouth of hers on mine. Her body moved convulsively, and for a moment it was difficult to consider other things. And then she pulled free of me, turned and ran into the saloon.

None of it made a great deal of sense, but then human actions seldom do. I moved along the starboard rail to the prow and paused to light a cigarette beside the Lewis gun, which was for the moment unmanned in its sandbagged emplacement.

There was a stack of forty-seven-round drum magazines ready for action at the side of the trim, deadly-looking gun. I sat down on the sandbags to examine it.

"The first gun ever fired from an aeroplane." Hannah appeared from the other side of the wheelhouse. "That was June 7, 1912. Shows how long they've been around."

"Still a lot around back home," I said. "We used them in Wapitis."

He nodded. "The Belgian Rattlesnake the Germans called it during the war. The best light aerial gun we had."

There was silence. Rain hissed into the river, ran from the brim of my wide straw sombrero. I couldn't think of a thing to say, didn't even know what he wanted. And even then, he surprised me by saying exactly the opposite of what I had expected.

"Look, kid, let's get it straight. She's my kind of woman. You saw her first, but I was there last and that's what counts, so hands off, understand?"

Which at least meant he expected me to survive the day's events. Unaccountably cheered, I smiled in his face. Poor Sam. For a moment I thought again he might hit me. Instead he turned wildly and rushed away.

The place was marked on the large-scale map for the area as Matamoros and we found it with no trouble at all. There was an old wooden jetty rotting into the river and a landing stage almost overgrown, but the track to the house, originally built wide enough to take a cart, was still plain.

We moved into the landing stage, a couple of men ready at each Lewis gun, another ten behind the canvas screen on the starboard side, rifles ready, my old comrade-in-arms Sergeant Lima in charge.

We bumped against the landing stage not twenty yards away from that green wall. A couple of men went over the rail and held her in on handlines, the engine gently ticking over, ready to take us out of trouble with a burst of power if necessary.

But nothing happened. A couple of alligators slid off a mud-bank, a group of howler monkeys shouted angrily from the trees. The rest was silence.

Alberto said, "Good, now we make ready."

We went into the saloon, where Joanna, Sister Maria Teresa and Hannah sat at the table talking in low voices. They stopped as we entered, Alberto, Pedro the half-breed interpreter and myself, and stood up.

I took off my yellow oilskin coat and Alberto opened the arms cupboard and produced a Thompson sub-machine-gun with a drum magazine, which we'd prepared earlier with a specially lengthened sling. I slipped it over my right shoulder, muzzle down, and Hannah helped me on with my coat again.

Alberto took a gun which was, I understood, his personal property—probably one of the most deadly hand-guns ever made: the Model 1932 Mauser machine-pistol, and he gave Pedro a .45 automatic to stick in his waistband under the ragged poncho he wore.

The interpreter was something of a surprise. I had expected at least some sign of his white blood but found none. He looked all Huna to me, in spite of his white man's clothing.

To finish, Alberto produced a couple of Mills grenades, slipped one in his pocket and handed the other to me. "Another little extra." He smiled lightly. "Just in case."

There was some confused shouting outside. As we turned, the saloon door was flung open and Sergeant Lima stood there, mouth gaping.

"What is it, man?" Alberto demanded. Hannah produced the .45 automatic from his shoulder holster with a speed which could only indicate considerable practice.

"The holy Sister, Colonel," Lima croaked. "She has gone into the jungle."

There was dead silence, and Joanna Martin slumped into a chair and started to whisper a Hail Mary, probably for the first time in years.

Alberto said savagely, "Good God, man, how could such a

thing be? You were supposed to be guarding the deck. You were in command."

"As God is my witness, Colonel." Lima was obviously terrified. "One second she was standing there, the next, she was over the rail and into the jungle before we realised what was happening."

Which was too much, even for the kind of rigidly correct professional soldier that Alberto was. He slapped him backhanded across the face, threw him into a chair and turned to Hannah.

"Captain Hannah, you will oblige me by taking charge here. I suggest you keep the launch in midstream till our return. If this miserable specimen gives you even a hint of trouble, shoot him." He turned to me. "And now my friend, I think we move very fast indeed."

Pedro was first over the rail and Alberto and I were not far behind. The launch was already moving out into the current as we reached the edge of the forest. I glanced back over my shoulder, caught a glimpse of Hannah standing in the stern under the awning, a machine-gun in his hands, Joanna Martin at his shoulder. God knows why, but I waved, some sort of final gallant gesture, I suppose, then turned and plunged into that green darkness after Alberto.

As I have said, the track had been built wide enough to accommodate reasonably heavy traffic. I now discovered that it had exceptionally solid foundations, logs of ironwood, embedded into the soft earth for its entire length. The jungle had already moved in on it to a considerable extent, but it still gave a quick, clear passage through the kind of country that would have been about as penetrable as a thorn thicket to a white man.

The branches above were so thickly intertwined that virtually no rain got through and precious little light either. The gloom was quite extraordinary and rather eerie.

Pedro was well ahead, running very fast and soon disappeared from sight. I followed hard on Alberto's heels. After a while, we heard a cry and a few yards farther on found Pedro and Sister Maria Teresa standing together.

Alberto kept his temper remarkably under the circumstance. He simply said, "This is foolishness of the worst kind, Sister. I must insist that you return with us at once."

"And I, Colonel, am as equally determined to carry on," she said.

I was aware of the forest foxes calling to each other in the jungle on either side and knew that it was already too late to go back, perhaps for all of us. The thing I was most conscious of was my contempt for her stupidity, a feeling not so much of anger, but of frustration at her and so many like her who out of their own pig-headed insistence on doing good ended up causing more harm than a dozen Avilas.

There was some sort of thud in the shadows a yard or two behind. My hand went through the slit in my pocket and found the grip and trigger guard of the Thompson. There was a Huna lance embedded in the earth beside the track, a necklace of monkey skulls hanging from it.

"What does it mean?" Sister Maria Teresa asked.

"That we are forbidden to go back," Alberto said. "The decision as to what to do with you is no longer mine to make, Sister. If it is of any consolation to you at all, you have probably killed us all."

At the same moment, a drum started to boom hollowly in the middle distance.

We put a bold face on it, the only thing to do, and moved on, Pedro in the lead, Sister Maria Teresa following. Alberto and I walked shoulder-to-shoulder at the rear.

We were not alone for the forest was alive with more than wild life. Birds coloured in every shade of the rainbow lifted out of the trees in alarm and not only at our passing. Parrots and macaws called angrily to each other.

"What did you say?" I murmured to Alberto. "A chief and five elders?"

131

"Don't rub it in," he said. "I've a feeling this is going to get considerably worse before it gets better."

The drum was louder now, and somehow the fact that it echoed alone made it even more sinister. There was the scent of wood-smoke on the damp air and then the trees started to thin and suddenly it was lighter, and then the gable of a house showed clear, and then another.

Not that it surprised me for in the great days of the Brazilian rubber boom, so many millions were being made that some of the houses on the plantations up-country were small palaces, with owners so wealthy they could afford to pay private armies to defend them against the Indians. But not now. Those days were gone, and Matamoros and places like it crumbled into the jungle a little bit more each year.

We emerged into a wide clearing, what was left of the house on the far side. The drumming stopped abruptly. Our hosts were waiting for us in the centre.

The *cacique*, or chief, was easily picked out and not only because he was seated on a log and had by far the most magnificent head-dress, a great spray of macaw feathers. He also sported a wooden disc in his lower lip which pushed it a good two inches out from his face, a sign of great honour amongst the Huna.

His friends were similarly dressed. Beautifully coloured feather head-dresses, a six-foot bow, a bark pouch of arrows, a spear in the right hand. Their only clothing, if that's what you could call it, was a bark penis sheath and various necklaces and similar ornaments of shells, stones or human bone.

The most alarming fact of all was that they were all painted for war, the entire skin surface being coated with an ochre-coloured mud peculiar to that section of the river. They were angry and showed it, hopping from one foot to the other, rattling on at each other like a bunch of old women in the curiously sibilant whispering that passed for speech amongst them. The anger on their flat, sullen faces was like the rage of children, and as unpredictable in its consequences.

The chief let loose a broadside. Pedro said, "He wants to know why the holy lady and Senhor Mallory are here? He's very worried. I'm not sure why."

"Maybe he intended to have us killed out of hand," I said to Alberto, "and her presence has thrown him off balance."

He nodded and said to Pedro, "Translate as I speak. Tell him the Huna have killed for long enough. It is time for peace."

Which provoked another outburst, the general gist of which was that the white men had started it in the first place which entitled the Huna to finish. If all the white men went from the Huna lands, then things might be better.

Naturally Alberto couldn't make promises of that kind and in any case, he was committed to a pretty attacking form of argument. The Huna had raided the mission at Santa Helena, had murdered Father Conté and many nuns.

The chief tried to deny this although he didn't stand much of a chance of being believed with a nun's rosary and crucifix hanging around his neck. His elders shuffled from foot to foot again, scowling like schoolboys in front of the headmaster so Alberto piled on the pressure. They had already seen what the government could do. Did they wish the white man's great bird to drop more fire from the sky on their villages?

One by one, more Indians had been emerging from the forest into the clearing. I had been aware of this for some time and so had Alberto, but he made no reference to it. They pressed closer, hanging together in small groups, shouting angrily. I won't say working up their courage for fear didn't enter their thinking.

I glanced once at Sister Maria Teresa and found her—how can I explain it?—transfixed, hands clasped as if in prayer, eyes shining with compassion, presumably for these brands to be plucked from the flames.

It was round about then that Alberto raised the question of the two missing nuns. The response was almost ludicrous in its simplicity. From denying any part in the attack on Santa Helena in the first place, the chief now just as vehemently denied taking

133

any female captives. All had been killed except for those who had got away.

Which was when Alberto told him he was lying because no one had got away. The chief jumped up for the first time and loosed off another broadside, stabbing his finger repeatedly at Pedro. I noticed the outsiders had crept in closer now in a wide ring, which effectively cut off our retreat to the forest.

Alberto gave me a cigarette and lit one himself nonchalantly. "It gets worse by the minute. He called me here to kill me, I am certain of that now. How many do you make it out there?"

"At least fifty."

"I may have to kill someone to encourage the others. Will you back me?"

Before I could reply, the chief shouted again. Pedro said, "He's getting at me now. He says I've betrayed my people."

In the same moment an arrow hissed through the rain and buried itself in his right thigh. He dropped to one knee with a cry and two of the elders raised their spears to throw, howling in unison.

I had already unbuttoned the front of my oilskin coat in readiness for something like this, but I was too slow. Alberto drew and fired the Mauser very fast, shooting them both in the body two or three times, the heavy bullets lifting them off their feet.

The rest turned and ran. I loosed off a quick burst to send them on their way, deliberately aiming to one side, ripping up the earth in fountains of dirt and stone.

Within seconds there was not an Indian to be seen. Their voices rose angrily from the jungle all the way round the clearing. When I turned, Pedro was on his feet, Sister Maria Teresa crouched beside him tugging at the arrow. "You're wasting your time, Sister," I told her. "Those things are barbed. He'll need surgery to get the arrowhead out."

"He's right," Pedro said, and reached down and snapped off the shaft as close to his thigh as possible.

"Right, let's get moving," Alberto said. "And be prepared to pick up your skirts and run if you want to live, Sister."

"A moment, please, Colonel."

One of the two men he had shot was already dead, but the other was having a hard time of it, blood bubbling between his lips with each breath. To my astonishment she knelt beside him, folded her hands and began to recite the prayers for the dying.

"Go, Christian soul, from this world, in the name of God the Father Almighty who created thee . . ."

Her voice moved on, Alberto shrugged helplessly and removed his cap. I followed suit with some reluctance, aware of the shrill cries of rage from the forest, thinking of that half-mile of green tunnel to the jetty. It suddenly came to me, with a sense of surprise, that I was very probably going to die.

Amazing what a difference that made. I was aware of the rain, warm and heavy, the blood on the dying man's mouth. No colour had ever seemed richer. The green of the trees, the heavy scent of wood-smoke from somewhere near at hand.

Was there much to regret? Not really. I had done what I wanted to do against all advice and every odds possible and it had been worth it. I could have been a junior partner in my father's law firm now and safe at home, but I had chosen to go to the margin of things. Well, so be it. . . .

The Huna's final breath eased out in a dying fall, Sister Maria Teresa finished her prayers, stood up and turned her shining face towards us.

"I am ready now, gentlemen."

I was no longer angry. There was no point. I simply took her arm and pushed her after Alberto who had turned and started towards the beginning of the track, Pedro limping beside him.

As we approached the forest I half expected a hail of arrows, but nothing came. Pedro said, "They will wait for us on the track, Colonel. Play with us for a while. It is their way."

Alberto paused and turned to me. "You agree with him?"

I nodded. "They like their fun. It's a game to them, remember. They'll probably try to frighten us to death for most of the way and actually strike when we think we are safe, close to the river."

"I see. So the main thing to remember is to walk for most of the way and run like hell over the last section?"

"Exactly."

He turned to Sister Maria Teresa. "You heard, Sister?"

"We are in God's hands," she said with that saintly smile of hers.

"And God helps those who help themselves," Alberto told her.

A group of Indians had filtered out of the forest perhaps fifty yards to the right. He took his Mills bomb from his pocket, pulled the pin and threw it towards them. They were hopelessly out of range, but the explosion had a more than salutary effect. They vanished into the forest and all voices were stilled.

"By God, I may have stumbled on something," he said. "Let them sample yours also, my friend."

I tossed it into the middle of the clearing, there was a satisfactorily loud explosion, birds lifted angrily out of the trees, but not one single human voice was to be heard.

"You like to pray, Sister?" Alberto said, taking her by the arm. "Well, pray that silence lasts us to the jetty."

It was, of course, too much to expect. The Huna were certainly cowed by the two explosions, it was the only explanation for their lack of activity, but not for long. We made it to the halfway mark and beyond in silence and then the forest foxes started to call to each other.

There was more than that, of course. The rattle of spear shafts drummed against war clubs, shrill, bird-like cries in the distance, bodies crashing through the undergrowth.

But I could hear the rushing of the river, smell the dank rottenness of it, and there was hope in that.

The sounds in the undergrowth on either side were closer now and parallel. We had a couple of hundred yards to go, no more, and there was the feeling that perhaps they were moving in for the kill.

Alberto said, "I'll take the left, you take the right, Mallory. When I give the word let them have a couple of bursts then we all run."

Even then, I didn't think we stood much of a chance, but there wasn't really much else we could do. I didn't hear what he shouted because he seemed to be firing that machine-pistol of his in the same instant. I swung, crouching, the Thompson gun bucking in my hands as I sprayed the foliage on my side.

We certainly hit something to judge by the cries, but I didn't stop to find out and ran like hell after Pedro and Sister Maria Teresa. For a man with an arrowhead embedded in his thigh he was doing remarkably well, although I presume the prospect of what would happen to him if he fell into their hands alive was having a salutary effect.

The cries were all around us again now. I fired sideways, still running and was aware of another sound, the steady rattle of a Lewis gun. A moment later we broke out on to the riverbank in time to see the launch moving in fast, Hannah himself working the gun in the prow.

I think it was about then that the arrows started to come, swishing through the trees one after the other, never in great numbers. One buried itself in the ground in front of me, another took Pedro full in the back, driving him forward. He spun around, took another in the chest and fell on his back.

I kept on running, ducking and weaving, for this was no place for heroes now, aware of the shooting from the launch, the hands helping Sister Maria Teresa over the rail. As Alberto followed her, an arrow pierced his left forearm. The force must have been considerable for he stumbled, dropping his Mauser into the river and I grabbed his other arm and shoved him over the rail. As I followed, I heard Hannah cry out, the engine note deepened and we started to pull away from the jetty.

Alberto staggered to his feet, and in the same moment, one

of his men cried out and pointed. I turned to see Pedro on his hands and knees like a dog back there on the landing stage, the stump of an arrow shaft protruding from his back. Behind him, the Huna broke from the forest howling like wolves.

Alberto snapped the shaft of the arrow in his arm with a convulsive movement, pulled it out and grabbed a rifle from the nearest man. Then he took careful aim and shot Pedro in the head.

The Launch turned downstream. Alberto threw the rifle on the deck and grabbed Sister Maria Teresa by the front of her habit, shaking her in helpless rage. "Who killed him, Sister, you or me? Tell me that. Something else for you to pray about."

She gazed up at him mutely, a kind of horror on her face. Perhaps for the first time in her saintly life she was realising that evil as the result of good intentions is just as undesirable, but I doubt it in view of subsequent events.

As for Alberto, it was as if something went out of him. He pushed her away and said in the tiredest voice I've ever heard, "Get away from me and stay away."

He turned and lurched along the deck.

10

Just One of Those Things

I came awake slowly, not at all certain that I was still alive and found myself in my hammock in the hangar at Landro. The kettle was boiling away on the spirit stove. Mannie was sitting beside it reading a book.

"Is it any good?" I asked him.

He turned, peering over the top of cheap spectacles at me, then closed the book, stood up and came forward, genuine concern in his eyes.

"Heh, what were you trying to do? Frighten me?"

"What happened?"

"You went out like a light, that's what happened, just after getting out of the plane. We carted you in here and Sister Maria Teresa had a look at you."

"What did she have to say?"

"Some kind of reaction to too much stress was all she could come up with. You crowded a lot of living into a small space in time today, boy."

"You can say that again."

He poured whisky into a glass—good whisky. "Hannah?" I said.

"He's been in and out of here at least a dozen times. You've been lying there for nearly six hours. Oh, and Joanna, she was here too. Just left."

I got out of the hammock and moved to the edge of the hangar and stared out into the night. It had stopped raining, but the air was fresh and cool, perfumed with flowers.

Piece by piece I put it all together again. Alberto's burning anger back there on the launch. He had even refused medical assistance from her—had preferred, he said, the comparatively clean hands of his medical orderly.

He had taken us straight back to the landing strip and had instructed Hannah to fly us back at once. And that just about filled in the blank pages, although I couldn't for the life of me actually remember fainting.

"Coffee!" Mannie called.

I finished my whisky and took the tin mug he offered. "Did Hannah tell you what happened up there?"

"As much as he could. Naturally there was little he could say about what took place at the actual confrontation."

So I told him and when I was finished, he said, "A terrible experience."

"I'll probably dream about that walk back through the jungle for the rest of my life."

"And this thing that took place between Sister Maria Teresa and the Colonel. A nasty business."

"He had a point, though. If she'd done as she was told and stayed on board things might have gone differently."

"But you can't be certain of that?"

"But she is," I said. "That's the trouble. Certain that whatever she does is because the good Lord has so ordained it. Certain that she's right in everything she does."

He sighed. "I must admit that few things are worse than a truly good person convinced they have the answer for all things."

"A female Cromwell," I said.

He was genuinely puzzled. "I don't understand."

"Read some English history, then you will. I think I'll take a walk."

He smiled slyly. "She will be alone, I think, except for that Huna girl she bought from Avila. The good Sister is awaiting delivery of another baby, I understand."

"Doesn't she ever give up? What about Hannah?"

"He said he would be at the hotel."

I found my flying jacket and walked across the landing strip towards Landro. When I reached the house, I actually paused, one foot on the bottom step of the veranda, but thought better of it.

The town itself was quiet. There was a little music through an open window from a radio and somewhere a dog barked a time or two, but otherwise there was just the night and the stars and the feeling of being alive here and now. *Here and now, in this place.*

I went up the steps to the hotel and opened the door. The bar was empty except for Hannah, who sat by an open shutter, feet on the table, a bottle of whisky in front of him and a glass.

"So the dead can walk after all," he said.

"Where is everybody?"

There had been a wedding, it seemed, a civil ceremony presided over by Figueiredo as he was empowered to do in the absence of a priest. The land agent's son, which meant there was money in it. Anyone who was anyone was at the party.

I went behind the counter and got a glass, then sat down and helped myself to whisky from his bottle. "You satisfied now?" he said. "After what you did back there? You feel like a man now?"

"You did a good job with the launch. Thanks."

"No medals, kid—I've already got everything, but the Congressional. Heh, you know what the Congressional is, you Limey bastard?"

I think it was only then that I realised that he had obviously drunk a great deal. I said gravely, "Yes, I think so."

And then he said a strange thing: "I used to know someone just like you, Mallory, back there in the old days at the Front. We were in a Pursuit Squadron together. Fresh kid from Harvard. Old man a millionaire—all the money in the world. He couldn't take it seriously. Know what I mean?"

"I think so."

"Hell, is that all you can say." He filled his glass again. "Know what he used to call me? The Black Baron, on account of von Richthofen was the Red Baron."

"He must have thought a hell of a lot about you."

He didn't seem to hear me. He said, "I used to tell him, 'Watch the sun. Never cross the line alone under ten thousand feet, and always turn and run for home if you see a plane on its own, because you can bet your sweet life it isn't.' "

"And he didn't listen?"

"Went after a Rumpler one morning and didn't notice three F.W.s waiting upstairs in the sun. Never knew what hit him." He shook his head. "Silly bastard." He looked up at me. "But a good flyer and all the guts in the world, kid, just like you."

His head sank on his hands, I got up and walked to the door. As I opened it he spoke without raising his head. "Show some sense, kid. She isn't for you. We're two of a kind, her and me."

I closed the door gently and went outside.

Light streamed out through the latticed shutters as I approached the house, golden fingers filtering into the darkness. I went up the steps to the veranda and paused. It was very quiet. Rain fluttered down, pattering on the tin roof. It was strange standing there, somehow on the outside of things, waiting for a sign that would probably never come, for the world itself to turn over.

I started to move away and on the porch a match flared, pulling her face out of the darkness. There was an old cane chair up there I had forgotten about. She lit a cigarette and flicked the match into the night.

"Why were you going to go away?"

To find a reason or give one, was difficult, but I tried. "I don't think there's anything here for me, that's all."

There was a slight creaking in the darkness as she stood up. The cigarette spun through the night in a glowing arc. I was not aware that she had moved, but suddenly she was there in front of me, the scent of her like flowers in the night. She was wearing some sort of robe or housecoat, which she pulled open to hold my hands against her naked breasts.

"There's this," she said calmly. "Isn't that enough for you?"

It wasn't, but there was no way of explaining that, and in any event, it didn't really seem to matter. She turned, holding me by the hand, and took me inside.

Naturally it was nothing like that first time, perfectly successful as a functional exercise, but no more than that. Afterwards, she was strangely discontented, which surprised me.

"What's wrong?" I demanded. "Wasn't I up to scratch?"

"Love," she said bitterly. "Why does every damned man I meet have to breathe that word in my ear while he's doing it. Do you need an excuse, you men?"

Which was a hell of a thing to say. I had no answer. I got up and dressed. She pulled on her robe and went and stood at the window smoking another cigarette.

I said, "You're a big girl now. Time you learned to tell the difference."

I moved behind her, slipping my arms about her waist, and she relaxed against me. Then she sighed. "Too much water under the bridge. I set my sights on what I wanted a long time ago."

"And nothing gets in the way?"

"Something like that."

"Then what are you doing here, a thousand miles from nowhere?"

She pulled away from me and turned. "That's different. Anna is all I've got. All that really counts."

And she was still speaking of her in the present tense. I held her arms firmly. "Listen to me, Joanna, you've got to face facts."

She pulled away from me violently. "Don't say it—don't ever say it. I don't want to hear."

We stood there in the pale darkness confronting each other. Outside, someone called her name; there was a crash on the veranda as a chair went over. As I went into the living-room, the door burst open and Hannah staggered in. He was soaked to the skin and just about as drunk as a man could be and still stand up. He reeled back against the wall and started to slide. I grabbed him quickly.

He opened his eyes and grinned foolishly. "Well, damn me if it isn't the boy wonder. How was it, kid? Did you manage to bring her off? When they've been around as long as she has it usually takes something special."

No rage—no anger. I stepped back, leaving him propped against the wall. Joanna said, "Get out, Sam."

He went down the wall in slow motion, head lolling to one side. I was aware of Christina, the Huna girl, standing in the entrance to the other bedroom wearing a silk nightdress a couple of sizes too large for her. The eyes were very round in that flat Indian face, the skin shining like copper in the lamp-light.

Joanna stirred Hannah with her toe, then folded her arms and leaned in the open doorway. "He's a bastard, your friend, king size, but he knows what he's talking about. I've been a whore all my life, one way or another."

"All right," I said. "Why?"

"Oh, there was Grantsville to get out of, and that's the way show business is. How do you think I got where I am?"

She took the cigarette from my mouth, inhaled deeply. "And then," she said calmly, "I've got to admit I like it. Always have."

Which was honest enough, God knows, but too honest for me. I said, "You can keep the cigarette," and moved out into the darkness.

I paused some little distance away and glanced back. She stood there in the doorway, silhouetted against the light, the outline of her body clear through the thin material of the house-coat. I was filled with the most damnable ache imaginable, but

144

for what I could not be certain. Perhaps for something which had never existed in the first place?

I heard Hannah call her name faintly, she turned and closed the door. I felt a kind of release, standing there in the rain. One thing was for certain—it was the end of something.

There was news when I returned to the hangar, word over the radio that Alberto had been ordered to evacuate Santa Helena forthwith and was to pull out the following day. It touched me in no way at all, meant absolutely nothing. I ignored Mannie's troubled glances and lay in my hammock staring up at the hangar roof for the rest of the night.

I suppose it would be easy to say with hindsight that some instinct warned me that I stood on the edge of events, but certainly I was aware that something was wrong and waited, filled with a vague unease, anticipating that what was to come was not pleasant.

There was no sign of Hannah when I left at nine the following morning for Manaus on the mail run. I was tired, too tired for that game, eyes gritty from lack of sleep and I had a hard day ahead. Not only the Manaus run, but two contract trips downriver.

Under the circumstances, I'd have taken the Hayley, but the military evacuation from Santa Helena made it more than likely that Hannah would be required up there when they managed to get him out of her bed.

I made the mail drop, re-fuelled and was off again with machine parts which were needed in a hurry by one of the mining companies a hundred and fifty miles downriver and a Portuguese engineer to go with them. He wasn't at all certain about the Bristol, but I got him there in one piece and was on my way back within the hour with ore samples for the assaye officer in Manaus.

My second trip was nothing like as strenuous, a seventy-mile hop with medical supplies to a Jesuit Mission and another quick turn-about, to the great disappointment of the priest in charge, a Dutchman called Herzog, who had hoped for a chess game or two and some conversation.

All in all, a rough day, and it was about six o'clock in the evening when I landed again at Manaus. A couple of mechanics were waiting and I helped them get the Bristol under cover.

The de Havilland Rapide I'd noticed a day or so earlier was parked by the end hangar again. A nice plane and as reliable as you could wish, so I'd been told. The legend *Johnson Air Transport* was neatly stencilled under the cabin windows.

One of the mechanics ran me into town in the old Crossley tender again. I dozed off in the cab and had to be awakened when we reached the Palace. Hardly surprising, when you consider that I hadn't slept at all the previous night.

I wanted a drink badly. I also needed about twelve hours in bed. I hesitated by the reception desk, considering the matter. The need for a very large brandy won hands down and I went into the bar. If I hadn't, things might have turned out very differently, but then, most of life, or what it becomes, depends upon such turns.

A small, wiry man in flying boots and leather jacket sat on the end stool constructing a tower of toothpicks on the base of an upturned glass. There was no barman as usual. I dropped my grip on the floor, went behind the counter and found a bottle of Courvoisier.

His left eye was fixed for all time, a reasonable facsimile of the real thing in glass. The face was expressionless, a wax-like film of scar tissues, and when he spoke the mouth didn't seem to move at all.

"Jack Johnson," he said in a hard Australian twang. "Not that I'm any bloody punch-up artist like the black fella."

I held up the brandy bottle, he nodded and I reached for another glass. "That your Rapide up on the field?"

"That's it, sport, Johnson Air Transport. Sound pretty good, eh?"

"Sounds bloody marvellous," I said and stuck out my hand. "Neil Mallory."

"Well, I'll come clean. That Rapide is Johnson Air Transport." He frowned suddenly. "Mallory? Say, are you the bloke who's been flying that old Bristol for the Baron?"

"The Baron?" I said.

"Sam Hannah, the Black Baron. That's what we used to call him at the Front during the war. I was out there with the R.F.C."

"You knew him well?"

"Hell, everybody knew the Black Baron. He was hot stuff. One of the best there was."

So it was all true, every damned word, and I had been convinced he had told me some private fantasy of long ago, a tissue of half-truths and exaggerations.

"But that was in another country, as they say," Johnson went on. "Poor old Sam's been on the long slide to nowhere ever since. By God, his luck certainly turned when you came along. You saved his bacon and no mistake. I hope he's paying you right?"

"The boot was on the other foot," I said. "If he hadn't taken me on when he did, I'd have ended up on the labour gang. He already had another pilot lined when I arrived."

It was difficult to come to terms with that face of his. There was no way of knowing what was going on behind the mask. There was just that hard Australian voice. In other words, he gave nothing away, and to this day I am still not certain whether what happened was by accident or design.

He said, "What other pilot? What are you talking about?"

"Portuguese, I think. I don't know his name. I believe he'd been flying for a mining company in Venezuela which went bust."

"First I've heard of it and pilots are like gold on the Amazon these days, what with the Spanish war and all this trouble coming up in Europe. You must have seemed like manna from heaven to poor old Sam dropping in like that after all those bad breaks he had. But he sure ran it close. A week left to get a second plane airborne and Charlie Wilson waiting to fly up from Belém and take over his government contract."

"Charlie Wilson?" I said.

"Haven't you met Charlie?" He helped himself to another brandy. "Nice bloke—Canadian—works the lower end of the river out of Belém with three Rapides. Sell his sister if he had to. Mind you, I always thought Sam would come up with something. Nobody in his right mind is going to let twenty thousand dollars slip through his fingers that easily."

It was all turning over inside me now, currents pulling every which way, explanations for some irrational things which had never made any sense rising to the surface.

"Twenty thousand dollars?" I said carefully.

"Sure, his bonus."

"I hadn't realised it was as much as that."

"I should know. I bid for the contract myself originally, then my partner went West in our other plane so that was that. I've been free-lancing since then in the middle section of the river operating from Colona about four hundred miles from here. I don't get into Manaus often."

He went on talking, but I didn't hear. I had other things on my mind. I went round the counter, picked up my canvas grip and moved to the door.

"See you around, sport," Johnson called.

I suppose I made some sort of answer, but I can't be certain for I was too busy reliving that first night in minutest detail. My meeting with Hannah, events at *The Little Boat*, Maria of the Angels and what had happened later.

For the first time, or at least for the first time consciously, it occurred to me that, to use one of Hannah's favourite phrases, I had been taken.

Strange how the body reacts according to circumstances. Sleep was the least of my requirements now. What I needed were answers and it seemed a reasonable assumption that I might get them at the place where it had all started.

I had a cold bath, mainly to sharpen myself up for it had occurred to me that I might well need my wits about me before the night was over. Then I dressed in my linen suit, creased as it was from packing, slipped the .45 automatic in one pocket, a handful of cartridges in the other and left.

It was eight o'clock when I reached *The Little Boat*, early by their standards and there wasn't much happening. I wanted one person, Hannah's old girl-friend, Lola of the red satin dress, and she was not there. Would not be in until nine-thirty at the earliest according to the barman.

I steeled myself to wait as patiently as possible. I'd had no more than a sandwich all day, so I went out on the private deck and ordered dinner and a bottle of Pouilly on Hannah's account, which gave me a perverse pleasure.

Lola arrived rather earlier than expected. I was at the coffee stage of things when the sliding door opened then closed again behind me, fingers gently ruffled my hair and she moved round to the other side of the table.

She looked surprisingly respectable for once in a well-fitting black skirt and a white cotton blouse which buttoned down the front.

"Tomas says you were asking for me." She pushed a glass towards me. "Any special reason?"

I filled her glass. "I was looking for a little fun, that's all. I'm in for the night."

"And Sam?"

"What about Sam?"

"He is with this—this woman who was here the other night? The American?"

"Oh, she seems to have become something of a permanent fixture up at Landro," I said.

The stem of the wineglass snapped in her hand. "God damn him to hell," she said bitterly.

"I know how you feel," I said. "I love him too."

She frowned instantly. "What do you mean?"

I stamped on the floor for the waiter. "Oh, come on now," I said. "Maria of the Angels, you remember her? The one who was so good at dropping out of sight? Mean to say you and Hannah had never clapped eyes on her before?"

149

The waiter appeared with another bottle. She said carefully, "And even if this were so, why should I tell you?"

"To get your own back on him. Much simpler from your point of view than sticking a knife in his back. Now that can be messy. That would get you at least ten years."

She laughed out loud, spilling her wine on the table. "You know, I like you, Englishman. I like you a lot."

She leaned across the table, her mouth opening as she kissed me, tongue probing. After a reasonably lengthy interval, she eased away. Her smile had faded slightly and there was a look of surprise on her face. She seemed to come to some decision and patted my cheek.

"I'll make a bargain with you. You give me what I want and I'll tell you what you want. A deal?"

"All right," I said automatically.

"Good. My place is just along the waterfront from here."

She walked out and I followed, wondering what in the hell I'd let myself in for now.

The room was surprisingly clean, with a balcony overlooking the river, the image of the Virgin and Child on the wall above a flickering candle. Lola herself was a surprise to say the least. She left me on the balcony with a drink and disappeared for a good fifteen minutes. When she returned, she was wearing a housecoat in plain blue silk. Every trace of make-up had been scrubbed from her face and she had tied back her hair.

I got up and put down my glass. She stood looking at me for a while then took off the housecoat and threw it on the bed. Few women are seen at their best in the nude. She had a body to thank God for.

She stood there, hands on hips, and said calmly, "I am beautiful, Senhor Mallory?"

"Few men would dispute that."

"But I am a whore," she said flatly. "Beautiful perhaps, but still a whore. Available to any man who can raise the price."

I thought of Joanna Martin, who had never actually taken cash on the barrel, which was the only difference between them.

"And I am tired of it all," she said. "Just for once I would like a man who can be honest with me as I am honest with him. Who will not simply use me. You understand?"

"I think so," I said.

She blew out the light.

It was late when I awakened. Just after two a.m. according to the luminous dial of my watch. I was alone in the bed, but when I turned my head I saw the glow of her cigarette out there on the terrace.

I started to get dressed. She called softly, "You are leaving?"

"I'll have to," I said. "I've things to do or had you forgotten?"

There was silence for a while, and then, as I pulled on my boots, she said, "There is a street opposite the last pier at the other end of the waterfront from here. The house on the corner has a lion carved over the door. You want the apartment at the top of the second flight of stairs."

I pulled on my jacket. "And what will I find there?"

"I wouldn't dream of spoiling the surprise."

I moved to the door, uncertain of what to say. She said, "Will you be back?"

"I don't think it very likely."

"Honest to the last," she said rather bitterly, then laughed, sounding for the first time since we had left *The Little Boat* like the old Lola. "And in the end, Senhor Mallory, I'm not at all certain that was what I really wanted. Don't you find that rather amusing?"

Which I didn't. I did what I suspected was the best thing in the circumstances, and got out of there fast.

I found the house with the lion above the door easily enough. It was one of those baroque monstrosities left over from the last century, probably built for some wealthy merchant and now in a state of what one might delicately term multiple occupation. The front door opened at once giving access to a large gloomy hall illuminated by a single oil lamp. There was a party going on in one of the downstairs back rooms. I heard a burst of noise and music as someone opened and closed a door.

I started up the stairs in the silence which followed. The first landing was illuminated like the hall below by a single oil lamp, but the next flight of stairs disappeared into darkness.

I went up cautiously, feeling my way along the wall, aware of the patter of tiny feet as the rats and lizards scattered out of the way. When I reached the landing, I struck a match and held it above my head. There was no name on the door opposite, and the lamp on the wall was cold.

The match started to burn my fingers. I dropped it and tried the door handle with infinite caution. It was locked, so I did the obvious thing and knocked gently.

After a while, a lamp was turned up, light seeping under the door, and there was movement, a man's voice and then a woman's. Someone shuffled towards the door. I knocked again.

"Who is it?" the woman demanded.

"Lola sent me," I answered in Portuguese.

The door started to open, and I moved back into the shadows. She said, "Look, I've got someone with me at the moment. Can't you come back a little later?"

I didn't reply. The door opened even wider and Maria of the Angels peered out. "Heh, where are you, man?"

I took her by the throat, stifling all sound, and ran her back into the room, shutting the door quietly behind. The man in the bed, who cried out in alarm, was a mountain of flesh if ever I've seen one. A great quivering jelly more likely to die of fright than anything else.

I produced the .45 and waved it at him. "Keep your mouth shut and you won't get hurt."

Then I turned to Maria. "I'd have thought you could have done better than that."

She was calmer now, a trifle arrogant even. She pulled the

old wrapper she was wearing closer around her and folded her arms. "What do you want?"

"Answers, that's all. Tell me what I want to know and I won't bring the police into this."

"The police?" She laughed at that one. Then shrugged. "All right, Senhor Mallory, ask away."

"It was a set-up our meeting that night, arranged by Hannah—am I right?"

"I'd just come upriver," she said. "I was new in town. Nobody knew me except Lola. We're second cousins."

"What did he pay you?"

"He told me to take whatever money was in your wallet and get rid of anything else."

The instant she said it, I knew that she had not done as she was told. She wasn't the sort. I said, "You've still got them, haven't you? My wallet and the passport."

She sighed in a kind of impatience, turned to a sideboard, opened the drawer and took out my wallet. The passport was inside, together with a few other bits and pieces and a photo of my mother and father. I was caught by that for a moment, then stowed it away and put the wallet in my breast pocket.

"Your parents, senhor?" I nodded. "They look like nice people. You will not go to the police?"

I shook my head and put the .45 back in my pocket. "That's one hell of a knee you have there."

"It's a hard world, senhor."

"You can say that again."

I let myself out and went down the stairs. It was very quiet on the waterfront, and I walked along the pier and sat on a rail at the end smoking a cigarette, feeling absurdly calm in the circumstances.

It was as if I had always known and had not wanted to face it, and perhaps that was so. But now it was out in the open. Now came the reckoning.

I got up and walked back along the pier, footsteps booming hollowly on the wood, echoing into the night.

11

Showdown

I had a contract run to make at nine o'clock, a mail pick-up which meant it could not be avoided. It was a tedious run. Sixty miles downriver, another fifty to a trading post at the headwaters of a small tributary to the west.

I cut it down to sixty-five miles by taking the shortest route between two points and flying across country over virgin jungle. A crazy thing to do and asking for trouble, but it meant I could do the round trip in a couple of hours. A brief pause to re-fuel in Manaus and I could be on my way to Landro by noon. Perhaps because of that, the elements decided to take a hand and I flew into Manaus, thunder echoing on the horizon like distant drums.

The rain started as I landed, an instant downpour that closed my world down to a very small compass indeed. I taxied to the hangar, and the mechanics ran out in rubber ponchos and helped me get her inside.

The mail was waiting for me, and they re-fuelled her quickly enough, but afterwards I could do nothing except stand at the edge of the hangar smoking cigarette after cigarette, staring out at the worst downpour since the rainy season.

After my meeting with Maria of the Angels I had felt surpris-

ingly calm in spite of her story. For most of the morning I'd
had things well under control, but now, out of very frustration,
I wanted to get to Landro so badly that I could taste it. Wanted
to see Hannah's face when I produced my wallet and passport,
confronted him with the evidence of his treachery. From the
start of things I had never really cared for him. Now it was a
question of hate more than anything else, and it was nothing to
do with Joanna Martin.

Looking back on it all, I think that what stuck in my throat
most was the feeling that he had used me quite deliberately to
further his own ends all along the line. There was a kind of
contempt in that, which did not sit easy.

According to the radio the situation at Landro was no better,
so more for something to do than anything else, I borrowed the
Crossley tender, drove into town and had a meal at a fish restau-
rant on the waterfront.

At the bar afterwards, halfway through my second large
brandy, I became aware of a stranger staring out at me from
the mirror opposite.

Small for his size as my grandmother used to say, long arms,
large hands, but a hard, tough, competent-looking young man
or was that only what I wanted to believe? The leather flying
jacket gaped satisfactorily revealing the .45 automatic in the
chest holster, the mark of the true adventurer, but the weary
young face had to be seen to be believed.

Was this all I had to show for two long years? Was this what
I'd left home for? I looked down through the rain at a stern-
wheeler making ready to leave for the coast. It came to me then
that I could leave now. Leave it all. Book passage using Hannah's
famous credit system. Once in Belém I would be all right. I had
a passport again. I could always work my passage to Europe
from there. Something would turn up.

I rejected the thought as instantly as I had considered it.
There was something here that had to be worked through to
the end and I was a part of it. To go now would be to leave the
story unfinished like a novel with the end pages missing, and

155

the memory of him would haunt me for the rest of my life. I had to lay Hannah's ghost personally; there could be no other way.

The rain still fell in a heavy grey curtain as I drove back to the airstrip, and so it continued for the rest of the afternoon. Most serious of all, by four o'clock the surface had turned into a thick, glutinous mud that would get worse before it got better. Much more of this, and it would be like trying to take off in a ploughed field.

Another half-hour and it was obvious that if I did not go then I would not get away at all. I had probably left it too late already. I told the mechanics it was now or never, and got ready to leave.

I started the engine while still inside the hangar and gave it plenty of time to warm up, an essential factor under the circumstances. When I taxied out into the open, the force of the rain had to be felt to be believed. At the very best it was going to be an uncomfortable run.

The strip was five hundred yards long. Usually two hundred was ample for the Bristol's take-off but not today. My tail skidded from side to side, the thick mud sucked at the wheels, showering up in great fountains.

At two hundred yards, I hadn't even managed to raise the tail, at two-fifty I was convinced I was wasting my time, had better quit while still ahead and take her back to the hangar. And then, at three hundred and for no logical reason that I could see, the tail came up. I brought the stick back gently and we lifted into the grey curtain.

It took me two hours but I made it. Two hours of hell, for the rain and the dense mist it produced from the warm earth covered the jungle and river alike in a grey blanket, producing some of the worst flying conditions I have ever known.

To stay with the river with anything like certainty, I had to fly at fifty feet for most of the way, a memorable experience for at that altitude, if that is what it can be termed, there was no room for even the slightest error in judgment and the radio had packed in; the rain, as it turned out, didn't help in the final stages, for conditions at Landro were no better than they had been at Manaus.

But by then I'd had it. I was soaked to the skin, bitterly cold and suffering badly from cramps in both legs. As I came abreast of the airstrip, Mannie ran out from the hangar. Everything looked as clear as it was ever going to be so I simply banked in over the trees and dropped her down.

It was a messy business, all hands and feet. The Bristol bounced once; then the tail slewed round, and we skidded forward on what seemed like the crest of a muddy brown wave.

When I switched off, the silence was beautiful. I sat there plastered with mud from head to toe, the engine still sounding inside my head.

Mannie arrived a few seconds later. He climbed up on the lower port wing and peered over the edge of the cockpit, a look of awe on his face. "You must be mad," he said. "Why did you do it?"

"A kind of wild justice, Mannie, isn't that what Bacon called it?" He stared at me, puzzled, as I stood and flung a leg over the edge of the cockpit. "Revenge, Mannie. Revenge."

But by then I was no longer in control, which was understandable enough. I started to laugh weakly, slid to the ground and fell headlong into the mud.

I sat at the table in the hangar wrapped in a couple of blankets, a glass of whisky in my hands and watched him make coffee over the spirit stove.

"Where's Hannah?"

"At the hotel, as far as I know. There was a message over the radio from Figueiredo to say he wouldn't be back till the morning because of the weather."

"Where is he?"

"Fifteen miles up-river, that's all. Trouble at one of the villages."

I finished the whisky and he handed me a mug of coffee. "What is it, Neil?" he said gravely. "What's happened?"

I answered him with a question. "Tell me something? Hannah's bonus at the end of the contract? How much?"

"Five thousand dollars." There was a quick wariness in his eyes as he said it and I wondered why.

I shook my head. "Twenty, Mannie."

There was a short silence. He said, "That isn't possible."

"All things are in this best of all possible worlds, isn't that what they say? Even miracles, it seems."

I took out my wallet and passport and threw them on the table. "I found her, Mannie—the girl who robbed me that night at *The Little Boat*—robbed me because Hannah needed me broke and in trouble. There was never any Portuguese pilot. If I hadn't turned up when I did, he would have been finished."

The breath went out from him like wind through the branches of a tree on a quiet evening. He slumped into the opposite chair, staring down at the wallet and passport.

After a while, he said, "What are you going to do?"

"I don't know. Finish this coffee, then go and show him those. Should produce an interesting reaction."

"All right," Mannie said. "So he was wrong. He shouldn't have treated you that way. But, Neil, this was his last chance. He was a desperate man faced with the final end of things. No excuse, perhaps, but it at least makes what he did understandable."

"Understandable?" I stood up, allowing the blankets to slip to the ground, almost choking on my anger. "Mannie, I've got news for you. I'll see that bastard in hell for what he's done to me."

I picked up the wallet and passport, turned and plunged out into the rain.

I hadn't the slightest idea what I was going to do when I saw him. In a way, I was living from minute to minute. I'd had virtually no sleep for two nights now, remember, and things seemed very much to be happening in slow motion.

As I came abreast of the house I saw the Huna girl, Christina standing on the porch watching me. I thought for a moment that Joanna or the good Sister might appear, not that it would have mattered.

I kept on going, putting one foot doggedly in front of the other. I must have presented an extraordinary sight, my face and clothing streaked with mud, painted for war like a Huna, soaked to the skin. People stopped talking on the verandas of the houses as I passed, and several ragged children ran out into the rain and followed behind me, jabbering excitedly.

As I approached the hotel I heard singing and recognised the tune immediately, a song I'd heard often sung by some of the old R.F.C. hands round the mess piano on those R.A.F. Auxiliary weekend courses.

I was damned if I could remember the title, another proof of how tired I was. My name sounded clear through the rain as I reached the bottom of the hotel steps. I turned and found Mannie hurrying up the street.

"Wait for me, Neil," he called. I ignored him, went up the steps to the veranda, nodded to Avila and a couple of men who were lounging there, and went inside.

Joanna Martin and Sister Maria Teresa sat at a table by the window drinking coffee. Figueiredo's wife stood behind the bar. Hannah sat on a stool at the far end, head back, singing for all he was worth.

> *So stand by your glasses steady,*
> *This world is a world of lies:*
> *A cup to the dead already,*
> *Hurrah for the next man who dies.*

He had, as the Irish say, drink taken, but he was far from drunk and his voice was surprisingly good. As the last notes died away the two women applauded, Sister Maria Teresa beaming enthusiastically, although the look on Joanna's face was more one of indulgence than anything else—and then she saw me and the eyes widened.

The door was flung open behind me as Mannie arrived. He was short of breath, his face grey, and clutched a shotgun to his chest.

Hannah said, "Well, damn me, you look like something the cat brought in. What happened?"

Mannie grabbed my arm. "No trouble, Neil."

I pulled free, went along the bar slowly. Hannah's smile didn't exactly fade away, it simply froze into place, fixed like a death mask. When I was close I took out the wallet and passport and threw them on the bar.

"I ran into an old friend of yours last night, Sam."

He picked up the wallet, considered it for a moment. "If this is yours I'm certainly glad you've got it back, but I can't say I know what in the hell you're talking about."

"Just tell me one thing," I said. "The bonus. For five thousand read twenty, am I right?"

Joanna Martin moved into view. "What is all this?"

I stiff-armed her out of the way and he didn't like that, anger sparking in those blue eyes, the smile slipping. The solution, when it came, was so beautifully simple. I picked up the passport and wallet and stowed them away.

"I'll do the Manaus mail run in the morning as usual," I said. "You can manage without me after that. I'll leave the Bristol there."

I started to turn away. He grabbed me by the arm and jerked me round to face him again. "Oh, no you don't. We've got a contract."

"I know; signed, sealed, delivered. You can wipe your backside on it as far as I'm concerned."

I think it was only then that he realised just how much trouble he was in. He said hoarsely, "But I've got to keep two planes in the air, kid, you know that. If I don't, those bastards in Belém

160

invoke the penalty clause. I'll lose that bonus. Everything. I'm in hock up to my ears. They could even take the Hayley."

"Marvellous," I said. "I hope that means they keep you here forever. I hope you never get out of this stinking hole."

He hit me then, a good, solid punch that caught me high on the cheek, sending me back against the bar, glasses crashing to the floor.

I have never been much of a fighting man. The idea of getting into the ring to have your face reduced to pulp by a more skillful boxer than yourself just to show you're a man has always struck me as a poor kind of sport, but the life I had been living for the past two years had taught me a thing or two.

I lashed out with my left foot, catching him under the knee. He cried out and doubled over, so I gave him my knee in the face for good measure.

He went back over a cane table with a crash. Both women cried out, there was a considerable amount of confused shouting which meant nothing to me for I had blood in my eye now with a vengeance.

I jumped on him as he started to get up and found him in better shape than he deserved, but then, I had forgotten that colossal strength of his. I got a fist under the ribs that almost took my breath away, another in the face and then my hands fastened around his throat.

We turned over and over, tearing at each other like a couple of mad dogs and then there was a deafening explosion that had us rolling apart in an instant.

Mannie stood over us clutching the shotgun, his face very pale. "Enough is enough," he said. "No more of this stupidity."

In the silence, I was aware of Avila and his friends outside on the terrace peering in, of the anguish on Sister Maria Teresa's face, of Joanna Martin, watchful and somehow wary, glancing first at Hannah and then at me.

We got to our feet together. "All right, have it your way, Mannie, but I'm still clearing out in the morning."

"We've got a contract." It was a cry of agony and Hannah

swayed, clutching at the table, blood streaming from his nose which, as I discovered later, I had broken with my knee.

I jerked my thumb at the shotgun. "I've got one of those too, Sam, remember? Try and stop me leaving in the morning and I'm just liable to use it."

When I turned and walked out, nobody got in my way.

It was growing dark as I ploughed my way back through the hangar. I lit the lamp and poured another whisky. I put my head on my hands and closed my eyes and fireworks sparked off in the darkness. My legs ached, my face ached. I wanted nothing so much as sleep.

I sat up and found Joanna Martin standing at the edge of the hangar looking at me. We stared at each other in silence for quite some time. Finally I said, "Did he send you?"

"If you do this to him he's finished," she replied.

"I'd say he's just about earned it."

Anger flared up in her suddenly. "Who in the hell do you think you are, Lord God Almighty? Haven't you ever made a mistake? The guy was desperate. He's sorry for what he's done. He'll make it up to you."

I said, "What are you supposed to do next? Take me back to bed?"

She turned and walked out. I sat there staring into the darkness, listening to the rain and Mannie moved out of the shadows.

"You too?" I said. "What are you going to do? Tell me some cosy Hassidic story about some saintly old rabbi who always turned the other cheek and smiled gratefully when they spat on him?"

I don't know whether he'd come with the intention of appealing to me to think again. If he had, then that little speech of mine made him certainly think twice. He simply said, "I think you're wrong, Neil, taking all the circumstances into account, but it's your decision." And he turned and followed Joanna Martin.

By then I not only didn't give a damn, I was past caring about anything. I was getting out and nothing on this earth was going to stop me. Let that be an end of it.

I changed into dry clothes, climbed into my hammock, hitched a blanket around my shoulders and was almost instantly asleep.

I don't know what time the rain stopped, but I awakened to a beautiful morning at eight o'clock, having slept for twelve solid hours. I was sore all over and cramp, that occupational disease of pilots, grabbed at my legs as I sat up. My face ached, and I peered in the mirror Mannie had fixed to one of the roof posts; I saw that both cheeks were badly swollen and discoloured with bruising.

There was a footstep behind me, and Mannie appeared, wiping his hands on some cotton waste. He was wearing overalls and there was grease on his face. The Bristol was parked out on the airstrip.

"How do you feel?" he asked.

"Terrible. Is there any coffee?"

"Ready on the stove. Just needs heating."

I turned up the flame. "What have you been doing?"

"My job," he said calmly. "You've got a mail run this morning, haven't you?"

"That's right," I said deliberately.

He nodded towards the Bristol. "There she is. Ready and waiting for you."

He turned away. I poured myself a mug of coffee and got ready to go. I had just finished packing my grip for the last time when Hannah arrived.

He looked terrible, the face badly bruised, the nose obviously out of alignment and the eyes were washed clean of all feeling. He wore his leather boots, breeches and an old khaki shirt, a white scarf looped around his neck. He carried the mail sack in his left hand.

He said calmly, "Are you still going through with this?"

"What do you think?"

"Okay," he said, still calm. "Suit yourself."

He walked across to the Bristol, climbed up and stowed the sack in the observer's cockpit. I followed slowly, my grip in one hand, zipping up my jacket with the other.

Mannie stayed in the hangar, which didn't make me feel too good, but if that was the way he wanted it, then to hell with him. Quite suddenly I had an overwhelming desire to get away from that place. I'd had Landro, I'd had Brazil.

I put my foot on the lower port wing and climbed into the cockpit. Hannah waited patiently while I fastened my helmet and went through the checks. He reached for the propeller, I began to wind the starting magneto and gave him the signal. And then he did a totally unexpected thing. He smiled or at least I think that's what it was supposed to be and called, "Happy landings, kid." Then he pulled the propeller.

It almost worked. I fought against the impulse to cut the engine, turned into the wind before I could change my mind and took off. As I banked across the trees, the government launch moved in to the jetty. Figueiredo was standing in the stern. He waved his hat to me, I waved back, took a final look at Landro then turned south.

I had a good fast run and raised Manaus in an hour and forty minutes. There were a couple of cars parked by the tower as I came in. A rather imposing black Mercedes and an Oldsmobile. As I taxied towards the hangar, they started up and moved towards me. When I stopped, so did they.

A uniformed policeman slid from behind the wheel of a Mercedes and opened the rear door for the *comandante*, who waved cheerfully and called a good morning. Three more policemen got out of the Oldsmobile, all armed to the teeth. *Hannah and that damned contract of ours.* So this was why he had been so cheerful?

I slid to the ground and took the hand the *comandante* so genially held out to me. "What's this? I don't usually rate a guard of honour."

His eyes behind the dark glasses gave nothing away. "A small matter. I won't keep you long, my friend. Tell me, Senhor Figueiredo has a safe at his place of business, you are aware of this?"

I knew at once that it was about as bad as it could be. I said, "Along with everyone else in Landro. It's under the bar counter."

"And the key? I understand Senhora Figueiredo can be regrettably careless regarding its whereabouts."

"Something else well known to everyone in Landro," I said. "She hangs it behind the bar. Look—what is this?"

"I had a message from Senhor Figueiredo over the radio half an hour ago to say that he opened his safe this morning to check the contents after his absence, he discovered a consignment of uncut diamonds was missing."

I took a deep breath. "Now, look here," I said. "Any one of fifty people could have taken them. Why pick on me?"

He nodded briefly, three of the policemen crowded in on me, the fourth climbed up into the observer's cockpit and threw out the mail sack and my grip, which the *comandante* started to search. The man in the cockpit said something briefly in Portuguese that I couldn't catch, and handed down a small canvas bag.

"Yours, senhor?" the *comandante* inquired politely.

"I've never seen it before in my life."

He opened the bag, peered inside briefly, then poured a stream of uncut diamonds into his left palm.

There was a terrible inevitability to it all after that, but I didn't go down without a struggle. The *comandante* didn't question me himself—not at first. I told my story from beginning to end and exactly as it had happened, to a surprisingly polite young lieutenant who wrote it all down and made no comment.

Then I was taken downstairs to a cell that was almost a parody of what you expected to find up-country in backward South American republics. There were at least forty of us crammed into a space fit for half that number. One bucket for urine,

165

another for excrement and a smell that had to be experienced to be believed.

Most of the others were the sort who were too poor to buy themselves out of trouble. Indians in the main, of the kind who had come to town to learn the white man's big secret and who had found only poverty and degradation.

I pushed towards the window and most of them got out of my way respectfully out of sheer habit. A large, powerful-looking Negro in a crumpled linen suit and straw sombrero sat on a bench against the wall. He looked capable of most things and certainly when he barked an order, the two Indians sitting beside him got out of the way fast enough.

He smiled amiably. "You have a cigarette for me, senhor?"

As it happened, I had a spare packet in one of my pockets and he seized them avidly. I had a distinct feeling I had made the right gesture.

He said, "What have they pulled you in for, my friend?"

"A misunderstanding, that's all," I told him. "I'll be released before the day's out."

"As God wills, senhor."

"And you?"

"I killed a man. They called it manslaughter because my wife was involved, you understand? That was six months ago. I was sentenced by the court yesterday. Three years at hard labour."

"I suppose it could have been worse," I said. "Better than hanging."

"It is all one in the end, senhor," he said with a kind of indifference. "They are sending me to Machados."

I couldn't think of a thing to say, for the very name was enough to frighten most people locally. A labour camp in the middle of a swamp two or three hundred miles from nowhere on the banks of the Negro. The sort of place from which few people seemed to return.

I said, "I'm sorry about that."

He smiled sadly, tilted his hat over his eyes and leaned back against the wall.

166

I stood at the window which gave a ground-level view of the square at the front of the building. There weren't many people about, just a couple of horse-drawn cabs waiting for custom, drivers dozing in the hot sun. It was peaceful out there. I decided this must all be a dream, that I'd wake very soon. The Crossley tender from the airstrip pulled up at the bottom of the steps, and Hannah got out.

They came for me about two hours later, took me upstairs and left me outside the *comandante*'s office with a couple of guards. After a while, the door opened and Hannah and the *comandante* emerged, shaking hands affably.

"You have been more than helpful, my friend," the *comandante* said. "A sad business."

Hannah turned and saw me. His face looked worse than ever for the bruising had deepened, but an expression of real concern appeared for all to see and he strode forward, ignoring the *comandante*'s hand on his shoulder.

"For God's sake, kid, why did you do it?"

I tried to take a swing at him and both guards grappled with me at once. "Please, Captain Hannah," the *comandante* said. "Better to go now."

He took him firmly to the outer door, and Hannah, a look of agony on his face now, called, "Anything, kid—anything I can do, just ask."

The *comandante* returned to his office, leaving the door ajar. After a couple of minutes, he called for me and the guards took me in. He sat at his desk examining a typed document for a while.

"Your statement." He held it up. "Is there anything you wish to change?"

"Not a word."

"Then you will please sign it. Please read it through first."

I found it a fair and accurate account of what I had said, something to be surprised at, and signed it.

He put it on one side, lit a cigarillo and sat back. "Right,

Senhor Mallory, facts only from now on. You have made certain accusations against my good friend Captain Hannah who, I may say, flew down especially at my request to make a statement."

"In which he naturally denies everything."

"I do not have to take his word for anything. The woman, Lola Coimbra—I have interviewed her personally. She rejects your story completely."

I was sorry about that, in spite of my position—sorry for Lola more than for myself.

"And this woman Maria," he went on. "The one you say assaulted you. Would it surprise you to know she is not known at the address you give?"

By then, of course, I had got past being surprised at anything, but still struggled to keep afloat. "Then where did I get the wallet and passport from?"

"Who knows, senhor? Perhaps you've never been parted from them. Perhaps the whole affair was an elaborate plot on your part to gain Captain Hannah's sympathy so that he would offer you employment."

Which took the wind right out of my sails. I struggled for words and said angrily, "None of this would stand up in a court of law for five minutes."

"Which is for the court to decide. Leaving all other considerations on one side, there is no question in my mind that you have a clear case to answer on the charge of being in unlawful possession of uncut diamonds to the value of . . ." Here, he checked a document before him. "Yes, sixty thousand *cruzeiros*."

Round about nine thousand pounds. I swallowed hard. "All right. I want to be put in touch with the British Consul in Belém and I'll need a lawyer."

"There will be plenty of time for that."

He reached for an official-looking document with a seal at the bottom and signed it. I said, "What's that supposed to mean?"

"The courts are under great pressure, my friend. This is a wild region. There are many wrongdoers. The scum of Brazil run here to hide. It may be at least six months before your case is heard."

I couldn't believe my ears. I said, "What the hell are you talking about?"

He carried on as if I had not spoken. "For the present, you will be committed to the labour camp at Machados until your case comes to trial. As it happens a new batch of prisoners go upriver in the morning."

He dismissed me, nodding at the guards to take me away, the last straw as far as I was concerned.

"Listen to me, damn you!" I reached across the desk, grabbing him by the front of the tunic.

It was about the worst thing I could have done. One of the guards jabbed the end of his club into my kidneys, and I went down like a stone. Then they grabbed an arm each and took me between them down the two flights of stairs to the basement, my feet dragging.

I was vaguely aware of the door of the cell being opened, of being thrown inside. I passed out for a while then and surfaced to find my Negro friend squatting beside me.

He held a lighted cigarette to my lips, his face expressionless. "The misunderstanding—it still exists?"

"I think you could say that," I told him weakly. "They're sending me to Machados in the morning."

He took it very philosophically. "Have courage, my friend. Sometimes God looks down through the clouds."

"Not today," I said.

I think the night which followed was the lowest point of my life, but the final humiliation was still to come. On the following morning, just before noon, the Negro, whose named turned out rather improbably to be Munro, a legacy from some Scottish plantation owner in the past, myself and about thirty other prisoners were taken out to the yard at the back to be fitted with leg and wrist irons for the trip upriver.

There was absolutely nothing to be done about it. I simply had to accept for the moment like everyone else, and yet when the sergeant in charge got to me and screwed the ankle bracelets up tight, it seemed like the final nail in my coffin.

Just after that it started to rain. They left us standing in the open for another hour, during which we got soaked to the skin, unnecessary cruelty but the sort of thing to be expected from now on. Finally, we were formed into a column and marched away at a brisk shuffle towards the docks.

There was a café-bar at the corner of the square, and plenty of people sat on the veranda having coffee and an aperitif before lunch. Most of them stood up to get a good view as we went past, chains clanking.

Hannah's face jumped out at me instantly for although he was standing at the back of the crowd, he was easily visible because of his height. He had a glass of something or other in his right hand, actually raised it in a silent toast, then turned away and strolled casually inside.

12

Hell on Earth

We were three days in the hold of an old stern-wheeler that worked its way upriver once a week, calling at every village on the way with a jetty large enough to lay alongside. Most people travelled on deck, sleeping in hammocks because of the heat. The guards let us up once a day for air, usually in the evening, but in spite of that two of the older men died.

One of the prisoners, a small man with skin like dried-up leather and hair that was prematurely white, had already served seven months at Machados while awaiting trial. He painted a harrowing picture of a kind of hell on earth, a charnel house where the whip was the order of the day and men died like flies from ill-treatment and disease.

But for me the present was enough. A nightmare, no reality to it at all. I found myself a dark little corner of my own and crouched there for two days in a kind of stupor, unable to believe that this was really happening to me. It was real enough, God knows, and the pain and the squalor and the hunger of it could not be evaded. It existed in every cruel detail and it was Hannah who had put me here.

Munro had done his best with me during this period, patiently continuing to talk, even when I refused to answer, feeding me cigarettes until the packet I'd given him was empty. In the end, he gave up the struggle in a kind of disgust and I recalled his final words clearly as he got up and shuffled away.

"Forgive me, senhor, I can see I've been talking to a man who is already dead."

It took a dead man to bring me back to life. On the evening of the third day I was awakened by the sound of the hatch being opened. There was a general movement instantly, everyone eager to be the first out into the clean air. The man next to me still slept on, leaning heavily against me, his head on my shoulder. I shoved him away and he went over in slow motion and lay still.

Munro pushed his way through the press and went down on his knees. After a while he shrugged and scrambled to his feet. "He's been dead for two or three hours."

My flesh crawled. I felt in some indefinable way unclean, for it was as if in taking this man death had touched me also. Someone called out, and a guard came down the ladder. He checked the body casually, then nodded to Munro and me. "You two—get him on deck."

Munro said, "I'll get on my knees and you put him over my shoulder. It's the easiest way."

He got down and I stood there, trapped by the horror of it all, filled with unutterable loathing at the idea of even touching that body.

The guard belted me across the shoulder blades with his club, the usual careless brutality. "Get moving, we haven't got all day."

Somehow I got the body across Munro's shoulders, followed him up the ladder, chains rattling against the wooden bars. There were only half a dozen passengers and they were all comfortably settled under an awning in the prow where they caught what breezes were going. The rest of the prisoners already squatted in the stern and a couple of guards lounged on a hatch-cover, smoking and playing cards.

One of them glanced up as we approached. "Over with him," he said. "And throw him well out. We don't want him getting into the paddle wheels."

I took him by the ankles, Munro by the shoulders. We swung him between us in an arc out over the rail. There was a splash, ibis rose in a dark cloud, black against the sky, the beating of their wings filling the air.

Munro crossed himself. I said, "You can still believe in God?"

He seemed surprised. "But what has God to do with this, senhor? This is Man and Man only."

"I've got a friend I'd like you to meet some time," I told him. "I think you'd get on famously."

He had one cigarette left, begged a light from the guard, and we went to the rail to share it. He started to crouch. I said, "No, let's stand. I've been down there long enough."

He peered at my face in the half-darkness, leaning close. "I think you are yourself again, my friend."

"I think so too."

We stood there at the rail looking out across the river at the jungle, black against the evening sky as the sun set. It was extraordinarily beautiful and everything was still. No bird called and the only sound was the steady swish of the paddles. Munro left me for a while and went and crouched beside Ramis, the man who had already spent some time at Machados.

When he returned he said quietly, "According to Ramis we'll be there in the morning. He says we leave the Negro about twenty miles from here. There's a river called the Seco which cuts into the heart of the swamp. Machados is on some kind of island about ten miles inside."

It was as if the gate was already swinging shut and I was filled with a sudden dangerous excitement. "Can you swim?"

"In these?" he said, raising his hands.

I stretched the chain between my wrists. There was about two and a half feet of it and the same between the ankles. "Enough for some sort of dog paddle. I think I could keep afloat long enough to reach the bank."

"You'd never make it, my friend," he said. "Look there by the stern."

I peered over the rail. Alligators' eyes glow red at night. Down there, tiny pin-pricks gleamed balefully in the darkness as they followed the boat like gulls at sea, waiting for the leavings.

"I have as great a desire for freedom as you," Munro said softly, "but suicide is another matter."

And suicide was the only word for it, he was right enough there. In any event, the moment had passed for the guards put their cards away, formed us into a line and put us back in the hold.

It was Ramis who saved me, by cutting his throat just after dawn with a razor blade he had presumably secreted on his person, since Manaus. He took several minutes to die and it wasn't pleasant listening to him gurgle his life away there in the semidarkness.

We were perhaps two or three miles into the Seco at the time, and it had an explosive effect on the rest of the prisoners. One man cracked completely, screaming like a woman, trampling his way through the others in an attempt to reach the ladder.

Panic swept through the group then, men kicking and cursing at each other, struggling wildly. The hatch went back with a crash, there was a warning shot into the air and everyone froze. A guard came halfway down the ladder, a pistol in his hand. Ramis sprawled face-down and everyone stood back from the body. The guard dropped in and turned him over with a foot. He was a ghastly sight, his throat gaping, the razor still firmly grasped in his right hand.

"All right," the guard said. "Let's have him up."

I moved before anyone else and got a hand to the body and Munro, by a kind of telepathy, was with me. He took the razor from the clenched hand and I heaved Ramis over his shoulder.

There was blood everywhere. My hands were smeared with it, and it splashed down on my head and face. I followed Munro up on deck.

The river was only thirty or forty yards wide and mangrove

swamp stretched away on either side, mist curling up from the surface of the water in the cold morning air. Even then, at that fixed point in time, I was not certain of what I intended to do. Things happened, I think, because they happened and very much by chance.

A miserable village, half a dozen huts constructed on sticks above a mudbank, drifted by. There were a couple of fishing nets stretched out on poles to dry and three canoes drawn up out of the water.

It was enough. I glanced at Munro. He nodded. As the village disappeared into the curling mist, we moved past the guards with our bloody burden and went to the rail.

"Go on, over with him," the sergeant in charge said. "Then get this deck cleaned up."

He was standing by the hatch smoking. Another guard sat beside him, a carbine across his knees. They were the only two on view, although there had to be others around. I took Ramis by the ankles, Munro took his arms. We swung him once, then twice. The third time we simply threw him at the sergeant and the guard on the hatch. I didn't even wait to see what happened, but flung myself awkwardly over the rail.

I started to kick wildly the moment the water closed over my head, aware of the constriction of the chains, aware also of the danger from the paddle wheel at the stern. Kicking with my feet was easy enough, and I clawed both hands forward in a frenzy, the turbulence all around me in the water as the boat slid past.

It would be some time before they could get it to stop, that would be one point in our favour, but they had already started firing. A bullet kicked water into the air a yard in front of me. I glanced over my shoulder, saw Munro some little way behind, the sergeant and three guards at the rail.

They all seemed to fire at once and Munro threw up his hands and disappeared. I took a deep breath and went under, clawing my way forward for all I was worth. When I surfaced I was into the first line of mangroves and in any case, the stern-wheeler had already faded into the mist.

I hung on to a root for a moment to get my breath, spitting out brackish, foul-tasting water. The general smell at that level was terrible and a snake glided by, reminding me unpleasantly of the hazards I was likely to meet if I stayed in the water too long. But anything was better than Machados.

I slid into the water again, struck out into the stream and allowed the current to take me along with it. I could already see the roofs of the huts above the trees for the mist at that point lay close to the surface of the water.

I grounded in the mud below the pilings a few moments later and floundered out of the water, tripping over my leg chains at one point and falling on my face. When I struggled up I found an old man staring at me from the platform of one of the huts, a wretched creature who wore only a tattered cotton shirt.

When I got hold of the nearest canoe and shoved it towards the water, he gave vent to some sort of cry. I suppose I was taking an essential part of his livelihood or some other poor wretch's. God knows what misery my action was leaving behind, but that was life. Somehow, in spite of the awkwardness of the chains I managed to get into the frail craft, picked up a paddle and pushed out into the current.

I didn't really think they would turn the stern-wheeler around and come downriver looking for me, but some sort of search would obviously be mounted as soon as possible. It would be when they discovered a canoe had been taken from the village that the fun would start.

It seemed essential that I got as much distance under me as possible. Whatever happened afterwards would have to be left to chance. Once into the Negro I would find plenty of riverside villages where people lived a primitive day-to-day life which didn't even recognise the existence of such trappings of civilisation as the police and the government. If I was lucky I'd find help and a little luck was something for which I was long overdue.

A couple of miles and I was obviously close to the confluence of the Negro. I was aware of the currents pulling, the surface turning over on itself. A mistake here and I was finished, for I had no hope of keeping afloat for long in such conditions in my chained state.

I turned the canoe towards the left-hand side for I was at least fifty yards from the shore and it certainly looked as if I would be safer there. It seemed to be working, and then, when I was a few yards from the mangrove trees, I seemed to slide down into a sudden turbulence.

It was like being seized in a giant hand, the canoe rocked from side to side, almost putting me over. I lost the paddle as I grabbed frantically at the sides to keep my balance, and then we spun round twice and turned over.

My feet touched the bottom instantly, but the current was too strong for me to be able to stand. However, the canoe, bottom up, barged into me a moment later and I was able to fling my arms across the keel.

Things slowed down a little after that and we finally drifted into quiet water amongst the mangrove trees farther along and grounded against a mudbank.

I righted the canoe and took stock of the situation. The mouth of the river was about a quarter of a mile away, and I didn't fancy my chances in the canoe, with or without a paddle. It seemed obvious that the best, indeed, the only thing to do was to attempt to cut through the mangroves on a diagonal course which would bring me out into the Negro down-river from the Seco.

I managed to get back into the canoe and pushed off, pulling myself along by the great roots of the trees until I came to a clump of bamboo where I managed to break myself off a length. From then on, it wasn't too bad. Henley, the Thames on a Sunday afternoon in summer. All I needed was a gramophone and a pretty girl. For a moment, I seemed to see Joanna Martin leaning back and laughing at me from under her parasol. But it was entirely the wrong kind of laughter. Some measure of the condition I was in by then, I suppose. I took a deep breath to brace myself up to what lay ahead and started to pole my way out of there.

13

Balsero

It took me four hours. Four hours of agony, tortured by mosquitoes and flies of every description, the iron bracelets rubbing my wrists raw so that each push on the pole became an effort of will.

The trouble was that every so often I ran into areas where the mangroves seemed to come closer together, branches crowding in overhead so that I couldn't see the sun which meant that I lost direction. And then there was the bamboo—gigantic walls of it that I could not possibly hope to penetrate. Each time, I had to probe for another way round or even retrace my route and try again from another direction.

When I finally saw daylight, so to speak, it was certainly more by accident than design. There were suddenly considerably fewer mangrove trees around, although I suppose it must have been a gradual process. And then I heard the river.

I came out of the trees and edged into the Negro cautiously. It rolled along quietly enough, and I had it to myself as far as I could see although as it was several hundred yards wide at that point, islands of various sizes scattered down the centre, it was impossible to be certain.

One thing I needed now above anything else. Rest, even sleep if possible. Someplace where I could lie up for a while in safety, for I could not continue in my present state.

It seemed to me then that one of those islands out there would be as good a place as any and I pushed out towards the centre of the river using the pole like a double-bladed paddle. It was slow work and I missed my first objective. By then there was hardly any strength left in me at all, and each movement of my arms was physical agony.

It was the current which helped me at last, pushing me into ground on a strip of the purest whitest sand imaginable. No south sea island could have offered more. I fell out of the canoe and lay beside it in the shadows for a while, only moving in the end because I would obviously drown if I stayed there, so I got up off my knees and hauled that bloody boat clear off the water . . . then fell on my face again.

I don't know how long I lay there. It may have been an hour or just a few minutes. There seemed to be some sort of shouting going on near by, all part of the dream, or so it seemed. Perhaps I was still back in the Seco after jumping from the stern-wheeler? I opened my eyes, and a child screamed.

There was all the terror in the whole world in that one cry. Enough to bring even me back to life. I got to my feet uncertainly, and it started again and didn't stop.

There was a high spit of sand to my right. I scrambled to the top and found two children, a boy and a girl, huddled together in the shadows on the other side, an alligator nosing in towards them.

They could not retreat any farther for there was deep water behind them and the little girl, who was hardly more than a baby, was screaming helplessly. The boy advanced on the beast, howling at the top of his voice, which, considering he looked about eight years of age, was probably one of the bravest things I've seen in my life.

I started down the slope, forgetting my chains and fell head-

179

long, rolling over twice and landing in about a foot of water which just about finished me off. I'm not really sure what happened then. Someone was yelling at the top of his voice, me, I suppose. The alligator shied away from the children and darted at me, jaws gaping.

I grabbed up the chain between my wrists and brought it down like a flail across that ugly snout again and again, shouting at the children in Portuguese, telling them to get out of it. I was aware of them scurrying by as I battered away, and then the alligator slewed round and that great tail knocked my feet from under me.

I kicked at it frantically, and then there was a shot and a ragged hole appeared in the alligator's snout. The sound it made was unbelievable, and it pushed off into deep water leaving a cloud of blood behind.

I lay on my back in the water for a while, then rolled over and got to my knees. A man was standing on the shore, small, muscular, brown-skinned. He might have passed for an Indian except for his hair, which was cut European style. He wore a denim shirt and cotton loincloth; the children clung to his legs, sobbing bitterly.

The rifle which was pointing in my direction was an old British Army Lee-Enfield. I didn't know what he was going to do with it, didn't even care. I held out my manacled wrists and started to laugh. I remember that, and also that I was still laughing when I passed out.

It was raining when I returned to life and the sky was the colour of brass, stars already out in the far distances. I was lying beside a flickering fire, there was the roof of a hut silhouetted against the sky beyond, and yet I seemed to be moving and there was the gurgle of water beneath me.

I tried to sit up and saw that I was entirely naked except for my chains. My body was blotched here and there with great black swamp leeches.

A hand pushed me down again. "Please to be still, senhor."

My friend from the island crouched beside me puffing on a

large cigar. When the end of it was really hot he touched it to one of the leeches which shrivelled at once, releasing its hold.

"You are all right, senhor?"

"Just get rid of them," I said, my flesh crawling.

He lit another cigar and offered it to me politely then continued his task. Beyond him in the shadows the two children watched, faces solemn in the firelight.

"Are the children all right?" I asked.

"Thanks to you, senhor. With children one can never turn the back, you have noticed this? I had put into that island to repair my steering oar. I turned my head for an instant and they are gone."

Steering oar? I frowned. "Where am I?"

"You are on my raft, senhor. I am Bartolomeo da Costa, *balsero*."

Balseros are the water gipsies of Brazil, drifting down the Amazon and Negro with their families on great balsa rafts up to a hundred feet long, the cheapest way of handling cargo on the river. Two thousand miles from the jungles of Peru down to Belém on occasion, taking a couple of months over the voyage.

It seemed as if that little bit of luck I had been seeking had finally come my way. The last leech gave up the ghost, and as if at a signal, a quiet, dark-haired woman wearing an old pilot coat against the evening chill emerged from the hut and crouched beside me holding an enamel mug.

It was black coffee, scalding hot. I don't think I have ever tasted anything more delicious. She produced an old blanket which she spread across me then suddenly seized my free hand and kissed it, bursting into tears. Then she got up and rushed away.

"My wife, Nula, senhor," Bartolomeo told me calmly. "You must excuse her, but the children—you understand? She wishes to thank you, but does not have the words."

I didn't know what to say. In any case, he motioned the children forward. "My son Flaveo and my daughter Christina, senhor."

181

The children bobbed their heads. I put a hand out to the boy, forgetting my chains and failed to reach him. "How old are you?"

"Seven years, senhor," he whispered.

I said to Bartolomeo, "Did you know that before I intervened, this one rushed on the *jacare* to save his sister?"

It was the one and only time during our short acquaintance that I saw Bartolomeo show any emotion on that normally placid face of his. "No, senhor." He put a hand on his son's shoulder. "He did not speak of this."

"He is a brave boy."

Bartolomeo capitulated completely, pulled the boy to him, kissed him soundly on both cheeks, kissed the girl and gave them both a push away from him. "Off with you—go help your mama with the meal." He got to his feet. "And now, senhor, we will see to these chains of yours."

He went into the hut and reappeared with a bundle under one arm which when unrolled, proved to be about as comprehensive a tool kit as I could have wished for.

"On a raft one must be prepared for all eventualities," he informed me.

"Are you sure you should be doing this?"

"You escaped from Machados?" he said.

"I was on my way there. Jumped overboard when we were on the Seco. They shot the man who was with me."

"A bad place. You are well out of it. How did they fasten these things?"

"Some sort of twist key."

"Then it should be simple enough to get them open."

It could have been worse, I suppose. The leg anklets took him almost an hour, but he seemed to have the knack after that and had my hands free in twenty minutes. My wrists were rubbed raw. He eased them with some sort of grease or other, which certainly got results, for they stopped hurting almost immediately. Then he bandaged them with strips of cotton.

"My wife has washed your clothes," he said. "They are almost

182

dry now, except for the leather jacket and boots which will take longer, but first we eat. Talk can come later."

It was a simple enough meal. Fish cooked on heated flat stones, cassava root bread, bananas. Nothing had tasted better. Never had my appetite been keener.

Afterwards I dressed. Nula brought more coffee, then disappeared with the children. Bartolomeo offered me a cigar, and I leaned back and took in the night.

It was very peaceful, whippoorwills wailed mournfully, tree frogs croaked, water rattled against the raft. "Don't you need to guide it?" I asked him.

"Not on this section of the river. Here, the current takes us along a well-defined channel and life is easy. In other places, I am at the steering oar constantly."

"Do you always travel by night?"

He shook his head. "Usually we carry green bananas, but this time we are lucky. We have a cargo of wild rubber. There is a bonus in it for me if I can have it in Belém by a certain date. Nula and I take turns, and turn about and watch during the night."

I got to my feet and looked out into the pale darkness. "You are a lucky man. This is a good life."

He said, "Senhor, I owe you more than sits comfortably on me. It is a burden. A debt to be repaid. We will be in Belém in a month. Stay with us. No one would look for you here if there should be a hue and cry."

It was a tempting thought. Belém and possibly a berth on a British freighter. I could even try stowing away if worse came to worst.

But then there was Hannah, and the fact that if I ran now, I would be running, in the most fundamental way of all, for the rest of my life. "When do you reach Forte Franco?"

"If things go according to plan, around dawn on the day after tomorrow."

"That's where I'll leave you. I want to get to Landro about fifty miles up the Rio das Mortes. Do you know it?"

"I've heard of the place. This is important to you?"

"Very."

"Good." He nodded. "Plenty of boats coming upriver and I know everyone in the game. We will wait at Franco till I see you safely on your way. It is settled."

I tried to protest, but he brushed it aside, went into the hut and reappeared with a bottle of what turned out to be the roughest brandy I'd ever tasted. It almost took the skin off my tongue. I fought for air, but the consequent effect was all that could be desired. All tiredness slipped away, I felt ten feet tall.

"Your business in Landro, senhor," he said, pouring more brandy into my mug. "It is important?"

"I'm going to see a man."

"To kill him?"

"In a way," I said. "I'm going to make him tell the truth for the first time in his life."

I slept like a baby for fourteen hours and didn't raise my head till noon the following day. During the afternoon I helped Bartolomeo generally around the raft in spite of his protests. There was always work to be done. Ropes chafing or some of the great balsa logs working loose which was only to be expected on such a long voyage. I even took a turn on the steering oar although the river continued so placidly that it was hardly necessary.

That night it rained and I sat in the hut and played cards with him in the light of a storm lantern. Surprisingly he was an excellent whist player—certainly a damned sight better than me. Eventually, he went out on watch and I wrapped myself in a blanket and lay in the corner smoking one of his cigars and thinking about what lay ahead.

The truth was that I was a fool. I was putting my head into a noose again, with no guarantee of any other outcome than a swift return to Machados, and this time, they'd see I got there.

But I had to face Hannah with this thing—had to make him admit his treachery, no matter what the consequences. I flicked my cigar out into the rain, hitched my blanket over my shoulder and went to sleep.

We reached the mouth of the Mortes about four in the morning. Bartolomeo took the raft into the left bank and I helped him tie her securely to a couple of trees. Afterwards, he put a canoe in the water and departed downriver.

I breakfasted with Nula and the children, then paced the raft restlessly, waiting for something to happen. I was too close, that was the thing, itching to be on my way and have it all over and done with.

Bartolomeo returned at seven, hailing us from the deck of an old steam barge, the canoe trailing behind on a line. The barge came alongside and Bartolomeo crossed over. The man who leaned from the deckhouse was thin and ill-looking with the haggard, bad-tempered face of one constantly in pain. His skin was as yellow as only jaundice can make it.

"All right, Bartolomeo," he called. "If we're going, let's go. I'm in a hurry. I've got cargo waiting upriver."

"My second cousin," Bartolomeo said. "Inside, he has a heart of purest gold."

"Hurry it up, you bastard," his cousin shouted.

"If you want to speak to him, call him Silvio. He won't ask you questions if you don't ask him any, and he'll put you down at Landro. He owes me a favour."

We shook hands. "My thanks," I said.

"God be with you, my friend."

I stepped over the rail to the steam barge and the two Indian deckhands cast off. As we pulled away, I moved to the stern and looked back towards the raft. Bartolomeo stood watching, an arm about his wife, the two children at his side.

He leaned down and spoke to them, and they both started to wave vigorously. I waved back, feeling unaccountably cheered. Then we moved into the mouth of the Mortes, and they disappeared from view.

14

Up the River
of Death

At two o'clock that afternoon the steam barge dropped me at Landro, pausing at the jetty only for as long as it took me to step over the rail. I waved as it moved away and got no reply which didn't particularly surprise me. During the entire trip, Silvio had not spoken to me once and the Indian deckhands had kept away from me. Whatever he was up to was no business of mine, but it was certainly illegal, I was sure of that.

A couple of locals were down on the beach beneath the jetty beside their canoes, mending nets. They looked casually up as I walked by, then carried on with their task.

There was something missing—something which didn't fit. I paused on the riverbank, frowning over it, then realised what it was. The mission launch was no longer tied up at the jetty. So they'd finally decided to get out? In a way, that surprised me.

An even bigger surprise waited when I crossed the airstrip. The Hayley stood in the open, ready for take-off as I would have expected, but when I reached the hangar, I saw to my amazement that the Bristol stood inside. Now how could that be?

There was no one about. Even the military radio section had been cleared. In fact, there was something of an air of desolation

186

to the place. I helped myself to a whisky from the bottle on the table, then climbed up to the observer's cockpit of the Bristol and found the 10-gauge still in its special compartment, and a couple of boxes of steel buckshot.

I loaded up as I crossed the airstrip. All very dramatic, I suppose, but the chips were down now with a vengeance. I was going to have the truth out of him for the whole world to see, nothing was more certain.

I tried the house first, approaching cautiously from the rear and entering by the back door. I needn't have bothered. There was no one there. There was another mystery here also. My old room had been cleared of any sign that Joanna Martin had ever inhabited it, but Mannie had very obviously not moved back in for neither of the two beds was made up.

It was a different story in Hannah's old room. It stank like a urinal, and from the look of things had very probably been used for that purpose. The bed had been recently slept in, sheets and blankets scattered to the floor, and someone had vomited by the window.

I got out of there fast, my stomach heaving, and moved towards Landro, the shotgun in the crook of my left arm. Again, there was this quality of déjà vu to everything. As if I had taken this same walk many times before, which, in a way, I had. The same hopeless faces on the veranda of the houses, the same dirty, verminous little children playing underneath. Time was a circle, no beginning, no end, and I would take this walk for all eternity. A disquieting thought, to say the least.

When I was ten or fifteen yards away from the hotel, I heard the crash of glass breaking; a woman screamed and a chair came through one of the windows. A moment later, the door was flying open and Mannie backed out slowly. Beyond him, Hannah stood inside the bar clutching a broken bottle by the neck.

It was Hannah who saw me first—saw a ghost walk before him. A look of stupefaction appeared on his face, his grip slackened, the bottle fell to the floor.

187

He was certainly a sight, no resemblance at all to the man I had met that first day beside the Vega. This was a human wreck. Bloodshot eyes, face swollen by drink, the linen suit indescribably filthy and soaked in liquor.

Mannie glanced over his shoulder. His eyes widened. "God in Heaven, we have miracles now? You're supposed to be dead in some swamp on the Seco. We had a message on the radio from Manaus last night. What happened?"

"My luck turned, that's what happened." I went up the steps to join him. "How long has he been like this?"

"Fifteen or sixteen hours. He's trying to kill himself, I think. His own judge and jury."

"And why should he do that?"

"You know as well as I do, damn you."

"Well, thanks for speaking up for me," I said. "You were a real friend in need."

He said instantly, "I didn't know till the night before last when he started raving. Didn't know for sure, anyway. Even then, what proof did I have? You were pretty mad when you left here, remember? Capable of most things."

Hannah had simply stood there inside the door during this conversation staring stupidly at me as if not comprehending. And then some sort of light seemed to dawn.

"Well, I'll be damned," he said. "The boy wonder. And how was Devil's Island?"

I moved in close, the barrel of the 10-gauge coming up. Mannie cried out in alarm, a woman screamed. Figueiredo's wife standing with her husband behind the bar. Hannah laughed foolishly, took a swipe at me and almost lost his balance, would have done if he hadn't fallen against me, knocking the barrel of the shotgun to one side.

He had a stink on him like an open grave, a kind of general corruption that was more total in its effect than any mere physical decay. I was seeing a human being disintegrate before my eyes.

I lowered my gun and pushed him away gently. "Why don't you sit down, Sam?"

He staggered back and flung his arms wide. "Well, if that don't beat all. Would you listen to the boy wonder turning the other cheek."

He blundered along the counter, sending glasses flying. "But I fixed you, wonder boy. I really fixed you good."

Figueiredo glanced at me, frowning. I said, "Nobody fixed me, Sam, I just caught, that's all."

The remark didn't seem to get through to him and in any event, was unnecessary for he condemned himself out of his own mouth with no prompting from me.

He reached across the counter, grabbing Figueiredo by the front of his jacket. "Heh, listen to this. This is good. Wonder boy here was running out on me, see? Leaving me in the lurch so I fixed him good. He thought he was taking his last mail run, but I slipped him a little extra something that sent him straight to Machados. Don't you find that funny?"

"Very funny, senhor," Figueiredo said, gently disengaging himself.

Hannah slid along the bar, laughing helplessly, glasses cascading to the floor. When he reached the other end he simply fell on his face and lay still.

Figueiredo went round the end of the bar. He sighed heavily. "A bad business this." He turned and held out his hand to me. "No one regrets what you have been through more than myself, Senhor Mallory, but by some miracle you are alive and that is all that matters. Naturally, I will make a full report to Manaus as soon as possible. I think you will find the authorites more than anxious to make amends."

It didn't seem to matter much anymore. I dropped to one knee beside Hannah and felt his pulse, which was still functioning.

"How is he?" Mannie demanded.

"Not good. He could probably do with a stomach wash. If it was me, I'd give him something to make him vomit, then I'd lock him in the steam house and leave him there till he sobered up."

"Which was exactly what we were trying to do when he at-

189

tacked us," Figueiredo said. "You have come at an opportune moment, my friend."

"How's that?"

He went behind the bar, found a bottle of his best whisky, White Horse no less, and poured me one. "The day after your unfortunate arrest, Sister Maria Teresa came to see me with as hare-brained a scheme as I have ever known. It seems this Huna girl, Christina, who Senhorita Martin purchased from Avila, had persuaded the good Sister that if she was returned to her people she could obtain news of Senhorita Martin's sister and her friend, perhaps even arrange for their return."

For a moment, I seemed to see again the Huna girl standing on the veranda of the house looking across at me, the flat, empty face, dark animal eyes giving nothing away.

"Good God, you surely didn't let her fall for that?"

"What could I do, senhor?" He spread his hands. "I tried to argue with her, but I had no authority to prevent her leaving and she persuaded Avila and four of his men to go with her. For a consideration, naturally."

"You mean they've actually gone to Santa Helena?" I said in astonishment.

"In the mission launch."

I turned to Mannie. "And Joanna?"

He nodded. "She and Sam had one hell of a row that day. I don't know what it was all about, but I can guess. She told him she was going with Sister Maria Teresa. That she never wanted to see him again."

Poor Sam. So in the end, he had lost all along the line?

"You've been in touch with them?" I said. "They have a radio?"

"Oh, yes, I insisted they take the one the military left in my care. It seems the girl went into the jungle the day they arrived and has not returned."

"And that doesn't surprise me."

"You think the whole thing could be some sort of trap to get them up there?" Mannie asked.

"On her part, perhaps, to put herself right with her people if she wants to return to them permanently. They'd catch on to the idea fast enough." I turned back to Figueiredo. "What's the latest development?"

"Huna have been seen near the mission for two days now. Some of Avila's men panicked and insisted on leaving. It seems Sister Maria Teresa stood firm."

"So they cleared out, anyway?"

"Exactly. Avila was on the radio just before noon. Reception was bad and he soon faded, but he managed to tell me that three of his men had cleared out at dawn in the mission launch, leaving the rest of them stranded."

"Anything else?"

"He said the drums had started."

"Which was why you were trying to sober up our friend?" I stirred Hannah with my foot. "Have you been in touch with Alberto?"

"He's on leave, but I spoke to a young lieutenant at Forte Franco an hour ago who said he'd contact Army Headquarters for instructions. In any case, what can they hope to do? This is something to be handled now or not at all. Tomorrow is too late."

"All right," I said. "I'll leave at once in the Hayley. Is she ready for take-off, Mannie?"

"Is now. She was having magneto trouble, but I've fixed that."

"How come the Bristol's here?"

"Sam went downriver by boat and flew her back. Had to just to keep a plane in the air while I fixed the Hayley. Once that penalty clause comes into operation he has a fortnight to find another pilot. He still hoped something would turn up or at least I thought he did."

He hurried out and Figueiredo said, "With four to bring back you must go alone, which could be dangerous. Would a machine-gun help?"

"The best idea I've heard today."

He beckoned and I went round the bar counter and followed

him through the bead curtain into the back room. He sat down, grunting, beside an old cabin trunk, took a key from his watch-chain and opened it. There were a dozen rifles, a couple of Thompson guns, a box of Mills bombs and quantities of ammunition.

"And where did you get this little lot?" I demanded.

"Colonel Alberto. In case of attack here. Take what you wish."

I slung one of the Thompson guns over my shoulder and stuffed half a dozen fifty-round clips of ammunition and a couple of Mills bombs into a military-type canvas haversack. "If this doesn't do it, nothing will."

I returned to the bar and paused beside Hannah. He moaned a little and stirred. I turned to Figueiredo who had followed me through. "I meant what I said. Lock him in the steam house and don't let him out till he's sober."

"I will see to it, my friend. Go with God."

I patted the butt of the Thompson gun. "I prefer something you can rely on. Don't worry about me. I'll be back. Keep trying to raise Avila. Tell him I'm on my way."

I smiled bravely, but inside, I felt considerably less sanguine about things as I went down the steps into the street.

I took the Hayley up and out of there fast. The last time I'd flown her to Santa Helena it had taken me forty minutes. Now, with the wind under my tail, I had every chance of doing it in half an hour.

When I was ten minutes away, I started trying to raise them on the radio without any kind of success. I kept on trying and then, when I was about three miles downriver from Santa Helena, I found the mission launch. I reduced speed, banked in a wide circle and went down low to take a look.

The launch was grounded on a mudbank, her deck tilted steeply to one side. The hull and wheelhouse were peppered with arrows and the man who hung over the stern rail had several in his back. There was no sign of the other two. I could only hope, for their sakes, that the Huna hadn't taken them alive.

So that was very much that. I carried on upriver, my speed right down, and passed low over the mission. There was no sign of life, and I tried calling them over the radio again. A moment later Avila's voice sounded in my ear, although weakly and with lots of static.

"Senhor Hannah, thanks be to God you have come."

"It's Mallory," I said. "How are things down there?"

"Senhorita Martin, the good Sister and I are in the church senhor. We are all that is left." In spite of the distortion, the astonishment in his voice was plain. "But you are here, senhor. How can this be?"

"Never mind that now. I found the launch downstream. They didn't get very far, those friends of yours. I'm going to land now. Get ready to bring the women across."

"An impossibility, senhor. There is no boat."

I told him to stand by and turned over the jetty. He was right enough, so I crossed the river and went in low over the airstrip. There was no sign of life there, but there was a canoe by the little wooden pier.

I circled the mission again and called up Avila. "There's a canoe at the landing strip pier. Have the women ready to go and I'll come over for you. I'm going down now."

I banked steeply and plunged in very fast, going in low over the trees. A final burst of power to level out and I was down. I taxied to the far end of the *campo*, turned the Hayley into the wind ready for a quick take-off and cut the engine.

I sat there for a couple of minutes waiting for something to happen. Nothing did, so I primed the two Mills bombs, shoved a clip into the Thompson, slipped the haversack over my shoulder, got out and started towards the river.

Except for the path which had been flattened by constant use as a landing strip, the grass over the rest of the *campo* was three or four feet high. Somewhere on the right, birds lifted in alarm. Enough to warn me in normal circumstances, but then it all happened so fast.

There were suddenly voices high and shrill, a strange crackling noise. When I turned, flames were sweeping across the *campo* from the edge of the jungle, the long, dry grass flaring like touch paper. Beyond, through the smoke, I caught sight of feathered head-dresses, but no arrows came my way. Presumably they thought me a moth to their flame.

It was certainly the end of the Hayley for as I turned to run, the flames were already flaring around the underbelly. I was halfway to the river when her tanks blew up, burning fuel and fuselage spraying out in a mushroom of flames. That really finished things off and within a few moments the entire *campo* was a kind of lake of fire.

But at least it put an impassable barrier between myself and the Huna, one flaw in their plan or so it seemed. I scrambled into the canoe at the jetty, pushed off and found half a dozen canoes packed with Huna coming downriver to meet me.

Even with the Thompson, there were too many to take on alone and in any case, I couldn't paddle and fire at the same time. There seemed to be only one thing to do which was to push like hell for the other side and that's exactly what I did.

A point in my favour was the numerous shoals and sandbanks in that part of the river. I got to the far side of a particularly large one, ibis rising in a great red cloud, putting what seemed like something of a barrier between us.

They were nothing if not resourceful. Two canoes simply grounded on the sandbank and their occupants jumped out and ran towards me, ankledeep in water. The other turned and paddled back upstream to cut me off.

The men on the sandbank were too close for comfort by now so I dropped my paddle in the bottom of the canoe for a moment, pulled the pin on one of the Mills bombs and tossed it towards them.

It fell woefully short, but as on a previous occasion, the explosion had exactly the effect I was looking for. They came to a dead stop, shouting angrily, so I gave them number two which turned them round and sent them running back the other way.

Even at that stage in the game I didn't want to kill any of them, but as I picked up my paddle again I saw that the others were rounding the tip of the sandbank a hundred yards north of me, effectively blocking the channel. Which only left the jungle on my left and I moved towards it as quickly as I could.

Undergrowth and branches spilled out over the bank in a kind of canopy. Inside, the light was dim, and I was completely hidden as far as anyone on the river was concerned. I paddled upstream for a little way, looking for a suitable landing place, and came to a shelving bank of sand where a creek emptied into the river.

I turned the canoe in towards it. I was aware of the Huna voices drawing nearer, and aware in the same moment of another canoe lying high on the mudbank inside the mouth of the creek, as if left there by floodwater. It was tilted to one side, so I could see it was not empty.

I splashed through the water towards it and knelt down, groping amongst the broken bones, the tattered scraps of what had once been nuns' habits. They were both there, but I could only find one identity chain. *Sister Anne Josepha L.S.O.P.* It was enough. One mystery was solved, at least. I dropped the disc and chain into my pocket, and started up the creek as the canoes moved in behind me.

I had about three hundred yards to go to the mission and it seemed sensible to get there as quickly as possible. I started to run, holding the Thompson at the high port, ready for action in case of trouble.

I kept as close to the riverbank as possible, mainly because the ground was clearer there and I could see what I was doing. I could hear their voices high and shrill, down on the river, and there was a crashing somewhere behind me in the brush. I turned and loosed off, raking the undergrowth, just to show them I meant business, then ran on, bursting out of the forest into the open a couple of minutes later.

The church was only thirty or forty yards away, and I put down my head and ran like hell, yelling at the top of my voice. An arrow whispered past me and buried itself in the door, then another as I went up the steps.

I turned and fired as a reflex action towards the dark shadows at the edge of the trees, each topped by a bright splash of colour. I couldn't tell if I'd hit anything. In any case, at that moment, the door opened behind me. A hand grabbed me by the shoulder and pulled me inside so forcibly that I lost my balance.

When I sat up, I found Avila leaning against the door clutching a carbine, Sister Maria Teresa and Joanna Martin on either side of him. The American girl was holding a rifle.

She leaned it against the wall and dropped to her knees beside me. "Are you all right, Neil?"

"Still in one piece as far as I can tell."

"What happened out there? We heard a terrific explosion."

"They set fire to the *campo* and the Hayley went up with it. I was lucky to get here."

"Then we are finished, senhor," Avila cut in. "Is that what you are saying? That there is nothing to be done?"

"Oh, I don't know," I said. "You could always ask Sister Maria Teresa to pray."

A drum started to beat monotonously in the distance.

15

The Last Show

There was still the radio. According to Avila, he had tried to raise Landro on several occasions since he'd last had contact at noon. I knew Figueiredo had been trying to get through to him, which meant something was wrong with the damn thing.

I did what I could, considering my limited technical knowledge, unscrewed the top and checked that no wires were loose and that all valves fitted tightly, which was very definitely my limit. I left Avila to keep trying and went and sat with my back against the wall beside Joanna Martin, who was making coffee on a spirit stove.

Sister Maria Teresa knelt at the altar in prayer. "Still at it, is she?" I said. "Faith unshaken."

Joanna gave me a cigarette and sat back, waiting for the water to boil. "What happened, Neil?"

"To me?" I said. "Oh, I jumped ship as the Navy say, before I got to where they were taking me."

"Won't they be after you—the authorities, I mean?"

"Not anymore. You see, strange to relate, I didn't do it. I was framed. Isn't that what Cagney's always saying in those gangster movies?"

She nodded slowly. "I think I knew from the beginning. It never did make any kind of sense."

"Thanks for the vote of confidence," I said. "You and Mannie both. I could have done with it a little earlier, mind you, but that's all water under the bridge."

"And Sam?"

"Poured out the whole story in front of Figueiredo and his wife and Mannie in the hotel bar earlier this afternoon when I confronted him. So drunk he didn't know what he was doing. He's finished, Joanna."

She poured coffee into a mug and handed it to me. "I think he was finished a long, long time ago, Neil."

She sat there, sitting on her heels, looking genuinely sad, a different sort of person altogether from the woman I was accustomed to. Somehow it seemed the right moment to break it to her.

"I've got something for you." I took the identity disc on its chain from my pocket and held it out to her.

The skin of her face tightened visibly before my eyes. She started to tremble. "Anna?" she said hoarsely.

I nodded. "I found what was left of her and her friend in a canoe on the riverbank. They must have been killed in the original attack after all and drifted downriver."

"Thank God," she whispered. "Oh, thank God."

She reached out for the disc and chain, got to her feet and fled to the other end of the church. Sister Maria Teresa turned to meet her and I saw Joanna hold out the identity disc to her.

At the same moment Avila called to me urgently. "I'm getting something. Come quickly."

He kept the headphones on and turned up the speaker for me. We all heard Figueiredo at once quite clearly in spite of some static.

"Santa Helena, are you receiving me?"

"Mallory here," I said. "Can you hear me?"

"I hear you clearly, Senhor Mallory. How are things?"

"As bad as they can be. The Huna were waiting for me when

I landed and set fire to the plane. I'm in the church at the mission now, with Avila and the two women. We're completely stranded. No boats."

"Mother of God." I could almost see him crossing himself.

"We've only one hope," I said. "You'll have to raise some sort of volunteer force and come upriver in that launch of yours. We'll try to hang on till you get here."

"But even if I managed to find men willing to accompany me, it would take us ten or twelve hours to get there."

"I know. You'll just have to do the best you can."

There was more from his end, but so drowned in static that I couldn't make any sense out of it, and after a while I lost him altogether. When I turned I found that Joanna and Sister Maria Teresa had joined Avila. They all looked roughly the same, strained, anxious, afraid. Even Sister Maria Teresa had lost her customary expression of quiet joy.

"What happens now, Neil?" Joanna said. "You'd better tell us the worst."

"You heard most of it. I've asked Figueiredo to try and raise a few men and attempt to break through to us in the government launch. At least twelve hours if everything goes right for him. To be perfectly frank, my own feeling is we'd be lucky to see them before dawn tomorrow."

Avila laughed harshly. "A miracle if they even started, senhor. You think they are heroes in Landro, to come looking for a Huna arrow in the back?"

"You came, Senhor Avila," Sister Maria Teresa said.

"For money, Sister," he told her. "Because you paid well and in the end what has it brought me? Only death."

I stood by the window, peering out through the half-open shutter across the compound, past the hospital and the bunga-lows to the edge of the forest, dark in the evening light. The sun was a smear of orange beyond the trees and the drum throbbed monotonously.

Joanna Martin leaned against the wall beside me smoking a

cigarette. In the distance, voices drifted on the evening air, mingling with the drumming, an eerie sound.

"Why are they singing?" she asked.

"To prepare themselves for death. It's what they call a courage chant. It means they'll have a go at us sooner or later, but there's a lot of ritual to be gone through beforehand."

Sister Maria Teresa moved out of the shadows. "Are you saying they welcome death, Mr. Mallory?"

"The only way for a warrior to die, Sister. As I told you once before, death and life are all part of a greater whole for these people."

Before she could reply, there was a sudden exclamation from Avila, who was sitting at the radio. "I think I've got Figueiredo again."

He turned up the speaker and the static was tremendous. I crouched beside it, aware of the voice behind all that interference, trying to make some sense of it all. Quite suddenly it stopped, static and all, and there was an uncanny quiet. Avila turned to me, removing the headphones slowly.

"Could you get any of that?" I said.

"Only a few words, senhor, and they made no sense at all."

"What were they?"

"He said that Captain Hannah was on his way."

"But that's impossible," I said. "You must have got it wrong."

Outside, the drum stopped beating.

The church was a place of shadows now. There was a lantern by the radio and the candles at the other end which Sister Maria Teresa had lit.

It was completely dark outside, just the faint line of the trees discernible against the night sky. There wasn't a sound out there. It was all quite still.

A jaguar coughed somewhere in the distance. Avila said, "Was that for real, senhor?"

"I don't know. It could be some sort of signal."

As long as we could keep them out we stood a chance. We

were both well armed. There was a rifle for Joanna Martin and a couple of spares laid out on a table next to the radio to hand for any emergency. But nothing stirred in all that silent world. The only sound was the faint crackle of the radio which Avila had left on with the speaker turned up to full power.

The light up at the altar was very dim now. The Holy Mother seemed to float out of the darkness, bathed in a soft white light, and Sister Maria Teresa's voice in prayer was a quiet murmur. It was all very peaceful.

Something rattled on the roof above my head. As I glanced up, a Huna swung in through one of the upper windows, poised on the sill, the light glistening on his ochre-painted body. He jumped with a cry like a soul in torment, a machete ready in his right hand.

I gave him a full burst from the Thompson, driving him back against the wall. Joanna screamed, and I was aware of Avila cursing savagely as he worked the lever of his old carbine, pumping bullet after bullet into another Huna who had dropped in on his side.

I moved to help him, Joanna screamed again and I turned, too late, to meet the new threat. The Thompson gun was knocked from my hand, I went down in a tangle of flying limbs, aware of the stink of that ochre-painted body, slippery with sweat, the machete raised to strike.

I got a hand to his wrist and planted an elbow solidly in the gaping mouth. God, but he was strong, muscles like iron as with most forest Indians. Stronger than I was. Suddenly his face was very close, the pressure too much for me. The end of things and the muzzle of a rifle jabbed against the side of his head, the top of his skull disintegrated, his body jumped to one side.

Joanna Martin backed away clutching her rifle, horror on her face. Beyond her, Sister Maria Teresa turned and a black wraith dropped from the shadows above her, landing in front of the altar. I grabbed for the Thompson, already too late and Avila shot him through the head.

He was gasping for breath, the sound of it hoarse in the silence as he feverishly reloaded his carbine. "Maybe some more on the roof, eh, senhor?"

"I hope not," I said. "We can't take much of this. Cover me and I'll take a look."

I rammed a fresh clip into the Thompson, opened the door and slipped outside. I ran some little distance away, turned and raked the roof with a long burst, ran to the other side and repeated the performance. There was no response—not even from the forest. I went back inside.

Sister Maria Teresa was on her knees again, prayers for the dead from what I could make out. Joanna had slumped down against the wall. I dropped to one knee beside her.

"You were pretty good in there. Thanks."

She smiled wanly. "I'd rather do it on Stage Six at MGM any day."

There was a sudden crackling over the loudspeaker, a familiar voice sounded harsh and clear. "This is Hannah calling Mallory! This is Hannah calling Mallory! Are you receiving me?"

I was at the mike in an instant and switched over. "I hear you, Sam, loud and clear. Where are you?"

"About five minutes away downriver if my night navigation's anything like as brilliant as it used to be."

"In the Bristol?"

"That's it, kid, just like old times."

There was something different in his voice, something I'd never heard before. A kind of joy, if you like, although I know that sounds absurd.

"I'm going to try and land on that big sandbank in the middle of the river. The one directly in front of the jetty, but I'm going to need some light on the situation."

"What do you suggest?"

"Hell, I don't know. What about setting fire to the bloody place?"

I glanced at Avila. He nodded. I said, "Okay, Sam, we're on our way."

His voice crackled back sharply, "Just one thing, kid. I can squeeze two in the observer's cockpit—no more. That means you and Avila lose out."

"I came floating downriver once," I said. "I can do it again."

But there was no hope of that. I knew it, and so did Joanna Martin. She put a hand on my sleeve and I straightened. "Neil, there must be a way. There's got to be."

It was Avila who answered for me. "If we don't go out now, senhor, there is no point in going at all."

There was a can of paraffin for the lantern in the vestry. I spilled some on the floor and ran a trail out to the front door. Avila slung his carbine over his shoulder, turned down the storm lantern and held it under his jacket. I opened the door and he slipped out into the darkness, making for the bungalows.

I gave him a moment, then went out myself, the can of paraffin in one hand, the Thompson in the other, my target the hospital and administrative building.

Somewhere quite close at hand, but as if from nowhere, there was the drone of the Bristol's engine. Time was running out. Of the Huna there was no sign. It was as if they had never existed. The door into the hospital was open. I unscrewed the cap of the can, splashed paraffin inside, then moved back out and flung the rest up over the roof.

On the other side of the compound, flames flowered in the night as one of the bungalows started to burn. I saw Avila quite clearly running to the next one, a burning brand in one hand, reaching up to touch the thatch.

I struck a match, dropped it into the entrance and jumped back hurriedly as a line of flames raced across the floor. With a sudden whoof and a kind of minor explosion, it broke through to the roof.

And then all hell broke loose. Those shrill Huna voices

buzzed angrily over there in the forest, like bees disturbed in the hive. They burst out in a ragged line. I loosed off a long burst, turned and ran towards the church as the arrows started to hum.

Avila was on a converging course. I heard him cry out, was aware, out of the corner of my eye, that he had stumbled. He kept on running for a while, then pitched on his face a few feet away from the church steps, an arrow in his back under the left shoulder blade.

I turned, dropping to one knee, and emptied the magazine in a wide arc across the compound, and yet there was nothing to see. Only the voices crying shrilly beyond the flames, the occasional arrow curving through the smoke.

Avila was hauling himself painfully up the steps. Joanna already had the door open. I took him by the collar and dragged him inside, kicking the door shut behind me. I rammed home the bolt, and when I turned, Sister Maria Teresa was on her knees beside him, trying to examine the wound. He turned over, snapping the shaft. There was blood on his mouth. He pushed her away violently and reached a hand out to me.

I dropped to one knee beside him. He said, "Maybe you can still make it, senhor. Torch the church and run for it. God won't mind." His other hand groped in his jacket pocket, came out clutching a small linen bag. "Have a drink on me, my friend. Good luck."

And then he brought up more blood than I would have thought possible, and lay still.

Hannah's voice boomed over the speaker. "Beautiful, kid, just beautiful. What a show. Are you getting this?"

I reached for the mike. "Loud and clear, Sam. Avila just bought it. I'm bringing the women out now."

"Wait on the bank and don't cross till I'm down," he said. "I've got the other Thompson with me. I'll give you covering fire. Christ, I wish I'd a couple of Vickers on this thing. I'd give the bastards something to remember." He laughed out loud. "I'll be seeing you, kid."

Sister Maria Teresa was on her knees beside Avila, lips moving in prayer. I dragged her up roughly. "No time for that now. We'll leave by the vestry door. Once you're outside, run for the river and don't look back. And I'd get that habit off if I were you, Sister, unless you want to drown."

She seemed dazed, as if not understanding what was happening, her mind, I think, temporarily rejecting the terrible reality. Joanna took charge then, literally tearing the habit off her, turning her within seconds into another person entirely. A small, frail woman in a cotton shift with iron-grey hair close-cropped to the head.

I hustled them into the vestry, opened the door cautiously and peered out. The Bristol was very close now, circling somewhere overhead. The river was perhaps sixty or seventy yards away.

I pushed them out into the darkness, struck a match, dropped it into the pool of paraffin I had left earlier. Flames roared across the floor into the church. I had a final glimpse of the altar, the Holy Mother standing above it, the Child in her arms, a symbol of something surely. Then I turned and ran.

I slid down the bank to join Joanna and Sister Maria Teresa in the shallows below. Flames danced in the dark waters, smoke drifted across in a billowing cloud, a scene from hell.

I could not hear the Huna, for there was only one sound then, the roaring of the engine as the Bristol came in low. And suddenly he was there, bursting out of the smoke a hundred feet above the river, the Black Baron coming in for his last show.

It needed a genius and there was one on hand that night. He judged the landing with absolute perfection, his wheels touched down at the very ultimate tip of the sandbank, giving himself the whole two-hundred-yard length to pull up in.

He rushed past, water spraying up from the wheels in two

great waves and I saw him clearly, the black leather helmet, the goggles, white scarf streaming out behind him.

I shoved the women out into the water, held the Thompson over my head and went after them. It wasn't particularly deep, four or five feet at the most, but the current was strong and it was taking them all their time to force a passage.

Hannah was already taxiing back to the other end of the sandbank. He turned into the wind, ready for take-off, and then the engine cut. Out of the night behind us, voices lifted high above the flames, the Huna in full cry.

Hannah was out of the Bristol now, standing at the edge of the sandbank, firing his Thompson gun across the channel. I didn't look back; I had other things on my mind. Sister Maria Teresa slipped sideways, caught by the current. I flung myself forward getting a hand to her just in time, another to Joanna. For a moment things hung in the balance, the current pushing against us and then we were ploughing through the shallows and up on to the sandbank.

There must have been a hundred Huna at least on the riverbank, outlined clearly against the flames. At that distance most of their arrows were falling short, but already some were sliding down into the water.

When the Thompson emptied, he slipped in another magazine and commenced firing again. I gave Joanna a leg up into the observer's cockpit, then shoved Sister Maria Teresa up after her.

Hannah backed up to join me. "Better get in and get this thing started, kid."

"What about you?"

"Can you turn that prop on your own?"

There was no argument there. I climbed up into the cockpit and made ready to go. He emptied the Thompson gun at the dark line now halfway across the channel, then dropped it to the sand and ran round to the front of the machine.

"Ready," he yelled.

I nodded and wound the starting magneto. He heaved on the propeller. The engine roared into life. Hannah jumped to one side.

I leaned out of the cockpit. "The wing," I cried. "Get on the wing."

He waved, ducked under the lower port wing and flung himself across it, grasping the leading edge with his gloved hands. There was a chance, just a chance that it might work.

I thrust the throttle open and started down the sandbank as the first of the Huna came up out of the water. Fifty or sixty yards and I had the tail up, but that was going to be all for the drag from his body was too much to take. I knew it and so did he—he was too good a pilot not to.

One moment he was there; the next he had gone, releasing his grip on the leading edge, sliding back to the sand. The Bristol seemed to leap forward. I pulled the stick back and we lifted off.

I had time for one quick glance over my shoulder. He had got to his feet, was standing, feet apart facing them, firing his automatic coolly.

And then the dark wave rolled over him like the tide covering the shore.

16

Downriver

"The *comandante* will not keep you waiting long, senhor. Please to be seated. A cigarette, perhaps?" The sergeant was very obviously putting himself out considerably on my behalf, so I met him halfway and accepted the cigarette.

Once again I found myself outside the *comandante*'s office in Manaus, and for one wild and uncertain moment, I wondered if it was then or now and whether anything had really happened.

A fly buzzed in the quiet, and then there were voices. The door opened and the *comandante* ushered Sister Maria Teresa out. She was conventionally attired again in a habit of tropical white, obtained, as I understood it, from some local nuns of another order.

Her smile faded slightly at the sight of me. The *comandante* shook hands formally. "Entirely at your service, as always, Sister."

She murmured something and went out. He turned to me beaming, the hand outstretched again. "My dear Senhor Mallory, so sorry to have kept you waiting."

"That's all right," I said. "My boat doesn't leave for an hour."

He gave me a seat, offered me a cigar, which I refused, then sat down himself behind the desk. "I have your passport and travel permit ready for you. All is in order. I also have two letters, both a long time in arriving, I fear." He pushed everything across to me in a little pile. "I was not aware that you held a commission in your Royal Air Force."

"Just in the Reserve," I said. "There's a difference."

"Not for much longer, my friend, if the newspapers have it right."

I put the passport and travel permit in my breast pocket and examined the letters, both of which had been originally posted to my old address in Lima. One was from my father and mother, I knew by the writing. The other was from the Air Ministry and referred to me as "Pilot Officer N. G. Malory." They could wait, both of them.

The *comandante* said, "So, you go home to England at last, and Senhor Sterne also. I understand his visa has come through?"

"That's right."

There was a slight pause, and he was obviously somewhat embarrassed, as if not quite knowing what to say next. He did the obvious thing, jumped up and came round the desk.

"Well, I must not detain you."

We moved to the door; he opened it and held out his hand. As I took it, his smile faded. It was as if he had decided it was necessary to make some comment, and perhaps, for him, it was.

He said, "In spite of everything, I am proud to have been his friend. He was a brave man. We must remember him as he was at the end, not by what went before."

I didn't say a word. What could I say? I simply shook hands, and his door closed behind me for the last time.

As I walked across the pillared entrance hall, I heard my name called. I turned and found Sister Maria Teresa moving towards me.

"Oh, Mr. Mallory," she said, "I was waiting for you. I just wanted the chance to say goodbye."

She seemed quite her old self again. Crisp white linen, the

cheeks rosy, the same look of calm eager joy about her as when we first met.

"That's kind of you."

She said, "In some ways I feel that we never really understood each other, and for that, I'm sorry."

"That's all right," I said. "It takes all sorts. I understand you're staying on here?"

"That's right. Others will be arriving from America to join me shortly."

"To go back upriver?"

"That's right."

"Why don't you leave them alone?" I said. "Why doesn't everybody leave them alone? They don't need us—any of us—and they obviously don't need what we've got to offer."

"I don't think you quite understand," she said.

I was wasting my time; I realised that suddenly and completely. "Then I'm glad I don't, Sister," I told her.

I think in that final moment, I actually got through to her. There was something in the eyes that was different, something undefinable, but perhaps that was simply wishful thinking. She turned and walked out.

I watched her go down the steps to the line of horse-drawn cabs whose drivers dozed in the hot sun. Nothing had changed, and yet everything was different.

I never saw her again.

Standing at the rail of the stern-wheeler in the evening light and half an hour out of Manaus, I remembered my letters. As I was reading the one from the Air Ministry, Mannie found me.

"Anything interesting?"

"I've been put on the active service list," I said. "Should have reported two months ago. This thing's been chasing me since Peru."

"So?" He nodded gravely. "The news from Europe seems to get worse each day."

"One thing's certain," I said. "They're going to need pilots back home. All they can get."

"I suppose so. What happens in Belém? Will you apply to your consul for passage home?"

I shook my head, took the small linen bag Avila had given me in the church at Santa Helena and handed it to him. He opened it and poured a dozen fair-sized uncut diamonds into his palm.

"Avila's parting present. I know it's illegal, but we should get two or three thousand pounds for them in Belém with no trouble. I'll go halves with you, and we'll go home in style."

He replaced them carefully. "Strange," he said. "To live as he did, and in the end, to die so bravely."

I thought he might take it further, attempt to touch on what had remained unspoken between us, but he obviously thought better of it.

"I've got a letter to write. I'll see you later." He patted me on the arm awkwardly and slipped away.

I had not heard her approach, and yet she was there behind me, like a presence sensed.

She said, "I've just been talking to the captain. He tells me there's a boat due out of Belém for New York the day after we get in."

"That's good," I said. "You'll be able to fly to California from there. Still make that test of yours at MGM on time."

The horizon was purple and gold, touched with fire. She said, "I've just seen Mannie. He tells me you've had a letter drafting you into the R.A.F."

"That's right."

"Are you pleased?"

I shrugged. "If there's going to be a war, and it looks pretty certain, then it's the place to be."

"Can I write to you? Have you got an address?"

"If you like. I've been posted to a place called Biggin Hill.

211

A fighter squadron. And my mother would always pass letters on."

"That's good."

She stood there, waiting for me to make some sort of move, and I didn't. Finally she said hesitantly, "If you'd like to come down later, Neil. You know my cabin."

I shook my head. "I don't think there would be much point."

He was between us still, always would be. She knew it, and so did I. She started to walk away, hesitated and turned towards me.

"All right. I loved him a little, for whatever that's worth, and I'm not ashamed of it. In spite of everything, he was the most courageous man I've ever known—a hero—and that's how I'll always remember him."

It sounded like a line from a bad play and he was worth more than that.

"He wasn't any hero, Joanna," I said. "He was a bastard, right from the beginning, only he was a brave bastard and probably the finest pilot I'm ever likely to meet. Let that be an end of it."

She walked away, stiff and angry, but somehow it didn't seem to matter anymore. Hannah would have approved and that was the main thing.

I turned back to the rail beyond the trees, the sun slipped behind the final edge of things, and night fell.

The
Savage Day

Between two groups of men that want to make inconsistent kinds of worlds I see no remedy except force. . . . It seems to me that every society rests on the death of men.

OLIVER WENDELL HOLMES

1

Execution Day

They were getting ready to shoot somebody in the inner court-yard, which meant it was Monday, because Monday was execution day.

Although my own cell was on the other side of the building, I recognized the signs: a disturbance from those cells from which some prisoners could actually witness the whole proceeding and then the drums rolling. The commandant liked that.

There was silence, a shouted command, a volley of rifle fire. After a while, the drums started again, a steady beat accompanying the cortege as the dead man was wheeled away, for the commandant liked to preserve the niceties, even on Skarthos, one of the most unlovely places I have visited in my life. A bare rock in the Aegean with an old Turkish fort on top of it containing three thousand political detainees, four hundred troops to guard them, and me.

I'd had a month of it, which was exactly four weeks too long, and the situation wasn't improved by the knowledge that some of the others had spent up to two years there without any kind of trial. A prisoner told me during exercise one day that the

217

name of the place was derived from some classical Greek root meaning "barren," which didn't surprise me in the slightest.

Through the bars of my cell you could see the mainland, a smudge on the horizon in the heat haze. Occasionally, there was a ship, but too far away to be interesting, for the Greek Navy ensured that most craft gave the place a wide berth. If I craned my head to the left when I peered out there was rock, thorn bushes to the right. Otherwise, there was nothing to see and nothing to do except lie on the straw mattress on the floor which was exactly what I was doing on that May morning when everything changed.

There was the grate of the key in the lock, quite unexpectedly, as the midday meal wasn't served for another three hours, then the door opened and one of the sergeants moved in.

He stirred me with his foot. "Better get up, my friend. Someone to see you."

Hope springing eternal, I scrambled to my feet as my visitor was ushered in. He was about fifty or so at a guess, medium height, good shoulders, a snow-white moustache, beautifully clipped and trimmed, very blue eyes. He wore a panama, a lightweight cream suit, an Academy tie, and carried a cane.

He was, or had been, a high-ranking officer in the Army; I was never more certain of anything in my life. After all, it takes an old soldier to know one.

I almost brought my heels together and he smiled broadly, "At ease, Major. At ease."

He looked about the cell with some distaste, poked at the bucket in the corner with his cane, and grimaced. "You really have got yourself into one hell of a bloody mess, haven't you?"

"Are you from the British Embassy in Athens?" I asked.

He pulled forward the only stool, dusted it, and sat down. "They can't do a thing for you in Athens, Vaughan. You're going to rot here till the colonels decide to try you. I've spoken to the people concerned. In their opinion, you'll get fifteen years if you're lucky. Possibly twenty."

"Thanks very much," I said. "Most comforting."

He took a packet of cigarettes from his pocket and threw them across. "What do you expect? Guns for the rebels, midnight landings on lonely beaches." He shook his head. "What are you, anyway? The last of the romantics?"

"I'd love to think so," I said. "But as it happens, there would have been five thousand pounds waiting for me in Nicosia if I'd pulled it off."

He nodded, "So I understand."

I leaned against the wall by the window and looked him over. "Who are you, anyway?"

"Name's Ferguson," he said. "Brigadier Harry Ferguson, Royal Corps of Transport."

Which I doubted, or at least the Corps of Transport bit, for with all due deference to that essential branch of the British Army, he just didn't look the type.

"Simon Vaughan," I said. "Of course, you'll know that."

"That's true," he said, "but then I probably know you better than you know yourself."

I couldn't let that one pass. "Try me."

"Fair enough." He clasped both hands over the knob of his cane. "Fine record at the Academy, second lieutenant in Korea with the Dukes. You earned a good M.C. on the Hook, then got knocked off on patrol and spent just over a year in a Chinese prison camp."

"Very good."

"According to your file, you successfully withstood the usual brainwashing techniques to which all prisoners were subjected. It was noted, however, that it had left you with a slight tendency to the use of Marxian dialectic in argument."

"Well, as the old master put it," I said. "Life *is* the actions of men in pursuit of their ends. You can't deny that."

"I liked that book you wrote for the War Office after Korea," he said. "*A New Concept of Revolutionary Warfare.* Aroused a lot of talk at the time. Of course the way you kept quoting from Mao Tse-tung worried a lot of people, but you were right."

"I nearly always am," I said. "It's rather depressing. So few other people seem to realize the fact."

He carried straight on as if I hadn't spoken. "That book got you a transfer to Military Intelligence, where you specialized in handling subversives, revolutionary movements generally, and so on. The Communists in Malaya, six months chasing Mau Mau in Kenya, then Cyprus and the E.O.K.A. The D.S.O. at the end of that little lot, plus a bullet in the back that nearly finished things."

"Pitcher to the well," I said. "You know how it is."

"And then Borneo and the row with the Indonesians. You commanded a company of native irregulars there and enjoyed great success."

"Naturally," I said, "because we fought the guerrillas on exactly their own terms. The only way."

"Quite right and now the climax of the tragedy. March 1963, to be precise. The area around Kota Baru was rotten with Communist terrorists. The powers that be told you to go in and clear them out once and for all."

"And no one can say I failed to do that," I said with some bitterness.

"What was it the papers called you? The Beast of Selangor? A man who ordered the shooting of many prisoners, who interrogated and tortured captives in custody. I suppose it was your medals that saved you, and that year in prison camp must have been useful. The psychiatrists managed to do a lot with that. At least you weren't cashiered."

"Previous gallant conduct," I said. "Must remember his father. Do what we can."

"And since then, what have we? A mercenary in Trucial Oman and Yemen. Three months doing the same thing in the Sudan and lucky to get out with your life. Since 1966 you've worked as an agent for several arms dealers, mostly legitimate. Thwaite and Simpson, Franz Baumann, Mackenzie Brown, and Julius Meyer among others."

"Nothing wrong with that. The British Government makes

several hundred million pounds a year out of the manufacture and sale of arms."

"Only they don't try to run them into someone else's country by night to give aid and succor to the enemies of the official government."

"Come off it," I said. "That's exactly what they've been doing for years."

He laughed and slapped his knee with one hand. "Damn it all, Vaughan, but I like you. I really do."

"What, the Beast of Selangor?"

"Good God, boy, do you think I was born yesterday? I know what happened out there. What really happened. You were told to clear the last terrorist out of Kota Baru and you did just that. A little ruthlessly perhaps, but you did it. Your superiors heaved a sigh of relief, then threw you to the wolves."

"Leaving me with the satisfaction of knowing that I did my duty."

He smiled. "I can see we're going to get along just fine. Did I tell you I knew your father?"

"I'm sure you did," I said, "but just now I'd much rather know what in hell you're after, Brigadier."

"I want you to come and work for me. In exchange I'll get you out of here. The slate wiped clean."

"Just like that?"

"Quite reasonable people to deal with—the Greeks—if one knows how."

"And what would I have to do in return?"

"Oh, that's simple," he said. "I'd like you to take on the I.R.A. in Northern Ireland for us."

Which was the kind of remark calculated to take the wind out of anyone's sails and I stared at him incredulously.

"You've got to be joking!"

"I can't think of anyone better qualified. Look at it this way. You spent years in Intelligence working against urban guerrillas, Marxists, anarchists, revolutionaries of every sort, the whole bagshoot. You know how their minds work. You're perfectly at

221

home fighting where the battlefield is back alleys and rooftops. You're tough, resourceful, and quite ruthless, which you'll need to be if you're to survive five minutes with this lot, believe me."

"Nothing like making it sound attractive."

"And then, you do have one or two special qualifications, you must admit that. You speak Irish, I understand, thanks to your mother, which is more than most Irishmen do. And then there was that uncle of yours, the one who commanded a flying column for the I.R.A. in the old days."

"Michael Fitzgerald," I said, "the Schoolmaster of Strad-balla."

He raised his eyebrows at that one. "My God, but they do like their legends, don't they? On the other hand, the fact that you're a half-and-half must surely be some advantage."

"You mean it might help me to understand what goes on in those rather simple peasant minds?"

He wasn't in the least put out. "I must say I'm damned if I can sometimes."

"Which is exactly why they've been trying to kick us out for the past seven hundred years."

He raised his eyebrows at that and there was a touch of frost in his voice. "An interesting remark, Vaughan. One which certainly makes me wonder exactly where you stand on this question."

"I don't take sides," I said. "Not anymore. Just tell me what you expect. If I can justify it to myself, I'll take it on."

"And if you can't, you'll sit here for another fifteen years?" He shook his head. "Oh, I doubt that, Major. I doubt that very much indeed."

And there was the rub for I doubted it myself. I took another of his cigarettes and said wearily. "All right, Brigadier, what's it all about?"

"The Army is at war with the I.R.A., it's as simple as that."
"Or as complicated."

"Exactly. When we first moved in troops in 'sixty-nine, it was to protect a Catholic minority who had certain just grievances, one must admit that."

"And since then?"

"The worst kind of escalation. Palestine, Aden, Cyprus. Exactly the same only worse. Increasing violence, planned assassinations, the kind of mad bombing incidents that usually harm innocent civilians more than the Army."

"The purpose of terrorism is to terrorize," I said. "The only way a small country can take on an empire and win. That was one of Michael Collin's favorite sayings."

"I'm not surprised. To make things even more difficult at the moment, the I.R.A. itself is split down the middle. One half call themselves official and seem to have swung rather to the left politically."

"How far?"

"As far as you like. The other lot, the pure nationalists, Provisionals, Provos, Bradyites, call them what you like, are the ones who are supposed to be responsible for all the physical action."

"And aren't they?"

"Not at all. The official I.R.A. is just as much in favor of violence when it suits them. And then there are the splinter groups. Fanatical fringe elements who want to shoot everyone in sight. The worst of that little lot is a group called the Sons of Erin, led by a man called Frank Barry."

"And what about the other side?" I asked. "The Ulster Volunteer Force?"

"Don't even mention them," he said feelingly. "If they ever decide to take a hand, it will be civil war and the kind of bloodbath that would be simply too hideous to contemplate. No, the immediate task is to defeat terrorism. That's the Army's job. It's up to the politicians to sort things out afterwards."

"And what am I supposed to be able to achieve that the whole of military intelligence can't?"

"Everything or nothing. It all depends. The I.R.A. needs

money if it's to be in a position to buy arms on anything like a large enough scale. They got their hands on some in rather a big way about five weeks ago."

"What happened?"

"The night mail boat from Belfast to Glasgow was hijacked by half a dozen men."

"Who were they? Provos?"

"No, they were led by a man we've been after for years. A real old timer. Must be sixty if he's a day. Michael Cork. The Small Man, they call him. Another of those Irish jokes as he's reputed to be over six feet in height."

"Reputed?"

"Except for a two-year sentence when he was seventeen or eighteen, he hasn't been in custody since. He did spend a considerable period in America, but the simple truth is we haven't the slightest idea what he looks like."

"So what happened on the mail boat?"

"Cork and his men forced the captain to rendezvous off the coast with a fifty-foot diesel motor yacht. They off-loaded just over half a million pounds worth of gold bullion."

"And slipped quietly away into the night?"

"Not quite. They clashed with a Royal Navy M.T.B. early the following morning near Rathlin Island, but managed to get away under cover of fog, though the officer in command thinks they were in a sinking condition."

"Were they sighted anywhere else?"

"A rubber dinghy was found on a beach near Stramore, which is a fishing port on the mainland coast south of Rathlin, and several bodies were washed up during the week that followed."

"And you think Michael Cork survived?"

"We know he did. In fact, thanks to that grand old Irish institution, the informer, we know exactly what happened. Cork was the only survivor. He sank the boat in a place of his own choosing, landed near Stramore in that rubber dinghy, and promptly disappeared with his usual sleight of hand."

I moved to the window and looked out over the blue Aegean

and thought of that boat lying on the bottom up there in those cold, gray northern waters.

"He could do a lot with that kind of money."

"An approach has already been made in his name to a London-based arms dealer who had the sense to contact the proper authorities at once."

"Who was it? Anyone I know?"

"Julius Meyer. You've acted for him on several occasions in the past, I believe."

"Old Meyer?" I laughed out loud. "Now there's a slippery customer if you like. I wonder why they chose him?"

"Oh, I should have thought he had just the right kind of shady reputation," the Brigadier said. "He's been in trouble often enough, God knows. There was all that fuss with the Spanish government last year when it came out that he'd been selling guns to the Free Basque movement. He was on every front page in the country for a day or two. The kind of thing interested parties would remember."

Which made sense. I said, "And where do I fit in?"

"You simply do exactly what you've done in the past. Act as Meyer's agent in this matter. They should find you perfectly acceptable. After all, your past stinks to high heaven very satisfactorily."

"Nice of you to say so. And what if I'm asked to act in a mercenary capacity? To give instruction in the handling of certain weapons. That can sometimes happen you know."

"I hope it does. I want you in there up to your ears, as close to the heart of things as possible because we want that gold, Vaughan. We can't allow them to hang on to a bank like that, so that's your primary task—to find out exactly where it is."

"Anything else?"

"Any information you can glean about the Organization: faces, names, places. All that goes without saying and it would be rather nice if you could get Michael Cork for us if the opportunity arises or indeed anyone else of similar persuasion that you meet along the way."

I said slowly, "And what exactly do you mean by get?"

"Don't fool about with me, boy," he said and there was iron in his voice. "You know exactly what I mean. If Cork and his friends want to play these kinds of games, then they must accept the consequences."

"I see. And where does Meyer fit into all this?"

"He'll cooperate in full. Go to Northern Ireland when necessary. Assist you in any way he can."

"And how did you achieve that small miracle? As I remember Meyer, he was always for the quiet life."

"A simple question of the annual renewal of his licenses to trade in arms," the Brigadier said. "There is one thing I must stress, by the way. Although you will be paid the remuneration plus allowances suitable to your rank, there can be no question of your being restored to the active list officially."

"In other words, if I land up in the gutter with a bullet through the head, I'm just another corpse?"

"Exactly." He stood up briskly and adjusted his panama. "But I've really talked for quite long enough and the governor's laid on an M.T.B. to run me back to Athens in half an hour. So what's it to be? A little action and passion or another fifteen years of this?" He gestured around the cell with his cane.

I said, "Do I really have a choice?"

"Sensible lad." He smiled broadly and rapped on the door. "We'd better get moving then."

"What, now?"

"I brought a signed release paper with me from Athens."

"You were that certain?"

He shrugged. "Let's say it seemed more than likely that you'd see things my way."

The key turned in the lock and the door opened, the sergeant saluted formally and stood to one side.

The Brigadier started forward and I said, "Just one thing."

"What's that?"

"You did say Royal Corps of Transport?"

He smiled beautifully. "A most essential part of the Service,

226

my dear Simon. I should have thought you would have recognized that. Now come along. We really are going to cut it most awfully fine for the R.A.F. plane I've laid on from Athens."

So it was Simon now? He moved out into the corridor and the sergeant stood waiting patiently as I glanced around the cell. The prospect was not exactly bright, but after all, anything was better than this.

He called my name impatiently once more from halfway up the stairs; I moved out and the door clanged shut behind me.

2

Meyer

I first met Julius Meyer in one of the smaller of the Trucial Oman States in June 1966. A place called Rubat, which boasted a sultan, one port town, and around forty thousand square miles of very unattractive desert which was inhabited by what are usually referred to in military circles as dissident tribesmen.

The whole place had little to commend it except its oil, which meant that besides the sultan's three Rolls-Royces, two Mercedes, and one Cadillac (our American friends not being so popular in the area that year), he could also afford a chief of police. I was glad of the work, however temporary the political situation made it look.

I was called up to the palace in a hurry one afternoon by the sultan's chief minister, Hamal, who also happened to be his nephew. The whole thing was something of a surprise, as it was the sort of place where nobody made a move during the heat of the day.

When I went into his office, I found him seated at his desk opposite Meyer. I never did know Meyer's age for he was one of those men who looked a permanent sixty.

Hamal said, "Ah, Major Vaughan, this is Mr. Julius Meyer."

"Mr. Meyer," I said politely.

"You will arrest him immediately and hold him in close confinement at central police headquarters until you hear from me."

Meyer peered shortsightedly at me through steel-rimmed spectacles. With his shock of untidy gray hair, the fraying collar, the shabby linen suit, he looked more like an unsuccessful musician than anything else. It was much later when I discovered that all these things were supposed to make him look poor which he certainly was not.

"What's the charge?" I asked.

"Import of arms without a license. I'll give you the details later. Now get him out of here. I've got work to do."

On the way to town in the Jeep, Meyer wiped sweat from his face ceaselessly. "A terrible, terrible thing, all this deceit in life, my friend," he said at one point. "I mean, it's really getting to the stage where one can't trust anybody."

"Would you by any chance be referring to our respected chief minister?" I asked him.

He became extremely agitated, flapping his arms up and down like some great shabby white bird. "I came in from Djibouti this morning with five thousand M.I. carbines, all in excellent condition, perfect goods. Fifty Bren guns, twenty thousand rounds of ammunition, all to *his* order."

"What happened?"

"You know what happened. He refuses to pay, has me arrested." He glanced at me furtively, trying to smile and failed miserably. "This charge? What happens if he can make it stick? What's the penalty?"

"This was a British colony for years, so they favor hanging. The Sultan likes to put on a public show in the main square, just to encourage the others."

"My God!" He groaned in anguish. "From now on, I use an agent, I swear it."

Which, in other circumstances, would have made me laugh out loud.

* * *

229

I had Meyer locked up, as per instructions, then went to my office and gave the whole business very careful thought which, knowing Hamal, took all of five minutes.

Having reached the inescapable conclusion that there was something very rotten indeed in the state of Rubat, I left the office and drove down to the waterfront, where I checked that our brand new fifty-foot diesel police launch was ready for sea, tanks full.

The bank, unfortunately, was closed, so I went immediately to my rather pleasant little house on the edge of town and recovered, from the corner of the garden by the cistern, the steel cash box containing five thousand dollars mad money put by for a rainy day.

As I started back to town, there was a rattle of machine gun fire from the general direction of the palace, which was comforting if only because it proved that my judgment was still unimpaired, Rubat, the heat, and the atmosphere of general decay notwithstanding.

I called in at police headquarters on my way down to the harbor and discovered, without any particular sense of surprise, that there wasn't a man left in the place, except Meyer, whom I found standing at the window of his cell listening to the sound of small arms fire when I unlocked the door.

He turned immediately, and there was a certain relief on his face when he saw who it was. "Hamal?" he inquired.

"He never was one to let the grass grow under his feet," I said. "Comes of having been a prefect at Winchester. You don't look too good. I suggest a long sea voyage."

He almost fell over himself in his eagerness to get past me through the door.

As we moved out of harbor, a column of black smoke ascended into the hot afternoon air from the palace. Standing beside me in the wheelhouse, Meyer shook his head and sighed.

"We live in an uncertain world, my friend." And then, dismissing Rubat and its affairs completely, he went on, "How good is this boat? Can we reach Djibouti?"

"Easily."

"Excellent. I have first class contacts there. We can even sell the boat. Some slight recompense for my loss, and I've a little matter of business coming up in the Somali Republic that you might be able to help me with."

"What sort of business?"

"The two thousand pounds a month kind," he replied calmly.

Which was enough to shut anyone up. He produced a small cassette tape recorder from one of his pockets, put it on the chart table, and turned it on.

The band which started playing had the unmistakably nostalgic sound of the thirties, and so did the singer who joined in a few moments later, reassuring me with "Every Day's a Lucky Day." There was complete repose on Meyer's face as he listened.

I said, "Who in the hell is that?"

"Al Bowlly," he said simply, "the best there ever was."

The start of a beautiful friendship in more ways than one.

I was reminded of that first meeting when I went down to Meyer's Wapping warehouse on the morning following my arrival back in England from Greece, courtesy of Ferguson and R.A.F. Transport Command, and for the most obvious of reasons, for when I opened the little judas gate in the main entrance and stepped inside, Al Bowlly's voice drifted like some ghostly echo out of the half-darkness to tell me "Everything I Have Is Yours."

It was strangely appropriate, considering the setting, for in that one warehouse Meyer really did have just about every possible thing you could think of in the arms line. In fact, it had always been a source of mystery to me how he managed to cope with the fire department inspectors, for, on occasion, he had enough explosives in there to blow up a sizable part of London.

"Meyer, are you there?" I called, puzzled by the lack of staff.

I moved through the gloom between two rows of shelving crammed with boxes of .303 ammunition and rifle grenades. There was a flight of steel steps leading up to a landing above, more shelves, rows and rows of old Enfields.

Al Bowlly faded, and Meyer appeared at the rail. "Who is it?"

As usual he had that rather hunted look about him, as if he expected the Gestapo to descend at any moment, which at one time in his youth had been a distinct possibility. He wore the same steel-rimmed spectacles he'd had on at our first meeting, and the crumpled blue suit was well up to his usual standard of shabbiness.

"Simon?" he said. "Is that you?" He started down the steps.

I said, "Where is everyone?"

"I gave them the day off. Thought it best when Ferguson telephoned. Where is he, by the way?"

"He'll be along."

He took off his glasses, polished them, put them back on, and inspected me thoroughly. "They didn't lean on you too hard in that place?"

"Skarthos?" I shook my head. "Just being there was enough. How's business?"

He spread his hands in an inimitable gesture and led the way toward his office at the other end of the warehouse. "How can I complain? The world gets more violent day by day."

We went into the tiny cluttered office and he produced a bottle of the cheapest possible British sherry and poured the ritual couple of drinks. It tasted like sweet varnish, but I got it down manfully.

"This man Ferguson," he said as he finished. "A devil. A cold-blooded, calculating devil."

"He certainly knows what he wants."

"He blackmailed me, Simon. Me, a citizen all these years. I pay my taxes, don't I? I behave myself. When these Irish nutcases approach me to do a deal, I go to the authorities straight away."

"Highly commendable," I said, and poured myself another glass of that dreadful sherry.

"And what thanks do I get? This Ferguson walks in here and gives me the business. Either I play the game the way he wants it or I lose my license to trade. Is that fair? Is that British justice?"

"Sounds like a pretty recognizable facsimile of it to me," I told him.

He was almost angry, but not quite. "Why is everything such a big joke to you, Simon? Is our present situation funny? Is death funny?"

"The sensible man's way of staying sane in a world gone mad," I said.

He considered the point and managed one of those funny little smiles of his. "Maybe you've got something there. I'll try it—I'll definitely try it. But what about Ferguson?"

"He'll be along. You'll know the worst soon enough." I sat on the edge of his desk and helped myself to one of the Turkish cigarettes he kept in a sandalwood box for special customers. "What have you got that works with a silencer? Really works."

He was all business now. "Hand gun or what?"

"And submachine gun."

"We'll go downstairs," he said. "I think I can fix you up."

The Mk IIS Sten submachine gun was especially developed during the war for use with commando units and resistance groups. It was also used with considerable success by British troops on night patrol work during the Korean war.

It was, indeed still is, a remarkable weapon, its silencing unit absorbing the noise of the bullet explosions to an amazing degree. The only sound when firing is the clicking of the bolt as it goes backwards and forwards, and this can seldom be heard beyond a range of twenty yards or so.

Many more were manufactured than is generally realized, and as they were quite unique in their field, the reason for the lack of production over the years has always been something of a mystery to me.

233

The one I held in my hands in Meyer's basement firing range was a mint specimen. There were a row of targets at the far end, life-size replicas of charging soldiers of indeterminate nationality, all wearing camouflage uniforms. I emptied a thirty-two-round magazine into the first five, working from left to right. It was an uncomfortably eerie experience to see the bullets shredding the target and to hear only the clicking of the bolt.

Meyer said, "Remember, full automatic only in a real emergency. They tend to overheat otherwise."

A superfluous piece of information as I'd used the things in action in Korea, but I contented myself with laying the Sten down and saying mildly, "What about a hand gun?"

I thought he looked pleased with himself, and I saw why a moment later, when he produced a tin box, opened it, and took out what appeared to be a normal automatic pistol, except that the barrel was of a rather strange design.

"I could get a packet from any collector for this little item," he said. "Chinese Communist silenced pistol. Seven point sixty-five millimeter."

It was certainly new to me. "How does it work?"

It was ingenious enough. Used as a semi-automatic, there was only the sound of the slide reciprocating and the cartridge cases ejecting, but it could also be used to fire a single shot with complete silence.

I tried a couple of rounds. Meyer said, "You like it?"

Before we could take it any further, there was a footstep on the stairs and Ferguson moved out of the darkness. He was wearing a dark gray double-breasted suit, Academy tie, bowler hat, and carried a briefcase.

"So there you are," he said. "What's all this?"

He came forward and put his briefcase down on the table, then he took the pistol from me, sighted casually, and fired. The result was as I might have expected. No fancy shooting through the shoulder or hand. Just a bullet dead center in the belly, painful but certain.

He put the gun down on the table and glanced at his watch.

"I've got exactly ten minutes, then I must be on my way to the War Office, so let's get down to business. Meyer, have you filled him in on your end yet?"

"You told me to wait."

"I'm here now."

"Okay." Meyer shrugged and turned to me. "I had a final meeting with the London agent for these people yesterday. I've told him it would be possible to run the stuff over from Oban."

"Possible?" I said. "That must be the understatement of this or any other year."

Meyer carried straight on as if I hadn't interrupted. "I've arranged for you to act as my agent in the matter. There's to be a preliminary meeting in Belfast on Monday night. They're expecting both of us."

"Who are?"

"I'm not certain. Possibly this official I.R.A. leader himself, Michael Cork."

I glanced at the Brigadier. "Your Small Man?"

"Perhaps," he said, "but we don't really know. All we can say for certain is that you should get some sort of direct lead to him, whatever happens."

"And what do I do between now and Monday?"

"Go to Oban and get hold of the right kind of boat." He opened the briefcase and took out an envelope which he pushed across the table. "You'll find a thousand pounds in there. Let's call it working capital." He turned to Meyer. "I'm aware that such an amount is small beer to a man of your assets, Mr. Meyer, but we wanted to be fair."

Meyer's hand fastened on the envelope. "Money is important, Briagadier, let nobody fool you. I never turned down a grand in my life."

Ferguson turned back to me. "It seemed to me that the most obvious place for your landing when you make the run will be the north Antrim coast, so Meyer will rent a house in the area. He'll act as a link man between us once you've arrived and are in the thick of it."

"You intend to be there yourself?"

"Somewhere at hand, just in case I'm needed, but one thing must be stressed. On no account are you to approach the military or police authorities in the area."

"No matter what happens?"

"You're on your own, Simon," he said. "Better get used to the idea. I'll help all I can at the right moment, but until then . . ."

"I think I get the drift," I said. "This is one of those jolly little operations that will have everybody from cabinet-level down clapping their hands with glee if it works."

"And howling for your blood if it doesn't," he said and patted me on the shoulder. "But I have every confidence in you, Simon. It's going to work, you'll see."

"At the moment, I can't think of a single reason why it should, but thanks for the vote of confidence."

He closed his briefcase and picked it up. "Just remember one thing. Michael Cork may be what some people would term an old-fashioned revolutionary, and I think they're probably right. In other words, he and his kind don't approve of the indiscriminate slaughter of the innocent for political ends."

"But he'll kill me if he has to, is that what you're trying to say?"

"Without a second's hesitation." He put a hand on my shoulder. "Must rush now, but do promise me one thing."

"What's that?"

"Get yourself a decent gun." He picked up the silenced pistol, weighed it in his hands, and dropped it on the table. "Load of Hong Kong rubbish."

"This one is by way of Peking," I told him.

"All the bloody same," he said cheerfully, and faded into the darkness. We heard him on the stairs for a moment, and then he was gone.

Meyer walked up and down, flapping his arms again, extremely agitated. "He makes me so uncomfortable. Why does he make me feel this way?"

"He went to what some people would term the right school. You didn't."

"Rubbish," he said. "You went to the right schools and with you I feel fine."

"My mother was Irish," I said. "You're forgetting. My one saving grace." I tried another couple of shots with the Chinese pistol and shook my head. "Ferguson is right. Put this back in the Christmas cracker where you found it, and get me a real gun."

"Such as?"

"What about a Mauser seven-point-sixty-three-millimeter Model 1932 with the bulbous silencer? The kind they manufactured for German counterintelligence during the second war. There must still be one or two around?"

"Why not ask me for the gold from my teeth while you're about it? It's impossible. Where will I find such a thing these days?"

"Oh, you'll manage," I said. "You always do." I held out my hand. "If you'll give me my share of the loot I'll be on my way. Oban is not just another station on the Brighton line you know. It's on the northwest coast of Scotland."

"Do I need a geography lesson?"

He counted out five hundred pounds, grumbling, sweat on his face as there always was when he handled money. I stowed it away in my inside breast pocket.

"When will you be back?" he asked.

"I'll try for the day after tomorrow."

He followed me up the stairs, and we paused at the door of his office. He said awkwardly, "Look after yourself then."

It was as near as he could get to any demonstration of affection. I said, "Don't I always?"

As I walked away, he went into his office and a moment later, Al Bowlly was giving me a musical farewell all the way to the door.

3

Night Sounds

They started shooting again as I turned the corner, the rattle of small arms fire drifting across the water through the fog from somewhere in the heart of the city. It was echoed almost immediately by a heavy machine gun. Probably an armored car opening up with its Browning in reply.

Belfast night sounds. Common enough these days, God knows, but over here on this part of the docks, it was as quiet as the grave. Only the gurgle of water among the wharf pilings to accompany me as I moved along the cobbled street past a row of warehouses.

I didn't see a soul, which was hardly surprising, for it was the sort of place to be hurried through if it had to be visited at all, and they'd obviously had their troubles. Most of the street lamps were smashed, a warehouse a little further on had been burned to the ground, and at one point rubble and broken glass carpeted the street.

I picked my way through and found what I was looking for on the next corner, a large Victorian public house, the light in its windows the first sign of life I'd seen in the whole area. The name was etched in acid on the frosted glass panel by the

238

entrance: *Cohan's Select Bar.* An arguable point from the look of the place, but I pushed open the door and went in anyway.

I found myself in a long narrow room, the far end shrouded in shadow. There was a small coal fire on the left, two or three tables and some chairs, and not much else except the old marble-topped bar with a mirror behind it that must have been quite something when clipper ships still used Belfast docks. Now it was cracked in a dozen places, the gold leaf on the ornate frame flaking away to reveal cheap plaster. As used by life as the man who leaned against the beer pumps reading a newspaper.

He looked older than he probably was, but that would be the drink if the breath on him was anything to go by. The neck above the collarless shirt was seamed with dirt, and he scratched the stubble on his chin nervously as he watched me approach.

He managed a smile when I was close enough. "Good night to you, sir. And what's it to be?"

"Oh, a Jameson, I think," I said. "A large one. The kind of night for it."

He went very still, staring at me, mouth gaping, and he was no longer smiling.

"English, is it?" he whispered.

"That's right. Another of those fascist beasts from across the water, although I suppose that depends upon which side you're on."

I put a cigarette in my mouth, and he produced a box of matches hastily and gave me a light, his hands shaking. I held his wrist to steady the flame.

"You're quiet enough in here, in all conscience. Where is everybody?"

There was a movement behind me, the softest of footfalls, wind over grass in a forest at nightfall, no more than that. Someone said quietly, "And who but a fool would be abroad at night in times like these, when he could be safe home, Major?"

He had emerged from the shadows at the end of the room, hands deep in the pockets of a dark blue double-breasted Melton overcoat, the kind much favored by undertakers, the collar turned up about his neck.

Five-foot-two or -three at the most—I took him for little more than a boy, although the white devil's face on him beneath the peak of the tweed cap, the dark eyes that seemed perpetually fixed on eternity, hinted at something more. A soul in torment if ever I'd seen one.

"You're a long way from Kerry," I said.

"And how would you be knowing that?"

"I mind the accent, isn't that what they say? My mother, God rest her, was from Stradballa."

Something moved in his eyes then. Surprise, I suppose. In any event, before he could reply a voice called softly from the shadows, "Bring the Major down here, Binnie."

There was a row of wooden booths, each with its own frosted glass door to ensure privacy, another relic of Victorian times. A young woman sat at a table in the end one. She wore an old trench coat and head scarf, but it was difficult to see much more than that.

Binnie ran his hands over me from behind presumably looking for some sort of concealed weapon, giving me no more than three opportunities of jumping him had I been so disposed.

"Satisfied?" I demanded. He moved back, and I turned to the girl. "Simon Vaughan."

"I know who you are well enough."

"And there you have the advantage of me."

"Norah Murphy."

More American than Irish, to judge from the voice. An evening for surprises. I said, "And are you for the Oban boat, Miss Murphy?"

"And back again."

Which disposed of the formalities satisfactorily, and I pulled a chair back from the table and sat down.

I offered her a cigarette, and when I gave her a light, the match flaring in my cupped hands pulled her face out of the shadows for a moment. Dark, empty eyes, high cheekbones, a wide, rather sensual mouth.

As the match died she said, "You seem surprised."

"I suppose I expected a man."

"Your sort would," she said with a trace of bitterness.

"Ah, the arrogant Englishman, you mean? The toe of his boot for a dog and a whip for a woman. Isn't that the saying? I would have thought it had possibilities."

She surprised me by laughing although I suspect it was in spite of herself. "Give the man his whiskey, Binnie, and make sure it's a Jameson. The Major always drinks Jameson."

He moved to the bar. I said, "Who's your friend?"

"His name is Gallagher, Major Vaughan. Binnie Gallagher."

"Young for his trade."

"But old for his age."

He put the bottle and single glass on the table and leaned against the partition at one side, arms folded. I poured a drink and said, "Well now, Miss Murphy, you seem to know all about me."

"Simon Vaughan, born 1931, Delhi. Father, a colonel in the Indian Army. Mother, Irish."

"More shame to her," I put in.

She ignored the remark and carried on. "Winchester, Sandhurst. Military Cross with the Duke of Wellington's Regiment in Korea, 1953. They must have been proud of you at the Academy. Officer, gentleman, murderer."

The American accent was more noticeable now along with the anger in her voice. There was a rather obvious pause as they both waited for some sort of reaction. When I moved, it was only to reach for the whiskey bottle, but it was enough for Binnie, whose hand was inside his coat on the instant.

"Watch yourself," he said.

"I can handle this one," she replied.

I couldn't be certain that the whole thing wasn't some prearranged ploy intended simply to test me, but the fact that they'd

241

spoken in Irish was interesting. It occurred to me that if the Murphy girl knew as much about me as she seemed to, she would be well aware that I spoke the language rather well myself, thanks to my mother.

I poured another drink and said to Binnie in Irish, "How old are you, boy?"

He answered in a kind of reflex. "Nineteen."

"If you're faced with a search, you can always dump a gun fast, but a shoulder holster . . ." I shook my head. "Get rid of it or you won't see twenty."

There was something in his eyes again, but it was the girl who answered for him, in English this time. "You should listen to the Major, Binnie. He's had a lot of practice at that kind of thing."

"You said something about my being a murderer?" I said.

"Borneo, 1963. A place called Selangor. You had fourteen guerrillas executed whose only crime was fighting for the freedom of their country."

"A debatable point considering the fact that they were all Communist Chinese," I said.

She ignored me completely. "Then there was a Mr. Hui Li, whom you had tortured and beaten for several hours. Shot while trying to escape. The newspapers called you the Beast of Selangor, but the War Office didn't want a stink so they put the lid on tight."

I actually managed a smile. "Poor Simon Vaughan. Never did really recover from the eighteen months he spent in that Chinese prison camp in Korea."

"So they didn't actually cashier you. They eased you out."

"Only the mud stuck."

"And now you sell guns."

"To people like you." I raised my glass and said gaily, "Up the Republic."

"Exactly," she said.

"Then what are we complaining about?" I took the rest of my whiskey down carefully. "Mr. Meyer is waiting to see you, not far from here. He simply wanted me to meet you first as a—a precautionary measure?"

"We know exactly where Mr. Meyer is staying. The Regent Hotel, Lurgan Street. You have room fifty-three at the Grand Central."

"Only the best," I said. "It's that public school education, you see. Now poor old Meyer, on the other hand, can never forget getting out of Germany in what he stood up in back in 'thirty-eight, so he saves his money."

Behind us the outside door burst open and a group of young men entered the bar.

There were four of them, all dressed exactly alike in leather boots, jeans, and pea jackets. Some sort of uniform I suppose, a sign that you belonged. That it was everyone else who were the outsiders. The faces and the manner of them as they swaggered in told all. Vicious young animals of a type to be found in any large city in the world from Belfast to Delhi and back again.

They were trouble and the barman knew it, his face sagging as they paused inside the door to look around, then started toward the bar, a red-haired lad of seventeen or eighteen leading the way, a smile on his face of entirely the wrong sort.

"Quiet tonight," he said cheerfully when he got close.

The barman nodded nervously. "What can I get you?"

The red-haired boy stood, hands on the bar, his friends ranged behind him. "We're collecting for the new church hall at St. Michael's. Everyone else in the district's chipping in and we knew you wouldn't like to be left out." He glanced around the bar again. "We were going to ask for fifty, but I can see things aren't so good, so we'll make it twenty-five quid and leave it at that."

One of his friends reached over the bar, helped himself to a pint pot, and pumped out a beer.

The barman said slowly. "They aren't building any church hall at St. Mick's."

The red-haired boy glanced at his friends inquiringly, then nodded gravely. "Fair enough," he said. "The truth, then. We're from the I.R.A. We're collecting for the Organization. More guns to fight the bloody British Army with. We need every penny we can get."

"God save us," the barman said. "But there isn't three quid in the till. I've never known trade as bad."

The red-haired boy slapped him solidly across the face sending him back against the shelves, three or four glasses bouncing to the floor.

"Twenty-five quid," he said. "Or we smash the place up. Take your choice."

Binnie Gallagher brushed past me like a wraith. He moved in behind them without a word. He stood there waiting, shoulders hunched, the hands thrust deep into the pockets of the dark overcoat.

The red-haired boy saw him first and turned slowly. "And who the hell might you be, little man?"

Binnie looked up, and I saw him clearly in the mirror, dark eyes burning in that white face. The four of them eased round a little, ready to move in on him, and I reached for the bottle of Jameson.

Norah Murphy put a hand on my arm. "He doesn't need you," she said quietly.

"My dear girl, I only wanted a drink," I murmured and poured myself another.

"The I.R.A., is it?" Binnie said.

The red-haired boy glanced at his friends, for the first time slightly uncertain. "What's it to you?"

"I'm a lieutenant in the North Tyrone Brigade myself," Binnie said. "Who are you lads?"

One of them made a break for the door on the instant and, incredibly, a gun was in Binnie's left hand, a nine-millimeter Browning automatic that looked like British Army issue to me. With that gun in his hand, he became another person entirely.

A man to frighten the devil himself. A natural-born killer if ever I'd seen one.

The four of them cowered against the bar, utterly terrified. Binnie said coldly, "Lads are out in the streets tonight spilling their blood for Ireland and bastards like you spit on their good name."

"For Christ's sake," the red-haired boy said, "we didn't mean no harm."

Binnie kicked him in the crotch. The boy sagged at the knees, turned, and clutched at the bar with one hand to stop himself from falling. Binnie reversed his grip on the Browning, the butt rose and fell like a hammer on the back of that outstretched hand, and I heard the bones crack. The boy gave a terrible groan and slipped to the floor, half-fainting, at the feet of his horrified companions.

Binnie's right foot swung back as if to finish him off with a kick in the side of the head and Norah Murphy called sharply, "That's enough."

He stepped back instantly like a well-trained dog and stood watching, the Browning flat against his left thigh. Norah Murphy moved past me and went to join them. I noticed that she was carrying in her right hand a square flat case, which she placed on the bar.

"Pick him up," she said.

The injured boy's companions did as they were told, holding him between them while she examined the hand. I poured myself another Jameson and joined the group as she opened the case. The most interesting item on display was a stethoscope. She rummaged around and finally produced a large triangular sling, which she tied about the boy's neck to support the injured hand.

"Take him into Casualty at the Infirmary," she said. "He'll need a plaster cast."

"And keep your mouth shut," Binnie put in.

They went out on the run, the injured boy's feet dragging between them. The door closed and there was only the silence.

As Norah Murphy reached for the case I said, "Is that just a front or the real thing?"

"Would Harvard Medical School be good enough for you?" she demanded.

"Fascinating," I said. "Our friend here breaks them up and you put them together again. That's what I call teamwork."

She didn't like that; she turned very pale and snapped the fastener of her case angrily, but I think she had determined not to lose her temper.

"All right, Major Vaughan," she said. "I don't like you either. Shall we go?"

She moved toward the door. I turned and placed my glass on the counter in front of the barman, who was standing there waiting for God knows what axe to fall.

Binnie said, "You've seen nothing, heard nothing. All right?"

There was no need to threaten. The poor wretch nodded dumbly, his lip trembling; and then, quite suddenly, he collapsed across the bar and started to cry.

Binnie surprised me then by patting him on the shoulder and saying with astonishing gentleness, "Better times coming, Da. Just you see."

But if the barman believed that, then I was the only sane man in a world gone mad.

It had started to rain, and fog rolled in across the docks as we moved along the waterfront, Norah Murphy at my side, Binnie bringing up the rear rather obviously.

Neither of them said a word until we were perhaps halfway to our destination, when Norah Murphy paused at the end of a mean street of terrace houses and turned to Binnie. "I've a patient I must see here. I promised to drop a prescription in this evening. Five minutes."

She ignored me and walked away down the street, pausing at the third or fourth door to knock briskly. She was admitted almost at once, and Binnie and I moved into the shelter of an arched passageway between two houses. I offered him a cigarette, which he refused. I lit one myself and leaned against the wall.

After a while he said, "Your mother—what was her maiden name?"

"Fitzgerald," I told him. "Nuala Fitzgerald."

He turned, his face a pale shadow in the darkness. "There was a man of the same name, schoolmaster at Stradballa during the Troubles."

"Her elder brother," I said.

He leaned closer as if trying to see my face. "You, a bloody Englishman, are the nephew of Michael Fitzgerald, the School-master of Stradballa?"

"I suppose I must be. Why should that be so hard to take?"

"But he was a great hero," Binnie said. "He commanded the Stradballa flying column. When the Tans came to take him, he was teaching at the school. Because of the children he went outside and shot it out in the open, one against fifteen, and got clean away."

"I know," I said. "A real hero of the revolution. All for the Cause. Only he never wanted it to end, Binnie, that was his trouble. Executed during the Civil War by the Free State Government. I always found that part of the story rather ironic myself, or had you forgotten that after they'd got rid of the English, the Irish set about knocking each other off with even greater enthusiasm?"

I could not see the expression on his face and yet the tension in him was something tangible between us.

I said, "Don't try it, boy. As the Americans would say, you're out of your league. Compared to me, you're just a bloody amateur."

"Is that a fact, now, Major?" he said softly.

"Another thing," I said. "Dr. Murphy wouldn't like it and we can't have that now, can we?"

She settled the matter for us by reappearing at that precise moment. She sensed at once that something was wrong, and paused.

"What is it?"

"A slight difference of opinion, that's all." I told her. "Binnie's just discovered I'm related to a piece of grand old Irish history, and it sticks in his throat—or didn't you know?"

"I knew," she said coldly.

"I thought you would," I said. "The interesting thing is, why didn't you tell him?"

I didn't give her a chance to reply and cut the whole business short by moving off into the fog briskly in the general direction of Lurgan Street.

The Regent Hotel didn't have a great deal to commend it, but then neither did Lurgan Street. A row of decaying terrace houses, a shop or two, and a couple of pubs making as unattractive a sight as I have ever seen.

The Regent itself was little more than a lodging house of a type to be found near the docks of any large port, catering mainly to sailors or prostitutes in need of a room for an hour or two. It had been constructed by simply joining three terrace houses together and sticking a sign above the door of one of them.

A merchant navy officer came out as we approached and clutched at the railings for support. A girl of eighteen or so in a black plastic macintosh emerged behind him, straightened his cap, and got a hand under his elbow to help him down the steps.

She looked us over without the slightest sense of shame and I smiled and nodded. "Good night, *a colleen*. God save the good work."

The laughter bubbled out of her. "God save you kindly."

They went off down the street together, the sailor breaking into a reasonably unprintable song and I shook my head. "Oh, the pity of it, a fine Catholic girl to come to that."

Binnie looked as if he would have liked to put a bullet into me, but Norah Murphy showed no reaction at all except to say, "Could we possibly get on with it, Major Vaughan? My time is limited."

We went up the steps and into the narrow hallway. There

was a desk of sorts to one side at the bottom of the stairs, and an old white-haired man in a faded alpaca jacket dozed behind it, his chin in one hand.

There seemed little point in waking him, and I led the way up to the first landing. Meyer had room seven at the end of the corridor. When I paused to knock, we could hear music from inside, strangely plaintive, something of the night in it.

Norah Murphy frowned. "What on earth is it?"

"Al Bowlly," I said simply.

"Al who?"

"You mean you've never heard of Al Bowlly, Doctor? Why he's indisputably number one in the hit parade to any person of taste and judgment, or he would be if he hadn't been killed in the London Blitz in 1941. Meyer listens to nothing else. Carries a cassette tape recorder with him everywhere."

"You've got to be kidding," she said.

I shook my head. "You're now listening to 'Moonlight on the Highway,' probably the best thing he ever did. Recorded with Lew Stone and his band on the twenty-first of March, 1938. You see, I've become something of an expert myself."

The door opened and Meyer appeared. "Ah, Simon."

"Dr. Murphy," I said. "And Mr. Gallagher. This is Mr. Meyer." I closed the door and Meyer, who could speak impeccable English when it suited him, started to act the bewildered Middle-European.

"But I don't understand, I was expecting to meet a Mr. Cork, commanding the official I.R.A. forces in Northern Ireland."

I walked to the window and lit a cigarette, aware of Binnie leaning against the door, hands in his pockets. It was raining harder than ever outside, bouncing from the cobblestones.

Norah Murphy said, "I am empowered to act for Michael Cork."

"You were to provide five thousand pounds in cash as an evidence of good faith. Where is it, please?"

She opened her case, took out an envelope and threw it on the bed. "Count it, please, Simon," Meyer said.

Al Bowlly was working his way through "I Double Dare You" as I reached for the envelope and Norah Murphy said quickly, "Don't waste your time, Major. There's only a thousand there."

There was a moment of distinct tension as Meyer reached for the tape recorder and cut Al Bowlly dead. "And the other four?"

"We wanted to be absolutely certain, that's all. It's ready and waiting, no more than ten minutes' walk from here."

He thought about it for a moment then nodded briefly. "All right. To business. Please sit down."

He offered her the only chair and sat on the edge of the bed himself.

"Will you have any difficulty in meeting our requirements?" she asked.

"The rifles will be no trouble at all. I am in the happy position of being able to offer you five hundred Chinese A.K. forty-sevens, probably the finest assault rifle in the world today. Extensively used by the Viet Cong in Vietnam."

"I'm aware of that," she said a trifle impatiently. "And the other items?"

"Grenades are no problem and we can offer you an excellent range of submachine guns. The early Thompsons still make a great deal of noise, but I would personally recommend you to try the Israeli Uzi. A remarkably efficient weapon. Absolutely first class, don't you agree, Simon?"

"Oh, the best," I said cheerfully. "There's a grip safety which stops it firing if dropped, so we find it goes particularly well with the peasant trade. They're usually inclined to be rather clumsy."

She didn't even bother to look at me. "And armor-piercing weapons?" she said. "We asked for those most particularly."

"Rather more difficult, I'm afraid," Meyer told her.

"But we must have them." She clenched her right hand and hammered it against her knee, the knuckles white. "They are absolutely essential if we are to win the battle in the streets. Petrol bombs make a spectacular show on color television, Mr.

250

Meyer, but they seldom do more than blister the paint of a Saracen armored car."

Meyer sighed heavily. "I can deliver between eighty and one hundred and twenty Lahti twenty-millimeter semi-automatic anti-tank cannons. It's a Finnish gun. Not used by any Western Powers, as far as I know."

"Is it efficient? Will it do the job?"

"Ask the Major; he's the expert."

She turned to me and I shrugged. "Any gun is only as good as the man using it, but as a matter of interest, someone broke into a bank in New York back in 1965 using a Lahti. Blasted a hole through twenty inches of concrete and steel. One round in the right place will open up a Saracen like a tin can."

She nodded, that hand still clenched, a strange, wild gleam in her eye. "You've used them? You've had experience with them in action, I mean?"

"In one of the Trucial Oman States and Yemen."

She turned to Meyer. "You must guarantee competent instruction in their use. Agreed?"

She didn't look at me. There was no need. Meyer nodded. "Major Vaughan will be happy to oblige, but for one week only and our fee will be an additional two thousand pounds on that agreed for the first consignment."

"Making twenty-seven thousand in all?" she said.

Meyer took off his glasses and started to polish them with a soiled handkerchief. "Good, then we can proceed as provisionally agreed with your representative in London. I have hired a thirty-foot motor cruiser, berthed at Oban at the present time, rigged for deep-sea fishing. Major Vaughan will leave next Thursday afternoon at high tide and will attempt the run with the first consignment."

"And where is it to be landed?" she asked.

Which was my department. I said, "There's a small fishing port called Stramore on the coast directly south from Rathlin Island. There's a secluded inlet with a good beach about five miles east. Our informant has been running whiskey in there from the Republic for the past five years without being caught so we should be all right. Your end is to make sure you have reliable people and transport on the spot to pick the stuff up and get the hell out of it fast."

"And what do you do?"

"Comply with my sailing instructions and call in at Stramore. I'll contact you there."

She frowned as if thinking about it and Meyer said calmly, "Is it to your satisfaction?"

"Oh, yes, I think so." She nodded slowly. "Except for one thing. Binnie and I go with him."

Meyer looked at me in beautifully simulated bewilderment and spread his hand in another of those Middle-European gestures. "But my dear young lady, it simply is not possible."

"Why not?"

"Because this is an extremely hazardous undertaking. Because of an institution known as the British Royal Navy which patrols the Ulster coast regularly these days with its M.T.B.'s. If challenged, Major Vaughan still stands some sort of a chance of getting away. He is an expert at underwater work. He carries frogman's equipment. An aqualung. He can take his chances over the side. With you along, the whole situation would be different."

"Oh, I'm sure we can rely on Major Vaughan to see that the Royal Navy doesn't catch us." She stood up and held out her hand. "We'll see you next Thursday in Oban, then, Mr. Meyer."

Meyer sighed, waved his arms about helplessly, then took her hand. "You're a very determined young woman. You will not forget, however, that you owe me four thousand pounds."

"How could I?" She turned to me. "When you're ready, Major."

Binnie opened the door for us, and I followed her out. As we went down the corridor Al Bowlly launched into "Good Night but Not Good-bye."

4

In Harm's Way

As we went down the steps to the street, a Land-Rover swept out of the fog followed by another, very close behind. They had been stripped to the bare essentials so that the driver and the three soldiers who crouched in the rear of each vehicle behind him were completely exposed. They were paratroopers, efficient, tough-looking young men, in red berets and flak jackets, their submachine guns held ready for instant action.

They disappeared into the fog, and Binnie spat into the gutter in disgust. "Would you look at that now, just asking to be chopped down, the dumb bastards. What wouldn't I give for a Thompson gun and one crack at them."

"It would be your last," I said. "They know exactly what they're doing, believe me. They perfected that open display technique in Aden. The crew of each vehicle looks after the other and without armor plating to get in their way they can return fire instantly if attacked."

"Bloody S.S.," he said.

I shook my head. "No, they're not, Binnie. Most of them are lads around your own age, trying to do a dirty job the best way they know how."

He frowned, and for some reason, my remark seemed to shut him up. Norah Murphy didn't say a word, but led the way briskly, turning from one street into another without hesitation.

Within a few minutes we came to a main road. There was a church on the other side, the Immaculate Heart according to the board, a Victorian monstrosity in yellow brick which squatted in the rain behind a fringe of iron railings. There were lights in the windows, the sound of an organ, and people were emerging from the open door in ones and twos to pause for a moment before plunging into the heavy rain.

As we crossed the road, a priest came out of the porch and stood on the top step trying to open his umbrella. He was a tall, rather frail-looking man in a cassock and black raincoat, and he wore a broad-brimmed shovel hat that made it difficult to see his face.

He got the umbrella up and started down the steps, then stopped suddenly. "Dr. Murphy," he called, "is that you?"

Norah Murphy turned quickly. "Hello, Father Mac," she said, then added in a low voice, "I'll only be a moment. The woman I saw earlier is one of his parishioners."

Binnie and I moved into the shelter of a doorway and she went under the shelter of the priest's umbrella. He glanced toward us once and nodded, a gentle, kindly man of sixty or so. Norah Murphy held his umbrella and talked to him while he took off his horn-rimmed spectacles and wiped rain from them with a handkerchief.

Finally he replaced the spectacles and nodded. "Fine, my dear, just fine," he said, and took a package from his raincoat pocket. "Give her that when you next see her and tell her I'll be along in the morning."

He touched his hat and walked away into the fog. Norah Murphy watched him go, then tossed the package to me so unexpectedly that I barely caught it. "Four thousand pounds, Major Vaughan."

I weighed the package in my hands. "I didn't think the Church was taking sides these days."

"It isn't."

"Then who in the hell was that?"

Binnie laughed out loud and Norah Murphy smiled. "Why, that was Michael Cork, Major Vaughan," she said sweetly, and walked away.

Which was certainly one for the book. The package was too bulky to fit in any pocket, so I pushed it inside the front of my trench coat and buttoned the flap as I followed her, Binnie keeping pace with me.

She waited for us on the corner of a reasonably busy intersection, four roads meeting to form a small square. There were plenty of people about, most of them emerging from a large supermarket on our left, which was ablaze with light to catch the evening trade; soft music, of the kind reputed to induce the right mood to buy, was drifting out through the entrance. There was also a certain amount of traffic about, private cars mostly, nosing out of the fog, pausing at the pedestrian crossing, then passing on.

It was a typical street scene of the kind you'd expect to find in any large industrial city, except for one thing. There was a police station on the other side of the square, a modern building in concrete and glass, and the entrance was protected by a sandbagged machine-gun post manned by Highlanders in Glengarry bonnets and flak jackets.

Norah Murphy leaned against the railing, clutching her case in both hands. "Occupied Belfast, Major. How do you like it?"

"I've seen worse," I said.

Two men came around the corner in a hurry, one of them bumping into Binnie, who fended him off angrily. "Would you look where you're going, now?" he demanded, holding the man by the arm.

He was not much older than Binnie, with a thin, narrow-jawed face and wild eyes. He wore an old trilby hat and carried an attaché case in his right hand; he tried to pull away.

His companion was a different proposition altogether, a tall, heavily built man in a raincoat and cloth cap. He was at least forty and had a craggy, pugnacious face. "Leave him be," he snarled, pulling Binnie round by the shoulder, and then his mouth gaped. "Jesus, Binnie, you couldn't have picked a worse spot. Get the hell out of it."

He pulled at his companion, they turned and hurried across the square through the traffic.

"Trouble?" Norah Murphy demanded.

Binnie grabbed her by the arm and nodded. "The big fella's Gerry Lucas. I don't know the other. They're Brady's."

That was the Belfast nickname for members of the Provisional branch of the I.R.A.—enough to make anyone move fast. We were already too late. A couple of cars had halted at the pedestrian crossing, and a woman in a head scarf was halfway across pushing a pram in front of her, a little girl of five or six trotting beside her. A young couple shared an umbrella behind.

Lucas and his friend reached the opposite pavement and paused behind a parked car. Lucas produced a Schmeisser machine pistol from beneath his raincoat and sprayed the machine-gun post.

In the same moment, his friend ran out into the open and tossed the attaché case in an arc through the rain and muffed things disastrously, for instead of dropping inside the machine-gun post, the case bounced from the sandbags to the gutter.

The two of them ran like hell for the shelter of the nearest side street and made it, the Highlanders being unable to open up with their machine gun for the simple reason that the square was suddenly filled with panic-stricken people running everywhere.

The case exploded a split second later, taking out half of the front of the machine-gun post, dissolving every window in the square in a snowstorm of flying glass.

People were running, screaming, some on their hands and knees, faces streaming with blood, cut by the flying glass. One of the cars at the pedestrian crossing had been blown onto its side; the crossing itself had been swept clean.

256

Norah Murphy ran out into the square in what I believe was a purely reflex action, and Binnie and I followed her toward the overturned car. A man was trying to climb out through the shattered side window, his face streaked with blood. I hauled him through, and he slipped to the ground and rolled over on his back.

The woman who had been pushing the pram was sprawled across the hood of another car, half the clothes torn off her. From the condition of the rest of her, she couldn't be anything else but dead. The young couple who had been behind her were in the gutter on the far side of the road, people clustering around.

The pram, miraculously, was intact, lying against the wall, but when I righted it, the condition of the baby still strapped inside was beyond description. The only good thing one could say was that death must have been instantaneous.

Norah Murphy was on her knees in the gutter beside the little girl who only a few moments before had gaily trotted beside her sister's pram. She was badly injured, smeared with blood and dust, but still alive.

Norah opened her case and took out a hypodermic. As troops emerged cautiously from the police station she gave the child an injection and said calmly, "Get out of it, Binnie, before they cordon off the whole area. Get to Kelly's if you can. Take the Major with you. He's too valuable to lose now. I'll see you there later."

Binnie gazed down at the child, those dark eyes blazing, and then he did a strange thing. He reached for one of the limp hands and held it tightly for a moment.

"The bastards," he said softly.

A Saracen swept into the square on the far side and braked to a halt effectively blocking the street.

"Will you get out of it, Binnie!" she said.

I jerked him to his feet. He stood looking down for a moment, not at her, but at the child, then turned and moved across the square away from the Saracen without a word. I went after him quickly, and he turned into a narrow alley and started to run. I followed at his heels, and we twisted and turned through a dark warren of mean streets, the sounds from the square growing fainter although never actually fading away altogether.

We finally came to the banks of a narrow canal of some description, moved along the towpath past an old iron footbridge and turned into a narrow alley. There was a high wooden gate at the end with a lamp bracketed to the wall above it. A faded sign read *Kelly's for Scrap.* Binnie opened the gate and I followed him through.

There was a small yard inside and another lamp high on the wall of the house giving plenty of illumination, which made sense for all sorts of reasons if this was a place of refuge as I suspected.

Binnie knocked on the back door. After a while, steps approached and he said in a low voice, "It's me, Binnie."

A bolt was withdrawn, the door opened. An old woman stood revealed, very old, with milk-white blind eyes and a shawl across her shoulders.

"It's me, Mrs. Kelly," Binnie said. "With a friend."

She reached for his face, cupped it in her hands for a moment, then smiled without a word, turned, and led the way inside.

When she opened the door at the end of the passage into the kitchen, Lucas and the bombthrower were standing shoulder to shoulder on the other side of the table, Lucas holding the Schmeisser at the ready, his friend clutching an old .45 Webley revolver that looked too big for him.

"Well would you look at this now?" Binnie said. "Rats will find a hole, so they say." He spat on the floor. "You did a fine job on the women and children back there."

The youth with the Webley turned wildly. "I told you," he said and Lucas struck him across the mouth, his eyes never leaving Binnie.

"Shut your mouth, Riley. And you just watch it, Binnie, or you might get some of the same. Who's your friend?"

"None of your affair."

"And what if I decide to make it mine?"

"Don't mind me," I put in.

For the first time Lucas lost some of that iron composure of his. He stared at me in astonishment. "A bloody Englishman, is it?"

"Or as much an Irishman as de Valera," I said. "It depends on your point of view."

"He's here on business for the Small Man," Binnie said. "For Cork himself, so keep your nose out of it."

They confronted each other for another tense moment. Then the old lady slipped in between them without a word and placed a pot of tea in the center of the table. Lucas turned away angrily, and I sat down against the wall and lit a cigarette. I offered Binnie one, but he refused. The old lady brought us a cup of tea each, then moved to the others.

"She doesn't have much to say for herself," I observed.

"She wouldn't," Binnie replied, "being dumb as well as blind."

He stared into space, something close to pain in his eyes, thinking of that child whose hand he had held, I suspect.

I said, "Remember what you were saying about my uncle coming out of the schoolhouse so the children wouldn't be harmed, to shoot it out with the Tans like a man?"

He turned to me with a frown. "So what?"

I said gently, "Times have changed, haven't they, Binnie?"

He stood up, walked over to the other side of the room, and sat down with his back to me.

I suppose it must have been all of two hours before there was a knock at the door. They each had a gun out on the instant, including Binnie, and waited while the old lady went to the door. Norah Murphy came into the kitchen. She paused, her eyes narrowing as she recognized Lucas; then she placed her case on the table.

"I'd love a cup of tea, Ma," she said in Irish as Mrs. Kelly followed her in.

She was as crisp and incisive as she had been at our first meeting. It was as if nothing at all had happened in between, and yet the skirts of her trench coat were stained with blood. I wondered if anything would ever really touch her.

Binnie said, "What happened?"

"I helped out till the ambulances arrived."

"How many were killed?" Lucas demanded.

"Five," she said, and turned to me. "I'll have that cigarette now, Major."

"And soldiers?" Young Riley leaned on the table with both hands, his eyes wilder than ever. "How many soldiers?"

Norah Murphy turned from the match I held for her and blew out a long column of smoke.

"And who might you be?" she inquired.

"Dennis Riley, m'am," he said in a low voice.

"Well then, Dennis Riley, you really will have to put in some practice before your next free show. The score this time was a mother and her two children and a couple of eighteen-year-olds who'd just got engaged. No soldiers, I'm afraid."

Riley collapsed into a chair and Binnie said quietly, "The little girl—she died then?"

"I'm afraid so."

He turned to Lucas and Riley and the look on his face was the same look I had seen in the pub earlier when he had confronted the hooligans.

"Women and kids now, is it?" He kicked the table over; the Browning was in his hand by a kind of magic. "You bloody bastards, here's for the two of you."

Norah Murphy had his arm up as he fired, a bullet ploughing through the ceiling. She slapped him across the cheek. He turned, a strange, dazed look on his face, and she grabbed him by the shoulders and shook him as one might shake a recalcitrant child.

"What's done is done, Binnie. Quarreling like this among ourselves won't help now."

Lucas stood with his back against the wall, the Schmeisser

260

ready, no more than a hairsbreadth away from cutting loose with it. Riley scrabbled on the floor at his feet for the Webley which he had lost when the table went over.

"Better to move on from here," Norah Murphy said. "All of us, and the sooner the better. Someone might have heard that shot." She turned to Mrs. Kelly. "I'm sorry, Ma."

The old woman smiled and touched her face. I said, "How are we going to work it?"

She shrugged. "We'll have to split up, naturally. Better to take your chances on your own, Major. Did you notice a foot-bridge over the canal on your way here?"

"I did."

"Cross over, take the towpath for a couple of hundred yards and a narrow passageway brings you into Delph Lane. Half a mile along that and you'll be in the center of the city."

"Why in the hell should he go first?" Lucas demanded.

She totally ignored him and said to Binnie, "We ought to leave separately. It would be the sensible thing."

"And how would I explain the loss of his niece to Michael Cork if anything happened to you?"

Which was an interesting disclosure. She actually smiled for him, then turned to me. "Off you go, then, Major."

The old woman went out ahead of me. I turned in the door-way. "Up the Republic!" I said. "Right up!" Then I closed the door gently and moved along the passage.

Mrs. Kelly had the door open. Beyond it, in the yard, rain fell in a silver curtain through the lamplight.

I turned up my collar. "Thanks for everything."

She had a strangely uncertain look, a slight frown on her face, as if there was something here she did not understand. The milk-white eyes stared past me vacantly and her fingers reached to touch my cheeks, to trace the line of my mouth.

And they found what they were searching for, those fingers, and fear blossomed on her face, the kind that a child might feel standing at the top of the stairs, aware of some nameless horror, some presence in the darkness below.

I said gently in Irish, "This is not on you, old woman. None of it."

She pushed me out into the rain and closed the door.

I found a dark corner of shadows near the footbridge with some bushes reaching over the wall above to give me some sort of shelter. I couldn't smoke. The smell would have been too distinctive on the damp air, so I waited as I had waited in other places than this. Different lands, hotter climates, but always the same situation.

There was the sound of cautious footsteps, and a moment later, two figures emerged from the alley. Binnie and Norah. I saw them clearly in the light of the lamp as they went up the steps to the bridge. Their footsteps boomed hollowly for a moment, then faded as they passed along the other side.

I returned to my waiting. Strange the tricks memory plays. The heavy rain, I suppose, reminding me of the monsoon. Borneo, Kota Baru, the ruins of the village, the stench of burning flesh, acrid smoke heavy on the rain, the dead school children. They, too, had been butchered for a cause, just like the little girl and her sister in the square tonight. The same story in so many places.

A stone rattled in the alleyway and they emerged a moment later. Lucas was well out in front. He stood under the lamp, then went up the steps to the footbridge alone, probably to test the ground.

Riley paused in the shadows and waited no more than a couple of yards away from me. I took him from behind with the simplest of headlocks, snapping his neck so quickly that he had no chance to make even the slightest cry.

I lowered him gently to the ground, found the Webley in his coat pocket, picked up his old trilby, and pulled it on. Then I moved toward the bridge.

Lucas was halfway across. "Will you get your bloody finger out, Dennis," he called softly.

I went up the steps head down, so that it was only at the last moment that instinct told him something was wrong and he swung to face me.

I said, "You're a big man with women and kids, Lucas. How do you feel now?"

He was trying to get the Schmeisser out from underneath his coat when I shot him in the right shoulder, the heavy bullet turning him around in a circle. The other two shots shattered his spine, driving him across the handrail of the bridge to hang, head down.

His raincoat started to smolder; there was a tiny tongue of flame. I leaned down, got him by the ankles with one hand, and tipped him over. Then I tossed the Webley and the trilby after him and continued across the bridge.

5

Storm Warning

Most of Oban seemed to be enveloped in a damp, clinging mist when I went out on deck, and there was rain on the wind which was hardly surprising for it had been threatening ever since my arrival two days previously.

Beyond Kercera the waters of the Firth of Lorn, when one could see them at all, seemed reasonably troubled and things generally looked as if they might get worse before they got better. Hardly the most comforting of thoughts with the prospect of the kind of passage by night I had in front of me.

For the moment, I was snug enough, anchored fifty yards from the main jetty in the inner harbor. I made a quick check to make certain that all my lines were secure and was just about to go below when a taxi pulled up on the jetty and Meyer got out.

He didn't bother to wave. Simply descended a flight of stone steps to the water's edge and stood waiting, so I dropped over the side into the rubber dinghy, started the outboard motor, and went to get him.

He looked distinctly out of place in his black Homburg and old Burberry raincoat, a parcel under one arm, a briefcase in his other hand, and obviously he felt it.

264

"Is it safe, this thing?" he demanded, peering anxiously through his spectacles at the dinghy.

"As houses," I said, taking the briefcase he passed to me.

He hung on to the parcel, stepped gingerly into the dinghy, and sat down in the prow. As we moved toward the motor cruiser, he turned to have a look at her.

"Are you satisfied?"

"Couldn't be better."

"The *Kathleen*, isn't that what they call her? I must say she doesn't look much."

"Which is exactly why I chose her," I said.

We bumped against the hull, I went up the short ladder and over the rail with the line. As I turned to help Meyer a curtain of rain drifted across the harbor. He darted for the shelter of the companionway and I followed him down to the saloon.

"What about some breakfast?" I said, as he took off his coat and hat.

"Breakfast?" He looked at me blankly. "But it's almost noon."

"So I got up late." I shrugged. "All right, tea then."

I went into the galley, and as I put on the kettle, Al Bowlly broke into "It's All Forgotten Now." When I went back into the saloon, Meyer was sitting at the table lighting one of the fat Dutch cigars he favored, the little cassette tape recorder in front of him.

"When are our friends due?"

I glanced at my watch. "About an hour. You're late. What kept you?"

"The Brigadier came to see me before I left so I had to get a later plane."

"What did he want?"

"A final briefing, that's all. He's flying to Northern Ireland himself this afternoon to be on hand in case he's needed."

The kettle started to whistle in the galley so I went in to make the tea. Meyer followed and leaned in the doorway, watching me.

"Perhaps I'm tired or maybe it's just that I'm getting old and

265

I didn't sleep so good last night and that's always a bad sign with me."

I poured milk and tea into two enamel mugs, topped them up with a largish measure of Jameson, and handed him one. "What are you trying to say, Meyer?"

"I don't feel so good about this, Simon."

"Like you said, you're tired, that's all."

He shook his head violently. "You know me. I get an instinct for these things and I'm never wrong. The first time I felt like this was when I was seventeen years of age, back in 1938."

"I know," I said. "You've told me often enough. You got out of Munich half an hour before the Gestapo came to arrest you. Your uncle and aunt wouldn't listen and died in Dachau."

He made a violent gesture, tea slopping out of his mug. "Don't mock me, Simon. What about that time in Casablanca? If you hadn't listened to me then and left on the next plane, they'd have arrested both of us."

"All right, so you've got second sight." I moved past him into the saloon. "Have you tried telling the Brigadier you don't feel so good about things?"

He shrugged helplessly and sat down at the table opposite me, "How do we get into such situations, Simon? It's crazy."

"Because we didn't have any choice," I said. "It's as simple as that. Did you bring what I asked?"

"In the parcel." I started to unwrap it and he added, "Where's the cargo?"

"The Lahtis are in the aft cabin. You're sitting on the Uzis."

I removed the last of the brown paper and opened the flat cardboard box it contained. Inside were several pounds of what looked like children's Plasticine, but was in fact a new and rather effective plastic explosive called ARI 7. There was a box of chemical fuses to go with it. There was also a cloth bundle tied with a string which, when I opened it, contained several clips of ammunition, and a Mauser automatic pistol with a rather strange bulbous barrel.

"That damn thing's almost a museum piece," Meyer observed as I hefted it on one hand. "You've no idea the trouble I had finding one."

"I know," I said. "But it's still the only really effective silenced hand gun ever made." I picked up the box and stood. "Let's go up top. I want to show you something."

It was raining harder than ever when we went out on deck. I led the way into the wheelhouse, put the box down on the chart table, reached underneath, and pressed a spring catch. A flap fell down which held an Mk IIS. There were several other spring clips and a shelf behind.

"A slight improvement," I said. "This is what kept me up so late last night."

I put the ARI 7 on the back shelf with the fuses and spare ammunition clips, loaded the Mauser and fitted it into place, then pushed the flap up out of sight.

"Very neat," Meyer observed.

"Nothing like being prepared."

He glanced at his watch. "I'll have to be away soon. I've got a hired car laid on by a local garage. They're going to run me down to Prestwich. I'll catch the evening plane to Belfast from there."

"Then what?"

He shrugged. "I'll get straight to the house I've rented and wait to hear from you."

"You'd better show me where it is."

I got out the right map for him and he found it soon enough. "Here we are. About ten miles out of Stramore on this road. Randall Cottage. It's right at the end of a farm track beside a small wood. A bit tumbledown, but rather nice. The sort of place they rent to holiday-makers in the season. Here's the telephone number."

It was easy enough to remember. I rolled the slip of paper into a ball and flipped it out through the side window. "What did you tell the agent?"

"I said I was a writer. Belfast was beginning to get me down and I felt in urgent need of a little peace and quiet. I used the name Berger, by the way, just in case."

I nodded. "It all sounds pretty neat to me."

He looked out across the Firth a trifle dubiously as rain drummed against the roof of the cabin with renewed vigor. "Do you really think you'll get across tonight? It doesn't look too good."

"According to the forecast, things should ease up considerably during the early evening and even if they don't, we'll still make it. This boat was built to stand most things."

There was a sudden hail across the water. "*Kathleen*, ahoy!"

Norah Murphy and Binnie Gallagher were standing on the jetty beside a taxi.

Meyer said, "Take me across with you and I'll be on my way. I don't want to talk to her any more than I can help."

He went below to get his hat and coat, and when he returned, he stowed Al Bowlly away in his briefcase. I helped him over the rail, slipped the line, and joined him.

His face was very pale as I started the outboard. I said, "Look, it's going to be all right. I promise you."

"Is that so?" he demanded. "Then tell me why I feel like I'm lying in my grave listening to earth rattling against the lid of my coffin!"

I couldn't think of a single thing to say that would have done any good. In any case, we were already coming in to the steps at the bottom of the jetty.

I stayed to tie up the dinghy and Meyer went up ahead of me to where Norah Murphy and Binnie waited beside the taxi. The boy was dressed exactly as he had been on that rather memorable night in Belfast, but Norah Murphy herself was all togged up for yachting in a yellow oilskin. Underneath she wore a navy blue Guernsey sweater, slacks, and rubber boots.

Meyer turned to me as I arrived. "I'm just making my excuses to Dr. Murphy, Simon, but I really must get moving now or I'll miss my plane."

"I'll be seeing you soon," I said and shook hands.

He got into the taxi quickly. The driver passed a suitcase out to Binnie, then drove away.

Norah Murphy said coolly, "So here we are again, Major."

"So it would appear."

I led the way down the steps to the dinghy and Binnie followed with the case. He didn't look too happy, but he got in after a moment's hesitation and sat in the prow. Norah Murphy perched herself in the stern beside me.

As we pulled away she said casually, "It's going to be a dirty night. Is the boat up to it?"

"Have you done much sailing?"

"One of my aunts was married to a retired sea captain. They had a house near Cape Cod."

"Then you should have learned by now not to be taken in by top show. Take the *Kathleen*. Underneath that rather drab coat of gray paint there's a steel hull by Akerboon."

"Only the best." She looked suitably impressed. "How is she powered?"

"Penta petrol engine. Twin screws. She'll do about twenty-five knots at full stretch. Depth sounder, radar, automatic steering. She's got the lot."

I cut the motor and we coasted in. Norah Murphy took the line and went over the rail nimbly enough. Binnie was nothing like so agile, and from the look on his face it was obvious that he was going to have a bad night of it whatever happened.

He was like a fish out of water. In fact, I doubt if he had ever been on a boat, certainly not a small boat of that type, in his life before. When he took off that sinister black overcoat of his he looked younger than ever, and the clothes he wore didn't help. A stiff white collar a size too large for him, a knitted tie, and an ill-fitting double-breasted suit of clerical gray.

Norah Murphy opened one of the saloon cupboards to hang the coat up for him and found a Neoprene wet suit, flippers and mask, and an aqualung inside.

She turned, one eyebrow raised. "Don't tell me you still intend to go over the rail if the situation arises."

"I'll take you with me if I do, I promise."

She put the suitcase on the table, opened it, and took out Binnie's Browning automatic. She held it in her right hand for a moment, looking at me, eyes narrowed slightly, then tossed it to Binnie, who was sitting down on one of the bench seats.

"Damn you, Vaughan," she said rather petulantly. "I never know which way to take you. You smile all the time. It isn't natural."

"Well, you've got to admit the world's a funny old place, love," I said. "Definitely a laugh a minute."

I went into the galley, got the bottle of Jameson and three mugs. When I returned she was sitting on the opposite side of the table from Binnie smoking a cigarette.

"Whiskey?" I said. "It's all I've got, I'm afraid."

She nodded, but Binnie shook his head. Admittedly we were dancing about, for quite a groundswell was building up inside the harbor, and he already looked ghastly. God knows what it was going to do to him when we ventured into the open sea.

Norah Murphy said, "Where's the cargo?" I told her and she nodded. "What are we carrying?"

"Fifty Lahti anti-tank cannon and fifty submachine guns."

She sat up straight, frowning deeply. "What goes on here? I expected more. A great deal more."

"Impossible in a boat this size," I said. "Those Lahtis are seven feet long. Have a look in the aft cabin and see for yourself. It will take a couple of trips to get all your first order across."

She went into the aft cabin. After a while she came back and sat down, picking up her mug again.

"Another thing," I said. "If we're challenged, if this boat is searched, we don't stand a cat in hell's chance, you realize that. As I'm not one of those captains who relishes the idea of going down with the ship, I'd appreciate it if you'd make it clear to Billy the Kid, here, that we don't want any heroics."

Poor Binnie couldn't even manage a scowl. He got up suddenly and made for the companionway.

Norah Murphy said, "I'm afraid he isn't much of a sailor. What time do we leave?"

"I've decided to make it a little later than I'd intended. Five o'clock, or even six. Give this weather a chance to clear a little."

"You're the captain. What about your friend Meyer? Will we be seeing him again?"

"I should imagine so—when the right time comes."

Binnie stumbled down the companionway and clutched at the wall to keep his balance. I said, "Never mind, Binnie. They say Nelson was sick every time he went to sea. Still, I don't suppose that's much comfort. Your lot didn't have much time for him either, did they?"

He ignored me completely and disappeared into the aft cabin. I started for the companionway, and Norah Murphy moved around the table to block my way. She seemed genuinely angry.

"Were you born a thoroughgoing bastard, Vaughan, or do you just work at it?"

The boat rocked hard, throwing her against me, so I did the obvious thing and kissed her. It was hardly all systems go, but I'd known worse.

When I finally released her, she shrugged, that strangely cruel mouth of hers twisted scornfully. "Only fair, Major," she observed.

"Now who's being a bastard?" I said, and went up the companionway fast.

We left just before six that evening, and although the weather hadn't improved all that much, at least it hadn't got any worse. As I pressed the starter and the engines rattled into life, the wheelhouse door opened, a flurry of wind lifted the chart like a sail, and Norah Murphy came in.

She stood at my elbow peering into the gloom of evening. "What's the forecast?"

"Nothing to get worked up about. Three- to four-mile winds with rain squalls. A light sea fog in the Rathlin Island area just before dawn."

"That should be useful," she said. "Can I take the wheel?"

"Later. How's Binnie?"

"Flat on his back. I'd better go and make sure he's all right. I'll see you later."

The door closed behind her, and I took *Kathleen* out through the harbor entrance in a long sweeping curve into the Firth.

The masthead light started to swing rhythmically from side to side as the swell started to roll beneath us and spray scattered across the window. A couple of points to starboard I could see the outline of a steamer against the slate gray evening sky, and her red and green navigation lights were clearly visible.

I reduced speed to twelve knots and we plunged forward into the gathering darkness, the sound of the engines a muted throbbing on the night air.

It must have been close to eleven o'clock when she returned. The door opened softly and she came in with a tray. I could smell the coffee and something more, the delicious scent of fried bacon.

"I'm sorry, Vaughan," she said. "I fell asleep. I've brought you some coffee and a bacon sandwich. Where are we?"

"Well on the way," I said. "There's Islay over there to the east of us. You can see a light occasionally between rain squalls."

"I'll spell you if you like."

"No need. I can put her on automatic pilot."

I checked the course, altered it a point to starboard, then locked the steering. When I turned and reached for my sandwich I found her watching me, a slight frown on her face.

"You know, I can't figure you, Vaughan. Not for one single minute."

"In what way?"

She lit a cigarette and turned to peer out into the darkness. "Oh, the Beast of Selangor bit."

"My finest hour," I said. "Believe me, MGM couldn't have improved on the part."

And I had made her angry again. "For God's sake, can't you ever be serious?"

"All right, keep your shirt on. What do you want to know? The gory details?"

"Only if it's the truth, no matter how unpleasant."

"And what's that?" I demanded and found that for no accountable reason, my throat had gone dry. I swallowed some of the coffee quickly, burning my mouth, and put the mug down on the chart table. "All right, you asked for it."

I sat down on the swivel chair, unlocked the automatic steering mechanism, and took the wheel again.

"There was an area in Borneo around Kota Baru that was absolutely controlled by terrorists back in 1963. Most of them were Chinese Communist infiltrators, not locals. They terrorized the whole area. Burned villages wholesale, coerced the Dyaks into helping them by butchering every second man and woman in some of the villages they took, just to encourage the others."

"And they put you in to do something about it?"

"I was supposed to be an expert on that kind of thing, so they gave me command of a company of irregulars, Dyak scouts, and told me to clean out the stable and not come back till I'd done it."

"A direct order?"

"Not on paper—not in those terms. We didn't have much luck at first. They burned two or three more villages, in one case after herding over fifty men, women, and children into a long-house beforehand. Finally, they burned the mission at Kota Baru, raped and murdered four nuns and eighteen young girls. That was it as far as I was concerned."

"What did you do?"

"Got lucky. An informer tipped me off that a Chinese merchant in Selangor named Hui Li was a Communist agent. I arrested him, and when he refused to talk, I handed him over to the Dyaks."

There was no horror on her face, and her voice was quite calm as she said, "To torture him?"

"Dyaks can be very persuasive. He only lasted a couple of hours, then he told me where the group I'd been chasing were holed up."

"And did you get them?"

"Eventually. They'd split into two, which didn't help, but we managed it."

"They said you shot your prisoners?"

"Only during the final pursuit, when I was hard on the heels of the second group. Prisoners would have delayed me."

"I see." She nodded with a kind of clinical detachment. "And Mr. Hui Li?"

"Shot trying to escape."

"You expect me to believe that?"

I laughed and without the slightest bitterness. "Absolutely true, and that's the most ironic part of it. I was quite prepared to take him down to the coast and let him stand trial, but he tried to make a break for it the night before we left."

There was silence for a while. I opened a window and took a deep breath of fresh sea air.

"Look, what I did to him he would have done to me. The purpose of terrorism is to terrorize, a favorite tag of Michael Collins, but Lenin said it first and it's on page one of every Communist handbook on revolutionary warfare. You can only fight that kind of fire with fire."

"You ruined yourself." There was a strange, savage, concerned note in her voice. "You fool, you threw everything away. Career, reputation, everything, and for what?"

"I did what had to be done," I said. "Malaya, Kenya, Cyprus, Aden. I'd seen it all and I was tired of people justifying the murder of the innocent by pleading that it was all in the name of the revolution. When I finished, there was no more terror by night in Kota Baru. No more butchering of little girls. That should count for something, God knows."

I was surprised at the feeling in my voice, the way my hands were shaking. I stood up and pulled her forward roughly. "You wanted to take the wheel. It's all yours. Stay on this course and wake me in three hours. Before, if the weather changes."

She grabbed my sleeve. "I'm sorry, Vaughan, I really am."

"You live long enough, you get over anything," I said. "I've learned that."

Or so I told myself as I went below. Perhaps if I repeated it often enough, I might really come to believe it.

I slept on one of the saloon bench seats, and when I awakened, it was almost three o'clock. Binnie was snoring steadily in the aft cabin. I peered in and found him flat on his back, collar and tie undone, mouth open. I left him to it and went up the companionway.

There was quite a sea, and cold spray stung my face as I moved along the heaving deck and opened the wheelhouse door. Norah Murphy was standing at the wheel, her face disembodied in the compass light.

"How are things going?" I asked.

"Fine. There's been a sea running for about half an hour now."

I glanced out. "Likely to get worse before it gets better. I'll take over."

She made way for me, her body brushing mine as we squeezed past each other. "I don't think I could sleep now if I wanted to."

"All right," I said. "Make some more tea and come back. Things might get interesting. And check the forecast on the radio."

I increased speed, racing the heavy weather that threatened from the east, and the waves grew rougher, rocking *Kathleen* from side to side. Visibility was rotten, utter darkness on every hand except for a slight phosphorescence from the sea. Norah Murphy seemed to be taking her time, but when she returned, she brought more bacon sandwiches as well as the tea.

"The forecast wasn't too bad," she said. "Wind moderating, intermittent rain squalls."

"Anything else?"

"Some fog patches toward dawn, but nothing to worry about."

I helped myself to a sandwich. "How's the boy wonder?"

She didn't like that, I could see, but she kept her temper and handed me a mug. "He's sitting up now in the saloon. I gave him tea with something in it. He'll be all right."

"Let's hope so. He could be needed."

She said, "Let me tell you about Binnie Gallagher, Major Vaughan. During the rioting that broke out in Belfast in August 1969, an Orange mob led by B-Specials would have burned the Falls Road to the ground, chased out every Catholic family who lived there—or worse. They were prevented by a handful of I.R.A. men who took to the streets led by Michael Cork himself."

"The Small Man again? And Binnie was one of that lot?"

"Don't tell me you're actually impressed?"

"Oh, but I am," I said. "They did a hell of a good job that night, those men. A great ploy, as my mother would have said. And Binnie was one of them? He must have been all of sixteen."

"He was staying with an aunt in the area. She gave him an old revolver, a war souvenir of her dead husband's, and Binnie went in search of the Small Man. Fought at his right hand during the whole of that terrible night. He's been his shadow ever since. His most trusted aide."

"Which explains why he guards the great man's niece." She lit a couple of cigarettes and passed one to me. I said, "How does an American come to be mixed up in all this anyway?"

"It's simple enough. My father spent around seventeen years in one kind of British prison or another, if you add up all his sentences. I was thirteen when he was finally released and we emigrated to the States to join my Uncle Michael. A new life, so we thought, but too late for my father. He was a sick man when they released him. He died three years later."

"And you never forgave them?"

"They might as well have hanged him."

"And you decided you ought to take up where he left off?"

"We have a right to be free," she said. "The people of Ulster have been denied their nationhood too long."

It sounded like the first two sentences of some ill-written political pamphlet and probably was.

I said, "Look, what happened in August '69 was a bad business, which was exactly why the Army was brought in—to protect the Catholic minority while the necessary political changes were put in hand. And it was working until the I.R.A. got up to their old tricks again."

"I wonder what your uncle would have thought if he could have heard you say that."

"The dear old Schoolmaster of Stradballa?" I said. "Binnie's particular hero? The saint who wouldn't see the children harmed at any price? He doesn't exist. He's a myth. No revolutionary leader could act like he was supposed to and survive."

"What are you trying to say?" she said.

"Among other things, that he had at least forty people executed, including several British officers, in reprisal for the execution of I.R.A. men, a pretty dubious action morally, I would have thought. On one particularly unsavory occasion, he was responsible for the shooting of a seventy-eight-year-old woman who was thought to have passed on information to the police."

In the light of the binnacle, her right fist was clenched so tightly that the knuckles gleamed white. "In revolutionary warfare, these things have to be done," she said. "There is no other choice."

"Have you tried telling Binnie that?" I said. "Or hadn't it occurred to you that that boy really believes with all his heart that it can be done with clean hands. I saw him at Ma Kelly's, remember. He'd have killed those two Provos himself if you hadn't stopped him, because he couldn't stomach what they'd done."

"Binnie is an idealist," she said. "There's nothing wrong in that. He'd lay down his life for Ireland without a second's hesitation."

"I'd have thought it more desirable all round if he'd lived for her," I said. "But then that's just my opinion."

"And why in the hell should he take any notice of that?" she demanded. "Who are you, anyway, Vaughan? A failure, a renegade who's willing to turn on his own side for the sake of a pound or two."

"That's me," I said. "Simon Vaughan, your friendly arms salesman."

I was smiling again although it was something of an effort and she couldn't stand that. "You arrogant bastard," she said angrily. "At least we'll have something to show for our struggles, people like Binnie and me."

"I know," I said. "A land of standing corpses."

She moved very close, a curious glitter in her eye and her voice was a sort of hoarse whisper. "Better that than what we had. I'd rather see the city of Belfast burn like a funeral pyre than go back to what we had."

And suddenly, for no sensible reason, I knew that I was close to the heart of things where she was concerned.

I said calmly, "And what was that, Norah? Tell me."

There was a vacant look on her face. The voice changed, became noticeably more Belfast than American; the lost-little-girl touch to it chilled my blood.

"When my father was released from jail that last time, he didn't want any more trouble, so he dropped out of sight till we were ready to leave for America. They came to our house looking for him several times."

"Who did?" I said.

"The B-Specials. One night while they were interrogating my mother, one of them took me out in the backyard. He said he believed there might be arms in the shed."

My stomach tightened as if to receive a blow. I said, "And were there?"

"I was thirteen," she said. "Remember that. He made me lie down on some old sacking. When he was finished, he told me there was no point in trying to tell anyone because I wouldn't be believed. And he made threats against my mother and the family. He said he wouldn't be responsible for what might happen. . . ."

There was a longish silence, the splutter of rain against the glass. She said, "You're the first person I've told, Vaughan. The only one. Not even a priest. Isn't that the strange thing?"

I said hoarsely, "I'm sorry."

"You're sorry?" And at that she exploded, broke apart at the seams. "By God, I'll see them in hell, Vaughan, every last one of them for what they did to me, do you understand?"

She stumbled outside; the door slammed. It occurred to me then, and not for the first time, that there were occasions when I despaired of humanity. And yet there was no sense of personal involvement, and any pity I felt was not so much for Norah Murphy as for that wretched, frightened little girl in the backyard of that house in Belfast so many years ago.

I lit a cigarette and, turning to flick the match through the open window on my left, found Binnie standing there as if turned to stone, the face contorted into a mask of agony, such suffering in the eyes as I never hope to see again.

I put a hand on his shoulder, which seemed to bring him back to life. He looked up at me in a strange daze, then turned and walked away along the deck.

We raised Rathlin Island just before four a.m., although I could only catch a glimpse of the lighthouse intermittently because of the bad visibility. From then on we were in enemy waters, so to speak, and I had both Norah Murphy and Binnie join me in the wheelhouse for a final briefing.

She seemed entirely recovered and so did he. I could not imagine for one moment that he had told her that he had overheard our conversation, or ever would, but in that bleak undertaker's coat of his, he certainly looked his old grim self again as he leaned over the chart.

279

I traced our course with a pencil. "Here we are. Another ten minutes and we round Crag Island and start the run-in to the coast. The channel through the reef is clearly marked and good deep water."

"Bloody Passage," Norah Murphy said. "Is that it?"

I nodded. "Apparently one of the biggest ships in the Spanish Armada went down there. According to old documents the bodies floated in for weeks." I glanced at my watch. "It's four twenty now and we're due in at five. First light's around six fifteen, which gives us plenty of time to get in and out. Let's hope your people are on time."

"They will be," she said.

"Once we're into the passage I'll have to kill the deck lights so I want both you and Binnie in the prow to look for the signal. A red light at two-second intervals on the minute or three blasts on a foghorn on the minute if visibility is really bad."

Which it was, there was no doubt about that as we crept in toward the shore, the engine throttled right back to the merest murmur. Not that it was particularly dangerous, even when I switched off the deck and masthead lights, for Bloody Passage was a good hundred yards across and there was little chance of coming to harm.

We were close now, very close, and I strained my eyes into the darkness, looking for that light, but it was hopeless in all that mist and rain. And then as I leaned out of the side window, a foghorn sounded three times in the distance.

Binnie appeared at the door. "Did you hear that, Major?"

I nodded and replied on our own foghorn with exactly the same signal. I told Binnie to return to the prow, throttled back, and coasted in gently. The foghorn sounded again, very close now, which surprised me, for by my reckoning we still had a good quarter of a mile to go.

I replied again as agreed. In the same moment, some strange instinct, the product, I suppose, of several years of rather hard living told me that something was very wrong indeed. Too late, of course, for a moment later, a searchlight picked us out of the darkness, there was a rumble of engines breaking into life, and an M.T.B. cut across our bow.

I was aware of the white ensign fluttering bravely in the dim light and then the sudden menacing chatter of a heavy machine gun above our heads.

As I ducked instinctively, she cut in again and an officer on the bridge called through a loud hailer, "I'm coming aboard. Heave to or I sink you."

Norah Murphy appeared in the doorway at the same moment. "What are we going to do?" she demanded.

"I should have thought that was obvious."

I cut the engines, switched on the deck lights, and lit a cigarette. Binnie had moved along the deck and was standing outside the open window.

I said, "Remember, boy, no heroics. Nothing to be gained."

As the M.T.B. came alongside, a couple of ratings jumped down to our deck, a line was thrown and quickly secured. The standard submachine gun in general use by the Royal Navy is the Sterling, so it was something of a surprise when a Petty Officer appeared at the rail above holding a Thompson gun ready for action, the 1921 model with the hundred-drum magazine. The officer appeared beside him, a big man in a standard reefer coat and peaked cap, a pair of night glasses slung about his neck.

Norah Murphy sucked in her breath sharply. "My God," she said. "Frank Barry."

It was a name I'd heard before and then I remembered. My cell on Skarthos and the Brigadier briefing me on the I.R.A. and its various splinter groups. Fanatical fringe elements who wanted to blow up everything in sight, and the worst of the lot were Frank Barry's Sons of Erin.

He leaned over the rail and grinned down at her. "In the flesh and twice as handsome. Good night to you, Norah Murphy."

Binnie made a sudden, convulsive movement and Barry said genially, "I wouldn't, Binnie, me old love. Tim Pat here would cut you in half."

One of the two ratings who had already boarded relieved Binnie of his Browning.

I leaned out of the window and said shortly, "Friends of yours, Binnie?"

"Friends?" he said bitterly. "Major, I wouldn't cut that bloody lot down if they were hanging."

6

Bloody Passage

The man with the Thompson gun, the one dressed as a Petty Officer whom Barry had called Tim Pat, came over the rail to confront us. On closer inspection he proved to have only one eye, but otherwise bore a distinct resemblance to the great Victor McLaglen in one of those roles where he looks ready to clear the bar of some waterfront saloon on his own at any moment.

Barry dropped down beside him, a handsome, lean-faced man with one side of his mouth hooked into a slight, perpetual half-smile as if permanently amused by the world and its inhabitants.

"God save the good work, Norah." He took off his cap and turned a cheek toward her. "Have you got a kiss for me?"

Binnie swung a punch at him, which Barry blocked easily. Tim Pat got an arm about the boy's throat and squeezed.

"I've told you before, Norah," Barry said, shaking his head. "You should never use a boy when a man's work is needed."

I think she could have killed him then. Certainly she looked capable of it, eyes hot in that pale face of hers, but always there was that iron control. God knows what was needed to break her, but I doubted whether Barry was capable.

He shrugged and lit a cigarette, turning to me as he flicked the match over the rail. "Now you, Major," he said, "look like a sensible man to me."

"And where exactly does that get us?"

"To you telling me where you've got the stuff stowed away. We'll find it in the end, but I'd rather it was sooner than later and Tim Pat here's the terrible impatient one if he's kept waiting."

Which seemed more than likely from the look of him, so I volunteered the necessary information.

"That's what I like about the English," he said. "You're always so bloody reasonable." He nodded to Tim Pat. "Put them in the aft cabin for the time being, and let's get moving. I want that gear transferred and us out of it in fifteen minutes at the outside."

He snapped his fingers and another half a dozen men, all in British naval uniform, came over the rail, but by then Tim Pat was already herding us toward the companionway. He took us below, shoved us into the big aft cabin, and locked us in.

I stood at the door listening to the bustle in the saloon, then turned to face my companions. "And who might this little lot be?"

"The walking ape is Tim Pat Keogh," Binnie said violently, "and one of these days . . ."

"Cool it, Binnie," Norah Murphy cut in on him sharply. "That kind of talk isn't going to help one little bit." She turned back to me. "The boss man is Frank Barry. He was my uncle's right-hand man until six or seven months ago, then he decided to go his own way."

"What is he—a Provo?"

She shook her head. "No, he runs his own show. The Sons of Erin, they call themselves. I believe there was a revolutionary organization under that name in Fenian times."

"He seems to be remarkably well informed," I said. "What else do he and his men get up to besides this kind of thing?"

"They'd shoot the Pope if they thought it was necessary," Binnie said.

I glanced at Norah Murphy in some surprise, and she shrugged. "And they're all good Catholic boys except for Barry himself. Remember the Stern gang in Palestine? Well, the Sons of Erin are exactly the same. They believe in the purity of violence if the cause is just."

"So anything goes? The bomb in the café? Women, kids, the lot?"

"That's the general idea."

"Well, it's a point of view, I suppose."

"Not in my book, it isn't," Binnie said quietly. "There's got to be another way—has to be or there's no point to any of it."

Which was the kind of remark that had roughly the same effect on one as being hit by a very light truck. The Brigadier had once accused me of being the last of the romantics, but I wasn't even in the running for that title with Binnie around.

The door opened and Frank Barry appeared, a bottle of my Jameson in one hand, four tin mugs from the galley hanging from his fingers. Behind him, they were passing the Lahtis out of the other cabin and up the companionway.

"By God, Major Vaughan, but you deal in good stuff and I don't just mean your whiskey," he said. "Those Lahtis are the meanest looking things I've seen in many a long day. I can't wait to try one out on a Weasel armored car."

"We aim to please," I said. "The motto of the firm."

"I only hope you've had your money."

He splashed whiskey into all four mugs. Norah and Binnie stood firm, but it seemed to me likely to be cold where I was going so I emptied one at a swallow and helped myself to another.

"The Small Man won't be pleased by this night's work," Barry said to Norah.

"At a guess I'd say he'll have your hide and nail it to the door."

"Chance would be a fine thing."

He toasted her, mug raised, that slight mocking smile hooked firmly into place, an immensely likable human being in every way, or so he appeared at that first meeting, and it seemed to

285

me more than a probability that he would be the end of me in the near future if I did not get to him first.

Tim Pat appeared in the doorway behind him. "We're ready to go, Frank."

Barry drained his mug, then turned casually without another word to us. "Bring them up," he said, and went out.

Norah followed him and I paused long enough to let Binnie go in front of me. As we went up the companionway I stumbled against him as if losing my footing and muttered quickly, "We'll only get one chance, if that, so be ready."

He didn't even glance over his shoulder as he moved out on deck. Tim Pat gave me a shove after him. Barry was standing by the rail, lighting another cigarette with some difficulty because of the heavy rain.

He nodded to Tim Pat. "Get Norah on board. We haven't much time."

She rushed forward as if to argue and Tim Pat handed his Thompson to one of the other men, grabbed her by the waist, and lifted her bodily over the rail of the M.T.B. Then he climbed up to join her.

Binnie and I stood waiting for sentence in the heavy rain. Only Barry and the two original ratings who had first boarded us were left now, one of them holding the Thompson.

"Now what?" I said.

Barry shrugged. "That depends." He turned to Binnie. "I could use you, boy. You're still the best natural shot with a hand gun I ever did see."

Binnie's hair was plastered to his forehead and he looked very young. He said quietly, but so clearly that everyone on the M.T.B. must have heard it, "I wouldn't sit on your deathbed."

Barry didn't stop smiling for a moment. Simply shrugged. "All right, Major, get back in the wheelhouse, start her up, and move out to sea again. We'll follow, and when I give the signal, you'll cut your engines and open the sea cocks."

He clambered up over the M.T.B.'s rail. One of the ratings

rammed a Browning into my side. I took the hint and moved along the deck into the wheelhouse.

The M.T.B.'s powerful engines rumbled into life. The Browning dug pointedly into my ribs again, and I pressed the starter button and looked out of the side window. Barry was walking across the deck to the short ladder which led up to the bridge. Norah ran after him and grabbed him by the arm.

I heard her cry, "No, you shan't. I won't let you."

He had her by both arms now and laughed softly as she started to struggle. "By God, Norah, but you have your nerve. All right, just to please you." He turned to Tim Pat Keogh. "I've changed my mind about Binnie. Pipe him on board."

I leaned out of the window. "And what about me, then?"

He paused halfway up the ladder and turned to smile at me. "Why damn me, Major, but I just took it for granted that the sum total of any real captain's ambition was to go down with his ship."

"We definitely operate on the same wavelength. That's exactly what I thought you'd say," I called, and added cheerfully, "The big moment, Binnie."

I put my left hand on the wheel; my right went under the chart table, found my secret button, and pressed. The flap fell, and I had the Mauser and shot my guard through the head at point-blank range, all in one continuous movement.

The silencer was really very effective, the only noise a dull thud audible at a range of three yards. The other guard was in the process of urging Binnie toward the rail, prodding him with the barrel of the Thompson.

I called softly, "Binnie!" and shot the man in the back of the head. He went down like a stone falling.

In an instant, as if by magic, Binnie had the Thompson in his hands, and was already firing as he turned. He caught the man who was standing by Norah Murphy with a long burst that drove him right back across the deck of the M.T.B. and over the far rail.

Then he went for Barry, who was still pulling hard for the top of the ladder. There was a flash of yellow oilskins on the far side of the rail. Binnie stopped firing as Norah Murphy ran crouching, then scrambled over.

When she reached the safety of our decks, he started to fire again, but by then Barry was over the top of the ladder and into the safety of the wheelhouse. A moment later, the engine note deepened at full throttle, and the M.T.B. surged away into the darkness.

A burst of submachine gun fire came our way, and I ducked as one of the side windows in the wheelhouse shattered. Binnie kept on firing until the Thompson jammed. He tossed it to the deck with a curse and stood listening, in the sudden silence, to the sound of the M.T.B.'s engines fade into the distance.

I replaced the Mauser in its clip, shoved the flap back into place, and went out on deck. Norah Murphy crouched by the rail on one knee, her face buried against her arm. I touched her gently on the shoulder and she looked up at me, a great weariness in her eyes.

"You had a gun?"

I nodded.

"But I don't understand. I thought they searched."

"They did." I pulled her to her feet.

Binnie said, "By God, but you're the close one, Major, and I didn't hear a damn thing."

"You wouldn't."

"I'd have had them if the Thompson hadn't jammed."

He kicked it toward me, and I picked it up and tossed it over the rail. "A bad habit they had, the early ones. Now let's get rid of the evidence." I turned to Norah Murphy. "Pump some water up and get the deck swabbed down. Make sure you clean off any bloodstains."

"My God," she said, a kind of horror on her face. "You must be the great original cold-blooded bastard of all time."

"That's me," I said. "And don't forget the broken glass in the wheelhouse. You'll find a broom in the galley."

Whatever she felt, she turned after that. Binnie and I dealt with the two guards, stripping their bodies of any obvious identification before putting them over the rail. Then I went back to the wheelhouse and examined the chart quickly.

Norah was sweeping the last of the glass out; she paused. "Now what?"

"We need a place to hole up in for a few hours," I told her. "Time to breathe again and work out the next move before we put in to Stramore." A moment later I found what I was looking for. "This looks like it. Small island called Magil, ten miles out. Uninhabited, and a nice secluded spot to anchor in. Horseshoe Bay."

Binnie was still at the rail at the spot where we had thrown the two bodies over. From where I stood it looked as if he was praying which didn't seem all that probable—or did it?

I leaned out of the window and called, "We're getting out of here."

He turned and nodded. I switched off the deck lights, took the *Kathleen* round in a tight circle, and headed out to sea again.

Magil was everything I could have hoped for, and Horseshoe Bay proved an excellent anchorage, being almost landlocked. It was still dark when we arrived, but dawn wasn't very far away, and in spite of the heavy rain there was a kind of pale luminosity to everything when I went out on deck.

When I went below, Binnie and Norah Murphy were sitting on either side of the saloon table, heads together.

"Secrets?" I said cheerfully. "From me? Now I call that very naughty."

I got the Jameson and a glass. Norah said harshly, "Don't you ever drink anything else? I've heard of starting early, but this is ridiculous. At least let me get you something to eat."

"Later," I said. "After I've had a good four hours' sleep you can wake me with another of those bacon sandwiches of yours."

I moved toward the aft cabin, and she said angrily, "For God's sake, Vaughan, cut out the funny stuff. We've got to decide what to do."

"What about?" I said, and poured myself a large Jameson, which for some reason—probably the time of day, as she had so kindly pointed out—tasted foul.

"The guns," she said, "what else? You are the most infuriating man I've ever met."

"All right," I said. "If you want to talk, let's talk, although I would have thought it simple enough. You'll want to get in touch with your Small Man to see about another consignment and I can assure you the price has gone up after last night's little fracas. The Royal Navy and ten years inside is one thing, but your friend Barry and his bloody Sons of Erin are quite another."

She glanced at me, white-faced. "How much?"

"A subject for discussion." I poured myself another drink. "On the other hand, maybe you don't have the funds."

"We have the funds," she said.

I tossed back the whiskey. Most of it, like the previous one, had actually gone down the leg of my left gumboot, and I tried to sound slightly tight when I laughed.

"I just bet you have." I poured another drink, spilling a little. "Maybe we'll ask for gold this time. Something solid to hang onto in this changing world of ours."

Binnie's hand went inside his coat, where the Browning once more safely nestled. Norah Murphy said fiercely, "What in the hell are you getting at?"

"Oh, come off it, angel," I said. "I know the Small Man was behind that bullion raid on the Glasgow mail boat. Word gets around. How much did he get away with? Half a million, or were they exaggerating?"

They both sat there staring at me, and I got to my feet. "Anyway, you go and see your uncle when we get in, and I'll have a word with Meyer. We'll sort something out, you'll see. Can I go to bed now?"

I moved toward the aft cabin, chuckling to myself. When I

reached the door I said, "You know, it really is very funny, whichever way you look at it. I'd love to see Frank Barry's face when he checks those submachine guns and the Lahtis and finds the firing pins are missing."

Her hands tightened on the edge of the table, and there was a look of incredulity on her face. "What are you talking about?" she whispered.

"Oh, didn't I tell you?" I said. "Meyer's got them. One of those little tricks of the trade we find useful, life being such a cruel hard business on occasion, especially in our game."

There was a look of unholy joy on Binnie's face, and he slammed a hand down hard across the table. "By Christ, Major Vaughan, but you're the man for me. For God's sake, take the oath and join us, and we'll have the entire thing under wraps in six months."

"Sorry, old lad," I said. "I don't take sides, not anymore. Ask the good doctor, she'll tell you."

And then Norah Murphy did the most incredible thing. She started to laugh helplessly, which was so unexpected that I closed the cabin door and actually poured myself a whiskey that I drank. Then I lay down on one of the bunks and, as is usual with the wicked and depraved of this world, was plunged at once into a deep and refreshing sleep.

7

When That Man
Is Dead and Gone

We came into Stramore just after noon. It was still raining, but the mist had cleared and according to the forecast brighter weather was on the way. It was little more than a village really, the sort of place which had lived off the fish for years and was now doing better out of weekend yachtsmen.

Expect for the side window missing in the wheelhouse and the odd chip where a bullet had splintered the woodwork, we showed little sign of the skirmish with Barry and his men. We anchored off the main jetty and used the dinghy to go ashore.

I arranged to meet Norah Murphy and Binnie in the local pub after I'd reported to the harbormaster—which was only an excuse, for I had something much more important to do.

I found a telephone box up a back street and dialed the number Meyer had given me. It was somehow surprising to hear the receiver picked up at the other end almost instantly, to hear the familiar voice, Al Bowlly belting out "Everything I Have Is Yours" in the background.

"Randall Cottage. Mr. Berger here."

"Mr. Berger?" I said. "You asked me to contact you the moment I got in about that consignment I was handling for you."

292

"Ah, yes," he said. "Everything all right?"

"I'm afraid not. Another carrier insisted on taking over the goods en route."

His voice didn't even flicker. "That is unfortunate. I think I'll have to contact my principal about this. Can you come to see me?"

"Anytime you say!"

"All right. Give me a couple of hours. I'll expect you around three thirty."

The receiver clicked into place, cutting Al Bowlly dead, and I left the phone box and moved back toward the waterfront. I wondered if he would have the Brigadier there by the time I arrived. It should prove an interesting meeting, or so I told myself as I turned the corner and walked toward the pub where I'd arranged to meet Norah and Binnie.

They were sitting in the snug by a roaring fire, a plate of meat sandwiches between them, pickles in a jar and two glasses of cold lager.

"And what am I supposed to do? Live off my fat?" I demanded as I sat down.

Norah reached for a small handbell and rang it. A pleasant-looking, middle-aged woman appeared a moment later with another plate of sandwiches.

"Was it the lager, sir, like the others?" she asked.

"That's it," I said.

She brought it and disappeared. "Satisfied?" Norah Murphy said.

"For the moment."

"And what did your friend Meyer have to say?" I tried to look puzzled, and she frowned in exasperation.

"Oh, be your age, Vaughan. It stood out a mile why you wanted to be alone. Did you think I was born yesterday?"

"Never that," I said, and held up my hands. "All right, I surrender."

"So when are you seeing him?" She frowned when I told her. "Why the delay?"

"I don't know. He's got things to do. It's only a couple of hours, after all, and we can reach him quickly enough. The place he's taken is no more than ten miles from here. What about your end of things?"

"Oh, that's all taken care of. I've been doing some telephoning, too." She glanced at her watch. "In fact, I'll have to get moving. I'm being picked up outside the schoolhouse in fifteen minutes by the local brigade commander. It was his people who were waiting for us on the beach last night. He wasn't too pleased."

"I can imagine. Will you be seeing your uncle?"

"I'm not sure. I don't know where he is at the moment, though I think they'll have arranged for me to speak to him on the phone."

I emptied my glass. Binnie picked it up without a word, went behind the bar, and got me another.

Norah Murphy put a cigarette in her mouth. As I gave her a light, the match flaring in my cupped hands, I said, "I'm surprised at you smoking those things, and you a doctor."

She seemed puzzled, a slight frown on her face, then glanced at the cigarette and laughed, that distinctive harsh laugh of hers. "Oh, what the hell, Vaughan, we'll all be dead soon enough."

In a sense, I had a moment of genuine insight there, saw deeper than I had seen before, but we were on dangerous ground and I had to go carefully.

I said, "What will you do when it's all over?"

"Over?" She stared at me blankly. "What in the hell are you talking about?"

"But you're going to win, aren't you, you and your friends? You must believe that or there wouldn't be any point to any of it. I simply wondered what you would do when it was all over and everything was back to normal."

She sat there staring at me, caught in some timeless moment like a fly in amber, unable to answer me for the simple and inescapable reason that there was only one answer.

294

I nodded slowly. "You remind me of that uncle of mine." Binnie put the pint of lager down on the table. "What was it they called him again, Binnie? The Schoolmaster of Stradballa?"

"That's it, Major."

I turned to Norah Murphy and said gently, but with considerable cruelty for all that, "He never wanted it to end, either. It was his whole life, you see. Trench coats and Thompson guns, action by night, a wonderful, violent game. He enjoyed it, Norah, if that's the right word. It was the only way he wanted to live his life—just like you."

She was white-faced, trembling, agony in her eyes, and she turned it all on me. "I fight for a cause, Major. I'll die for it if necessary, and proud to, like thousands before me." She placed both hands flat on the table and leaned toward me. "What did you ever believe in, Major Simon bloody Vaughan? What did you kill for?"

"You mean what was my excuse, don't you?" I nodded. "Oh, yes, doctor, we all need one of those."

She sat back in the chair, still trembling, and I said softly, "You'll be late for the pick-up. Better get going."

She took a deep breath as if to pull herself together, and stood up. "I want Binnie to go with you."

"Don't you trust me?"

"Not particularly, and I'd like the address and telephone number of this place where your friend Meyer is staying. I'll phone you at four o'clock. Whatever happens, don't leave till you hear from me." She turned to Binnie. "I'm counting on you to see that he does as he's told, Binnie."

He looked more troubled than I'd ever seen him, torn between the two of us, I suspect, for it had become more than obvious that the events of the previous night had considerably enlarged his respect for me. On the other hand, he loved Norah Murphy in his own pure way. She had been put into his charge by the Small Man; he would die, if necessary, to protect her. It was as simple or as complicated as that.

A great deal of this Norah Murphy saw, and her mouth

tightened. I wrote Meyer's address and phone number on a scrap of paper and gave it to her.

"Ask for Mr. Berger," I said. "If anything goes adrift, we'll meet back at the boat."

She said nothing. Simply glanced at the piece of paper briefly, dropped it into the fire, and walked out.

Binnie said, "When I was a kid on my Da's farm in Kerry I had the best-looking red setter you ever saw."

I tried some more lager. "Is that so?"

"There was a little flatcoat retriever bitch on the next place and whenever he went over there, she used to take lumps out of him. You've never seen the like." There was a heavy pause, and then he went on. "When he was run over by the milk lorry one morning, she lay in a corner, that little bitch, for a week or more. Would neither drink nor eat. Now wasn't that the strange thing?"

"Not at all," I said. "It's really quite simple. She was a woman. Now get the hell out of here with your homespun philosophy, and hire us a car at the local garage. I'll wait here for you."

"Leave it to me, Major," he said, his face expressionless, and went out.

The door closed with a soft whuff, wind lifted a paper off the bar, the fire flared up.

What was my reason for killing, that's what she had said. I tried to think of Kota Baru, of the burned-out mission, the stink of roasting flesh. It had seemed enough at the time—more than enough, but there was nothing real to it anymore. It was an echo from an ancient dream, something that had never happened.

And then it was quiet. So quiet that I could hear the clock ticking on the mantelpiece. For no logical reason whatsoever, my stomach tightened, fingers seemed to crawl across my skin; I suddenly knew exactly what Meyer meant by having a bad feeling.

There had been no car available at the town's only garage, but Binnie had managed to borrow an old Ford pickup truck from them, probably by invoking the name of the Organization, although I didn't inquire too closely into that.

He did the driving, and I sat back and smoked a cigarette and stared morosely into the driving rain. It was a pleasant enough ride. Green fields, high hedges, rolling farmland, with here and there gray stone walls that once had been the boundaries of the great estates, or still were.

He had picked up an ordnance survey map of the area, and I found Randall Cottage again. The track leading to it was perhaps a quarter of a mile long, and the place was entirely surrounded by trees. The right kind of hidey-hole for an old fox like Meyer.

I gave Binnie the sign when we were close and he started to slow. A car was parked on the grass verge at the side of the road a hundred yards from the turning, a large green Vauxhall estate with no one inside.

God knows why, that instinct again for bad news, I suppose, the product of having lived entirely the wrong sort of life, but something was wrong, I'd never been more certain of anything. I clapped a hand on Binnie's shoulder and told him to pull up.

I got out of the car, walked back to the Vauxhall, and peered inside. The doors were locked and everything seemed normal enough. Rooks called in the elm trees beyond the wall that enclosed the plantation and Randall Cottage.

I walked back to the van through the rain, and Binnie got out to meet me. "What's up?"

"That car," I said. "It worries me. It could be that it's simply broken down and the driver's walking on to the next village for help. Pigs could also fly."

"On the other hand," he said slowly, "if someone wanted to walk up to the cottage quiet-like . . ."

"That's right."

"So what do we do about it?"

I gave the matter some thought, and then I told him.

* * *

The track to the cottage wasn't doing the van's springs much good, and I stayed in bottom gear, sliding from one pothole to the next in the heavy rain. It was a gloomy sort of a place that wood, choked with undergrowth, pine trees unthinned over the years, cutting out all light.

The track took a sharp right turn that brought me out into a clearing suddenly and there was Randall Cottage, a colonial-style wooden bungalow with a wide verandah running along the front.

It was unexpectedly large but quite dilapidated, and the paved section at the foot of the verandah steps was badly overgrown with grass and weeds of every description.

As I got out of the van, thunder rumbled overhead, a strange, menacing sound, and the sky went very dark so that standing there in the clearing among the trees, it seemed as if the day was drawing to a close and darkness was about to fall.

I went up the steps and knocked on the front door, which stood slightly ajar. "Hey, Meyer, are you there?" I called cheerfully.

There was no reply, but when I pushed the door wide, Al Bowlly sounded faintly and rather eerily from somewhere at the rear of the house.

The song he was singing was "When That Man Is Dead and Gone," a number he's reputed to have dedicated to Adolf Hitler. It was the last thing he ever recorded, because a couple of weeks later he was killed by a bomb during the London Blitz.

None of which was calculated to make me feel any happier as I moved in and advanced along a dark, musty corridor, following the sound of the music.

The door at the far end stood wide, and I paused on the threshold. There were French windows on the far side, curtains partially drawn so that the room was half in darkness. Meyer sat in a chair beside a table on which the cassette tape recorder was playing.

"Hey, Meyer," I said. "What in the hell are you up to?"

And then I moved close enough to see that he was tied to

the chair. I tilted his chin and his eyes stared up at me blankly, fixed in death. His cheeks were badly blistered, probably from repeated application of a cigarette lighter flame. There was froth on his lips. He'd had a bad heart for some time now. It seemed pretty obvious what had happened.

Poor old Meyer. To escape the Gestapo by the skin of his teeth so young, and all these years later to end in roughly the same way. And yet I was not particularly angry, not filled with any killing rage, for anger stems from frustration, and I knew with complete certainty that Meyer would not go unavenged for long.

The door slammed behind me, as I had expected, and when I turned, Tim Pat Keogh was standing there, flanked by two hard-looking men in reefer coats who both held revolvers in their hands.

"Surprise, surprise," Tim Pat said laughing. "This just isn't your day, Major."

"Did you have to do that to him?" I asked.

"A tough old bastard, I'll give him that, but then I wanted him to tell me where those firing pins were and he was stubborn as Kelly's mule."

One of his friends came forward and ran his hands over me so inexpertly that I could have taken him and the gun in his hand in any number of ways. But there was no need.

He moved back, slipping his gun in his pocket, and the three of them faced me. "Where's Binnie, then, Major?" Tim Pat demanded. "Did you lose him on the way?"

The French windows swung in with a splintering crash, the curtains were torn aside, and Binnie stood there, crouching, the Browning ready in his left hand.

There was a sudden silence, the one curtain remaining fluttered in the wind; rain pattered into the room. Thunder rumbled on the horizon of things.

Binnie said coldly, "Here I am, you bastard."

Tim Pat's breath went out of him in a dying fall. "Well, would you look at that now?"

299

One of the other two men was still holding his gun. Binnie extended the Browning suddenly, the revolver dropped to the floor, the hands went up.

"What about Mr. Meyer?"

"Look for yourself," I pulled Meyer's head back.

A glance was enough. The boy's eyes became empty, devoid of all feeling for a moment, the same look as on that first night in Belfast, and then something moved there, some cold spark, and the look on his face was terrible to see.

"You did this?" he said in a strange dead voice. "In the name of Ireland?"

"For God's sake, Binnie," Tim Pat protested. "The old bugger wouldn't open his mouth. Now what in the hell could I do?"

Binnie's glance flickered once again to Meyer. The man with his hands raised dropped to one knee and grabbed for his revolver. In the same moment, Tim Pat and the other man went for their guns.

One of the finest shots in the world once put five .38 specials into a playing card at fifteen feet in half a second. He would have met his match in Binnie Gallagher. His first bullet caught the man who had dropped to one knee between the eyes; he put two into the head of the other one that could not have had more than two fingers' span between them.

Tim Pat fired once through the pocket of his raincoat; then a bullet shattered his right arm. He bounced back against the wall, staggered forward, mouth agape, and blundered out through the French windows.

Binnie let him reach the bottom of the steps, start across the lawn, then shot him three times in the back so quickly that to anyone other than an expert it must have sounded like one shot.

Al Bowlly was into "Moonlight on the Highway" now. I switched off the cassette recorder, then I walked past Binnie and went down the steps. Tim Pat lay on his face. I turned him over and felt in his pocket for the gun. It was a Smith & Wesson automatic and when I pulled it out, a piece of cloth came with it.

Binnie stood over me, reloading the Browning. I held up the Smith & Wesson. "Let that be a lesson to you. Never fire an automatic from your pocket. The slide usually catches on the lining, so you can only guarantee to get your first shot off, just like our friend here."

"You learn something new every day," he said.

From inside the house the phone started ringing. I went back in at once and found it in the darkness of the hall on a small table.

I lifted the receiver and said, "Randall Cottage."

Norah Murphy's harsh, distinctive voice sounded at the other end. "Who is this?"

"Vaughan."

"Is Meyer there?"

"Only in a manner of speaking. I'm afraid the opposition got here first. Three of them."

There was silence for a moment and then she said, "You're all right—both of you?"

"Fine," I said. "Binnie handled it with his usual efficiency. I hope our friends have got funeral insurance. This one's going to be expensive for them. Where shall we meet?"

"Back at the boat," she said. "I can be there in fifteen minutes. We'll talk then."

The receiver clicked into place, and I hung up and turned to Binnie. "All right, back to Stramore."

We went out into the rain and I paused beside the van. "Are you okay? Do you want me to drive?"

"God save us, why shouldn't I, Major. I'm fit as a hare. You sit back and enjoy your cigarette."

As we went down the farm track, his hands were steady as a rock on the wheel.

The green Vauxhall still waited on the grass verge at the side of the road as we passed, might stand there for some time before anyone thought to do any checking, although that was not all that probable in times like these.

About five miles out of Stramore we had a puncture in the left rear tire. Binnie managed to pull off the road, and we got out together to fix it, only to discover that while there was a reasonably serviceable spare, there was no jack.

He gave the offending wheel an angry kick. "Would you look at that? Two quid that dirty bowser took off me. Wait, now, till I see him. We'll be having a word and maybe more."

We started to walk side by side in the heavy rain. I wasn't particularly put out at what had happened. I needed time to think and this was as good a chance as any. I had a problem on my hands—a hell of a problem. Meyer had been the pipeline to the Brigadier and had probably spoken to him as soon as he had heard from me, if Tim Pat Keogh and his friends had given him time.

So now I was nicely adrift, for the Brigadier had made it plain that under no circumstances was I to get involved with the military. Whichever way you looked at it, it seemed obvious that if I was ever to get in touch with him at all, which seemed pretty essential now, I would have to disregard that part of my instructions.

I suppose we had been walking for about half an hour when we were picked up by a traveling shop. The driver was going to Stramore and was happy to take us there if we didn't mind a roundabout route, as he had calls to make at a couple of farms on the way.

The end result was that we were a good two hours later into Stramore than I had calculated, and it was past six o'clock when the van dropped us at the edge of town. We had to pass the garage on the way down to the harbor, and as it was still open, Binnie went in. I waited for him, and five minutes later he emerged, face grim.

"What happened?" I asked him.

He held up two one-pound notes. "He saw reason," he said. "A decent enough man with the facts before him."

I wondered if the Browning had figured in the proceedings,

but that was none of my affair. We went down the narrow cobbled street together and turned along the front.

Binnie tugged at my sleeve quickly. "The boat's gone."

He was right enough, but when we went down to the jetty itself, we found the *Kathleen* moored at the bottom of a flight of wide stone steps on the far side.

"Now what in the hell would she do that for?" Binnie asked.

I led the way down the steps without replying. There was something wrong here, I sensed that, but in view of the time and place, it didn't seem likely to be anything to do with Frank Barry and his merry men.

We reached the concrete landing strip at the bottom and I called, "Norah? Are you there?"

She screamed high and clear from inside the cabin, "Run for it, Vaughan! Run for it!"

But we were already too late. A couple of stripped-down Land-Rovers roared along the jetty in the same instant and a moment later, there were at least eight paratroopers lining the jetty above us plus the same number of submachine guns pointing in our direction. Binnie's hand was already inside his coat, and I barely had time to grab his arm before he could draw.

"I told you before, boy, no heroics. There's no percentage in it. There'll be another time."

He looked at me, eyes glazed, that strange, dazed expression on his face again, and then they were down the steps and onto us.

They put us up against the wall none too gently, which was only to be expected, legs astraddle for the search. The sergeant in charge found the Browning, of course, but nothing on me.

After that, we waited until someone said, "All right, Sergeant, turn them round."

A young paratrooper captain was standing by the wheelhouse wearing a red beret, camouflaged uniform, and flak jacket, just like his men. He was holding the Browning in one hand. Norah Murphy stood beside him, her face very white.

The captain had the lazy, rather amiable face of the kind of man who usually turns out to be as tough as old boots underneath. He looked me over with a sort of mild curiosity.

"You are Major Simon Vaughan?"

"That's right, Captain."

I laid a slight emphasis on my use of his handle, which he didn't fail to notice, for he smiled faintly. "Your wheelhouse would appear to have been in the wars, Major. Window gone, wood splintered, and a couple of nine-millimeter rounds embedded in one panel. Would you care to comment?"

"It was a rough trip," I said. "Or didn't you hear the weather report?"

He shrugged. "Under the circumstances, I have no alternative but to take you all into custody."

Norah Murphy said, "I'm an American citizen. I demand to see my consul."

"At the earliest possible moment, ma'am," he assured her gravely.

Another vehicle turned on to the jetty and braked to a halt above us. I heard a door slam, and a cheerful, familiar voice called, "Now then, Stacey, what's all this? What have we got here?"

The captain sprang to attention and gave the kind of salute that even the Guards only reserve for very senior officers as the Brigadier came down the steps resplendent in camouflaged uniform, flak jacket, and dark blue beret, a Browning in the holster on his right hip, a swagger stick in his left hand.

8

Interrogation

In happier times Stramore had only needed one constable, which meant that the local police station was a tiny affair—little more than an office and a single cell, which from the look of it had been constructed to accommodate all the local drunks at the same time. It was clean enough, with green-painted brick walls, four iron cot beds, and a single narrow window, heavily barred as was to be expected.

The door was unlocked by the police constable and Captain Stacey led the way in. "I'm sorry we can't offer separate accommodations in your case, Dr. Murphy," he said, "but it won't be for long. Tonight at the most. I would anticipate moving you first thing in the morning."

Norah Murphy said calmly, "I'm not going anywhere till I hear from the American consul."

Stacey saluted and turned to leave. Binnie and I had both been handcuffed, and I held out my hands. "What about these?"

"Sorry," he said. "I've had my orders."

The door closed, the key turned. I moved to the window and tried to peer outside, but there was nothing to see. The glass was misted with rain and it was almost dark.

Norah Murphy said softly, "Are we wired for sound?"

"In this place?" I couldn't help laughing. "That only happens on Stage Six at MGM. Get me a cigarette. Left-hand pocket."

She put one in my mouth and gave me a light, then took one herself. "All right, what went wrong?"

"Tim Pat Keogh and a couple of Barry's goons were waiting for us."

"What happened?"

"They killed the old man," Binnie told her. "Burned his face with a cigarette lighter to make him tell them where the firing pins were. And that bastard Tim Pat tried to justify it." He spat in the corner. "May he roast in hell."

She turned back to me. "What did happen to the firing pins, then? Are they still at the cottage?"

"They're in Scotland, sweetheart," I said. "That's the irony of it. In an old garage Meyer rented in Oban. We intended bringing them over with the rest of the stuff on the second trip if everything had gone all right this time."

Her eyes widened in horror. "Then Meyer died for nothing."

"Exactly." I moved to the window and peered out again. It was quite dark. "Of course the really interesting question is, How did they know where he was?" When I turned she was watching me closely, a slight frown on her face. "Or to put it another way: Who told them?"

Binnie had been sitting on one of the beds. He stood up quickly. "What are you trying to say, Major?"

Norah Murphy cut him off with a quick gesture. "No, Binnie, let him have his say."

"All right," I said. "It's straightforward enough. I was the only one who knew Meyer's address until I gave it to you in the pub on a piece of paper Binnie didn't even see. In fact he didn't know where we were going till we were on our way. In any case, as he's knocked off four of Barry's men by now, he's hardly likely to be working for him."

"Which leaves me?" she said calmly.

"The only possibility. You even knew there was plenty of

306

time for action, because Meyer didn't want to see me till three thirty. A quick phone call was all it took. It also explains how they came to be waiting for us in Bloody Passage last night, which was also reasonably coincidental. I mean, we'd hardly advertised the trip, now had we?"

All this, of course, was right out of the top of my head. It made sense, there was a sort of logic to it and yet I was whistling in the dark to a certain extent, attempting, more than anything else, to provoke some kind of reaction.

I was totally unprepared for the violence of her reply. Her face was contorted with rage on the instant, and she flung herself at me, one hand catching me solidly across the face, the other on the rebound, and she could punch her weight.

"I'll kill you for saying that," she cried. "I'll kill you, Vaughan." She grabbed me by the lapels and shook me furiously.

I couldn't do all that much to defend myself what with the handcuffs and the unexpectedness of the attack, but as she clawed at my face again Binnie moved in behind her, pulled her away with both hands, and got between us.

He looked at me over his shoulder. "You shouldn't have said that, Major. You've done a bad thing here."

She collapsed on the bed, dry sobs racking her body, her face in her hands, and Binnie crouched beside her like a dog, his handcuffed hands in her lap. She ran her fingers through his hair. After a while she looked up. Her face was calm again, but the eyes were somehow weary and the voice was very tired.

"I spoke to the commander of the North Antrim Brigade of the official I.R.A. this afternoon. He was the man whose people were waiting for us on that beach last night. As a matter of interest, he was notified within one hour of your friend Meyer's arrival at Randall Cottage yesterday, just as he's told immediately of any stranger moving into a house anywhere in his district these days. Unfortunately, Frank Barry and his organization hold just as much sway in this area."

"And last night?"

"All right." She nodded heavily. "There was a leak, but at

least twenty people were on that beach. It could have been any one of them. If I know my Barry he would be cunning enough to leave a sympathizer or two within the ranks of the official I.R.A. when he broke away."

It was all plausible enough. In fact, the truth of the matter was that it was beginning to look as if I had been about as wrong as a man could be.

I said, "All right, then. Did you speak to your uncle?"

"I did."

"Where is he?"

The hate in her eyes when she looked up at me was really quite something. "I'd burn in hell before I'd tell you that now."

I don't know where the thing might have gone after that, but as it happened, the door opened and the police constable appeared.

"Would you be good enough to come with me, ma'am," he said to Norah.

"Where are you taking me?" she demanded.

"To the nearest wall," I said, "where they have a firing party waiting for you. A bad habit the British Army have—or don't you believe your own propaganda?"

She went out fast, like a clipper under full sail; the police constable closed the door. When I turned, Binnie was sitting on the edge of the bed watching me.

"What did you have to go and say a thing like that for, Major?"

"I don't really know." I shrugged. "It seemed like a good idea at the time. There has to be some explanation."

"She gave it to you, didn't she?" he said violently. "Christ Jesus, but I will hear no more of this."

He jumped to his feet, eyes staring, the handcuffed hands held out in front of him and for a moment I thought he might have a go at me. And then the door opened and the police constable appeared again, this time with the paratroop sergeant at his shoulder.

"Major Vaughan, sir. Will you come this way, please?"

Everyone was being too bloody polite to be true, but I winked at Binnie and went out, the police constable leading the way, the paratroop sergeant falling in behind me.

We went straight out of the front door and hurried through the teeming rain across the yard to what looked like a church hall. The entrance was sandbagged and a sentry stood guard beside a heavy machine gun. We moved past him along a short corridor and paused outside a door at the far end. The sergeant knocked and when he opened it, I saw the Brigadier seated behind a desk in a tiny cluttered office.

"Major Vaughan, sir," the sergeant said.

The Brigadier looked up. "Thank you, Grey. Bring the Major in and wait outside—and see that we're not disturbed."

I advanced into the room, the door closed behind me. The Brigadier leaned back in his chair and looked me over. "Well, you seem to have survived so far."

"Only just."

He stood up, got a chair from the corner, and put it down beside me. "Sorry about the handcuffs, but you'll have to hang on to those for the time being, just for the sake of appearances."

"I understand."

"But I can offer you a cigarette and a glass of Scotch."

He produced a bottle of White Horse and two glasses from a cupboard in the desk and I sat down. "This place seems snug enough."

He pushed a glass across to where I could reach it and half-filled it. "Used to be the Sunday school. This was the superintendent's office. Rum kind of soldiering."

"I suppose so."

He leaned across the desk to give me a cigarette. "You'd better fill me in on what happened on the run from Scotland."

Which didn't take long in the telling. When I had finished he said, "And when you got in this morning you phoned Meyer?"

"That's it. He told me he'd get in touch with you straight away. He asked me to be at the cottage by three thirty."

"Was he dead when you arrived?"

I nodded. "You've been there?"

He opened the bottle of White Horse and splashed more whiskey into my glass. "I arrived at Randall Cottage at four twenty precisely, which was the earliest I could manage. I'd told Meyer to hold you till I got there."

"And all you found was a butcher's shop in hell."

"Exactly. I hoped you'd gone back to the boat, naturally."

"With the pipeline cut it seemed the only thing to do."

"Which was why I phoned through to Captain Stacey, who's in charge here, and got him to lay on a reception party for you and your friends. An elaborate device for getting us together again, but there didn't seem any other way and time is of the essence after all. Who were the other three at the cottage, by the way?"

"Some of Barry's men. They were after the firing pins."

"Which explains the condition of poor old Meyer's face." He nodded. "I see now. Did you kill them?"

"No, the boy took care of that department. He didn't like what they'd done to Meyer."

"He's that good?"

"The best I ever saw with a hand gun. The complete idealist. He honestly thinks you can fight this kind of a war and come out of it with clean hands." I swallowed my whiskey and shook my head. "God help him, but he's going to get one hell of a shock before he's through."

"You sound as if you like him."

"Oh, I like him, all right. The only trouble is that one of us will very probably end up by knocking off the other before this little affair is over."

"There was a bad explosion in Belfast this afternoon, in one of the big public offices."

"Many casualties?"

"Thirty or more. Mostly young girls from the typing pool and half of them were Catholic, there's the irony. The Provisionals have already claimed credit, if that's the right word. A nasty business."

"Binnie Gallagher would be the first to agree with you."

Which seemed to have little or no effect on him for he sat staring down at the desk, whistling softly to himself while he traced complicated patterns on a memo pad with a pencil.

I said, "Look, I'm not too happy about what you might call the security aspects of the affair. The fact that Barry and his men were waiting for us out there in Bloody Passage. The way they turned up at Meyer's cottage just like that."

He looked up. "Have you any ideas on the subject?"

I told him about my confrontation with Norah Murphy and when I was finished he shook his head. "Michael Cork's niece selling him down the river? It doesn't make any kind of sense."

"What does then?"

"The girl's own explanation. What I told you about I.R.A. splinter groups at your briefing in London is absolutely true. They're not only having a go at the British, they're fighting each other. Each group had its own spies out, believe me. On top of that, it's almost impossible to keep any kind of security the way things are. There isn't a post office or shop or telephone exchange in the county that doesn't have sympathizers working in it. Ordinary, decent people on the whole, who probably hate the violence, but are willing to pass on interesting information for all that. And then there's always intimidation."

He poured me another whiskey and sat back, holding his glass up to the light. "On the whole, I'd say things are going very well. You've got Frank Barry and one of the most wanted terrorist squads in Ireland sniffing at your heels and as long as you stick with the girl, you've a direct line to the Small Man himself. Do you think she knows where the bullion is?"

"My hunch is no, but I couldn't be definite at this stage. You could always try pulling out her fingernails."

"Your sense of humor will be the death of you one of these fine days, Simon, just like your father. Did I ever tell you that I knew him back in the old days in India?"

"Several times."

"Is that so?"

311

He dropped into that brown study of his again. I said patiently, "All right, sir, what happens now?"

He drained his glass, rolled the last of the whiskey around his tongue. "That's easy enough." He glanced at his watch. "It's just after seven thirty. At nine o'clock precisely, I'm taking the three of you back to Belfast with me escorted by Captain Stacey and Sergeant Grey."

"Do we get there?"

"Of course not. About ten miles out on the road to Ballymena we'll have engine trouble."

"Which means that Stacey and Sergeant Grey will know what they're about?"

"Exactly. I'll come round to the rear of the vehicle to check your handcuffs, giving you an excellent chance to grab my Browning. Only make damn sure it's you and not that lad. From the way he's been carrying on, he'd leave the three of us lying in the nearest ditch."

"Then what?"

"You play the game as the cards fall. If you want me, you get in touch with the following Belfast telephone number. It'll be manned day and night."

He gave it to me and I memorized it quickly. "And the bullion is still number one on the agenda?"

"Followed by the apprehension of Michael Cork himself, with Frank Barry and his men number three."

I stood up. "That's about it, then."

He chuckled suddenly as if to himself. "Sons of Erin. Why on earth do they choose such ridiculous bloody names?"

"You know how it is." I said. "The Celtic Twilight and all that sort of rubbish."

"You know, you really have got me wrong, my boy," he said. "I like the Irish. No, I do. Finest soldiers in the world."

"Next to the English, of course."

"Well, as a matter of fact, I was going to give pride of place to the Germans. Terribly unpatriotic, I know, but truth must out."

I retired, defeated, and Sergeant Grey took me back to my cell.

Norah Murphy was standing at the window peering out into the night when I went in. There was no sign of Binnie.

She said, "What happened?"

"I had a chat with the Brigadier. Ferguson his name is. Very pleasant. What about you?"

"Captain Stacey. Cigarettes, coffee, and lots of public school charm. I just kept asking for the American consul. He gave up in the end. He's talking to Binnie now."

"He won't get very far there."

She sat down on the bed, crossed one knee over the other, and looked up at me. "What did you tell the Brigadier then?"

"That I'd hired the *Kathleen* in Oban and that as far as I was concerned, any bullet holes must date from some previous occasion. I also told him in confidence, one gentleman to another, that you and I were very much in love and that the passage of Stramore had just been designed as a kind of pre-wedding honeymoon trip, just to make certain we were physically suited."

There was that look on her face again of helpless rage and yet there was something else in her eyes—something indefinable.

"You what?"

I crouched down in front of her and laid my manacled hands on her knees. "Actually, I'd say the idea had a great deal to commend it."

And once again, the humor welled up from deep inside her, breaking the mask into a hundred pieces. She laughed harshly and cupped my face in her two hands. "You bastard, Vaughan, what am I going to do with you?"

"You could try kissing me."

Which she did, but before I could appreciate the full subtlety of the performance, the key rattled in the lock. I got to my feet as the door opened and Binnie and Captain Stacey entered followed by the Brigadier.

Binnie moved to join us and Norah stood up so that we confronted them in a tight little group. The Brigadier brushed his moustache with the back of a finger.

"I'm afraid I'm not satisfied with the answers any of you have

313

given. Not satisfied at all. Under the circumstances, I intend to transfer you to Military Intelligence H.Q. outside Belfast where you may be properly interrogated. We leave at nine o'clock. You'll be given something to eat before then."

He turned and went out followed by Stacey. The door clanged shut with a kind of grim finality and when Norah Murphy turned to me, there was real despair on her face for the first time since I'd known her.

We left exactly on time in an army Land-Rover, Captain Stacey driving, the Brigadier beside him, and the three of us behind them, all handcuffed now, including Norah. Sergeant Grey crouched in the rear with a Sterling submachine gun.

The rain was really bad now, the road a ribbon of black wet tarmac in the powerful headlights. There was a moment of excitement about two miles out of Stramore when Grey announced suddenly that we were being followed.

I glanced over my shoulder. There were headlights there certainly, but a moment later as he cocked his submachine gun, they turned off into a side road.

"Never mind, Sergeant," Captain Stacey said. "Keep your eyes skinned just the same. One never knows."

I sat there in the darkness waiting for the big moment, Norah's knees rubbing against mine. I tried a little pressure. After a moment's hesitation, she responded. I dropped my manacled hands on hers. It was all very romantic.

From somewhere up ahead there was one hell of a bang, and orange flames blossomed in the night. We came round a corner to find a Ford van slumped against a tree, petrol spilling out to where a man lay sprawled in the middle of the road, a tongue of flame sweeping toward him with the rapidity of a burning fuse.

I didn't fall for it, not for a minute, but Stacey and the sergeant were already out of the vehicle and running toward the injured man.

There were several bursts of submachine-gun fire from the

wooded hillside to our right, knocking the sergeant sideways into the ditch. Stacey managed to get his Browning out, fired twice desperately, then turned and ran back toward the Land-Rover, head down.

They all seemed to be firing at him then, pieces jumping out of his flak jacket as the bullets hammered into him. His beret flew off, his face was suddenly a mask of blood. He fell against the hood and slid to the ground.

The Brigadier went out head first, Browning in one hand, crouched beside the Land-Rover, waiting in the sudden silence. There was laughter up there in the trees and then submachine gun fire sprayed across the road again.

There seemed no point in letting the old boy do a Little Bighorn, so I did the most sensible thing I could think of in the circumstances, opened the rear door and hit him in the back of the neck with my two clenched fists.

He went flat on his face and lay there groaning. I picked up the Browning in both hands and stood up. "You can come out now, whoever you are."

"Put the Browning down and stand back," a voice called.

I did as I was told. There was a rustle in the bushes to our right and Frank Barry stepped into the light.

The Ford truck was going well by now, the kind of blaze that seemed likely, on a conservative estimate, to attract every soldier and policeman in a mile radius, but Barry and his men didn't seem disposed to hurry.

There were six of them, and at one point, he took a small walkie-talkie from his pocket and murmured something into it which seemed to indicate that he had other forces not too far away.

He noticed me watching and grinned as he put it away. "Grand things, these, Major. A great comfort on occasion. The minute you left the police post in Stramore I knew." He lit a cigarette and said, "What about my firing pins? Now there's a dirty trick."

"You're wasting your time," I said. "They're in Oban."

"Is that a fact?" He turned to Binnie, who stood beside me. "You've been a bad boy, Binnie. Tim Pat, Donal McGuire, and Terry Donaghue, all at one blow just like the tailor in the fairy tale. I can see I'm going to have to do something about you."

"I'm frightened to death," Binnie told him.

"You will be," Barry told him genially. He turned suddenly as the Brigadier groaned and tried to get up.

"What's this then, one of them still kicking?"

He took a revolver from inside his coat and I said quickly, "Seems like a hell of a waste to me, Barry. I mean Brigadier Generals aren't all that thick on the ground."

He lowered the revolver instantly and crouched down. "Is that what he is? By God, you're right." He straightened and nodded to a couple of his men. "Get the old bugger on his feet. We'll take him with us. I might find a use for him."

Someone brought the handcuff keys found on Stacey's body and Barry slipped them in his pocket. Then he turned and peered inside the Land Rover where Norah Murphy still sat.

"Are you there, Norah, me love? It's your favorite man."

A large van came round the corner, reversed across the road, and braked to a halt beside us.

Barry pulled her out of the Land-Rover and put an arm about her. "Nothing mean about me, Norah. See, I even provide transport to take you home—my home, of course."

She struggled in his grasp, furiously angry, and he tightened his grip and kissed her full on the mouth.

"We've such a lot to talk over, Norah. Old times, you, me, the Small Man, cabbages and kings, ships and sealing wax, gold bullion."

She went very still, staring up at him fixedly, shadows dancing across her face in the firelight as he laughed softly.

"Oh, yes, Norah, that too." Then he picked her up in his arms and carried her across to the van.

9

Spanish Head

Our destination, as I discovered later, was only a dozen miles along the coast from Stramore, yet such was the circuitous back country route that we followed that it took us almost an hour to get there.

There were a couple of small plastic windows in the side of the van. For most of the time there wasn't much to see, but then the rain stopped and by the time we turned on to the coast road it had become a fine, clear night with a half-moon lighting the sky.

The road seemed to follow the contours of the cliff edge exactly, and as far as I could judge, there was a drop on our left beyond the fence of a good two hundred feet.

We finally took a narrow road to the left and braked to a halt so that one of the men could get out to open a gate. There was a notice to one side. I craned my neck and managed to make out the words "Spanish Head" and "National Trust" before the gate opened and we drove through.

"Spanish Head," I murmured in Norah's ear. "Does that mean anything to you?"

"His uncle's place."

One of the guards leaned forward and prodded me on the shoulder. "Shut your face."

An inelegant phrase, but he made his point. I contented myself after that with the view from the window, which was interesting enough. We went over a small rise, and the road dropped away to a wooded promontory. There was a castle at the very end above steep cliffs, battlements and towers black against the night sky, like something out of a children's fairy tale.

It was only as we drew closer that I saw that I was mistaken. That it was no more than a large country house, built, from the look of it, during that period of Victoria's reign when Gothic embellishments were considered fashionable.

The van came to a halt, the door was opened, and when I scrambled out, I found myself in a courtyard at the rear of the main building. Barry himself came round to hand Norah Murphy down, and he also unlocked her handcuffs.

"Now be a good girl and you'll come to no harm, as my old grannie used to say." He took her by the arm firmly and led her toward the door. "Stick the others in the cellar," he said carelessly over his shoulder. "I'll have them up when I need them."

After he'd gone, a couple of his men took us in through the same door. There was a long, dark, flagged passage inside, presumably to the kitchen quarters. At the far end a flight of stairs obviously gave access to the rest of the house. There was a stout oaken door beside it, which one of the men opened to disclose steps leading into darkness. He switched on a light and we went down. There was a series of cellars below, one leading into another, and there were wine racks everywhere, most of them empty.

We finally arrived at what looked suspiciously like a cell door straight out of some Victorian prison. It was sheathed in iron plate and secured by steel bolts so large that the guard who opened them needed both hands.

A cell indeed it was, as we found when we went in. Bare,

lime-washed walls oozing damp, no window of any description, an iron cot with no mattress, a wooden table, and two stools.

The door shut; the bolts rammed home solidly. The steps of the two guards faded away along the passage outside. There was a zinc bucket in one corner, presumably for the purposes of nature, and I gave it a kick.

"Every modern convenience."

Binnie sat on the edge of the bed, the Brigadier limped to one of the stools and sat down, massaging the back of his neck.

"Are you all right, sir?" I asked politely.

"No thanks to you."

He glared up at me, and I said, "If I hadn't done what I did, you'd be dead meat by now. Be reasonable."

I managed to fish out my cigarettes with some difficulty, as I was still handcuffed, and offered him one.

"Go to the devil," he said.

I turned to Binnie and grinned. "No pleasing some people."

But he simply lay down on the bare springs of the cot without a word, staring up at the ceiling, unable, I suspect, to get Norah Murphy out of his mind.

I managed to light a cigarette then sat down against the wall, suddenly rather tired. When I looked across at the Brigadier his right eyelid moved fractionally.

It must have been about an hour later that the door was unbolted and a couple of men entered, both of them armed with Sterling submachine guns. One of them jerked his thumb at me without a word—a squat, powerful-looking individual whose outstanding feature was the absence of hair on his skull. I went out, the door was closed and bolted again, and we set off in echelon through the cellars, the gentleman with the bald head leading the way.

When we reached the kitchen area again we kept right on going, taking the next flight of stairs, coming out through a green baize door at the top into an enormous entrance hall, all pillars and Greek statues, a great marble staircase drifting up into the half-darkness above our heads.

We mounted that, too, turned along a wide corridor at the top, and climbed two more flights of stairs, the last being narrow enough for only one man at a time.

When the final door opened I found myself on the battlements at the front of the house. Frank Barry sat at a small ironwork table at the far end. I caught the fragrance of cigar smoke as I approached and there was a glass in his hand.

I could see him clearly enough in the moonlight, and he smiled. "Well, what do you think of it, Major? The finest view in Ireland, I always say. You can see the whole of the North Antrim coast from here."

It was certainly spectacular enough, and in the silvery moonlight it was possible to see far, far out the lights of some ship or other moving through the passage between the mainland and Rathlin.

He took a bottle dripping with water from a bucket on the floor beside him. "A glass of wine, Major? Sancerre. One of my favorites. There's still two or three dozen left in the cellar."

I held up my wrists and he smiled with that immense charm of his. "There I go again, completely forgetting my manners."

He produced the keys from his pocket, I held out my hands, and he unlocked the cuffs. The second of the two guards had faded away, but my friend with the bald head still stood watchfully by, the Sterling ready.

A boat came round the headland a hundred yards or so to our right, the noise of its engine no more than a murmur in the night. It started to move into an inlet in the cliffs below and disappeared from sight, presumably into some harbor or anchorage belonging to the house.

"That should be your *Kathleen*," Barry said. "I sent a couple of my boys round to Stramore to lift her from the harbor as soon as it was dark."

"Do you usually think of everything?"

"Only way to live." He filled a glass for me. "By the way,

old lad, let's keep it civilized. Dooley, here, served with me in Korea. He's been deaf, dumb, and minus his hair since a Chinese trench mortar blew him forty feet through the air. That means he only has his eyes to think with and he's apt to be a bit quick off the mark."

"I'll remember. What were you in?"

"Ulster Rifles. Worst National Service second lieutenant in the Army."

I tried some of the wine. It was dry, ice-cold, and I sampled a little more with mounting appreciation. "This is really quite excellent."

"Glad you like it." He refilled my glass. "What would you say if I offered to let you go?"

"In return for what?"

"The firing pins and the rest of the arms you have stored away over there in Oban somewhere." He sampled some of his wine. "I'd see you were suitably recompensed. On delivery, naturally."

I laughed out loud. "I just bet you would. I can imagine what your version of payment would be. A nine-millimeter round in the back of the head."

"No, really, old lad. As one gentleman to another."

He was quite incredible. I laughed again. "You've got to be joking."

He sighed heavily. "You know, nobody, but nobody, takes me seriously, that's the trouble." He emptied his glass and stood up. "Let's go downstairs. I'll show you over the place."

I hadn't the slightest idea what his game was, but on the other hand, I didn't exactly have a choice in the matter with Dooley dogging my heels, that submachine gun at the ready.

We went down to the main corridor leading to the grand stairway. Barry said, "My revered uncle, my mother's brother, made the place over to the National Trust on condition he could continue to live here. It has to be open to the public from May to September. The rest of the time you could go for weeks without seeing a soul."

"Very convenient for you, but doesn't it ever occur to the military to look the place over once in a while in view of the special relationship?"

"With my uncle? A past grand master of the Orange lodge? A Unionist since Carson's day? As a matter of interest, he threw me out on my ear years ago. A well-known fact of Ulster life."

"Then how does he allow you to come and go as you please now?"

"I'll show you."

We paused outside a large double door. He knocked, a key turned, and it was opened by a small, wizened man in a gray alpaca jacket who drew himself stiffly together at once and stood to one side like an old soldier.

"And how is he this evening, Sean?" Barry asked.

"Fine, sir. Just fine."

We moved into an elegant, book-lined drawing room which had a large four-poster bed in one corner. There was a marble fireplace, logs burning steadily in the hearth, and an old man in a dressing gown sat in a wing chair before it, a blanket around his knees. He held an empty glass in his left hand and there was a decanter on a small table beside him.

"Hello, uncle," Barry said. "And how are we this evening?"

The old man turned and stared at him listlessly, the eyes vacant in the wrinkled face, lips wet.

"Here, have another brandy. It'll help you sleep."

Barry poured a good four fingers into the glass, steadied the shaking hand as it was raised. In spite of that, a considerable amount dribbled from the loose mouth as the old man gulped it down greedily.

He sank back in the chair, and Barry said cheerfully, "There you are, Vaughan, Old Lord Palsy himself."

I had found him likable enough until then, in spite of his doings, but a remark so cruel was hard to take. Doubly so when one considered that it was being made about his own flesh and blood.

There was a silver candelabrum on a sideboard with half a dozen candles in it. He produced a box of matches, lit them one by one, then moved to the door, which the man in the alpaca jacket promptly opened for him.

Barry turned to look back at his uncle. "I'll give you one guess who the heir is when he goes, Vaughan." He laughed sardonically. "My God, can you see me taking my seat in the House of Lords? It raises interesting possibilities, mind you. The Tower of London, for instance, instead of the Crumlin Road jail if they ever catch me."

I said nothing, simply followed him out and walked at his side as he went down the great stairway to the hall. It was a strange business, for as we moved from one room to another, Dooley keeping pace behind, the only light was the candelabrum in Barry's hand, flickering on silver and glass and polished furniture, drawing the faces of those long dead out of the darkness as we passed canvas after canvas in ornate gilt frames. And he talked ceaselessly.

He stopped in front of a portrait of a portly, bewigged gentleman in eighteenth-century hunting dress. "This is the man who started it all, Francis the First, I always call him. Never got over spending the first twenty years of his life slaving on a Galway potato patch. Made his fortune out of slaves and sugar in Barbados. His plantation out there was called Spanish Head. When he'd got enough, he came home, changed his religion, bought a peerage, and settled down to live the life of an Irish Protestant gentleman."

"What about your father's side of things?"

"Ah, now there you have me," he said. "He was an actor whose looks outstripped his talent by half a mile, and in their turn were only surpassed by his capacity for strong liquor, which actually allowed him to survive to the ripe old age of forty."

"Was he a Catholic?"

"Believe it or not, Vaughan, but I'm not the first Protestant to want a united Ireland." He held a candle up to an oil painting that was almost life-size. "There's another. Wolfe Tone. He started it all. And that's my favorite relative beside him. Francis the Fourth. By the time he was twenty-three he'd killed three men in duels and had it off with every presentable female in the county. Had to flee to America."

The resemblance to Barry himself was quite remarkable. "What happened to him?"

"Killed at a place called Shiloh, during the American Civil War."

"On which side?"

"What do you think? Gray brought out the color of his eyes, that's what he said in a letter home to his mother. I've read it."

We had turned and were making a slow promenade back toward the entrance hall. I said, "When I look at all this, you don't make sense."

"Why exactly?"

"Your present activities."

"I like a fight." He shrugged. "Korea wasn't all that bad if it hadn't been for the bloody cold. And life gets so damn boring, don't you think?"

"Some people might think that was a pretty poor excuse."

"My reasons don't matter, Vaughan, it's what I'm doing for the Cause that counts."

We had reached the hall and he put the candelabrum down on the table and took out the handcuffs. I held out my wrists.

He said, "Thirty years ago, if I'd been doing exactly what I'm doing today for the resistance in France or Norway, I'd have been looked upon as a gallant hero. Strange how perspective changes with the point of view."

"Not mine," I said.

He looked at me closely, "And what do you believe in, Vaughan?"

"Nothing. I can't afford to."

"A man after my own heart." He turned to Dooley and jerked his thumb downward. "Take him back to the others for now."

He picked up the candelabrum and went upstairs. I stood

watching him for a moment, then Dooley put the muzzle of the Sterling in my back and prodded me toward the door.

When I was returned to the cell, Bennie was fast asleep on the cot, his head to one side, mouth open. When the door closed, he stirred slightly, but did not waken. The Brigadier put a finger to his lips, moved to check that the boy was genuinely asleep, then crossed to the table. We both sat down.

"A pretty kettle of fish," he said. "What's been happening to you?"

I told him and in detail, for in some way, almost everything Barry had said to me seemed important, if only because of the way in which it threw some light on the man himself.

When I'd finished, the Brigadier nodded. "It makes sense that he would ask you to go to Oban. After all, you're on call to the highest bidder as far as he knows, and you couldn't very well go running to the police."

"He said he'll be seeing me later, presumably to discuss the deal further. What do I say?"

"You accept, of course, all along the line."

"And what about you?"

"God knows. What do you think he'd do if you told G.H.Q. where I was and they sent the Royal Marine Commandos to get me out?"

"He'd use you as a hostage. Try to bargain."

"And if that failed—and it would fail because the moment the government gives in to that kind of blackmail it's finished—what would he do then?"

"Put a bullet through your head."

"Exactly."

The bolts rattled again, the door was flung open with a crash that brought Binnie up off the cot to his feet. He stood there, swaying slightly, wiping sleep from his eyes with the back of a hand.

Dooley was back again with a couple of men this time. "Outside, all of you," one of them ordered roughly.

325

We followed the same route as before, up through the green baize door to the hall, then up the marble stairs to the main landing and along the corridor. We paused at another of those tall double doors, Dooley opened it and led the way in.

It was rather similar to the old man's room, though without a bed, but it was pleasantly furnished in Regency style. Norah Murphy sat in a chair by the fire, her hands tightly folded in her lap. Barry stood beside her, a hand on the back of the chair.

"Good, then, as we're all here, we can get started. I should tell you gentlemen that Dr. Murphy is being more than a trifle stubborn. She has certain information I need rather badly which she stupidly insists on keeping to herself." He put a hand on her shoulder. "Shall we try again? What happened to the bullion, Norah? Where's he hidden it?"

"You go to hell," she said crisply. "If I did know, you're the last man on earth I'd tell."

"A great pity." He nodded to Dooley, speaking slowly, enunciating the words so that he could read his lips. "Come and hold her."

Dooley slung his Sterling over one shoulder and moved behind the chair. Norah tried to get up, and he shoved her down and twisted her arms back cruelly, holding her firm.

Barry leaned down to the fire. When he turned, he was holding a poker, the end of which was red-hot. Binnie gave a desperate cry, took a step forward, and got the butt of a Sterling in the kidneys.

He went down on one knee and Barry said coldly, "If any one of them makes a move, put a bullet in him."

He turned to Norah, grabbed her hair, turning her face up to him and held the poker over her. "I'll ask you once more, Norah. Where's the bullion?"

"I don't know," she said. "You're wasting your time. This will get you nowhere."

He touched her cheek with the tip of the poker, there was a plume of smoke, the smell of burning flesh. She gave a terrible cry and fainted.

326

Binnie forced himself up on one knee and put out a hand in appeal. "It's the truth she's telling you. Nobody knows where that gold is except the Small Man himself. Not even here because that's the way he wanted it."

Barry looked down at him, frowning for a long moment. Then he nodded. "All right, I'll buy that. Where is he now?"

Binnie got to his feet and stood swaying, a hand to his back, not saying a word. Barry grabbed the unconscious girl by the hair again, the poker raised in threat.

"You tell me, damn you, or I'll mark the other side of her face."

"All right," Binnie said. "But much good it'll do you. He's in the old hidey-hole in the Sperrins, and there's nothing he'd like better than for you and your men to try and take him there."

Barry underwent another personality change, became once again the smiling, genial man I'd taken wine with earlier. He dropped the poker into the fireplace and nodded to Dooley.

"Take her into the bedroom."

Dooley picked her up effortlessly, crossed the room, and kicked open a door on the far side. Barry moved to a sideboard and poured himself a whiskey. When he turned he was smiling. "I wouldn't get within ten miles of that farmhouse. There isn't a farm laborer or shepherd or snotty-nosed little boy in any village you touch on up there who isn't another pair of eyes for the Small Man."

"Exactly," Binnie said.

"I know," Barry nodded. "But you, Binnie, they'd welcome with open arms."

Binnie stared at him, amazement on his face. "You must be mad."

"No, I'm not, old love, I've never been saner in my life. You're going to go and see my old friend Michael for me, and you're going to point out the obvious and unpleasant fact that I'm holding his favorite niece. If I get the gold or details of its whereabouts, he gets her back in one piece. If I don't . . ."

"By God, they broke the mold when they made you," Binnie said. "I'll kill you for this, Barry. Before God, I will."

Barry sighed heavily and patted the boy's face. "Binnie, Cork's milk and water religion, his let's-sit-down-and-talk, isn't going to win this war. It's people like me who are willing to go all the way."

"And to hell with the cost?" the Brigadier put in. "The slaughter of the innocents all over again."

When Barry turned to him there was a madness in his eyes that chilled the blood.

"If that's what's needed," he said. "We won't shirk the price, any price, because we are strong and you are weak." He turned back to Binnie. "With that gold I can buy enough arms to take on the whole British Army. What will the Small Man do with it?"

Binnie stared at him, that slightly dazed look on his face again, and Barry, calmer now, patted him on the shoulder. "You'll leave at dawn, Binnie. It's a good time on the back roads. Nice and quiet. It shouldn't take you more than a couple of hours to get there. I'll give you a good car."

Binnie's shoulders sagged. "All right." It was almost a whisper.

"Good lad." Barry patted him again and looked straight at me. "And we'll send the Major along, just to keep you company. That public school accent of his should be guaranteed to get you past any roadblocks you run into, especially with the kind of papers I'll provide him with. All right, Major Vaughan?"

"Do I have any choice?"

"I shouldn't think so."

He gave me that lazy, genial smile of his, looking more than ever like Francis the Fourth of the portrait up there in the gallery. I didn't smile back because I was thinking of Norah, remembering the stink of her flesh burning, considering with some care exactly how I was going to give it to him when the time came.

10

Run for Your Life

Barry himself disappeared and a great deal seemed to happen after that. The Brigadier was hauled off to his cell. Binnie and I, rather puzzlingly, had our pictures taken by one of Barry's men using a flash camera.

Afterwards, we were taken by way of the back stairs to a bedroom on the next floor. It was comfortable enough, with dark mahogany furniture and brass bedstead, a faded Indian carpet on the floor. There was a familiar-looking suitcase on the bed. As I approached it, Barry came into the room.

"I had your stuff brought up from the boat, old lad. I don't think those sea-going togs of yours will be exactly appropriate for this little affair. Suit, collar and tie, raincoat—or something of that order. Can you oblige?"

"Everything except the raincoat."

"No problem there."

"What about Binnie?"

Barry turned to look at him. "As impeccable as usual. All done up to go to somebody's funeral."

"Yours maybe?" Binnie said. I noticed that his forehead was damp with sweat.

Barry chuckled, not in the least put out. "You always were a comfort, Binnie boy." He turned to me. "There's a bathroom through there. Plenty of hot water. No bars on the window, but it's fifty feet down to the courtyard and two men on the door so behave yourselves. I'll see you later."

The door closed behind him. Binnie went to the window, opened it, and stood there breathing deeply of the damp air as if to steady himself.

I said, "Are you all right?"

He turned, that look on his face again. "For what he has done to Norah Murphy he is a dead man walking, Major. He is mine for the taking when the time comes. Nothing can alter that."

Something cold moved inside me then, fear, I suppose, at his utter implacability, which went so much beyond mere hatred. There was a power in this boy, an elemental force that would carry him through most things.

A dead man walking, he had called Frank Barry, and I wondered what he would call me on that day of reckoning when he discovered my true motives.

Which was all decidedly unpleasant, so I left him there by the window staring out to sea, went into the bathroom, and ran a bath.

I dressed in a brown polo neck sweater, Donegal tweed suit, and brown brogues. The result, after the bath and a shave, was something of an improvement. Binnie, who seemed to have recovered his spirits a little, sat on the edge of the bed watching me. As I pulled on my jacket and checked the general effect in the wardrobe mirror, he whispered softly.

"By God, Major, but you look grand. Just like one of them fellas in the whiskey adverts in the magazines."

I had the distinct impression that he might break into laughter at any moment, an unusual event indeed. "And the toe of my boot to you too, you young bastard."

We were prevented from carrying the conversation any further, for at that moment the door opened and the guards ordered us outside.

This time we were taken all the way down to the kitchen, where we were given a really excellent meal with another bottle of the Sancerre that Barry had liked so much. It was all rather pleasant in spite of the guards in the background.

As we were finishing, Barry appeared, the formidable Dooley at his back. He had an old trench coat over one arm, which he dropped across the back of a chair.

"That should keep out the weather, and these should get you past any roadblocks you run into, military or police."

There were two Military Intelligence identity cards, each with its photo, which explained the camera work earlier. Binnie was a Sergeant O'Meara; I had become Captain Geoffrey Hamilton. There was also a very authentic-looking travel permit authorizing me to proceed to Strabane to interrogate an I.R.A. suspect named Malloy being held at police headquarters there.

I passed Binnie his I.D. card. "These are really very good indeed."

"They should be. They're the real thing." He turned to Binnie. "The boys will take you down to the garage now so you can check the car. The Major and I will be along in a few minutes."

Binnie glanced at me briefly. I nodded and he got up and went out followed by two of the guards. Dooley stood by the door watching me woodenly, his Sterling at the ready. I pulled on the trench coat.

Barry took a couple of packets of cigarettes from his pocket and shoved them across the table. "For the journey."

He stood watching me, hands in pockets, as I stowed them away. "Very nice of you," I said. "Now what do you want?"

"Binnie is inclined to be a little emotional where Norah is concerned, but I'm not."

"I must say I had rather got that impression," I said.

"As far as I'm concerned she's just a medium of exchange. You make that clear to Cork, just in case Binnie doesn't get the message across." He turned and nodded to Dooley who went out of the room immediately. "The first sign of anything untoward at all, Dooley puts a bullet in her head."

"In other words, you mean business?"

"I hope I've made that clear enough."

"And Norah?"

"She's okay," he said callously. "When last seen she was giving herself an injection from that bag of hers. Of course she'll have a fair old scar from now on, but then I always say that kind of thing gives a person character."

He was baiting me, I think, but I played him at his own game. "Just like a broken nose?"

"Exactly." He laughed and yet frowned a little. "By God, but you're a cold fish, Vaughan. What does it take to get you roused?"

"That usually comes halfway through the second bottle of Jameson," I said. "There's this click inside my head and . . ."

He raised a hand. "All right, you win. We'd better see how Binnie is getting on. You haven't got much time."

The garage had obviously been the coach house in other days and stood on the far side of the courtyard. Binnie was checking the engine of a green Cortina GT when I went in, watched impassively by the guards. He dropped the hood and wiped his hands on a rag.

"Where did you knock this off?" he demanded.

Barry grinned. "According to the papers in the glove compartment it's on loan from a car hire firm in Belfast, which is exactly as it should be. When they're in plain clothes the Field Security boys don't like to use military vehicles."

"You think of everything," I said.

"I try to, old lad, it's the only way." He glanced at his watch. "It's just after four so you should be there by seven at the outside. Six o'clock tonight is your deadline. Nothing to come for after that, which I trust you'll make plain to the Small Man for me."

Binnie slid behind the wheel without a word and I got in the passenger seat. Barry leaned down to the window. "By the way, Field Security personnel are supposed to go armed during the present emergency so you'll find a couple of Brownings in the glove compartment. Army issue, naturally, only don't try turning round at the gate and coming back in like a two-man commando. That really would be very silly."

Binnie slipped the handbrake and took the Cortina away with a burst of speed that wouldn't have disgraced the starting line at Monza, and Barry had to jump for it pretty sharply.

The needle was flickering at fifty as we left the courtyard and it kept on climbing. The result was that we were skidding to a halt in a shower of gravel at the private gate giving access to the main road within no more than a couple of minutes.

I got out, opened the gate, and closed it again after Binnie had driven through. When I returned to the car, the glove compartment was open and he was checking a Browning, a grim look on his face in the light from the dashboard.

I said, "I wouldn't if I were you, Binnie. He meant it. Dooley is her shadow from now on, with orders to kill at even a hint of trouble."

For a moment, he clutched the Browning so tightly that his knuckles turned white and then something seemed to go out of him and he pushed it into his inside breast pocket.

"You're right," he said. "Only the Small Man can help now. We'd better get moving."

"Can I ask where?"

"He has a place in the Sperrins—an old farmhouse in a valley near a mountain called Mullaclogha. We need to be on the other side of Mount Hamilton on the Plumbridge Road."

"Do you anticipate a clear run?"

"God knows. I'll use what back roads I can. For the rest, we'll just have to take it as it comes."

He drove away at a much more moderate speed this time and I dropped the seat back a little, closed my eyes, and went to sleep.

I was out completely for the first hour and dozed fitfully during the next half. It must have been somewhere around five thirty when he nudged me sharply in the ribs with his left elbow.

"We've got company, Major. Looks like a roadblock up ahead."

I raised my seat as he started to slow. It was raining again, a slight, persistent drizzle. There were two Land-Rovers forming a barrier across the road and half a dozen soldiers, all wearing rubber capes against the rain and looking thoroughly miserable which, in view of the time and the weather, was understandable enough.

I leaned out of the window, identity card and movement order in hand, and called, "Who's in charge here?"

A young sergeant got out of the nearest Land-Rover and crossed to the Cortina. He was wearing a flak jacket and camouflaged uniform, but no cape. He was prepared to be belligerent, I could see by the set of his jaw, so I forestalled him quickly.

"Captain Hamilton, Field Security, and I'm in one hell of a hurry so get the barrier out of the way, there's a good chap."

It worked like a charm. He took one look at the documents, saluted swiftly as he passed them back, then turned to bark an order at his men. A moment later and the lights of the roadblock were fading into the darkness.

"Like taking toffee off a kid," Binnie crowed. "I can see now what Barry meant about you having the right manner, Major."

As a junior officer I once served with an old colonel who had spent a hair-raising three months on a journey to the Swiss border after escaping from a Polish prison camp. Three miles from his destination he paused in a village inn to wait for darkness. He was arrested by a colonel of mountain troops who only happened to be there because his car had broken down on the way through. It seems he had been a member of a party of German officers who had visited Sandhurst in 1934, when the old boy was an instructor there. He had been recognized instantly in spite of the circumstances, the years between, and the brevity of the original meeting.

334

Time and chance, the right place at the wrong time or vice versa. Fate grabbing you by the trouser leg. How could I speak to Binnie of things like these? What purpose would it serve?

The truth is, I suppose, that I was experiencing one of poor old Meyer's famous bad feelings, which didn't exactly help because it simply made me think, with some sadness, of him and other good men dead on somber gray mornings like this.

We pulled in at a filling station, which was closed as far as I could see. In any case, according to the gauge there was plenty of petrol in the tank.

"What's this?" I demanded.

"I need to make a phone call," Binnie said as he opened the door. "Ask a friend to tell a friend we'll meet him in a certain place."

He was beginning to sound more like an I.R.A. man in one of those old Hollywood movies by the minute. I watched him go into the telephone box at the side of the building. He wasn't long. I noticed it was six o'clock and switched on the radio to get the news.

To my astonishment, the first thing I heard was my own name, then Norah Murphy's.

Binnie got back in the car. "That's all right, then. We're expected."

"Shut up and listen," I said.

The announcer's voice moved on. "The police are also anxious to trace James Aloysius Gallagher." There followed as accurate a description of Binnie as any hard-working police officer could reasonably have hoped for.

He was behind the wheel in an instant, and we were away. I kept the radio on, and it couldn't have been worse. The bodies of Captain Stacey and Sergeant Grey had been discovered by a farmer during the past hour, and the absence of the Brigadier and the three of us could lead to only one conclusion.

"God save us, Major," Binnie said as the broadcast finished. "At a conservative estimate I'd say they've got half the British Army out on this one."

"And then some," I said. "How much further?"

"Ten or fifteen miles, that's all. I bypassed Draperstown just before I stopped. You'd see the mountains on the right here if it wasn't for the rain and mist."

"Have we any more towns to pass through?"

"Mount Hamilton, and there's no way around it. We take a road up into the mountains about three miles on the other side."

"All right," I said. "So we go through, nice and easy. If anything goes wrong, put your foot down and drive like hell and never mind the gun play."

"Ah, go teach your grandmother to suck eggs, Major," he said.

The young bastard was enjoying it, that was the thing. This was meat and drink to him, a great, wonderful game that was for real. Always for real. He sat there, hunched over the wheel, cap over his eyes, the collar of his undertaker's overcoat turned up, and there was a slight pale smile on his face.

We were entering Mount Hamilton now. I said, "You'd have gone down great during Prohibition, Binnie. Al Capone would have loved you."

‹ "Ah, to hell with that one, Major. Wasn't there some Irish lad took that Capone fella on?"

"Dion O'Bannion," I said.

"God save the good work. With a name like that he must have gone to mass every day of his life."

"And twice on Sundays."

We slowed behind a few farm trucks and a milk truck, all waiting their turn to pass through the checkpoint. There were four or five Land-Rovers, at least twenty paratroopers, and a couple of R.U.C. constables who leaned against a police car and chatted to a young paratroop lieutenant.

The milk truck moved on through the gap between the Land-Rovers and I repeated my previous performance, holding my identity card and movement order out of the window and calling to the young officer.

"Lieutenant, a moment, if you please."

He came at once, instantly alert, for whatever else I had become, I had spent twenty years of my life a soldier and as they say in the Army, it takes an old Academy man to recognize one.

"Captain Hamilton, Field Security," I said. "We're in a hell of a hurry. They've got a terrorist in custody in Strabane who might be able . . ."

I didn't get any further because one of the policemen who had moved to join him, a matter of idle curiosity, no more than that, leaned down at my window suddenly and stared past me, the eyes starting from his head.

"God love us, Binnie Gallagher!"

I put my fist in his face, Binnie gunned the motor, wheels spinning, and we shot through the space between the two Land-Rovers, bouncing from one to the other in the process.

But we got through. As he accelerated I screamed, "Head down."

A Sterling chattered, glass showering everywhere, and the Cortina skidded wildly. And then he had her in full control again; we were round a bend in the road and away.

It was raining harder now, mist rolling down the slopes of the mountains, reducing visibility considerably. Beyond that first bend the road ran straight as a die for about a mile. We were no more than a hundred and fifty yards into it when the police car came round the bend closely followed by the Land-Rovers.

Binnie had the Cortina up to eighty now, the needle still mounting, and the wind and rain roared in through the shattered windshield so that I had to shout to be heard.

"How far?"

"A couple of miles. There's a road to the right which takes us up into the hills. Tanbrea, they call the place. We'll be met there."

We were almost at the end of the straight now and when I glanced back, the police car seemed, if anything, to have closed the gap.

"They're moving up," I yelled.

"Then discourage them a little, for Christ's sake."

When it came right down to it, I had little choice in the matter. As far as the police or the Army were concerned, I was an I.R.A. terrorist on the run, or as good as, so they would have no qualms about putting a bullet into me if necessary.

I wondered what the Brigadier would have said. Probably shoot the policeman and be damned at the consequences on the grounds that the end justified the means.

But life, after all, is a matter of compromise so when I drew my Browning, turned, and fired back through the shattered rear window at the pursuing vehicles, I took care to aim as far above them as possible.

The policeman who fired back at us out of his side window had understandably different intentions and he was good. One bullet passed between Binnie and me shattering the speedometer, another ricocheted from the roof.

We skidded violently. Binnie cursed and dropped a gear as we drifted broadside on into the next bend. In the end it was his undoubted driving skill that saved us, plus a little of the right kind of luck. For a moment things seemed to be going every which way, but when we finally came out of the bend into the next straight we were pointing in the right direction.

The police car was nothing like as fortunate. It bounced right across the road, turned in a circle twice, and ended halfway through a thorn hedge on the left-hand side of the road.

Binnie could see all this for himself, for strangely enough, the rearview mirror had survived intact, and he laughed out loud. "There's one down for a start."

"And two to go," I shouted as the first Land-Rover came round the corner, followed by the second.

A signpost on the left-hand side of the road seemed to be rushing toward us at a rate of knots. Binnie braked violently and dropped into third, the car drifting into another of those long-angled slides and then, miraculously, we were into a narrow country lane that climbed steeply between gray stone walls.

Things became a little calmer there. Such were the twists and turns that he had to drop right down for it was the sort of road where thirty miles an hour would have been construed as dangerous driving in some places.

"How far now?" I demanded.

"To Tanbrea? Five miles, but how in the hell can we stop there with the British Army snapping at our heels and the Small Man waiting? Might as well serve up his head with an apple between the teeth. We'll have to drive straight on through."

I leaned out of the window and looked down through the mist and rain to where the road twisted between gray stone walls below. I caught a brief glimpse of one of the Land-Rovers and then another. They were several hundred yards in the rear now.

I said to Binnie, "Is this the only road through the mountains?"

He nodded. "On this section."

"Then we'll never make it. I've got news for you. Marconi has very inconveniently invented a thing called radio. By the time we get to the other side of the mountains they'll have every soldier and policeman for miles around waiting." I shook my head. "We'll have to do better than that."

"Such as?"

I thought about it for a moment and came up with the one obvious solution. "We'll have to die, Binnie, rather nastily, or at least make them think we have for an hour or two and preferably on the other side of Tanbrea."

Tanbrea was a couple of streets, a pub, a small church, a scattering of gray stone houses on the hillside. The only sign of life was a dog in the center of the main street who got out of the way fast as we roared through. The road lifted steeply on the other side, climbing the mountain through what looked like a Forestry Commission fir plantation.

About half a mile beyond the village, we rounded a sharp bend and Binnie braked to a halt in the center of the road. There was a wooden fence on the left-hand side. I got out of the Cortina and glanced over. There was a drop of a hundred feet or more through fir trees to a stream bed below.

"This is it," I said. "Let's get moving."

I'd intended a good solid push, but Binnie surprised me to the end. Instead of getting out, he moved into gear and drove straight at the fence. For a heart-stopping moment I thought he'd left it too late, and then, as the Cortina smacked through the fence and disappeared over the edge, I saw him rolling over and over on the far side.

As he picked himself up there was the noise of metal tearing somewhere down below, a tremendous thud, and then the kind of explosion that sounded as if someone had detonated fifty pounds of gelignite. Pieces of metal cascaded into the air like shrapnel. When I peered over the edge, what was left of the Cortina was blazing furiously in the ravine below.

Somewhere near at hand I could hear engines roaring as the Land-Rovers started to climb the hill. When I turned, Binnie was already running for the fence on the other side of the road. I scrambled over, no more than a yard behind him, and we plunged into the undergrowth.

We were halfway up the hillside when the two Land-Rovers braked to a halt on the bend below, one behind the other. The paratroopers got out and ran to the edge of the road, the young lieutenant from the checkpoint in Mount Hamilton well to the fore.

We didn't hang about to see what happened. Binnie tugged at my sleeve, we went over a small rise and followed a stream that dropped down through a narrow ravine to the village.

As we came out of the trees at the back of the church, one of the Land-Rovers came down the road fast. I grabbed Binnie by the arm, we dropped behind the graveyard wall and waited until the Land-Rover had disappeared between the houses.

"Come on," he said. "Follow me, Major, and do exactly as I tell you."

We went through the graveyard cautiously, moving from

tombstone to tombstone. When we were almost at the rear entrance of the church, a couple of paratroopers appeared on the street side of the far wall. We dropped down behind a rather nice Victorian mausoleum and waited in the steady rain, a gray angel leaning over us protectively.

Binnie said, "Sure and there's nothing better than a nice cemetery. Have you ever seen your uncle's grave at Stradballa, Major?"

"Not since I was a boy. There was just a plain wooden cross, as I remember."

"Not now." He shook his head. "They bought a stone by public subscription about ten years ago. White marble. It says, 'Michael Fitzgerald, Soldier of the Irish Republican Army. He died for Ireland.' By God, but that would suit me."

"A somewhat limited ambition, I would have thought." He stared at me blankly, so I pulled him to his feet, the soldiers having moved elsewhere. "Come on, let's get out of this. I'm soaked to the bloody skin."

A moment later we were into the shelter of the back porch. He opened the massive oak door, motioning me to silence, and led the way in.

It was very quiet, winking candles and incense heavy on the cold morning air, and down by the altar the Virgin seemed to float out of darkness, a slight fixed smile on her delicate face.

Half a dozen people waited by a couple of confessional boxes. An old woman with a scarf bound around her head, peasant-fashion, turned and looked at us blankly. Binnie put a finger to his lips as, one by one, the others sitting there turned to look at us. Beyond the great door at the far end a voice shouted an order; steps approached outside.

Binnie grabbed me by the arm and dragged me toward the nearest confessional box. In a moment we were jammed together inside, the curtain drawn.

There was a movement on the other side of the grill and a quiet voice said, "My son?"

"I have sinned most grievously, Father, and that's a fact,"

Binnie told him, "but even hellfire and damnation would be preferable to what the bastards who're coming in now are likely to dish out if they lay hands on us."

There was silence, then the main church door opened and steps approached, the boots ringing out on the flagstones. There was a movement on the priest's side of the grill and I turned to peer through the curtain, aware that Binnie had drawn his Browning.

The young paratroop officer from the roadblock was there, a gun in his hand. He paused, and then my view of him was blocked as a priest appeared in alb and black cassock, a violet confessional stole around his shoulders.

"Can I help you, lieutenant?" he asked quietly.

The young officer murmured something, I couldn't catch what, and the priest laughed. "No one here except a few back-sliders as you can see, anxious to be confessed in time for early mass."

"I'm sorry, Father."

He holstered his gun, turned, and walked away. The priest stood watching him go. When the door closed behind him, he said calmly and without turning round, "You can come out now, Binnie."

Binnie jerked back the curtain. "Michael?" he said. "Is it you?"

The priest turned slowly, and I was face to face, at last, with the Small Man.

11

The Small Man

I waited in a small, cold annex outside the vestry, aware of the murmur of voices inside, but unable to hear a thing through that stout oaken door. Not that it mattered. For the moment, I'd lost interest. Too much had happened in too short a time, so I smoked a cigarette, sacrilege or no, and slumped into a chair in the corner.

After a while, the door opened and Cork appeared. I could see Binnie sitting on the edge of a table behind him. I knew he was in his sixties, but when he took off his horn-rimmed spectacles and cleaned them with a handkerchief he looked older— much older.

He said, "I'd like to thank you, Major Vaughan. It seems we owe you a great deal."

"Binnie's told you, then?" I said.

"About Norah and Frank Barry." He replaced his spectacles. "Oh, yes, I think you could say he's put me in the picture."

"So what do you intend to do about it?"

There were the sounds of more vehicles arriving in the street outside, a shouted command.

He smiled gravely. "From the looks of things I wouldn't say

we're in a position to do much about anything at the moment, Major. Wait here."

He took a shovel hat down from a peg, put it on, and went out through the church briskly. The front door clanged. There was silence.

I said, "Does he do this often? The priest bit, I mean?"

"It gets him around," Binnie said. "You know how it is. Nuns and priests—everybody trusts them and the Army has to be careful in its dealings with the Church. People take offense easy over things like that."

"What about the local priest?"

"They don't have one here. A young Jesuit comes up from Strabane once a week."

"So Cork's performance isn't official?"

He laughed harshly. "The Church has never been exactly a friend of the I.R.A., Major. If they knew about this there would be hell to pay."

"What do you think he'll do? About Norah, I mean?"

"He didn't say."

He lapsed into silence after that, staring moodily into space. Reaction, I supposed, and hardly surprising. I went back to my chair and stared blankly at the wall opposite, more tired than I had ever been in my life.

After a while, the front door of the church opened again, then closed, the candles by the altar flickering wildly. We flattened ourselves against the wall, Binnie with that damned Browning ready in his hand, but it was only Cork and a small, gnarled old man in cloth cap, tattered raincoat, and muddy boots.

"More troops have arrived." Cork hung up his shovel hat. "And more to come I fancy. Paratroops in the main. I've been talking to that young lieutenant. Gifford, his name is. Nice lad."

He frowned in a kind of abstraction and Binnie said, "And what's happening, for God's sake?"

"They seem to think you're down in the ravine in the wreckage of that car. They're still searching. I think you'd better go

344

up to the farm for the time being till I sort this thing out. Sean here will take you." He turned to me. "It's only half a mile up the valley at the back of the church, Major. You'll be safe there. There's a hidey-hole for just this kind of occasion that they've never discovered yet."

"And Norah," Binnie demanded urgently. "What about her?"

"All in good time, Binnie lad." Cork patted him on the shoulder. "Now be off with you."

He took down his hat and went out again. The door clanged, the candles flickered, only this time most of them went out. I hoped it wasn't an omen.

The old man, Sean, took us out through the graveyard and plunged into the trees at the back of the church, walking strongly in spite of his obvious age. What with the rain and the mist, visibility was reduced to a few yards, certainly excellent weather to turn and run in. Not that it was necessary, for we didn't see a soul and within fifteen minutes came out of the trees above a small farm in a quiet valley.

It was a poor sort of place and badly in need of a coat of whitewash. Broken fences everywhere and a yard that looked more like a ploughed field after heavy rain than anything else.

There didn't seem to be anyone about and old Sean crossed to a large, two-story barn built of crumbling gray stone, opened one-half of the double door, and led the way in. There was the general air of decay I might have expected, a rusted threshing machine, a broken down tractor, and several holes in the roof where slates were missing.

There was also a hayloft, a ladder leading up to it. At first I thought the old man intended climbing it, but instead he moved it to the other side of the barn and leaned it against the wall which was constructed of wooden planking. Then he stood back.

Binnie said, "Follow me, Major. The Black Hole of Calcutta, we call it."

He went up the ladder nimbly, paused halfway, reached to

one side, got a finger into a knothole and pulled. The door which opened was about three feet square. He ducked inside and I followed him.

The old man was already moving the ladder back to its original position by the loft as Binnie closed the door. Light streamed in through various nooks and crannies, enough for me to see that we were in a small, narrow room barely large enough to stand up in.

He said, "Follow me and watch it. It's thirty feet down and no place to find yourself with a broken leg."

I could see the top of a ladder protruding through some sort of trapdoor, waited until he was well on his way and went after him, dropping into the kind of darkness that is absolute.

Binnie said softly, "Easy does it, Major, you're nearly there."

My feet touched solid earth again a moment later. I turned cautiously; there was the scrape of a match and as it flared, I saw him reaching to an oil lamp that hung from a hook in the wall.

"All the comforts of home," he said.

Which was a fair enough description, for there was a rough wooden table, chairs, two old Army cots and plenty of blankets, a shelf stocked with enough tinned food to feed half a dozen men for a week or more.

"Where are we, exactly?" I demanded, unbuttoning my trench coat.

"Underneath the barn. This place has been used by our people since the 1920s and never discovered once."

The far end of the room was like a quartermaster's store. There were at least two dozen British Army issue automatic rifles, a few old Lee-Enfields, several Sterlings, and six or seven boxes of ammunition—all stamped War Department. There were camouflage uniforms, flak jackets, several tin hats, a few paratroop berets.

"What in the hell is all this lot for?" I demanded. "The great day?"

"Mostly stuff we've knocked off at one time or another—

some of the lads wore the uniforms when we raided an arms dump a few months back." He draped his wet overcoat carefully across a chair and sprawled out on one of the beds. "Christ, but I'm bushed, Major. I could sleep for a week and that's a fact."

I think he was asleep before he knew it, to judge by the regularity of his breathing, but in the circumstances, it seemed the sensible thing to do. I tried the other bed. Nothing had ever felt so comfortable. I closed my eyes.

I don't know what brought me awake, some slight noise perhaps, but when I opened my eyes, Cork was sitting on the other side of the table from me reading a book.

As I stirred, he peered over the top of his spectacles. "Ah, you're awake."

My watch had stopped. "What time is it?"

"Ten o'clock. You've been asleep maybe three hours."

"And Binnie?"

He turned and glanced toward the other bed. "Still with his head down. A good thing, too, while he has the chance. In our line of work a man should always snatch forty winks at every opportunity, but there's no need to tell an old soldier like you that, Major."

I joined him at the table and offered him a cigarette, but he produced a pipe and an old pouch. "No, thanks, I prefer this."

The book was St. Augustine's *City of God*. "Heavy stuff," I commented.

He chuckled. "When I was a lad, my father sent me to Maynooth to study for the priesthood. A mistake, as I realized after a year or two and got out, but old habits die hard."

"Was that before you were in prison or after?"

"Oh, after, a desperate attempt by the family to rehabilitate me. They were a terrible middle-class lot, Major. Looked upon the I.R.A. as a kind of Mafia."

"And none of it did any good?"

"Not a bit of it." He puffed at his pipe until it was going. "Mind you, a couple of years in the Crumlin Road jail was enough. I've managed to stay out of those places since then, thank God."

"I know what you mean."

He nodded. "As I remember, the Chinese had you for a spell in Korea."

There was a slight pause. He sat there puffing away at his pipe, staring into the distance in that rather abstracted way that seemed characteristic of him.

I said, "What are you going to do?"

"About Norah, you mean?" He sighed. "Well, now, it seems to me I'd better go to Stramore myself and see exactly what's in Frank's mind."

"Just like that?"

"With a little luck, of course, and God willing."

I said, "He's a bad bastard. I think he means what he says. He'll kill her if you don't tell him where the bullion is."

"Oh, I'm sure he will, Major Vaughan. In fact, I'm certain of it. There isn't much you can tell me about Frank Barry. We worked together for too long."

"What caused the split?"

"As the times change, all men change with them, or nearly all." He sighed and scratched his head. "I suppose I'm what you'd call an old-fashioned kind of revolutionary. Oh, I'll use force if I have to, but I'd rather sit round a table and talk."

"And Barry?"

"A different story altogether. Frank has this idea about the purity of violence. He believes anything is justified to gain his end."

There was another of those silences. I said, "Will you tell him what he wants to know?"

"I'd rather not."

"No answer."

His smile had great natural charm, and I suddenly realized what an enormously likable man he was.

I said, "How could you ever have worked with a man like Barry or the others that are like him, for that matter? The kind who think it helps the cause to slaughter indiscriminately. Women, kids, anyone who happens to be around."

He sighed and scratched his head again, another characteristic gesture. "Revolutionaries, Major, like the rest of humanity, are good, bad, and indifferent. I think you'll find that's held true in every similar situation since the war. We have our anarchists, the bomb-happy variety who simply want to destroy, and one or two who enjoy having a sort of legal excuse for criminal behavior."

"Like Barry?"

"Perhaps. We also have a considerable number of brave and honest men who've dedicated their lives to an ideal of freedom."

I didn't have any real answer to that except the most obvious one. "I suppose it all depends on your point of view."

He chuckled. "You know, I knew your uncle, Michael Fitzgerald of Stradballa. Now there was a man."

"Who just didn't know when to stop fighting."

"Ah, but you've got quite a look of him about you." He put another match to his pipe then glanced at me quizzically over the tops of his glasses. "You're a funny kind of gun runner, boy, and that's a fact. Now what exactly would your game be, I wonder?"

Dangerous ground indeed, but I was saved from an unexpected quarter. There were three distinct blows against the floor above our heads. Binnie awoke in an instant, and Cork jumped up and climbed the ladder in the corner.

Binnie swung his legs to the floor and ran a hand through his hair. "What's going on?"

"I'm not sure," I said.

Cork came back down the ladder and returned to the table. "Right," he said. "It's time to be off."

Binnie stared at him blankly. "What's all this?"

"You're going back to Stramore, Binnie," Cork told him patiently, "and I'm going with you."

Binnie turned to me. "Is he going crazy or am I? Isn't half the British Army scouring the hills for us out there?"

"True enough," Cork said, "and with paratroopers by the dozen in every country lane, who'll notice two more?"

He walked to the other end of the room, picked up one of the camouflaged uniforms, and tossed it onto the table; then he rummaged in one of the boxes for a moment. When he returned, he was holding a couple of Major's crowns in his open palm.

"Stick those in your epaulettes and you've got your old rank back again, Major. You'll have to make do with corporal, Binnie. You don't have the right kind of face for a British officer."

Binnie gave a kind of helpless shrug. I said to Cork, "All right, what's the plan?"

"Simplicity itself. You and Binnie get into uniform and go back down to the village. Keep to the woods and if anyone sees you, they'll think you're simply searching the area like everyone else. I'll pick you up at the roadside on the other side of the village in my car. You can't miss it. It's an old Morris Ten. Rather slow, I'm afraid, but I find that an asset in my line of work. No one ever seems to think a car that will only do forty miles an hour is worth chasing."

"Will you still be playing the priest?"

"Oh, yes, that's all part of the plan. Once we reach the bottom road, the story, if we're stopped, is that you're escorting me to Plumbridge to make an identification. If we get through there in one piece, we'll change direction. From there on you'll be escorting me to Dungiven. After that, Coleraine. Sure and we'll be at Stramore before you know it. The military have a terrible respect for rank, Major. With a modicum of luck we won't get stopped for more than a minute at any one time."

It had a beautiful simplicity that made every kind of sense. "God help me," I said, "but it's just daft enough to work."

He glanced at his watch. "Good, I'll pick you up as arranged in exactly half an hour."

He climbed the ladder and disappeared. Binnie stared at me wildly. "He's mad, Major. He must be."

"Maybe he is," I said, "but unless you can think of another way out of this mess, you'd better get into uniform and fast. We haven't got much time."

I was dressed in one of the camouflaged uniforms and a flak jacket in five minutes and that included fixing the Major's crowns to the epaulettes. Binnie, once he started moving, wasn't far behind. When he was ready, I moved close to check that everything was in order and adjusted the angle of his red beret.

"Christ Jesus, Major, but you're the sight for sore eyes." There was a small broken mirror on the wall and he tried to peer into it. "My old da would spin in his grave if he could see this."

I found a webbing belt and holster to hold my Browning. Binnie stowed his out of sight inside his flak jacket and we each took a Sterling from Cork's armory. When I followed Binnie out through the trapdoor to the barn, old Sean was waiting at the bottom of the ladder. He showed not the slightest surprise at our appearance, simply picked up the ladder when I reached the ground and carried it across to the hayloft again. It was only as we went out into the rain and started across the farmyard that I realized he hadn't spoken a single word to us since that first meeting in the church.

Binnie led the way at a brisk pace, cutting up into the trees on the opposite side of the valley from the way we had come. It was quiet enough up there; the only sound was the rain swishing down through the branches or the occasional noise of an engine from the road. Once, through a clear patch in the mist, I saw a red beret or two in the trees on the other side of the valley, but there was no one on our side.

We bypassed the village altogether, keeping high in the trees, only moving down toward the road when we were well clear of the last houses.

We crouched in the bushes and waited. A Land-Rover swished past moving toward the village. The old Morris Ten appeared perhaps three minutes later and we stood up and showed ourselves instantly. Binnie scrambled into the rear seat; I got in beside Cork and he drove away.

In his shovel hat, clerical collar, and shabby black raincoat he was as authentic-looking a figure as one could have wished for, a thought which, for some reason, I found rather comforting.

I said, "So far so good."

"Just what I was after telling myself." He glanced in the driving mirror and smiled. "Binnie, you look lovely. If they could see you in Stradballa now."

"Get to hell out a' that," Binnie told him.

"Come on now, Binnie," I said. "I thought any sacrifice was worth making for the cause."

Which made Cork laugh so much he almost put us into a ditch. He recovered just in time and the Morris proceeded sedately down the hill at a good twenty-five miles an hour.

The first few miles were uneventful enough. Several military vehicles passed us going the other way, but we didn't run into a roadblock until we reached the outskirts of Plumbridge. There was the usual line of vehicles and Cork joined at the end.

I said, "We're on military business aren't we? Straight through to the head of the queue."

He didn't argue, simply pulled out of line and did as I told him. As a young sergeant came forward, I leaned out of the window. He took one look at those Major's crowns and sprang to attention.

"For God's sake, clear a way for us, Sergeant," I said. "We're due in Stramore in half an hour to make a most important identification."

It worked like a charm. They pulled aside the barrier and the spiked chain they had across the road a yard or two further on to rip open the tires of anyone who tried to barge their way through.

"Now I know what they mean by audacity," Cork said.

We were already moving out into the countryside and Binnie laughed delightedly. "It worked. It actually worked."

I think it was at that precise moment that the right rear tire burst. Not that we were in any danger, considering the relatively slow speed at which we were traveling. The Morris wobbled slightly, but responded to the wheel reasonably enough as Cork turned in toward the grass.

"What they used to call Lag's Luck when I was in prison," he said as he switched off the engine.

"Never mind that," I said. "Let's have that wheel off and the spare on and out of here double quick. I've somehow got a feeling that it's healthier to stay on the move."

Binnie handled the jack while I got the spare out of the trunk. As I wheeled it round to him, a Land-Rover passed us going toward Plumbridge. It vanished into the mist, but a moment later reappeared, reversing toward us.

The driver got out and came round to join us. He was no more than eighteen or nineteen. A lance corporal in the Royal Corp of Transport.

He saluted smartly. "Anything I can do, sir?"

His attitude was natural enough at the sight of a Major getting his hands dirty. I made the first mistake by trying to get rid of him. "No, everything's under control, corporal. Off you go."

There was a flicker of surprise in his eyes. He hesitated, then leaned down to Binnie, who reacted violently. "You heard what he said, didn't you? Clear off."

It was an understandable reaction to stress but, delivered as it was in that fine Kerry accent of his, it compounded my original error.

The corporal hesitated, seemed about to speak, then thought better of it. He saluted punctiliously, then moved back to the Land-Rover. He started to get inside, or so it seemed, then turned and I saw that he was holding a Sterling.

"I'd like to see your identity card, if you don't mind, sir," he said firmly.

"Now look here," I said.

Binnie straightened slowly and the lad, who knew his business, I'll say that for him, said, "Hands on top of the car."

353

Cork walked straight toward him, a puzzled smile on his face. "For heaven's sake, young man," he said. "Control yourself. You're making a terrible mistake."

"Stand back," the young corporal said. "I warn you."

But he had hesitated for that one fatal second that seemed to give Cork his opportunity. He flung himself forward, clutching at the Sterling. There was the briefest of struggles. I had already taken a couple of strides to join him when there was a single shot. Cork staggered back violently with a terrible cry and fell on his back.

I put my fist into the corporal's stomach, then a knee in his face as he doubled over laid him unconscious beside the Land-Rover; it was better than a bullet in the head from Binnie.

Binnie was already on his knees beside Cork, who was obviously in great pain and barely conscious, blood on his lips. I ripped open the front of his cassock and looked inside. It was enough.

"Is it bad?" Binnie demanded.

"Not good. From the looks of it, I'd say he's been shot through the lungs. He needs a doctor badly. Where's the nearest hospital? Stramore?"

"And life imprisonment if he pulls through?" Binnie said.

"Have you got a better idea?"

"We could try to get him over the border into the Republic."

"That's crazy. Even if we could pull it off, it's too far. There isn't time. He needs skilled treatment as soon as possible."

"Twelve miles," he said clutching my flak jacket. "That's all, and I know a farm track south of Clady that runs clear into the Republic. There's a hospital no more than three miles on the other side run by the Little Sisters of Pity. They'll take him in."

One thing was certain. Another vehicle might appear from the mist at any moment so whatever we were going to do had to be done fast. "Right. Get him into the Land-Rover," I said.

We lifted him in between us, putting him out of sight behind the rear seat; then I got out again, knelt beside the unconscious corporal and tied his hands behind his back with his belt.

Binnie joined me as I finished. "What are we going to do with him?"

"We'll have to take him with us. Can't afford to have anybody find him too soon."

Binnie's anger boiled over suddenly and he kicked the unconscious man in the side. "If he got his deserts, I'd put a bullet in him."

"For God's sake, get his feet and shut up," I said. "If you want your precious Small Man to live, you'd better get him where we're going fast."

We bundled the corporal into the Land-Rover, putting him on the floor between the front and rear seats. I got into the back with Cork and left the driving to Binnie.

I wasn't really conscious of the passing of time, although I was aware that wherever we were going, we were going there very fast indeed. I was too occupied with keeping Cork as upright as possible, an essential where lung wounds are concerned. I had found the vehicle's first-aid box easily enough and held a field dressing over the wound tightly in an effort to staunch the bleeding.

Gradually his condition grew worse. All color had faded from his face, the breathing sounded terrible, and there was a kind of gurgling inside his chest as he inhaled, one of the nastiest sounds I have ever heard.

As I say, I was not conscious of the passage of time and yet I realize now that until that moment, I had not spoken a word to Binnie since we had left the scene of the shooting.

Blood trickled from the corner of Cork's mouth and I said desperately, "For God's sake, Binnie, when do we reach the border? The man's dying on us."

"Hang on to your hat, Major," he replied over his shoulder. "For the past mile and a half you've been inside the Republic."

12

The Race North

The convent looked more like a seventeenth-century country house than anything else, which was very probably what it had once been. It was surrounded by a fifteen-foot wall of mellow brick and the main gate was closed.

Binnie braked to a halt, jumped out, and pulled on a bell rope. After a while, a small judas gate opened and a nun peered out. It was not unknown for British patrols to cross the ill-marked border in error on occasion, which probably explained the expression of shocked amazement on her face at the sight of the uniform.

"Good heavens, young man, don't you realize where you are? You're in the Irish Republic. Turn round and go back where you came from this instant."

"For God's sake, Sister, will you listen to me?" Binnie demanded. "We're not what we seem. We've a man near dying in the back here."

She came through the gate without hesitation and approached the Land-Rover. Binnie ran in front of her and got the rear door open. She looked in and was immediately confronted with the sight of the wounded man held upright in my arms. He chose that exact moment to cough, blood spurting from his mouth.

She turned and ran, picking up her skirts; the gates swung open a moment later and Binnie drove into the courtyard.

The anteroom was surprisingly well furnished with padded leather club chairs and a selection of magazines laid out on a coffee table. There was a glass partition at one side, and I could see into the reception room where they had taken Cork. He lay on a trolley covered with a blanket, and four nuns in nursing uniform busied themselves in giving him a blood transfusion, among other things.

The door opened and another nun appeared, a tall, plain-looking woman in her forties. The others got out of her way fast and she examined him.

Within a moment or so she was giving orders and Cork was being wheeled out, one nun keeping pace with the trolley, the bottle of blood held high. The one who had examined him turned to glance at us through the glass wall, then followed them out. A moment later, the door opened behind us and she entered.

"I am Sister Teresa, Mother Superior here." Her voice was well-bred, pleasant, more English than Irish. Very definitely someone who had known the better things of life and I wondered, in a strange, detached way, what her story was. What had she given up for this?

There was an edge to her voice when she spoke again. "Who are you?"

Binnie glanced at me briefly, then shrugged. "I.R.A., from across the border."

"And that man in there? Is he a priest?" He shook his head and she went on. "Who is he, then?"

"Michael Cork," I said. "Otherwise known as the Small Man. Perhaps you know of him?"

Her eyes widened, closed briefly, then opened again. "I have heard of Mr. Cork. He is extremely ill. The bullet has penetrated the left lung and lodged under the shoulder blade. I think the heart has also been touched, but I can't be sure until I operate."

"You operate?" Binnie said, taking a step toward her.

"I would imagine so," she replied calmly. "I am senior surgeon here and a case like this requires experience."

"The bullet was fired at point blank range, sister," I informed her.

"I had imagined that must be so from the powder burns. What caliber?"

"Nine-millimeter. Sterling submachine gun."

She nodded. "Thank you. You must excuse me now."

Binnie caught her sleeve. As she turned, he said, "No need to inform the authorities about this is there, sister?"

"On the contrary," she said. "The moment more pressing matters are taken care of I shall make it my first duty to inform the area military commander of Mr. Cork's presence. You gentlemen, I presume, will have had the good sense to take yourselves back where you came from by then."

"We'd like to stay for a while, sister," I said. "Until after the operation, if you've no objection?"

She hesitated, then made her decision. "Very well, I'll send for you when it's all over." She opened the door, paused, a hand on the knob, and turned to Binnie who had slumped into a chair, shoulders bowed. "I spent five years at a mission hospital in the Congo, young man, so gunshot wounds are not unknown to me. A small prayer might be in order, however."

But I was long past that kind of thing myself. Perhaps there was a God who cared, although from my own experience, I doubted it. But I knew a professional when I saw one and beyond any shadow of a doubt, if Sister Teresa couldn't save him, no one could.

I left Binnie and went out to the Land-Rover to check on our prisoner. When I opened the door I found that he was not only conscious again, but had managed to roll over on his back. His face was streaked with dried blood and his nose, from the look of it, was very possibly broken.

He looked up at me, dazed and more than a little frightened. "Where am I?"

I said, "You're on the wrong side of the border in the hands of the I.R.A. Lie very still and quiet, there's a good lad, and you might come out of this with a whole skin."

He seemed to shrink inside himself. I got up and went back to the anteroom.

We weren't left alone for very long. After twenty minutes or so, a nun appeared and took us down the corridor to a washroom where we could clean up. Then we were taken to a large dining room with several rows of tables. We had the whole place to ourselves, two nuns standing patiently by to serve us while we ate.

Afterward, we were escorted back to the anteroom. It was a long wait, in fact a good two hours, before a nun appeared and beckoned us.

We followed her along the corridor to another small room at the far end. Again there was a glass wall, this time looking in at a side ward. There were half a dozen beds, but only one occupant, Michael Cork, and he was in an oxygen tent.

A couple of nuns knelt at the end of the bed in prayer, two more leaned over the patient. One of them turned and came toward us. It was Sister Teresa and she still wore a surgeon's white cap and gown, a mask suspended around her neck.

She looked tired, lines etched deeply from either side of her nose to the limits of her mouth. I think I knew what she was going to say even before she opened the glass door and joined us.

"He's going to be all right?" Binnie asked.

"On the contrary," she told him calmly. "He's going to die, and very soon now. As I had feared, there was damage to the heart as well as to the lungs, but much worse than I would have thought possible."

Binnie turned away. I said, "He's a good man, sister. A fine man. I know the Church does not approve of the I.R.A.'s actions, but he deserves a priest."

"I've sent for one," she said simply. "But first, he wishes to speak to you."

"Are you certain?"

"He is quite rational though very weak. He said I was to bring the Major quickly. There isn't much time."

She opened the glass door and I followed her through. I paused beside the oxygen tent and waited, the voices of the nuns in prayer a soft murmur. Cork opened his eyes and looked up at me. Sister Teresa unzipped the plastic flap that we might speak.

"I'm going, Vaughan," he whispered. "At the end of things at last and full of doubts. I'm not sure if I've been right—if it's all been worthwhile. Do you follow me?"

"I think so."

"Connolly and Pearse—Big Mick Collins. They were names to conjure with, but what came after? Did it really measure up to their sacrifice?" He closed his eyes. "I could have been wrong all these years. I can't risk another death on my conscience."

"Norah?" I said.

He opened his eyes. "Get back to Stramore if you have to walk through hell to do it. Tell Barry that if he wants that bloody gold he'll have to swim for it. It's six fathoms down in the middle of Horseshoe Bay on Magil Island. That's where I sank the launch. I haven't been back since."

Which was interesting, and for a second I got a flash of the place again in my mind's eyes as I had last seen it, gray, windswept, and lonely beneath the barren rocks of the island in the morning rain.

He stared up at me in mute appeal. "I'll see to it," I said and something made me add in Irish, "I'll settle Barry for you, Small Man."

His eyes opened again. "Who are you, boy? What are you?"

I said nothing and he continued to stare up at me, a slight frown on his face and then his eyes widened and I think a kind of understanding dawned.

"Holy Saints," he said. "There's irony for you. My God, but I call that rich."

He started to laugh weakly, and Sister Teresa pulled me gently away. "Please leave now," she said, "as you promised."

"Of course, Sister."

She turned back to the bed as the priest was ushered in and I went into the anteroom and took Binnie by the arm. "Let's get out of here. No sense in prolonging the agony."

He looked once toward the bed where the priest leaned over Cork, then turned and walked out. I followed him along the corridor and out of the front door to the courtyard where the Land-Rover still waited at the bottom of the steps.

Binnie said, "What now?"

"Stramore," I said. "Where else?"

His eyes widened. "He told you, then, where the stuff is?"

"Not ten miles from Spanish Head. Remember that island we stopped at yesterday morning—Magil? He sank the launch in the bay there."

Binnie glanced at his watch, then slammed a fist against his thigh in a kind of impotent fury. "Much good will it do us."

His despair was absolute, which was understandable enough. He had just lost the one man he respected above all others, and was now faced with the knowledge that Norah Murphy would almost certainly end the same way and there was nothing he could do about it.

"No chance of reaching Stramore by six o'clock now, Major. No chance at all."

"Oh, yes, there is," I said. "If we don't waste time dodging round the back country, stay on main roads all the way."

"But how?" he demanded. "It's asking to be lifted."

"Bluff, Binnie," I said. "Two paratroopers in an Army Land-Rover taking a chance on the Queen's Highway. Does the prospect please you?"

He laughed suddenly, much more his old self again. "By God, Major, but there are times when I think you're very probably the Devil himself."

361

I opened the rear door and pulled the young corporal up and out into the open. He seemed unsteady on his feet, the skin around the swollen nose and eyes blackening into bruises. I sat him down carefully on the convent steps.

Binnie said, "What are we going to do with him?"

"Leave him here. By the time the nuns have patched him up and fed him and reported his presence to the Garda, it'll be evening. He can't do us any harm, but if we're going, we've got to go now."

The nun on the gates had got them open. As we drove through I called, "We've left you another patient back there on the steps, Sister. Tell Sister Teresa I'm sorry."

Her mouth opened as if she was trying to say something, but by then it was too late and we were out into the road and away. Five minutes later we bumped over the farm track that took us into Ulster and turned along the road to Strabane.

The streets of Strabane were jammed with traffic, and there seemed to be roadblocks everywhere, which was pretty much what I had expected. The authorities must have known for some considerable time that we were not in the wreckage of that burned-out Cortina at the bottom of the ravine.

Getting through proved unbelievably easy for the obvious reason that there were soldiers everywhere and we were just two more. I told Binnie to simply blast his way through, which he did, on several occasions taking to the pavement to get past lines of cars and trucks waiting their turn.

At every checkpoint we came to we were waved on without the slightest hesitation and within ten minutes of entering the town, we were clear again and moving along the main road to Londonderry.

Binnie was like some kid out for the day, excitement and laughter bubbling out of him. "I'd say they were looking for somebody back there, wouldn't you, Major?"

"So it would seem."

"That's the bloody British Army for you." He snapped his

fingers and took us down the center of the road, overtaking everything in sight.

I said mildly, "Not so much of the bloody, Binnie. I used to be a part of it remember."

He glanced at me, surprise on his face as if he had genuinely forgotten, and then he laughed out loud. "But not now, Major. Now, you're one of us. Christ, but you'll be taking the oath next. It's all that's needed."

He started to sing the "Soldier's Song" at the top of his voice, hardly the most appropriate of choices considering he was wearing a British uniform, and concentrated on his driving. I lit a cigarette and sat back, the Sterling across my knees.

I wondered what kind of face he'd show me at that final, fatal moment when, as they used to say in the old melodramas, all was revealed. He would very probably make me kill him, if only to save my own skin, something I very definitely did not want to do.

Binnie and I had come a long way since that first night in Cohan's Select Bar in Belfast and I'd learned one very important thing. The I.R.A. didn't just consist of bomb-happy Provos and Frank Barry and company. There were also genuine idealists there in the Pearse and Connolly tradition. Always would be. People like the Small Man, God rest him, and Binnie Gallagher.

Whether one agreed with them or not, they were honest men who believed passionately that they were engaged in a struggle for which the stake was nothing less than the freedom of their country.

They would lay down their lives if necessary, they would kill soldiers, but not children—never that. Whatever happened, they wanted to be able to face it with clean hands and a little honor. Their tragedy was that in this kind of war that just was not possible.

Frank Barry, of course, was a different proposition altogether, which brought me right back to the Brigadier and Norah Murphy and the present situation at Spanish Head.

The Brigadier had told me quite clearly that I was to avoid

contact with the military on any official level at all costs and it
seemed to me that no purpose was to be gained by disregarding
his instructions in the present circumstances. If the Guards
Parachute Company itself was dropped in on Spanish Head,
the Brigadier and Norah would be the first to go.

Not that I believed for one moment that Barry would keep
his promise and release the girl, and the Brigadier, of course,
had never been a party to the agreement in the first place.

No, whichever way you looked at it, the only thing to do was
to go in and play it by ear in the hope of extracting every possible
advantage from the fact that I had something he wanted very
badly indeed.

We were somewhere past Londonderry on the coast road
before we ran into any kind of trouble. When it came, it was
from the most unexpected quarter.

We went around a bend and Binnie had to brake hard, for
the road in front of us was jammed with vehicles. In the distance
I could see the roofs of houses among the trees, and smoke
drifted across them in a black pall.

There were two or three isolated shots followed by the rattle
of a submachine gun as Binnie pulled out to bypass the line of
traffic. I heard confused shouting faintly in the distance.

"This doesn't look good," I said. "Is there a way round?"

"No, there's a central square to the place and everything goes
through it."

I told him to keep on going and we reached the outskirts of
the village to find a couple of M.P. Land-Rovers blocking one-
half of the road. As Binnie braked to a halt, a corporal came
forward and saluted.

I said, "What's going on in there?"

"Riot situation, sir. Local police arrested a youth they found
painting slogans on the walls of the church hall. After half an
hour, a mob collected outside the police barracks demanding
he should be freed. When the petrol bombs started coming in
they sent for us."

"Who's handling it?"

"Half a company of Highlanders, sir, but there are more on the way."

I turned to Binnie. "All right, drive on."

As we started to move, the corporal ran alongside. "You want to watch it on the way in, sir. That crowd is in a bloody ugly mood."

Binnie accelerated and we moved down the center of the street. People stood outside the small terrace houses, huddled together in groups. As we passed, heads turned and the insults started to come thick and fast. A stone bounced from the canopy and then another.

But worse was to come, for when we turned the corner, the street was jammed with an angry mob and beyond them in the square the Highlanders were drawn up in a phalanx, transparent riot shields held out before them. A petrol bomb curved through the air and exploded, carpeting the area in front of the troops with orange flame. They moved back in good order and the crowd surged forward.

Binnie said, "This doesn't look too good. What do we do?"

"Drive like hell and don't stop for anything. If that lot get their hands on us it's a length of rope and the nearest lamppost."

At that moment someone at the rear of the crowd turned and saw us and raised the alarm. The howl that went up was enough to chill the blood. I ducked instinctively as a shower of stones came toward us, though most of them rattled harmlessly enough from the bodywork of the Land Rover.

A petrol bomb soared through the air. Binnie swerved violently as it exploded to one side. And then we were into the crowd. He slowed instinctively, couldn't help it as they crowded in, men, women, even children, howling like wolves, hands tearing at the Land-Rover as we passed. Some madman jumped into our direct path, arms wide, bounced from the hood into the crowd like a rubber ball. Binnie slammed his foot on the brake.

It was like that last great wave one reads about sweeping in.

I did the only possible thing, leaned out of the window and fired a burst from the Sterling above their heads. The effect was all that I could have hoped for and everyone scattered.

I shook Binnie by the shoulder. "Now let's get moving."

We shot forward, swerving to avoid someone lying on the ground, narrowly missed a lamppost, and drove through the debris of the square toward the line of Highlanders. They opened their ranks to receive us and Binnie pulled in beside an ambulance and an armored troop carrier.

A young lieutenant in camouflaged uniform, flak jacket, and Glengarry bonnet came forward and saluted formally. "A near thing, sir. For a while there I thought we might have to come and get you. My name's Ford."

"Major Parker, Second Paras." I held out my hand. "Sorry to descend on you like this, but I didn't have much option. I've been ordered to report to police headquarters in Coleraine as soon as possible to have a look at someone they've picked up in connection with the Brigadier Ferguson kidnapping. If it's the man they think it is, I can identify him positively. Can we get through?"

"I should think so, sir," Ford said. "Only a church and a few almshouses on that side. Not many people around."

There was a sudden cry and as we turned, at least half a dozen petrol bombs burst in front and behind his men. There seemed to be flames everywhere, smoke billowing across the square. For a moment, there was considerable confusion and the Highlanders scattered.

One young soldier ran toward us screaming, his legs ablaze, still clutching his transparent shield in one hand, a riot stick in the other. Binnie got to him before I did, sticking out a foot deftly to trip him up. We beat at the flames with our hands, then someone appeared with a fire extinguisher from one of the Land-Rovers and sprayed his legs.

The young soldier lay there crying helplessly, his face screwed up in agony, and a couple of medics ran across from the ambulance with a stretcher. One of them got a morphine ampule out of his first-aid kit and jabbed it in the boy's arm.

Binnie stayed on one knee watching, his face very white, the eyes full of pain. I pulled him up. "Are you all right?"

"It was the stink of his flesh burning," he said as they carried the lad away. "It reminded me of Norah."

"Now you see how the other half lives," I said.

The Highlanders were on the offensive now, firing rubber bullets into the crowd, following this up with a wild baton charge to drive them back. It was a scene from hell, pools of fire all over the square from the petrol bombs, black greasy smoke billowing everywhere, shouts and screams from the crowd where hand-to-hand fighting was taking place.

Binnie was looking anything but happy, which was understandable enough, I gave him a push toward the Land-Rover. "Time to go."

He got behind the wheel and started the engine. As I climbed in beside him, Lieutenant Ford approached. "Ready for off, sir?"

"That's right."

"I think we've got things under control here now and another company's due to assist. I'll just put you on your way."

He stood on the running board, hanging on to the door as Binnie drove away. The square was, in fact, L-shaped, and we moved round a corner and looked across to a church, the entrance to a narrow street beside it.

"That's where you want to be, sir," Ford said, and pointed.

There was a single shot, a high powered rifle from the sound of it; he gave a grunt and went sideways. I dropped out, grabbed him by the flak jacket, and dragged him around the corner as another bullet chipped a cobblestone a yard to one side. As Binnie reversed to join us, a third round punched a hole in the left-hand side of the windshield.

The bullet had gone straight through Ford's right thigh and he lay there on the cobbles clutching it with both hands, blood spurting between his fingers. The medics appeared on the run. There was a rumble of thunder above us and it started to rain, a sudden drenching downpour that put out the petrol fires almost instantly.

One of the medics slapped a couple of field dressings on either side of Ford's thigh and started to bandage it tightly. Binnie had gotten out of the Land-Rover and was crouched against the wall beside me.

"Now what?" he whispered.

I heard Ford say, "Johnson, take a look and see if you can spot him."

Johnson, a stocky young sergeant, crawled to the corner and peered around cautiously. Nothing happened. Even the crowd on the other side of the square had gone quiet. Johnson eased forward, there was a single shot, and he was lifted bodily backward.

He cannoned against me and rolled over, gasping, but when a couple of his men lifted him into a sitting position we saw that the bullet had mushroomed against his flak jacket and he was simply winded by the blow.

Another round chipped the corner and a second ricocheted from the cobbles on the other side of the Land-Rover. Someone tried a steel helmet on the end of a stick around the corner and the moment it appeared a bullet drilled a neat hole through it.

The medics were trying to persuade Ford to get on a stretcher so they could take him to the ambulance and he was telling them exactly what to do about it in crisp Anglo-Saxon.

"By God, but he's doing a great job whoever he is," Binnie whispered. "He's got every bastard here neatly pinned down."

"Including us," I said. "Or had you forgotten that? We've got just over an hour to get to Spanish Head, Binnie, which means that if we're not out of here within the next ten minutes, Norah Murphy's had it."

He stared at me aghast. I picked up the helmet with the hole through and handed it to him. "When I give the word, toss that out into the square."

I pulled off my beret, then crawled to the corner on my belly and peered around at ground level. The most likely spot seemed to be the church tower opposite. I was proven right a moment later, for when Binnie threw the helmet there was some sort of movement up there in the belfry and the helmet jumped twenty feet as another round pumped into it. A second shot chipped the corner just above my head and I withdrew hurriedly.

"What's the situation, sir?" Ford called.

"He's in the belfry," I said, "and he's good. He'll kill any man stone dead who tries to make it to that church door."

Ford nodded wearily. "We'll have to wait till B Company gets here. We'll smoke him out soon enough then."

As I stood up, Binnie whispered urgently, "We can't stand around here doing nothing while Norah's life's ticking away by the minute."

"Exactly," I said, "and the only way out of here is by knocking out the lad up there in the tower."

"But he's one of our own."

"It's either him or Norah Murphy. Make up your mind."

His face was very pale now, sweat on his brow. He glanced about him wildly as if looking for some other way out, then nodded. "All right, damn you, what do we have to do?"

"It's simple," I said. "I want you to draw his fire by driving the Land-Rover out into the square. I'll handle the rest."

He turned from me at once, went to the Land-Rover, and got behind the wheel. As he started the engine, I took the rifle from a young private who was kneeling beside me.

I said to Ford, "Perhaps we won't have to wait for B Company after all, Lieutenant." Then I flattened myself against the corner and gave Binnie the nod.

He roared out into the square and the sniper in the tower went to work instantly. I allowed him two shots, then ran out into the open, raised the rifle to my shoulder, and fired six or seven times up into the belfry very rapidly.

It was enough. The bells started to ring a hideous clamor, as bullets ricocheted from them, a rifle jumped into the air, a man

369

in a trench coat seemed to poise there for a moment then dived head first to the cobbles.

I handed the rifle back to its owner and started across the square. Binnie had braked to a halt in the center. As I reached him, the Highlanders moved past me toward the body. The smoke seemed suddenly to grow thicker, from the rain, I suppose, choking the square so that visibility was reduced to a few yards.

I climbed in beside Binnie. "I think this would be as good a time as any to get out of here."

The skin was drawn tightly over his cheekbones so that his face was skull-like and it was as if Death himself stared out at me when he turned.

"I didn't look," he said. "I couldn't. Is he dead?"

"Drive on, Binnie," I told him gently. "There's a good lad."

"Oh, my God," he said as he drove away, his eyes were wet and I do not think it was from the smoke alone.

13

May You Die in Ireland

We turned in through the gate leading to the private road to Spanish Head at about ten minutes to six. The final part of the run had proved completely uneventful, for although we had run across two more roadblocks near Coleraine, we had been waved through without the slightest hesitation.

It had stopped raining for the moment, but there was a dampness to the air that seemed to indicate more rain was to come. Out to sea, heavy gray clouds crowded in toward a horizon that was touched with a weird orange glow.

The house seemed dark and somber, waiting for us at the edge of the cliff in the pale evening light. There was no sign of life at all as we rolled into the courtyard and braked to a halt.

So, here we were again at the final, dangerous edge of things. I lit a cigarette and turned to Binnie, "We made it."

"So it would appear, Major." He rested his forehead on the steering wheel as if suddenly very weary.

There was a slight eerie creaking as the garage door eased open. I said softly, "Don't let's do anything drastic. It's Vaughan and Binnie Gallagher."

I turned slowly and found Dooley and three of his chums standing abreast, each man covering us with a submachine gun.

When we went into the drawing room on the first floor, Frank Barry was standing with his back to the fire, a glass of brandy in one hand. He looked us over with obvious amusement.

"My, my, but this is one for the book. I've never seen you so well dressed, Binnie. You should wear it all the time."

Binnie said quietly, "Where's Norah?"

"You can see her when I'm good and ready. Now, what did Cork have to say?"

"You heard him," I said. "First Norah, then we talk."

I think that for a moment there, he was going to argue about it, but instead he shrugged and nodded to Dooley who went into the next room. He returned leading Norah by the arm. She looked pale and ill, her cheek covered by a padded dressing held in place by surgical tape. She seemed stunned at the sight of Binnie and tried to take a step toward us. Frank Barry pulled her back and shoved her down into a chair.

"All right," he said. "What about Cork?"

"He died earlier this afternoon," I said simply.

Barry stared at me, thunderstruck. "You're lying. I would have heard. It would have been on the news. He's too important."

"He was shot during a struggle with a British soldier near Plumbridge," I said. "Binnie and I took him to a convent hospital just across the border into the Republic."

"You know the place," Binnie said. "Gleragh."

Barry glanced at him briefly, then turned back to me. "Go on."

"They operated; he died; it's as simple as that. But before he went he told me what you wanted to know."

I turned to Norah Murphy, who sat gazing fixedly at me, the eyes dark and tragic in that ravaged face.

"He said he didn't want you on his conscience, too, Norah, when he died."

She buried her face in her hands, and Barry said impatiently, "Come on, old lad, out with it. Where is the stuff?"

"Not so fast," I said. "You gave us a promise. You said you'd free us all if we got you the information you wanted. What guarantee do we have that you intend to keep your word?"

He stood there staring at me, a slight, fixed frown on his face. "Guarantee?" he said.

He laughed suddenly and it was not a pleasant sound. "I'll tell you what I will guarantee." He grabbed Norah Murphy by the hair and yanked her head back. "That I'll give her a repeat performance on the other cheek if you don't come clean."

He ripped the dressing away brutally and the girl cried out in pain. I caught my breath at the sight of that hideous, swollen burn.

I think Binnie went a little mad there for a moment for he flung himself at Barry, hands reaching for the throat. Dooley moved in fast and gave him the butt of his Sterling in the back. Binnie went down on his knees and Barry booted him in the stomach.

He shoved the wretched girl back into her chair and turned to me. "All right, make up your mind. I haven't got all night."

"There's an island about ten miles out from here called Magil," I told him. "Cork said he sank the launch containing the gold in five or six fathoms of water in Horseshoe Bay. He said that if you wanted it, you'd have to swim for it."

"Well, the old bastard. The cunning old fox." He threw back his head and laughed uproariously. "Now that's what I call very, very funny."

"I'm glad you think so," I said. "Though I must say the point of the joke escapes me."

"Oh, you'll see it soon enough," he said. "You see, you're going to get that gold for me, Vaughan. After all, you're the expert in the diving department. I've seen all that gear you keep on the *Kathleen*."

"And afterwards?"

He spread his arms wide. "I let you go, all of you, and no hard feelings."

"And what guarantee do I have that you'll keep your promise this time?"

"None," he said. "None at all, but then, you don't really have any choice in the matter, do you?"

The final screw in the coffin, or so it seemed. I suppose it showed in my face for he laughed harshly, turned, and walked out, still laughing.

They took Binnie downstairs, presumably to the cellars, and Dooley and another man escorted me up the back stairs and locked me in the room with the dark mahogany furniture and the brass bedstead.

My suitcase was still there exactly as I had left it. It was almost like coming home. I ran a bath, got rid of the flak jacket and camouflaged uniform, and wallowed in water as hot as I could bear for half an hour and tried to think things out.

It was a mess, whichever way you looked at it. Barry had gone back on his promise once. What possible hope was there that he would keep his word now? The more I considered the matter, the more likely it appeared that once I'd raised the gold for him, he'd put me back over the side double quick with about forty pounds of old chain around my ankles.

I dried off and got a change of clothes from my suitcase: corduroy slacks, blue flannel shirt, and a sweater. Then I opened the window and had a look out there.

Barry had warned me on an earlier occasion that there was no need for bars and I could see why. There was a clear drop of fifty feet to the courtyard at the rear and the walls on either side were beautifully smooth. Not even the hint of a toehold between the stonework, no drainpipes within reaching distance, nothing.

The door opened behind me and Dooley appeared, the ever-present Sterling at the ready. He jerked his head and I took the hint and moved out past him. He was on his own and on the way downstairs. I wondered, for one wild moment, about having a go at him, missed a step deliberately, and allowed myself to stumble, dropping to one knee.

My God, but he was quick, the Sterling rammed up against the back of my head in an instant. I managed a smile with some

374

difficulty, but there was no response at all on that bleak stone face. Discretion very definitely being the better part of valor, I got up and continued down the stairs.

When we entered the drawing room Barry was sitting alone at the table by the fire finishing a meal. There was a decanter and several glasses on a silver tray and he nodded toward it.

"Have a glass of port, old lad."

The logs spluttered cheerfully in the Adam fireplace. It was all quite splendid, with the oil painting on the wall, the silver and crystal on the table. Rather like the officers' mess in one of the better regiments.

An Admiralty chart for the coastal area was opened out across the lower end of the table. I glanced at it casually as I poured a couple of glasses of port and pushed one across to him. He was, I think, mildly surprised, but took it all the same.

"Very civil of you."

I raised my glass. "Up the Republic."

He laughed out loud, head thrown back. "By God, but I like you Vaughan. I really do. You have a sense of humor, that's what it is, and so few of us do. The Irish, in spite of their reputation, are a sad race."

"All that rain," I said. "Now, what do you want?"

"A few words about the job in hand, that's all. I had that chart brought up from the *Kathleen*. As far as I can judge there aren't more than five fathoms anywhere in Horseshoe Bay."

I had a look at the chart. "So it would appear."

"It should be easy enough," he said. "I mean, you can stay down there at that depth for as long as it takes. You won't need to decompress or anything like that?"

It seemed likely that he was simply testing me so I decided to be honest. "Not really."

A slow smile spread across his face. "You told the truth. That's encouraging."

"My mother always said I should."

"I'm glad you decided to follow her advice." He took a small book from a drawer and tossed it on the table. "I found that on the boat with your diving gear so I was able to check the situation for myself."

It was a Board of Trade pamphlet containing various tables relating to diving depths, decompression rates, and so on.

I said, "One thing that doesn't tell you is that I only have about an hour's air left in my aqualung."

"Then you'll have to work fast, won't you?"

He obviously hadn't bothered to check how many ingots went into half a million in gold bullion. There didn't seem to be any point in trying to tell him, because I didn't know myself, although I suspected it must be a considerable number.

I said, "All right, when do we go?"

"Not me, old lad, you," he said. "With Dooley and another of my men to keep you company. Anything smaller than the *Queen Elizabeth* brings out the worst in me. If you leave at five you'll be there by first light."

The more I thought about it the less I liked it, for I could imagine what Dooley's orders would be the moment I delivered the goods.

"One small change," I said. "Binnie goes with me."

He shook his head sorrowfully. "Still don't trust me, old lad, do you?"

"Not one damn bit."

"All right," he said cheerfully. "If it makes you feel any happier, Binnie you shall have."

"With a Browning in his pocket?"

"Now that really would be expecting too much."

He went back to the table, poured two more glasses of port, and handed one to me. "Well, almost at the end of things now, Vaughan, eh? What shall we drink to?"

"Why, to you," I said, and gave him, in Irish, that most ancient of all toasts: "May you die in Ireland."

I had expected another of those laughs of his, but instead saw only a brief, reflective smile. "A fine toast, Major Vaughan, an excellent sentiment. Better by far than Shiloh and another man's war."

376

He drew himself up proudly, looking more like Francis the Fourth than ever, and raised his glass. "Up the Republic!"

It was only then, I think, that I realized just how seriously he took himself.

Dooley took me back up to the bedroom and locked the door on me again. I stood at the window smoking a cigarette and looked out at the night, an old Irish custom.

It was raining again now and I could smell the sea, although I couldn't see it. For a moment I saw the waters of Horseshoe Bay, gray in the dawn light. It would be cold down there and lonely with only a dead ship waiting. . . .

The Celt in me again. I shivered involuntarily and the door opened behind me. As I turned, Binnie was pushed into the room. He was dressed in a pair of faded jeans and an old turtleneck sweater, but still wore the paratroop boots.

I said, "Where have they been keeping you?"

"Down in the cellar with the old Brigadier."

"He's still in one piece then?"

"As far as I could see. What's all this about, Major?"

"I'm supposed to leave for Magil in the *Kathleen* just before dawn with Dooley and one of his cronies to keep me company. It seemed to me more than likely they'd put me over the side when I'd done the necessary so I told Barry I wouldn't go unless you went with me."

"And he agreed? Why?"

"A couple of reasons. One, he wanted to keep me happy—for the time being, that is."

"And two?"

"He's probably decided Dooley might just as well take care of you at the same time as he disposes of me."

There was still that sense of strain about him, the skin too tightly drawn across the cheekbones, and he was very pale, but when he spoke, his voice was calm, almost toneless.

"And what are we going to do about it?"

"I haven't the slightest idea because so much depends on

unknown factors. Will either of us be allowed in the wheelhouse, for example?"

"And why should that be so important?"

I told him about the secret flap under the chart room table. "Whatever happens," I went on, "if you see the slightest chance of grabbing one of those guns, take it. They're both silenced, by the way."

But for once, technical detail, even when concerned with his favorite subject, failed to interest him. "And what if they keep us out of the wheelhouse entirely? What if we don't get anywhere near those guns?"

"All right," I said. "Let's say I come up from the wreck twice. As I go down for the third time, you create a diversion of some sort. I'll surface on the other side of the boat and try to board and get into the wheelhouse undetected."

He thought about it for quite some time and then nodded slowly, "I don't suppose we have a great deal of choice, do we, Major? And afterward?"

"Now you are running ahead of the game. There may be no afterward anyway. On the other hand, there is one interesting thing I've noticed. The ranks of the Sons of Erin seem to be thinning rapidly. Since we've been back I've only seen Dooley and four other men. Even if one supposes another watching Norah's door, it still makes the odds bearable."

His face seemed paler than ever at the mention of her name, and his eyes seemed to recede into the sockets. "Have you seen her again?" he asked.

I shook my head. "No."

"Did you see her face, Major, the spirit in her broken utterly?" His hands tightened over the brass rail at the end of the bed. "By Christ, but I will have the eyes out of his head for doing that to her."

From the look on his face, I'd say he meant every word of it.

The tiny harbor in the inlet below Spanish Head was reached by a road that zigzagged down the side of the cliff in a reasonably hair-raising way. We were taken down in the back of the Ford truck and when it stopped, we got out to find ourselves on a long stone jetty. The cliffs towered above us on either side and from that vantage point, it was impossible to see anything of Spanish Head.

At the far end of the inlet there was a massive boathouse which I presumed contained the M.T.B., although I could not be sure as the great wooden doors were closed. The *Kathleen* was tied up at the bottom of a flight of stone steps, and Dooley pushed us down in front of him.

His companion was already on board, a squat, rough-looking man with a shock of red hair and a tangled beard who wore fisherman's boots turned down at the knees and an Aran sweater. As I stepped over the rail, the Land-Rover we'd come all the way from Plumbridge in braked to a halt on the jetty above and Frank Barry got out.

"Everything all right, old lad?" he called. "McGuire, there, knows these waters like the back of his hand so he'll run the ship or boat or whatever you call it. We don't want to overwork you."

So that was very much that. I said, "Just as you say, Barry."

He smiled beautifully. "Thought you'd see it my way. Now for the surprise. Norah's come to see you off."

He pulled her out of the Land-Rover so forcefully that she lost her balance and almost fell over. Binnie put a foot on the rail and Dooley raised his Sterling ominously. At the same moment the engines rumbled into life and McGuire leaned out of the wheelhouse and told us to cast off.

I looked up and had a final glimpse of Norah Murphy standing under the lamp in the rain, a pale shadow of her former self, so frail that, from the looks of her, she would have fallen down had it not been for Barry's supporting arm.

And then they suddenly receded into darkness as McGuire increased speed and we moved out to sea.

14

Dark Waters

Magil Island was as bleak a sight as I have ever seen as we nosed into Horseshoe Bay in the gray light of dawn. At the height of summer the place could never hope to seem more than it was, a bare, black rock, but just now in the morning mist, rain driving across the bay in a gray curtain, it looked about the last place there was on top of earth.

I'd been preparing on the way over and was already wearing my wetsuit as McGuire cut the engines and dropped anchor as close to the center of the bay as he could gauge.

Standing at my side in an old reefer coat, the collar turned up against the driving rain, Binnie shivered visibly as he looked down at the dark waters.

"Rather you than me, Major. Will it take long to find, do you think? It doesn't look to me as if you've a hope of seeing a thing down there. It's as dark as the grave."

"Cork said the center," I reminded him, "and we can't be too far out, whatever happens. The damn bay is only about seventy-five yards across, as far as I can see."

He started to help me on with my equipment while McGuire rigged the winch to start hauling, which was, I suppose, the

380

right kind of optimistic attitude. As I strapped my cork-handled diver's knife to my leg I noticed Dooley watching from a distance, the Sterling, as always, ready for action.

"Any objection, you great stupid bastard?" I demanded.

The stone mask he called a face didn't move a muscle. I turned away, stood up, and Binnie helped me into my aqualung. As he tightened the straps I whispered, "Don't forget—when I go down for the third time."

He handed me a diver's lamp without a word. I pulled down my mask, got a firm grip on my mouthpiece, and went over the rail.

I paused briefly to adjust my air supply and went down quickly. It wasn't anything as bad as I'd thought it would be. The water was strangely clear, like black glass. I was reminded suddenly and with a touch of unease of those dark pools of Celtic mythology into which heroes were constantly diving to seek out monstrous beasts that preyed on lesser men.

The bottom of the bay at that point was covered with seaweed, great, pale fronds reaching out toward me like tentacles, five or six feet in length. I hovered beside the anchor chain for a moment, turning full circle, but in spite of the almost unnatural clearness of the water, my visibility range was only a few yards.

There was nothing for it, then, but to start looking. I swam toward the shore, staying close to the seabed, and found the launch almost instantly, lying tilted to one side in the center of a patch of clear white sand.

I went down to deck level, grabbed hold of the rail, and hung on. The signs of the fight with the Royal Navy M.T.B. were plain to see. Two largish holes in the superstructure where cannon shells had hit and dozens of bullet holes in the hull that could only have been made by heavy machine gun fire.

I went up fast and surfaced a good thirty yards nearer the shore than the *Kathleen*. Binnie was the first to see me and waved his hand. They hauled in the anchor, McGuire started the engines and coasted toward me.

"You've found it?" Binnie asked as they slowed beside me and McGuire let the anchor out again.

I nodded. "I'm making my first dive now to assess the situation."

I got a grip on my mouthpiece again and went down fast, hanging onto the deck rail while I adjusted my air supply. Then I switched on the lamp and went headfirst down the companionway.

A small amount of gray light filtered in through the portholes, and it was as eerie as hell in that passage. One of the cabin doors swung gently to and fro. I shoved it open with my foot and a body lifted gently off the bunk opposite in the sudden turbulence and subsided again, but not before I'd seen the face, swollen to incredible proportions like something out of a nightmare. Another drifted above my head, pinned to the cabin roof. I got out and closed the door hurriedly.

I found what I wanted the moment I entered the main saloon, for several large boxes were jumbled together in the angle between the center table and the bulkhead where the boat had tilted. Most of them were padlocked, but one had been opened and the contents spilled out in an untidy pile like children's blocks.

Gold is heavy stuff and the ingot I picked up must have weighed a good twenty pounds, but I was conscious of no particular elation as I moved back along the companionway. The chips were down now with a vengeance and a hell of a lot depended on what happened during the next ten or fifteen minutes.

I surfaced beside the ladder McGuire had put over the rail and held up the ingot. Binnie came down the ladder and stood knee-deep in water to take it from me, hanging on with one hand. It was a heaven-sent opportunity and as I passed the ingot to him, I slipped my diver's knife from its sheath and pushed it down inside one of his paratrooper's boots.

His face, as usual, gave nothing away. He handed the ingot

over the rail to McGuire who turned excitedly to show it to Dooley. Dooley was more interested in watching me.

"Are you all right, Major?" Binnie asked.

"It's bloody cold," I said, "so let's have that net down pretty damn quick. I want to get out of here."

McGuire, helped by Binnie, pushed the winch arm out over the rail. They had already fixed a heavy net to the pulley hook, which they now let down. I adjusted my mouthpiece and went after it.

Filling the net was a laborious process for, as I needed the lamp to negotiate the interior of the wreck, I could only carry one ingot at a time. It took me a good twenty minutes to move six. Which was very definitely enough, so I hauled on the line and followed them up.

As I surfaced they were already swinging the net in over the deck. "Jesus, man, this is the best you can do?" McGuire called.

"It's bloody hard work," I told him.

"Well, you'd better get on with it or we'll be here all day."

I glanced at Binnie who was crouched over the rail, busily engaged in moving the ingots. Dooley stood against the rail toward the prow watching me so I gave him two fingers and dived.

I went nearly all the way to the bottom before changing direction and striking for the surface again, keeping directly under the keel the *Kathleen*. When I was almost there, I unbuckled the straps of my aqualung and got rid of it, surfacing gently on the other side of the *Kathleen*.

I heard Binnie say angrily, "Will you watch what you're doing, you stupid bastard, or you'll get my fist in your teeth."

"You little runt," McGuire answered. "I'll break your bloody neck."

I could see none of this, of course, as I hauled myself under the rail and slipped inside the wheelhouse. My finger found the button under the chart table, the flap fell.

I reached for the Mauser with my left hand. As I pulled it

from the clip, there was the faintest of sounds behind me. I turned, very carefully, to find Dooley standing in the open doorway.

What sixth sense had brought him there I'll never know, but there was no expression on his face as he stood covering me with the Sterling. I dropped the Mauser, having little option in the matter. He smiled beautifully, then shot me through the left forearm.

I lay on my back in the corner for a moment. There was some sort of disturbance taking place on the other side of the wheelhouse, for I could hear McGuire cursing.

Gunshot wounds seldom hurt straight away, but the shock to the nervous system is considerable so that I was understandably not quite myself as I struggled to my feet.

I fully expected Dooley to finish me off there and then, but instead he moved outside and beckoned me to follow. I must have looked quite a sight as I paused in the doorway, dazed and shocked, blood pouring from my left arm, because he gave me that smile again and lowered the Sterling.

I think it was the smile that did it, but then I learned a long time ago that you survive in my line only by seizing each chance as it comes. I moved out of the door swaying, ready to fall down at any moment, and gave him the edge of my right hand across his throat. He dropped the Sterling and staggered back against the companionway.

By rights such a blow should have put him on his back, but the heavy collar of his reefer coat, turned up against the rain, saved him. As I leaned down and tried to pick up the Sterling, he came for me.

I kicked the Sterling under the rail, which seemed the sensible thing to do, and put a fist into his mouth when he got close enough. It was like hitting the Rock of Gibraltar, and his own blow in return was of such devastating power that I felt at least two ribs go in my right side.

384

He wrapped those great arms around me and started to squeeze. Perhaps he'd some pleasant little idea in mind like breaking my back across the rail. If so, it was his last mistake, for when he pushed me up against it, I let myself go straight over, taking him with me.

And the sea was my element, not his. I kicked hard, taking us down, clutching at his reefer coat as he tried to pull away. My back scraped against the anchor chain. I grabbed hold of it with my left hand, ignoring the pain, and clamped my right forearm across his throat.

God, how he struggled, but he was already half-gone and nothing on top of earth or beneath it could have made me let go. My lungs were near to bursting when I finally released him and followed him up.

Binnie reached for me as I surfaced beside Dooley. I sucked in air and shook my head. "Give me a line. I'll pass it under his arms."

"Christ Jesus, Major, the bastard's dead. You've only got to look at him."

"Do as I say," I insisted. "I'll explain later."

Binnie got a line as I requested, I passed it under the dead man's arms, and he hauled him over the rail. I followed a moment later and collapsed on the deck, my back against the wheelhouse.

"Jesus, but you look in a bad way, Major," Binnie said anxiously as he leaned over me.

"Never mind that. What happened to McGuire?"

"I put the knife to him and shoved him over the side."

"Good lad. Now bring me a bottle of Jameson up from the saloon, and the first-aid kit. You've got some patching up to do."

I moved into the wheelhouse and he cut me out of the wet suit and set to work. By the time I was on my third large Jameson, he'd bandaged the forearm, but the ribs were a different proposition. He taped them up as best he could, but each time I breathed it felt like a knife in the lungs. After that, he gave me two shots of morphine under my instructions and helped me dress.

I poured another large Jameson and he said anxiously, "Sure, now, and didn't I read somewhere that booze and that stuff don't mix too well?"

"Maybe not," I said. "But I need them both for what I've got to do."

"And what would that be, Major?"

"Oh, get back to Spanish Head and sort out that bastard, Barry, once and for all." I managed a grin. "He's really beginning to annoy me, Binnie."

"I'm with you there all the way," he said.

"All right, then let's have a look at the situation. When we take the *Kathleen* in, there are two possibilities. The first is that Barry will be waiting on the jetty in person, eager for his first sight of the gold."

"And the second?"

"He'll stay up at the house and leave his men, or some of them, to do the welcoming."

"But they'll know something is wrong the moment they see either of us at the wheel as we come in," Binnie pointed out.

I shook my head and fought hard to keep control of the pain in my side. "But neither of us will be at the wheel, Binnie, that's the point."

I looked out to where Dooley sprawled on his back on the deck, eyes wide for all eternity.

15

Fire from Heaven

We moved in toward the inlet below Spanish Head, Dooley in the helmsman's seat in the wheelhouse, his hands on the wheel. The ropes which held him in place were concealed by his reefer coat and I was satisfied that he would pass muster at any but the closest range.

I steered on my hands and knees, peering out through a hole I had kicked in the paneling of the wheelhouse for that very purpose. The pain wasn't so bad now, but I felt strangely numb. It was as if nothing was real and anything could happen. The effects of mixing morphine, Jameson, and nine-millimeter bullets before breakfast. A dangerous combination.

We must certainly have been under surveillance for some considerable time, for the mist had cleared now and visibility was quite good although it was still raining heavily.

The Ford truck was parked halfway along the jetty at the end of the road, but there was no sign of the Land-Rover. Two of Barry's men waited at the jetty's edge. One was smoking a cigarette. They both carried Sterlings.

I called softly to Binnie who waited in the shelter of the companionway. "No sign of Barry. Just the two of them. About a minute to go and when you hit, hit hard. We can't afford any mistakes at this stage."

One of them called, "Hey, Mac, where are you?"

And then the other leaned forward and stared at Dooley, an expression of horror on his face. "My God," I heard him say, "what's wrong with him?"

As something like the truth dawned on them, I yelled, "Now, Binnie!"

He sprang from the shelter of the companionway, the Sten gun bucking in his hands as he sprayed the top of the jetty. As I have said, the Sten Mk IIS is probably one of the most remarkable submachine guns ever invented; the only sound as it fired being the bolt clicking backward and forward. As that is not audible above a distance of twenty yards, there was no danger that anyone at Spanish Head would be alerted to the holocaust below.

Binnie cut them both down in that instant, knocking one of them clean over the edge of the jetty into the water, using all thirty-two rounds in the magazine as far as I could make out. He went over to the rail to make the *Kathleen* fast, then started up the steps.

"You get the truck started," I called. "I want to immobilize the engine, just in case anyone gets ideas."

I got what I needed from the wheelhouse, went aft, and took off the engine hatch and did what I had to do. It only took me two or three minutes, but in spite of that Binnie was waiting in an agony of impatience at the edge of the jetty.

"For God's sake, Major, will you hurry!"

The second of the two men he had killed was lying face down near the truck. There was a Browning on the ground beside him. I picked it up, slipped it into my pocket, and heaved myself painfully into the cab.

"Now what?" Binnie demanded as he drove away.

I felt strangely lightheaded and my side was beginning to hurt like hell again, and for some reason, I found his question rather irritating.

I said, "As I don't happen to have my Tarot cards with me, I can't answer that one. So just get us up to the house in one piece, there's a good lad, and we'll take it from there."

He glanced at me, frowning, opened his mouth to speak, and obviously thought better of it. I leaned back in my seat and fought against the tiredness which threatened to overwhelm me.

We drove into the courtyard at the rear of the house very fast indeed and braked to a halt outside the back door. Binnie jumped down and was inside in a second. I summoned up my last reserves of will power and energy and followed him.

He kicked open the kitchen door and went in, crouching. There was only one occupant, a man in shirt sleeves who sat at the table drinking tea and reading a newspaper.

Binnie had him against a wall in a flash and ran his hand over him, removing a Browning from his hip pocket and shoving it into his own waistband. He turned the man around and slapped him across the face.

"Right, Keenan, you bastard. Tell us what we want to know, or I'll give it to you right now."

Keenan stared Death in the face and started to tremble. "For God's sake, Binnie, take it easy, will you?"

"All right," I said. "Speak up and you won't get hurt. Who else is in the house at the moment?"

"Just Barry."

"And who's guarding the girl?" Binnie demanded, ramming the muzzle of the Browning up under Keenan's chin.

"No one, Binnie, no one." Keenan was shaking with fear. "There's no need, and her with Barry himself like always."

Binnie was beside himself with rage and grabbed Keenan by the shirt. "Come on, then, lead us to them. Make any kind of wrong move and I'll kill you."

"Just a moment, Binnie," I said, and turned to Keenan. "What about the Brigadier? Is he still in the cellar?"

"That's right."

"Where's the key?"

"Hanging on that nail there."

I took it down. "We'll get him out now before we go any further."

"Why should we, for Christ's sake?" Binnie exploded.

"He could be useful. If not now, later."

Which was pretty thin, but the best I could do on short notice. I went out before he could argue, opened the door at the end of the passage, and went down the cellar steps.

When I unlocked the door of the cell, the Brigadier was lying on the cot reading a book which looked suspiciously like the Bible. He looked at me calmly for a long moment over the top of it, then sat up.

"I must say you've taken your own sweet time about it. What kept you?"

"Oh, little, unimportant things like being shot in the arm and having my ribs kicked in, not to mention being chased over large parts of Ulster by what seemed, on occasion, to be the entire strength of the present British Army."

"And at exactly what stage in the affair are we now?"

"Michael Cork is dead, I've found your gold, and Binnie Gallagher and I are about to see what we can do about Barry right now." I took the spare Browning from my pocket and offered it to him. "If you'd care to join in the fun, follow me, only keep out of sight for the moment. I'm afraid Binnie thinks I'm Pearse, Connolly, and Michael Collins all rolled into one. Very sad."

He was looking at me strangely, which didn't surprise me for my voice seemed to be coming from somewhere outside me. I turned and led the way out through the wine cellars, and mounted the stairs to where Binnie waited impatiently with Keenan.

"What kept you, for God's sake?" he demanded, then turned on the Brigadier without waiting for a reply. "You follow close behind and keep your mouth shut, do you understand?"

"Perfectly," the Brigadier assured him.

390

We went up, Keenan in the lead, and emerged through the green baize door into the hall. It was very quiet. He paused for a moment, listening, then started up that great stairway.

We moved along the corridor, past the stiff ladies and gentlemen of bygone years, set in canvas for all time. Someone was playing a piano, I could hear it plainly, a Bach Prelude, lovely, ice-cold stuff, even at that time in the morning. The music was coming from inside Frank Barry's sitting room and when we stopped at the door, I paused, caught by the beauty of it.

"They're in there," Keenan whispered.

Binnie put a knee into his crotch, turned as Keenan slipped to the floor with a groan, and burst into the room, the Sten at the ready.

Barry was seated at the piano and stopped playing instantly. Norah Murphy was in a chair by the fire. She jumped to her feet and turned to us, the dressing on her right cheek making her face seem misshapen and ugly.

"Norah?" Binnie cried. "Are you all right?"

She stood staring at us, a strange, dazed expression on her face and then suddenly she ran forward and flung her arms around him. "Oh, Binnie, Binnie. I've never been so glad to see anyone in my whole life."

In the same moment, she yanked the Browning from his waistband and moved back to a point where she could cover all of us comfortably.

"I would advise complete stillness, gentlemen, if you want to live, that is," she said crisply, in the harsh, pungent tones of the Norah Murphy I knew and loved.

Frank Barry stayed where he was, but drew a revolver from a shoulder holster. The Brigadier and I, being sensible men, raised our hands, although I didn't get very far with my left.

"You know, I wondered about you from the beginning, sweetheart," I said. "The fact that Barry and his boys were waiting for us on the way in and the speed with which they ran poor old Meyer to earth. That really was rather hard to swallow."

"But you took it."

"Not really. It was the branding that finally persuaded me I must have been wrong. Now that was quite a show. What did you do, Barry, fill her up with pain killer beforehand?"

"Just like going to the dentist," he said. "But it needed something as drastic as that to persuade Binnie she was in real danger. To send him running to the Small Man."

"But she never was?" I said.

"We wanted to know where the bullion was, old lad, and Cork wouldn't even tell Norah that. Had a thing about holding it in reserve as a last resort if the talking failed and he needed more arms."

"Talk," Norah Murphy said. "That's all he ever wanted to do and what good was it? He'd had his day, he and his kind. Now we'll try our way."

"Force and even more force," the Brigadier said. "Terror on terror, and what have you left after that little lot?"

"It's the only way," she said. "The only way we can make them see we mean business. Frank understands."

"Which is why you've been working together?" I asked her.

During all this, Binnie had stood as if turned to stone, the Sten gun hanging from one hand by its sling. But this final remark seemed to bring him back to life.

"You mean you're one of them?" he whispered. "You've been working for Frank Barry all along? A man who would murder— has murdered—women, kids, anyone who happens to stand in his road at the wrong moment for them."

"Sometimes it's the only way, Binnie." There was a pleading note in her voice as if she would make him understand. "We can't afford weakness now. We must be strong."

"You bloody murdering bitch," he cried, and took a step toward her, the Sten coming up.

She shot him twice at close quarters; he staggered back, spun around, and fell on his face.

*   *   *

She stood there, the Browning ready in her hand for anyone else who made a move, very pale but quite composed, showing no evidence of even the slightest remorse for what she had done.

But it was Frank Barry who took over now. "Answers, Vaughan, and quickly, or you get the same here and now. Dooley, McGuire—the men I sent down to the jetty to meet the boat?"

"All gone," I said. "Very sad."

"And the gold?"

"On board the *Kathleen.*"

"All of it?"

"All that I could find."

He stood there, thinking for a moment, then said to Norah, "All right, we've leaving now in the boat. You get the Land-Rover from the garage and meet me out front."

She went out quickly, stepping over Keenan, who still lay in the corridor moaning softly to himself and clutching his privates.

I said, "What about us?"

"Behave yourselves and I'll let you go just before we leave. Now clasp your hands behind your necks and start walking."

I didn't believe him, of course, not for a moment, but there didn't seem to be anything we could do about it. We went along the corridor, down the great stairway, and out through the front door.

There was no sign of Norah, and Barry marched us across the gravel drive to the patch of grass with a balustrade from which one could look down into the inlet below. He finally told us to halt and we turned to face him.

"Is this where we get it?" the Brigadier asked him.

"I'm afraid so," Barry said. "But then I thought you'd prefer to have it outdoors and it really is a splendid view, you must admit."

The Land-Rover came round the corner and braked to a halt

a few yards away. Norah Murphy sat behind the wheel looking at us, waiting for him to get on with it.

"And behold how the evil ones shall reap fire from heaven," I called. "That's what the good book says. You'll get yours, Norah, never fear."

Frank Barry smiled and opened his mouth to make some last bon mot, I suppose, but the words were never uttered. The air was full of a strange metallic chattering, bullets shredding his jacket, blood spurting from a dozen places, sending him staggering sideways in a mad, drunken dance of death, to fall head first over the balustrade and disappear from view.

Binnie Gallagher lurched down the steps, clutching the Sten, and started across the gravel drive toward the Land-Rover. Norah sat there staring at him, frozen, waiting for the ax to descend.

He paused a yard or two away, stood there swaying, then suddenly said contemptuously, "Oh, get to hell out o' that, why don't you? You're not worth spitting on."

It took a moment for it to sink in and then she switched on the engine quickly and drove away, turning into the corkscrew road that led down to the inlet.

Binnie dropped the Sten and moved past me, grabbing at the balustrade to keep himself from falling. "A hell of a view, I'll give the bastard that much."

I ran to catch him as he started to fall, and we went down together. His sweater was soaked in blood, the face very pale. He said, "It was fun while it lasted, Major. Sure and the two of us could wrap the whole British Army up between us in six months. Isn't that the fact?"

I nodded. "It is surely."

He smiled for the last time. "Up the Republic, Simon Vaughan," he cried and then he died.

The Brigadier said, "I'm sorry about this. You liked him, didn't you?"

"You could say that."

He coughed awkwardly. "What about the girl?"

"She isn't going anywhere. I immobilized the engine, just in case. There are only a few bars of gold on board anyway. It's going to take a Navy diver to get the rest. I'll show him where."

He coughed again as if to clear his throat. "It's beginning to look as if we owe you rather a lot. If there's anything I can do . . ."

"I'll tell you one thing you are going to do," I said. "You're going to pull the right kind of strings in the Republic so that you and I take this boy here back to Stradballa, which, in case you don't know it, is the village in Kerry where my mother was born."

"I see," he said. "I suppose it could be arranged."

"Oh, you'll arrange it all right," I told him, "or I'll know the reason why. Just like you'll arrange for him to be buried next to my sainted uncle, Michael Fitzgerald. And we'll have a stone. The finest marble you can buy."

"And what will it say on it?"

"Binnie Gallagher, Soldier of the Irish Republican Army. He died for Ireland." I looked down at Binnie. "He'd like that."

I turned away and lit a cigarette. The sky was dark and gray, swollen with rain. It seemed set for the day.

I said, "Do you think we've accomplished anything? Really and truly?"

"We've won a little more time, that's all. In the end that's what soldiers are for. The rest is up to the politicians."

"God help us all, then."

There was a slight pause, and he said, "Vaughan, I've got a confession to make. The night you were arrested in Greece running those guns—I'm afraid I arranged the whole thing."

"That's all right," I said. "I decided that was a distinct possibility within ten minutes of meeting you. Anyway, it got me out, didn't it?"

Or had it? I stood there at the balustrade, staring out into the gray morning, and down below at the jetty, hidden by the overhang in the cliffs, the *Kathleen*'s engine burst into life.

Ferguson moved beside me quickly, "My God, she's getting away. I thought you said you immobilized the engine."

The *Kathleen* appeared in the inlet far below, heading out to sea. I saw the bow wave as Norah Murphy increased speed. A moment later, the whole vessel seemed to split apart, orange flame spurting outward as the fuel tanks went up. What was left went down like a stone.

"Fire from heaven," I said. "I warned her, but she wouldn't listen."

"Oh my God," whispered the Brigadier.

I gazed down at the dark waters, searching for some sign of Norah Murphy, the merest hint that she had ever existed, and found none. Then I turned and walked away through the rain.

A Prayer for the Dying

For Philip Williams,
the Expert

1

Fallon

When the police car turned the corner at the end of the street, Fallon stepped into the nearest doorway instinctively and waited for it to pass. He gave it a couple of minutes and then continued on his way, turning up his collar as it started to rain.

He walked on towards the docks keeping to the shadows, his hands pushed deep into the pockets of his dark-blue trenchcoat, a small dark man of five-feet-four or -five who seemed to drift rather than walk.

A ship eased down from the Pool of London sounding its foghorn, strange, haunting—the last of the dinosaurs moving aimlessly through some primeval swamp, alone in a world already alien. It suited his mood perfectly.

There was a warehouse at the end of the street facing out across the river. The sign said *Janos Kristou—Importer*. Fallon opened the little judas gate in the main entrance and stepped inside.

The place was crammed with bales and packing cases of every description. It was very dark, but there was a light at the far end and he moved towards it. A man sat at a trestle table beneath a naked light bulb and wrote laboriously in a large, old-fashioned ledger. He had lost most of his hair and what was left stuck out in a dirty white fringe. He wore an old sheepskin jacket and woollen mittens.

Fallon took a cautious step forward and the old man said without turning around, "Martin, is that you?"

Fallon moved into the pool of light and paused beside the table. "Hello, Kristou."

There was a wooden case on the floor beside him and the top was loose. Fallen raised it and took out a Sterling submachine gun thick with protective grease.

"Still at it, I see. Who's this for? The Israelis or the Arabs, or have you actually started taking sides?"

Kristou leaned across, took the Sterling from him and dropped it back into the box. "I didn't make the world the way it is," he said.

"Maybe not, but you certainly helped it along the way." Fallon lit a cigarette. "I heard you wanted to see me."

Kristou put down his pen and looked up at him speculatively. His face was very old, the parchment-colored skin seamed with wrinkles, but the blue eyes were alert and intelligent.

He said, "You don't look too good, Martin."

"I've never felt better," Fallon told him. "Now what about my passport?"

Kristou smiled amiably. "You look as if you could do with a drink." He took a bottle and two paper cups from a drawer. "Irish whiskey—the best. Just to make you feel at home."

Fallon hesitated and then took one of the cups. Kristou raised the other. "May you die in Ireland. Isn't that what they say?"

Fallon swallowed the whiskey down and crushed the paper cup in his right hand. "My passport," he said softly.

Kristou said, "In a sense it's out of my hands, Martin. I mean to say, you turning out to be so much in demand in certain quarters—that alters things."

Fallon went round to the other side of the table and stood there for a moment, head bowed, hands thrust deep into the pockets of the blue trenchcoat. And then he looked up very slowly, dark empty eyes burning in the white face.

"If you're trying to put the screws on me, old man, forget it. I gave you everything I had."

Kristou's heart missed a beat. There was a cold stirring in his bowels. "God help me, Martin," he said, "but with a hood on you'd look like Death himself."

Fallon stood there, eyes like black glass staring through and beyond, and then suddenly something seemed to go out of him. He turned as if to leave.

Kristou said quickly, "There is a way."

Fallon hesitated. "And what would that be?"

"Your passport, a berth on a cargo boat leaving Hull for Australia, Sunday night." He paused. "And two thousand pounds in your pocket to give you a fresh start."

"What do I have to do? Kill somebody?" Fallon said incredulously.

"Exactly," the old man answered.

Fallon laughed softly. "You get better all the time, Kristou. You really do."

He reached for the whiskey bottle, emptied Kristou's cup on the floor and filled it again. The old man watched him, waiting. Rain tapped against the window as if somebody was trying to get in. Fallon walked across and peered down into the empty street.

A car was parked in the entrance to an alley on his left. No lights—which was interesting. The foghorn sounded again, farther downriver this time.

"A dirty night for it." He turned. "But that's appropriate."

"For what, Martin?" Kristou asked.

"Oh, for people like you and me."

He emptied the cup at a swallow, walked back to the table and put it down in front of Kristou very carefully.

"All right," he said. "I'm listening."

Kristou smiled. "Now you're being sensible." He opened a

manila folder, took out a photo and pushed it across the table. "Take a look at that."

Fallon picked it up and held it under the light. It had obviously been taken in a cemetery and in the foreground there was a rather curious monument. A bronze figure of a woman in the act of rising from a chair as if to go through the door which stood partly open between marble pillars behind her. A man in a dark overcoat, head bare, knelt before her on one knee.

"Now this." Kristou pushed another photo across.

The scene was the same except for one important fact. The man in the dark overcoat was now standing, facing the camera, hat in hand. He was massively built, at least six-foot-two or -three, with chest and shoulders to match. He had a strong Slavic face with high flat cheekbones and narrow eyes.

"He looks like a good man to keep away from," Fallon said.

"A lot of people would agree with you."

"Who is he?"

"His name's Krasko—Jan Krasko."

"Polish?"

"Originally—but that was a long time ago. He's been here since before the war."

"And where's here?"

"Up North. You'll be told where at the right time."

"And the woman in the chair?"

"His mother." Kristou reached for the photo and looked at it himself. "Every Thursday morning without fail, wet or fine, there he is with his bunch of flowers. They were very close."

He put the photos back in the manila folder and looked up at Fallon again. "Well?"

"What's he done to deserve me?"

"A matter of business, that's all. What you might call a conflict of interests. My client's tried being reasonable, only Krasko won't play. So he'll have to go, and as publicly as possible."

"To encourage the others?"

"Something like that."

Fallon moved back to the window and looked down into the

street. The car was still there in the alley. He spoke without turning around.

"And just what exactly is Krasko's line of business?"

"You name it," Kristou said. "Clubs, gambling, betting shops . . ."

"Whores and drugs?" Fallon turned round. "And your client?"

Kristou raised a hand defensively. "Now you're going too far, Martin. Now you're being unreasonable."

"Good night, Kristou." Fallon turned and started to walk away.

"All right, all right," Kristou called, something close to panic in his voice. "You win."

As Fallon moved back to the table, Kristou opened a drawer and rummaged inside. He took out another folder, opened it and produced a bundle of newspaper clippings. He sorted through them, finally found what he was looking for and passed it to Fallon.

The clipping was already yellowing at the edges and was dated eighteen months previously. The article was headed "The English Al Capone."

There was a photo of a large, heavily-built man coming down a flight of steps. He had a fleshy, arrogant face under a Homburg hat and wore a dark-blue, double-breasted melton overcoat, a handkerchief in the breast pocket. The youth at his shoulder was perhaps seventeen or eighteen; he wore a similar coat but was bare-headed. He was an albino, with white shoulder-length hair that gave him the look of some decadent angel.

The caption under the photo read: *Jack Meehan and his brother Billy leaving Manchester Central Police Headquarters after questioning in connection with the death of Agnes Drew.*

"And who was this Agnes Drew?" Fallon demanded.

"Some whore who got kicked to death in an alley. An occupational hazard. You know how it is?"

"I can imagine." Fallon glanced at the photo again. "They look like a couple of bloody undertakers."

405

Kristou laughed until the tears came to his eyes. "That's very funny, you know that? That's exactly what Mr. Meehan is. He runs one of the biggest funeral concerns in the north of England."

"What, no clubs, no gambling? No whores, no drugs?" Fallon put the clipping down on the table. "That's not what it says here."

"All right," Kristou leaned back, took off his spectacles and cleaned them with a soiled handkerchief. "What if I told you Mr. Meehan is strictly legitimate these days? That people like Krasko are leaning on him. Leaning hard—and the law won't help."

"Oh, I see it all now," Fallon said. "You mean give a dog a bad name?"

"That's it." Kristou slammed a fist against the table. "That's it exactly." He adjusted his spectacles again and peered up at Fallon eagerly. "It's a deal then?"

"Like hell it is," Fallon said coldly. "I wouldn't touch either Krasko or your friend Meehan with a bargepole. I might catch something."

"For God's sake, Martin, what's one more on the list to you?" Kristou cried as he turned to go. "How many did you kill over there? Thirty-two? Thirty-four? Four soldiers in Londonderry alone."

He got up quickly, his chair going backwards, darted round the table and grabbed Fallon by the arm.

Fallon pushed him away. "Anything I did, I did for the cause. Because I believe it was necessary."

"Very noble," Kristou said. "And the kids in that school bus you blew to a bloody pulp. Was that for your cause?"

He was back across the table, a hand of iron at his throat, staring up into the muzzle of a Browning automatic and behind it Fallon and the white devil's face on him. There was the click of the hammer being cocked.

Kristou almost fainted. He had a partial bowel movement,

the stench foul in the cold, sharp air of the warehouse and Fallon pushed him away in disgust.

"Never again, Kristou," he whispered and the Browning in his left hand was rock-steady. "Never again." The Browning disappeared into the right-hand pocket of his trenchcoat. He turned and walked away, his footsteps echoing on the concrete floor. The judas gate banged.

Kristou got up gingerly, tears of rage and shame in his eyes. Someone laughed and a harsh, aggressive Yorkshire voice said from the shadows, "Now that's what I call really being in the shit, Kristou."

Jack Meehan walked into the light, his brother Billy at his heels. They were both dressed exactly as they had been in the newspaper photo. It really was quite remarkable.

Meehan picked up the clipping. "What in the hell did you want to show him that for? I sued the bastard who wrote that article and won."

"That's right." Billy Meehan giggled. "The judge would have made it a farthing damages only there's no such coin any more." His voice was high-pitched, repellent—nothing masculine about it at all.

Meehan slapped him casually, back-handed across the mouth, and said to Kristou, his nose wrinkling in disgust, "Go and wipe your backside, for Christ's sake. Then we talk."

When Kristou returned, Meehan was sitting at the table pouring whiskey into a clean paper cup, his brother standing behind him. He sampled a little, spat it out and made a face. "All right. I know the Irish still have one foot in the bog, but how can they drink this muck?"

"I'm sorry, Mr. Meehan," Kristou said.

"You'll be a bloody sight sorrier before I'm through with you. You cocked it up proper, didn't you?"

Kristou moistened dry lips and fingered his spectacles. "I didn't think he'd react that way."

"What in the hell did you expect? He's a nutcase, isn't he? I mean, they all are over there, going round shooting women and blowing up kids. That's civilized?"

Kristou couldn't think of a thing to say, but was saved by Billy who said carelessly, "He didn't look much to me. Little half-pint runt. Without that shooter in his fist he'd be nothing."

Meehan sighed heavily. "You know there are days when I really despair of you, Billy. You've just seen hell on wheels and didn't recognize it." He laughed harshly again. "You'll never come closer, Kristou. He was mad at you, you old bastard. Mad enough to kill, and yet that shooter didn't even waver."

Kristou winced. "I know, Mr. Meehan. I miscalculated. I shouldn't have mentioned those kids."

"Then what are you going to do about it?"

Kristou glanced at Billy, then back to his brother, frowning slightly. "You mean you still want him, Mr. Meehan?"

"Doesn't everybody?"

"That's true enough."

He laughed nervously. Meehan stood up and patted him on the face. "You fix it, Kristou, like a good lad. You know where I'm staying. If I haven't heard by midnight, I'll send Fat Albert to see you and you wouldn't like that, would you?"

He walked into the darkness followed by his brother and Kristou stood there, terrified, listening to them go. The judas gate opened and Meehan's voice called, "Kristou?"

"Yes, Mr. Meehan."

"Don't forget to have a bath when you get home. You stink like my Aunt Mary's midden."

The judas banged shut and Kristou sank down into the chair, fingers tapping nervously. God damn Fallon. It would serve him right if he turned him in.

And then it hit him like a bolt from the blue. The perfect solution and so beautifully simple.

He picked up the telephone, dialled Scotland Yard and asked to be put through to the Special Branch.

* * *

It was raining quite heavily now, and Jack Meehan paused to turn up his collar before crossing the street.

Billy said, "I still don't get it. Why is it so important you get Fallon?"

"Number one, with a shooter in his hand he's the best there is," Meehan said. "Number two, everybody wants him. The Special Branch, Military Intelligence—even his old mates in the IRA, which means—number three—that he's eminently disposable afterwards."

"What's that mean?" Billy said as they turned the corner of the alley and moved towards the car.

"Why don't you try reading a few books, for Christ's sake?" Meehan demanded. "All you ever seem to think of is birds."

They were at the front of the car by now, a Bentley Continental, and Meehan grabbed Billy by the arm and pulled him up quickly.

"Here, what the hell's going on? Where's Fred?"

"A slight concussion, Mr. Meehan. Nothing much. He's sleeping it off in the rear seat."

A match flared in a nearby doorway pulling Fallon's face out of the darkness. There was a cigarette between his lips. He lit it, then flicked the match into the gutter.

Meehan opened the door of the Bentley and switched on the lights. "What are you after?" he said calmly.

"I just wanted to see you in the flesh, so to speak, that's all," Fallon said. "Good night to you."

He started to move away and Meehan grabbed his arm. "You know, I like you, Fallon. I think we've got a lot in common."

"I doubt that."

Meehan ignored him. "I've been reading this German philosopher lately. You wouldn't know him. He says that for authentic living what is necessary is the resolute confrontation of death. Would you agree with that?"

"Heidegger," Fallon said. "Interesting you should go for him. He was Himmler's bible."

He turned away again and Meehan moved quickly in front of him. "Heidegger?" he said. "You've read Heidegger?" There was genuine astonishment in his voice. "I'll double up on the original offer and find you regular work. Now I can't say fairer than that, can I?"

"Good night, Mr. Meehan," Fallon said and melted into the darkness.

"What a man," Meehan said. "What a hard-nosed bastard. Why, he's beautiful, Billy, even if he is a fucking Mick." He turned. "Come on, let's get back to the Savoy. You drive and if you put as much as a scratch on this motor I'll have your balls."

Fallon had a room in a lodging-house in Hanger Street in Stepney just off the Commercial Round. A couple of miles, no more, so he walked, in spite of the rain. He hadn't the slightest idea what would happen now. Kristou had been his one, his only hope. He was finished, it was as simple as that. He could run, but how far?

As he neared his destination, he took out his wallet and checked the contents. Four pounds and a little silver, and he was already two weeks behind with his rent. He went into a cheap wine shop for some cigarettes then crossed the road to Hanger Street.

The newspaper man on the corner had deserted his usual pitch to shelter in a doorway from the driving rain. He was little more than a bundle of rags, an old London Irishman, totally blind in one eye and only partially sighted in the other.

Fallon dropped a coin in his hand and took a paper. "Good night to you, Michael," he said.

The old man rolled one milky-white eye towards him, his hand fumbling for change in the bag which hung about his neck.

"Is it yourself, Mr. Fallon?"

"And who else? You can forget the change."

The old man grabbed his hand and counted out his change

laboriously. "You had visitors at number thirteen about twenty minutes ago."

"The law?" Fallon asked softly.

"Nothing in uniform. They went in and didn't come out again. Two cars waiting at the other end of the street—another across the road."

He counted a final penny into Fallon's hand. Fallon turned and crossed to the telephone-box on the other corner. He dialled the number of the lodging-house and was answered instantly by the old woman who ran the place. He pushed in the coin and spoke.

"Mrs. Keegan? It's Daly here. I wonder if you'd mind doing me a favor?"

He knew at once by the second's hesitation, by the strain in her voice, that old Michael's supposition had been correct.

"Oh, yes, Mr. Daly."

"The thing is, I'm expecting a phone call at nine o'clock. Take the number and tell them I'll ring back when I get in. I haven't a hope in hell of getting there now. I ran into a couple of old friends and we're having a few drinks. You know how it is."

There was another slight pause before she said, as if in response to some invisible prompt, "Sounds nice. Where are you?"

"A pub called The Grenadier Guard in Kensington High Street. I'll have to go now. See you later."

He replaced the receiver and left the phone-box, and moved into a doorway from which he had a good view of number 13 halfway down the short street.

A moment later, the front door was flung open. There were eight of them. Special Branch from the look of it. The first one on the pavement waved frantically and two cars moved out of the shadows at the end of the street. The whole crew climbed inside, the cars moved away at speed. A car that had been parked at the curb on the other side of the main road went after them.

Fallon crossed to the corner and paused beside the old newspaper seller. He took out his wallet, extracted the four remaining pound notes and pressed them into his hand.

"God bless you, Mr. Fallon," Michael said, but Fallon was already on the other side of the road, walking rapidly back towards the river.

This time Kristou didn't hear a thing although he had been waiting for something like an hour, nerves taut. He sat there at the table, ledger open, the pen gripped tightly in his mittened hand. There was the softest of footfalls, wind over grass only, then the harsh, deliberate click as the hammer of the Browning was cocked.

Kristou breathed deeply to steady himself. "What's the point, Martin?" he said. "What would it get you?"

Fallon moved round to the other side of the table, the Browning in his hand. Kristou stood up, leaning on the table to stop from shaking.

"I'm the only friend you've got left now, Martin."

"You bastard," Fallon said. "You sicked the Special Branch on to me."

"I had to," Kristou said frantically. "It was the only way I could get you back here. It was for your own good, Martin. You've been like a dead man walking. I can bring you back to life again. Action and passion, that's what you want. That's what you need."

Fallon's eyes were black holes in the white face. He raised the Browning at arm's length, touching the muzzle between Kristou's eyes.

The old man closed them. "All right, if you want to, go ahead. Get it over with. This is a life, the life I lead. Only remember one thing. Kill me, you kill yourself because there *is* no one else. Not one single person in this world that would do anything other than turn you in or put a bullet in your head."

There was a long pause. He opened his eyes to see Fallon gently lowering the hammer of the Browning. He stood there holding it against his right thigh, staring into space.

Kristou said carefully, "After all, what is he to you, this Krasko? A gangster, a murderer. The kind who lives off young girls." He spat. "A pig."

Fallon said. "Don't try to dress it up. What's the next move?"

"One phone call is all it takes. A car will be here in half an hour. You'll be taken to a farm near Doncaster. An out-of-the-way place. You'll be safe there. You make the hit on Thursday morning at the cemetery like I showed you in the photo. Krasko always leaves his goons at the gate. He doesn't like having them around when he's feeling sentimental."

"All right," Fallon said. "But I do my own organizing. That's understood."

"Of course. Anything you want." Kristou opened the drawer, took out an envelope and shoved it across. "There's five hundred quid there in fives, to be going on with."

Fallon weighed the envelope in his hand carefully for a moment, then slipped it into a pocket. "When do I get the rest?" he said. "And the passport?"

"Mr. Meehan takes care of that end on satisfactory completion."

Fallon nodded slowly. "All right, make your phone call."

Kristou smiled, a mixture of triumph and relief. "You're doing the wise thing, Martin. Believe me you are." He hesitated. "There's just one thing if you don't mind me saying so?"

"And what would that be?"

"The Browning—no good to you for a job like this. You need something nice and quiet."

Fallon looked down at the Browning, a slight frown on his face. "Maybe you have a point. What have you got to offer?"

"What would you like?"

Fallon shook his head. "I've never had a preference for any particular make of handgun. That way you end up with a trademark. Something they can fasten on to, and that's bad."

Kristou unlocked a small safe in the corner, opened it and took out a cloth bundle which he unwrapped on the table. It contained a rather ugly automatic, perhaps six inches long, a

413

curious-looking barrel protruding a farther two inches. The bundle also contained a three-inch silencer and two fifty-round cartons of ammunition.

"And what in the hell is this?" Fallon said, picking it up.

"A Czech Ceska," Kristou told him. "Seven point five mm. Model twenty-seven. The Germans took over the factory during the war. This is one of theirs. You can tell by the special barrel modification. Made that way to take a silencer."

"Is it any good?"

"SS Intelligence used them, but judge for yourself."

He moved into the darkness. A few moments later, a light was turned on at the far end of the building and Fallon saw that there was a target down there of a type much used by the army. A life-size replica of a charging soldier.

As he screwed the silencer on to the end of the barrel, Kristou rejoined him. "Anytime you're ready."

Fallon took careful aim with both hands, there was a dull thud that outside would not have been audible above three yards. He had fired at the heart and chipped the right arm.

He adjusted the sight and tried again. He was still a couple of inches out. He made a further adjustment. This time he was dead on target.

Kristou said, "Didn't I tell you?"

Fallon nodded. "Ugly, but deadly, Kristou, just like you and me. Did I ever tell you I once saw a sign on a wall in Derry that said: Is there a life before death? Isn't that the funniest thing you ever heard?"

Kristou stared at him, aghast. Fallon turned, his arm swung up, and fired twice, apparently without taking aim, and shot out the target's eyes.

2

Father da Costa

... The Lord is my Shepherd, I shall not want. Father Michael da Costa spoke out bravely as he led the way up through the cemetery, his words almost drowned in the rush of heavy rain.

Inside, he was sick at heart. It had rained heavily all night, was raining even harder now. The procession from chapel to graveside was a wretched affair at the best of times, but this occasion was particularly distressing.

For one thing, there were so few of them. The two men from the funeral director's, carrying the pitifully small coffin between them. And the mother, already on the point of collapse, staggering along behind, supported by her husband on one side and her brother on the other. They were poor people. They had no one. They turned inward in their grief.

Mr. O'Brien, the cemetery superintendent, was waiting at the graveside, an umbrella over his head against the rain. There was a gravedigger with him who pulled off the canvas cover as they arrived. Not that it had done any good for there was at least two feet of water in the bottom.

O'Brien tried to hold the umbrella over the priest, but Father da Costa waved it away. Instead, he took off his coat and handed

415

it to the superintendent and stood there in the rain at the graveside, the old red and gold cope making a brave show in the gray
morning.

O'Brien had to act as server and Father da Costa sprinkled
the coffin with holy water and incense and as he prayed, he
noticed that the father was glaring across at him wildly like
some trapped animal behind bars, the fingers of his right hand
clenching and unclenching convulsively. He was a big man—
almost as big as da Costa. Foreman on a building site.

Da Costa looked away hurriedly and prayed for the child,
face upturned, rain beading his tangled grey beard:

"Into your hands, O Lord, we humbly commend our sister.
Lead her for whom you have shown so great a love into the joy
of the heavenly paradise."

Not for the first time, the banality of what he was saying
struck him. How could he explain to any mother on this earth
that God needed her eight-year-old daughter so badly that it
had been necessary for her to choke to death in the stinking
waters of an industrial canal. To drift for ten days before being
found.

The coffin descended with a splash and the gravedigger
quickly pulled the canvas sheet back in place. Father da Costa
said a final prayer, then moved round to the woman who was
now crying bitterly.

He put a hand on her shoulder, "Mrs. Dalton, if there's
anything I can do . . ."

The father struck his arm away wildly. "You leave her alone!"
he cried. "She's suffered enough. You and your bloody prayers.
What good's that? I had to identify her, did you know that? A
piece of rotting flesh that was my daughter after ten days in the
canal. What kind of a God is it that could do that to a child?"

O'Brien moved forward quickly, but Father da Costa put up
an arm to hold him back. "Leave it," he said calmly.

A strange, haunted look appeared on Dalton's face as if he
suddenly realized the enormity of his offense. He put an arm

about his wife's shoulders and he and her brother hurried her away. The two funeral men went after them.

O'Brien helped da Costa on with his coat. "I'm sorry about that, Father. A bad business."

"He has a point, poor devil," da Costa said. "After all, what am I supposed to say to someone in his position?"

The gravedigger looked shocked, but O'Brien simply nodded slowly. "It's a funny old life sometimes." He opened his umbrella. "I'll walk you back to the chapel, Father."

Da Costa shook his head. "I'll take the long way round if you don't mind. I could do with the exercise. I'll borrow the umbrella, if I may."

"Certainly, Father."

O'Brien gave it to him, and da Costa walked away through the wilderness of marble monuments and tombstones.

The gravedigger said, "That was a hell of an admission for a priest to make."

O'Brien lit a cigarette. "Ah, but then da Costa is no ordinary priest. Joe Devlin, the sacristan at St. Anne's, told me all about him. He was some sort of commando or other during the war. Fought with Tito and the Yugoslav partisans. Afterwards, he went to the English College in Rome. Had a brilliant career there—could have been anything. Instead, he decided to go into mission work after he was ordained."

"Where did they send him?"

"Korea. The Chinese had him for nearly five years. Afterwards they gave him some administrative job in Rome to recuperate, but he didn't like that. Got them to send him to Mozambique. I think it was his grandfather who was Portuguese. Anyway, he speaks the language."

"What happened there?"

"Oh, he was deported. The Portuguese authorities accused him of having too much sympathy with rebels."

"So what's he doing here?"

"Parish priest at Holy Name."

"That pile of rubble?" the gravedigger said incredulously. "Why, it's only standing up because of the scaffolding. If he gets a dozen for Mass on a Sunday he'll be lucky."

"Exactly," O'Brien said.

"Oh, I get it." The gravedigger nodded sagely. "It's their way of slapping his wrist."

"He's a good man," O'Brien said. "Too good to be wasted."

He was suddenly tired of the conversation and, for some strange reason, unutterably depressed. "Better get that grave filled in."

"What, now, in this rain?" The gravedigger looked at him bewildered. "It can wait till later, can't it?"

"No, it damn well can't."

O'Brien turned on his heel and walked away. The gravedigger, swearing softly, pulled back the canvas sheet and got to work.

Father da Costa usually enjoyed a walk in the rain. It gave him a safe, enclosed feeling. Some psychological thing harking back to childhood, he supposed. But not now. Now, he felt restless and ill at ease. Still disturbed by what had happened at the graveside.

He paused to break a personal vow by lighting a cigarette, awkwardly because of the umbrella in his left hand. He had recently reduced his consumption to five a day, and those he smoked only during the evening, a pleasure to be savored by anticipation, but under the circumstances . . .

He moved on into the oldest part of the cemetery, a section he had discovered with delight only a month or two previously. Here amongst the pines and the cypresses were superb Victorian Gothic tombs, winged angels in marble, bronzed effigies of Death. Something different on every hand and on each slab of pious, sentimental, implacable belief in the hereafter was recorded.

He didn't see a living soul until he went round a corner between rhododendron bushes and paused abruptly. The path divided some ten yards in front of him and at the intersection stood a rather interesting grave. A door between marble pillars, partially open. In front of it the bronze figure of a woman in the act of rising from a chair.

A man in a dark overcoat, head bare, knelt before her on one knee. It was very quiet—only the rushing of the rain into wet earth and Father da Costa hesitated for a moment, unwilling to intrude on such a moment of personal grief.

And then an extraordinary thing happened. A priest stepped in through the eternity door at the back of the grave. A youngish man who wore a dark clerical raincoat over his cassock and a black hat.

What took place then was like something out of a nightmare, frozen in time, no reality to it at all. As the man in the dark overcoat glanced up, the priest produced an automatic with a long black silencer on the end. There was a dull thud as he fired. Fragments of bone and brain sprayed out from the rear of his victim's skull as he was slammed back against the gravel.

Father da Costa gave a hoarse cry, already seconds too late, "For God's sake, no!"

The young priest, in the act of stepping towards his victim, looked up, aware of da Costa for the first time. The arm swung instantly as he took deliberate aim, and da Costa looked at Death, at the white devil's face on him, the dark, dark eyes.

And then, unaccountably, as his lips moved in prayer, the gun was lowered. The priest bent down to pick something up. The dark eyes stared into his for a second longer and then he slipped back through the door and was gone.

Father da Costa threw the umbrella to one side and dropped to his knees beside the man who had been shot. Blood trickled from the nostrils, the eyes were half-closed and yet, incredibly, there was still the sound of labored breathing.

He began to recite in a firm voice, the prayers for the dying: *Go, Christian Soul, from this world, in the Name of God the Father Almighty Who created thee* . . . Then, with a hoarse rattle, the breathing stopped abruptly.

* * *

Fallon followed the path at the north end of the cemetery, walking fast, but not too fast. Not that it mattered. He was well screened by rhododendron bushes and it was unlikely that there would be anyone about in such weather.

The priest had been unfortunate. One of those time and chance things. It occurred to him, with something like amusement and not for the first time in his life, that no matter how well you planned, something unexpected always seemed to turn up.

He moved into a small wood and found the van parked in the track out of sight as he had left it. There was no one in the driver's seat and he frowned.

"Varley, where are you?" he called softly.

A small man in a raincoat and cloth cap came blundering through the trees, mouth gaping, clutching a pair of binoculars in one hand. He leaned against the side of the van, fighting for breath.

Fallon shook him roughly by the shoulder. "Where in the hell have you been?"

"I was watching." Varley gasped. He raised the binoculars. "Mr. Meehan's orders. That priest. He saw you. Why didn't you give it to him?"

Fallon opened the van door and shoved him in behind the wheel. "Shut up and get driving!"

He went round to the rear, opened the doors, got in and closed them again as the engine roared into life and they lurched away along the rough track.

He opened the small window at the rear of the driver's compartment. "Steady," he said. "Easy does it. The slower the better. A friend of mine once robbed a bank and made his escape in an ice-cream van that couldn't do more than twenty miles an hour. They expect you to move like hell after a killing so do the other thing."

He started to divest himself of the raincoat and cassock. Underneath he wore a dark sweater and grey slacks. His navy blue trenchcoat was ready on the seat and he pulled it on. Then he took off the rubber galoshes he was wearing.

Varley was sweating as they turned into the dual carriageway. "Oh, God," he moaned. "Mr. Meehan will have our balls for this."

"Let me worry about Meehan." Fallon bundled the priest's clothing into a canvas holdall and zipped it shut.

"You don't know him, Mr. Fallon," Varley said. "He's the devil himself when he's mad. There was a fella called Gregson a month or two back. Professional gambler. Bent as a corkscrew. He took one of Mr. Meehan's clubs for five grand. When the boys brought him in, Mr. Meehan nailed his hands to a table top. Did it himself, too. Six-inch nails and a five-pound hammer. Left him like that for five hours. To consider the error of his ways, that's what he said."

"What did he do to him after that?" Fallon asked.

"I was there when they took the nails out. It was horrible. Gregson was in a terrible state. And Mr. Meehan, he pats him on the cheek and tells him to be a good boy in the future. Then he gives him a tenner and sends him to see this Paki doctor he uses." Varley shuddered. "I tell you, Mr. Fallon, he's no man to cross."

"He certainly seems to have his own special way of winning friends and influencing people," Fallon said. "The priest back there? Do you know him?"

"Father da Costa?" Varley nodded. "Has a broken-down old church near the center of the city. Holy Name, it's called. He runs the crypt as a kind of doss house for down-and-outs. About the only congregation he gets these days. One of these areas where they've pulled down all the houses."

"Sounds interesting. Take me there."

The car swerved violently, so great was Varley's surprise and he had to fight to regain control of the wheel. "Don't be crazy. My orders were to take you straight back to the farm."

"I'm changing them," Fallon said simply and he sat back and lit a cigarette.

421

* * *

The Church of the Holy Name was in Rockingham Street, sandwiched between gleaming new cement and glass office blocks on the one hand and shabby, decaying warehouses on the other. Higher up the street there was a vast brickfield where old Victorian slum houses had been cleared. The bulldozers were already at work digging the foundation for more tower blocks.

Varley parked the van opposite the church and Fallon got out. It was a Victorian Gothic monstrosity with a squat, ugly tower at its center, the whole networked with scaffolding although there didn't seem to be any work in progress.

"It isn't exactly a hive of industry," Fallon said.

"They ran out of money. The way I hear it the bloody place is falling down." Varley wiped sweat from his brow nervously. "Let's get out of it, Mr. Fallon—please."

"In a minute."

Fallon crossed the road to the main entrance. There was the usual board outside with da Costa's name there and the times of Mass. Confession was at one o'clock and five on weekdays. He stood there, staring at the board for a moment and then he smiled slowly, turned and went back to the van.

He leaned in the window. "This funeral place of Meehan's— where is it?"

"Paul's Square," Varley said. "It's only ten minutes from here on the side of the town hall."

"I've got things to do," Fallon said. "Tell Meehan I'll meet him there at two o'clock."

"For Christ's sake, Mr. Fallon," Varley said frantically. "You can't do that," but Fallon was already halfway across the road going back towards the church.

Varley moaned, "You bastard!" and he moved into gear and drove away.

Fallon didn't go into the church. Instead, he walked up the side street beside a high, greystone wall. There was an old cemetery inside, flat tombstones mainly and a house in one corner, presumably the presbytery. It looked to be in about the same state as the church.

It was a sad, grey sort of place, the leafless trees black with a century of city soot that even the rain could not wash away, and he was filled with a curious melancholy. This was what it all came to in the end whichever way you looked at it. Words on cracked stones. A gate clicked behind him and he turned sharply.

A young woman was coming down the path from the presbytery, an old trenchcoat over her shoulders against the rain. She carried an ebony walking stick in one hand and there was a bundle of sheet music under the other arm.

Fallon judged her to be in her late twenties with black shoulder-length hair and a grave, steady face. One of those plain faces that for some strange reason you found yourself looking at twice.

He got ready to explain himself as she approached, but she stared straight through him as if he wasn't there. And then, as she went by, he noticed the occasional tap with the stick against the end of a tomb—familiar friends.

She paused and turned, a slight, uncertain frown on her face. "Is anyone there?" she called in a calm, pleasant voice.

Fallon didn't move a muscle. She stayed there for a moment longer, then turned and continued along the path. When she reached a small door at the end of the church, she took out a Yale key, opened it and went inside.

Fallon went out through the side gate and round to the main entrance. When he pushed open the door and went inside he was conscious of the familiar odor and smiled wryly.

"Incense, candles and the holy water," he said softly. His fingers dipped in the bowl as he went past in a kind of reflex action.

It had a sort of charm and somewhere in the dim past, somebody had obviously spent a lot of money on it. There was Victorian stained glass and imitation medieval carvings everywhere. Gargoyles, skulls, imagination running riot.

Scaffolding lifted in a spider's web to support the nave at the altar end and it was very dark except for the sanctuary lamp and candles flickering about the Virgin.

The girl was seated at the organ behind the choir stalls. She started to play softly. Just a few tentative chords at first and then, as Fallon started to walk down the center aisle, she moved into the opening of the Bach Prelude and Fugue in D Major.

And she was good. He stood at the bottom of the steps, listening, then started up. She stopped at once and swung round.

"Is anyone there?"

"I'm sorry if I disturbed you," he told her. "I was enjoying listening."

There was that slight, uncertain smile on her face again. She seemed to be waiting, so he carried on. "If I might make a suggestion?"

"You play the organ?"

"Used to. Look, that trumpet stop is a reed. Unreliable at the best times, but in a damp atmosphere like this—" He shrugged. "It's so badly out of tune it's putting everything else out. I'd leave it in if I were you."

"Why, thank you," she said. "I'll try that."

She turned back to the organ and Fallon went down the steps to the rear of the church and sat in a pew in the darkest corner he could find.

She played the Prelude and Fugue right through and he sat there, eyes closed, arms folded. And his original judgment still stood. She *was* good—certainly worth listening to.

When she finished after half an hour or so, she gathered up her things and came down the steps. She paused at the bottom and waited, perhaps sensing that he was still there, but he made no sign and after a moment, she went into the sacristy.

And in the darkness at the back of the church, Fallon sat waiting.

3

Miller

Father da Costa was just finishing his second cup of tea in the cemetery superintendent's office when there was a knock at the door and a young police constable came in.

"Sorry to bother you again, Father, but Mr. Miller would like a word with you."

Father da Costa stood up. "Mr. Miller?" he said.

"Detective Superintendent Miller, sir. He's head of the CID."

It was still raining heavily when they went outside. The forecourt was crammed with police vehicles and as they walked along the narrow path, there seemed to be police everywhere, moving through the rhododendron bushes.

The body was exactly where he had left it although it was now partially covered with a groundsheet. A man in an overcoat knelt on one knee beside it making some sort of preliminary examination. He was speaking in a low voice into a portable dictaphone and what looked like a doctor's bag was open on the ground beside him.

There were police here everywhere, too, in uniform and out. Several of them were taking careful measurements with tapes. The others were searching the ground area.

The young detective inspector who had his statement was called Fitzgerald. He was standing to one side, talking to a tall, thin, rather scholarly-looking man in a belted raincoat. When he saw da Costa, he came across at once.

"There you are, Father. This is Detective Superintendent Miller."

Miller shook hands. He had a thin face and patient brown eyes. Just now he looked very tired.

He said, "A bad business, Father."

"It is indeed," da Costa said.

"As you can see, we're going through the usual motions and Professor Lawlor here is making a preliminary report. He'll do an autopsy this afternoon. On the other hand, because of the way it happened you're obviously the key to the whole affair. If I might ask you a few more questions?"

"Anything I can do, of course, but I can assure you that Inspector Fitzgerald was most efficient. I don't think there can be anything he overlooked."

Fitzgerald looked suitably modest and Miller smiled. "Father, I've been a policeman for nearly twenty-five years and if I've learned one thing, it's that there's always something and it's usually that something which wins cases."

Professor Lawlor stood up. "I've finished here, Nick," he said. "You can move him." He turned to da Costa. "You said, if I got it right from Fitzgerald, that he was down on his right knee at the edge of the grave." He walked across. "About here?"

"That's correct."

Lawlor turned to Miller. "It fits, he must have glanced up at the crucial moment and his head would naturally be turned to the right. The entry wound is about an inch above the outer corner of the left eye."

"Anything else interesting?" Miller asked.

"Not really. Entry wound a quarter of an inch in diameter. Very little bleeding. No powder marking. No staining. Exterior wound two inches in diameter. Explosive type with disruptions of the table of the skull and lacerations of the right occipital lobe of the brain. The wound is two inches to the right of the exterior occipital protuberance."

"Thank you, Doctor Kildare," Miller said.

Professor Lawlor turned to Father da Costa and smiled. "You see, Father, medicine has its jargon, too, just like the Church. What I'm really trying to say is that he was shot through the skull at close quarters—but not too close."

He picked up his bag. "The bullet shouldn't be too far away, or what's left of it," he said as he walked off.

"Thank you for reminding me," Miller called ironically.

Fitzgerald had crossed to the doorway and now he came back, shaking his head. "They're making a plaster cast of those footprints, but we're wasting our time. He was wearing galoshes. Another thing, we've been over the appropriate area with a fine-tooth comb and there isn't a sign of a cartridge case."

Miller frowned and turned to da Costa. "You're certain he was using a silencer?"

"Absolutely."

"You seem very sure."

"As a young man I was lieutenant in the Special Air Service, Superintendent," da Costa told him calmly. "The Aegean Islands, Yugoslavia. That sort of thing. I'm afraid I had to use a silencer pistol myself on more than one occasion."

Miller and Fitzgerald glanced at each other in surprise and then Father da Costa saw it all in a flash of blinding light. "But of course," he said, "it's impossible to use a silencer with a revolver. It has to be an automatic pistol, which means the cartridge case would have been ejected." He crossed to the doorway. "Let me see, the pistol was in his right hand, so the cartridge case should be somewhere about here."

"Exactly," Miller said. "Only we can't find it."

And then da Costa remembered. "He dropped to one knee and picked something up, just before he left."

Miller turned to Fitzgerald who looked chagrined. "Which wasn't in your report."

"My fault, Superintendent," da Costa said. "I didn't tell him. It slipped my mind."

"As I said, Father, there's always something," Miller took out a pipe and started to fill it from a worn leather pouch. "I know one thing. This man's no run-of-the-mill tearaway. He's a professional right down to his fingertips, and that's good."

"I don't understand," Father da Costa said.

"Because there aren't many of that calibre about, Father. It's as simple as that. Let me explain. About six months ago somebody got away with nearly a quarter of a million from a local bank. Took all weekend to get into the vault. A beautiful job—too beautiful. You see we knew straight away that there were no more than five or six men in the country capable of that level of craftsmanship and three of them were in jail. The rest was purely a matter of mathematics."

"I see," da Costa said.

"Now take my unknown friend. I know a hell of a lot about him already. He's an exceptionally clever man because that priest's disguise was a touch of genius. Most people think in stereotypes. If I ask them if they saw anyone they'll say no. If I press them, they'll remember they saw a postman or—as in this case—a priest. If I ask them what he looked like, we're in trouble because all they can remember is that he looked like a priest—any priest."

"I saw his face," da Costa said. "Quite clearly."

"I only hope you'll be as certain if you see a photo of him dressed differently." Miller frowned. "Yes, he knew what he was doing, all right. Galoshes to hide his normal footprints, probably a couple of sizes too large, and a crack shot. Most people couldn't hit a barn door with a handgun at twelve feet. He only needed one shot and that's going some, believe me."

"And considerable nerve," Father da Costa said. "He didn't forget to pick up that cartridge case, remember, in spite of the fact that I had appeared on the scene."

"We ought to have you in the Department, Father." Miller turned to Fitzgerald. "You carry on here. I'll take Father da Costa down town."

Da Costa glanced at his watch. It was twelve-fifteen and he said quickly, "I'm sorry, Superintendent, but that isn't possible. I hear confessions at one o'clock. And my niece was expecting me for lunch at twelve. She'll be worried."

Miller took it quite well. "I see. And when will you be free?"

"Officially at one-thirty. It depends, of course."

"On the number of customers?"

"Exactly."

Miller nodded good-humoredly. "All right, Father, I'll pick you up at two o'clock. Will that be all right?"

"I should imagine so," da Costa said.

"I'll walk you to your car."

The rain had slackened just a little as they went along the path through the rhododendron bushes. Miller yawned several times and rubbed his eyes.

Father da Costa said, "You look tired, Superintendent."

"I didn't get much sleep last night. A car salesman on one of the new housing estates cut his wife's throat with a bread knife, then picked up the phone and dialed nine-nine-nine. A nice, straightforward job, but I still had to turn out personally. Murder's important. I was in bed again by nine o'clock and then they rang through about this little lot."

"You must lead a strange life," da Costa said. "What does your wife think about it?"

"She doesn't. She died last year."

"I'm sorry."

"I'm not. She had cancer of the bowel," Miller told him calmly, then frowned slightly. "Sorry, I know you don't look at things that way in your Church."

Father da Costa didn't reply to that one, because it struck him with startling suddenness that in Miller's position, he would have very probably felt the same way.

They reached the car, an old grey Mini van in front of the chapel, and Miller held the door open for him to get in.

Da Costa leaned out the window. "You think you'll get him, Superintendent? You're confident?"

"I'll get him all right, Father," Miller said grimly. "I've got to if I'm to get the man I really want—the man behind him. The man who set this job up."

"I see. And you already know who that is?"

"I'd put my pension on it."

Father da Costa switched on the ignition and the engine rattled noisily into life. "One thing still bothers me," he said.

"What's that, Father?"

"This man you're looking for—the killer. If he's as much a professional as you say, then why didn't he kill me when he had the chance?"

"Exactly," Miller said. "Which is why it bothers me too. See you later, Father."

He stood back as the priest drove away and Fitzgerald appeared round the corner of the chapel.

"Quite a man," he said.

Miller nodded. "Find out everything you can about him and I mean everything. I'll expect to hear from you by a quarter to two." He turned on the astonished Fitzgerald. "It should be easy enough for you. You're a practising Catholic, aren't you, and a Knight of St. Columbia or whatever you call it, or is that just a front for the IRA?"

"It damn well isn't," Fitzgerald told him indignantly.

"Good. Try the cemetery superintendent first and then there's the Cathedral. They should be able to help. They'll talk to you."

He put a match to his pipe and Fitzgerald said despairingly, "But why, for God's sake?"

"Because another thing I've learned after twenty-five years of being a copper is never to take anything or anyone at face value," Miller told him.

He walked across to his car, climbed in, nodded to the driver and leaned back. By the time they reached the main road, he was already asleep.

4

Confessional

Anna da Costa was playing the piano in the living-room of the old presbytery when Father da Costa entered. She swung round on the piano stool at once and stood up.

"Uncle Michael, you're late. What happened?"

He kissed her cheek and led her to a chair by the window. "You'll hear soon enough so I might as well tell you now. A man was murdered this morning at the cemetery."

She gazed up at him blankly, those beautiful, useless, dark eyes fixed on some point beyond, and there was a complete lack of comprehension on her face.

"Murdered? I don't understand."

He sat down beside her and took both her hands in his. "I saw it, Anna. I was the only witness."

He got up and started to pace up and down the room. "I was walking through the old part of the cemetery. Remember, I took you there last month?"

He described what had happened in detail, as much for himself as for her, because for some reason it seemed suddenly necessary.

"And he didn't shoot me, Anna!" he said. "That's the strangest thing of all. I just don't understand it. It doesn't make any kind of sense."

She shuddered deeply. "Oh, Uncle Michael, it's a miracle you're here at all."

She held out her hands and he took them again, conscious of a sudden, overwhelming tenderness. It occurred to him, and not for the first time, that in some ways she was the one creature he truly loved in the whole world, which was a great sin, for a priest's love, after all, should be available to all. But then, she was his dead brother's only child, an orphan since her fifteenth year.

The clock struck one and he patted her head. "I'll have to go. I'm already late."

"I made sandwiches," she said. "They're in the kitchen."

"I'll have them when I get back," he said. "I won't have much time. I'm being picked up by a detective superintendent called Miller at two o'clock. He wants me to look through some photos to see if I can recognize the man I saw. If he's early, give him a cup of tea or something."

The door banged. It was suddenly very quiet. She sat there, thoroughly bewildered by it all, unable to comprehend what he had told her. She was a quiet girl. She knew little of life. Her childhood had been spent in special schools for the blind. After the death of her parents, music college. And then Uncle Michael had returned and for the first time in years, she had somebody to care about again. Who cared about her.

But as always, there was solace in her music and she turned back to the piano, feeling expertly through Braille music transcripts for the Chopin prelude she was working on. It wasn't there. She frowned in bewilderment and then suddenly remembered going across to the church earlier to play the organ and the stranger who'd spoken to her. She must have left the piece she wanted over there with her organ transcripts.

She went out into the hall, found a raincoat and a walking stick and let herself out of the front door.

432

* * *

It was still raining hard as Father da Costa hurried through the churchyard and unlocked the small door which led directly into the sacristy. He put on his alb, threw a violet stole over his shoulder and went to hear confession.

He was late—not that it mattered very much. Few people came at that time of day. Perhaps the odd shopper or office worker who found the old church convenient. On some days he waited the statutory half an hour and no one called at all.

The church was cold and smelt of damp, which wasn't particularly surprising as he could no longer meet the heating bill. A young woman was just lighting another candle in front of the Virgin, and as he moved past he was aware of at least two other people, sitting waiting by the confessional box.

He went inside, murmured a short prayer and settled himself. The prayer hadn't helped, mainly because his mind was still in a turmoil, obsessed with what he had seen at the cemetery.

The door clicked on the other side of the screen and a woman started to speak. Middle-aged, from the sound of her. He hastily forced himself back to reality and listened to what she had to say. It was nothing very much. Sins of omission in the main. Some minor dishonesty concerning a grocery bill. A few petty lies.

The next was a young woman, presumably the one he had seen lighting the candle to the Virgin. She started hesitantly. Trivial matters on the whole. Anger, impure thoughts, lies. And she hadn't been to Mass for three months.

"Is that all?" he prompted her in the silence.

It wasn't, of course, and out it came. An affair with her employer, a married man.

"How long has this been going on?" da Costa asked her.

"For three months, Father."

The exact period since she had last been to Mass.

"This man has made love to you?"

"Yes, Father."

"How often?"

"Two or three times a week. At the office. When everyone else has gone home."

There was a confidence in her voice now, a calmness. Of course bringing things out into the open often made people feel like that, but this was different.

"He has children?"

"Three, Father." There was a pause. "What can I do?"

"The answer is so obvious. Must be. Leave this place, find another job. Put him out of your mind."

"I can't do that."

"Why?" he said, and added with calculated brutality, "Because you enjoy it?"

"Yes, Father," she said simply.

"And you're not prepared to stop?"

"I can't!" For the first time she cracked, just a little, but there was panic there now.

"Then why have you come here?"

"I haven't been to Mass in three months, Father."

He saw it all then and it was really so beautifully simple, so pitifully human.

"I see," he said. "You can't do without God either."

She started to cry quietly. "This is a waste of time, Father, because I can't say I won't go with him again when I know damn well my body will betray me every time I see him. God knows that. If I said any different I'd be lying to Him as well as you and I couldn't do that."

How many people were that close to God? Father da Costa was filled with a sense of incredible wonder. He took a deep breath to hold back the lump that rose in his throat and threatened to choke him.

He said in a firm, clear voice, "May Our Lord Jesus Christ absolve you, and I, by his authority, absolve you from every bond of excommunication and interdict, so far as I can, and you have need. Therefore, I absolve you from your sins, in the name of the Father and of the Son and of the Holy Spirit."

434

There was silence for a moment, and then she said, "But I can't promise I won't see him again."

"I'm not asking you to," da Costa said. "If you feel you owe me anything, find another job, that's all I ask. We'll leave the rest up to God."

The longest pause of all followed. He waited, desperately anxious for the right answer, aware of an unutterable sense of relief when it came.

"Very well, Father, I promise."

"Good. Evening Mass is at six o'clock. I never get more than fifteen or twenty people. You'll be very welcome."

The door clicked shut as she went and he sat there feeling suddenly drained. With any luck, he'd said the right thing, handled it the right way. Only time would tell.

It was a change to feel useful again. The door clicked, there was the scrape of the chair being moved on the other side of the grille.

"Please bless me, Father."

It was an unfamiliar voice. Soft. Irish—an educated man without a doubt.

Father da Costa said, "May our Lord Jesus bless you and help you to tell your sins."

There was a pause before the man said, "Father, are there any circumstances under which what I say to you now could be passed on to anyone else?"

Da Costa straightened in his chair. "None whatsoever. The secrets of the confessional are inviolate."

"Good," the man said. "Then I'd better get it over with. I killed a man this morning."

Father da Costa was stunned. "Killed a man?" he whispered. "Murdered, you mean?"

"Exactly."

With a sudden, terrible premonition, da Costa reached forward, trying to peer through the grille. On the other side, a match flared in the darkness and for the second time that day, he looked into the face of Martin Fallon.

435

*   *   *

The church was still when Anna da Costa came out of the
sacristy and crossed to the choir stalls. The Braille transcripts
were where she had left them. She found what she was looking
for with no difficulty. She put the rest back on the stand and
sat there for a few moments, remembering the stranger with
the soft Irish voice.

He'd been right about the trumpet stop. She put out a hand
and touched it gently. One thing putting everything else out of
joint. How strange. She reached for her walking stick and stood
up and somewhere below her in the body of the church, a door
banged and her uncle's voice was raised in anger. She froze,
standing perfectly still, concealed by the green curtains which
hung beside the organ.

Father da Costa erupted from the confessional box, flinging
the door wide. She had never heard such anger in his voice
before.

"Come out—come out, damn you, and look me in the face
if you dare!"

Anna heard the other door in the confessional box click open.
There was the softest of footfalls, and then a quiet voice said,
"Here we are again, then, Father."

Fallon stood beside the box, hands in the pockets of the navy
blue trenchcoat. Father da Costa moved closer, his voice a
hoarse whisper.

"Are you a Catholic?"

"As ever was, Father." There was a light mocking note in
Fallon's voice.

"Then you must know that I cannot possibly grant you absolu-
tion in this matter. You murdered a man in cold blood this
morning. I saw you do it. We both know that." He drew himself
up. "What do you want with me?"

"I've already got it, Father. As you said, the secrets of the
confessional are inviolate. That makes what I told you privileged
information."

436

There was an agony in Father da Costa's voice that cut into Anna's heart like a knife. "You used me!" he cried. "In the worst possible way. You've used this church."

"I could have closed your mouth by putting a bullet between your eyes. Would you have preferred that?"

"In some ways I think I would." Father da Costa had control of himself again now. He said, "What is your name?"

"Fallon—Martin Fallon."

"Is that genuine?"

"Names with me are like the Book of the Month. Always changing. I'm not wanted as Fallon. Let's put it that way."

"I see," Father da Costa said. "An interesting choice. I once knew a priest of that name. Do you know what it means in Irish?"

"Of course. Stranger from outside the campfire."

"And you consider that appropriate?"

"I don't follow you."

"I mean, is that how you see yourself? As some romantic desperado outside the crowd?"

Fallon showed no emotion whatsoever. "I'll go now. You won't see me again."

He turned to leave and Father da Costa caught him by the arm. "The man who paid you to do what you did this morning, Fallon? Does he know about me?"

Fallon stared at him for a long moment, frowning slightly, and then he smiled. "You've nothing to worry about. It's taken care of."

"For such a clever man, you really are very foolish," Father da Costa told him.

The door at the main entrance banged open in the wind. An old woman in a headscarf entered. She dipped her fingers in the holy water, genuflected and came up the aisle.

Father da Costa took Fallon's arm firmly. "We can't talk here. Come with me."

At one side of the nave there was an electric cage hoist,

obviously used by workmen for access to the tower. He pushed Fallon inside and pressed the button. The cage rose through the network of scaffolding, passing through a hole in the roof.

It finally jerked to a halt, and da Costa opened the gate and led the way out on to a catwalk supported by the scaffolding that encircled the top of the tower like a ship's bridge.

"What happened here?" Fallon asked.

"We ran out of money," Father da Costa told him.

Neither of them heard the slight whirring of the electric motor as the cage dropped back to the church below. When it reached ground level, Anna da Costa entered, closed the gate and fumbled for the button.

The view of the city from the catwalk was magnificent, although the grey curtain of the rain made things hazy in the middle distance. Fallon gazed about him with obvious pleasure. He had changed in some subtle, indefinable way and smiled slightly.

"Now this I like. 'Earth hath not anything to show more fair'—isn't that what the poet said?"

"Great God in heaven, I bring you here to talk seriously and you quote Wordsworth to me? Doesn't anything touch you at all?"

"Not that I can think of." Fallon took out a packet of cigarettes. "Do you use these?"

Father da Costa hesitated, then took one angrily. "Yes, I will, damn you."

"That's it, Father, enjoy yourself while you can," Fallon said as he struck a match and gave him a light. "After all, we're all going to hell the same way."

"You actually believe that?"

"From what I've seen of life it would seem a reasonable conclusion to me."

Fallon leaned on the rail, smoking his cigarette, and Father da Costa watched him for a moment, feeling strangely helpless. There was obvious intelligence here—breeding, strength of character—all the qualities and yet it seemed impossible to reach through and touch the man in any way.

"You're not a practising Catholic?" he said at last.

Fallon shook his head. "Not for a long time."

"Can I ask why?"

"No," Fallon told him calmly.

Father da Costa tried again. "Confession, Fallon, is a Sacrament. A Sacrament of Reconciliation."

He suddenly felt rather silly, because this was beginning to sound dangerously like one of his Confirmation classes at the local Catholic school, but he pressed on.

"When we go to confession we meet Jesus, who takes us to himself, and because we are in Him and because we are sorry, God our Father forgives us."

"I'm not asking for any forgiveness," Fallon said. "Not from anybody."

"No man can damn himself for all eternity in this way," Father da Costa said sternly. "He has not the right."

"Just in case you hadn't heard, the man I shot was called Krasko and he was the original thing from under a stone. Pimp, whoremaster, drug-pusher. You name it, he had a finger in it. And you want me to say sorry? For him?"

"Then he was the law's concern."

"The law!" Fallon laughed harshly. "Men like him are above the law. He's been safe for years behind a triple wall of money, corruption and lawyers. By any kind of logic I'd say I've done society a favor."

"For thirty pieces of silver?"

"Oh, more than that, Father. Much more," Fallon told him. "Don't worry, I'll put something in the poor box on the way out. I can afford it." He flicked his cigarette out into space. "I'll be going now."

He turned, and Father da Costa grabbed him by the sleeve, pulling him round. "You're making a mistake, Fallon. I think you'll find that God won't let you have it your way."

Fallon said coldly, "Don't be stupid, Father."

"In fact, he's already taken a hand," Father da Costa continued. "Do you think I was there in that cemetery at that particular moment by accident?" He shook his head. "Oh, no, Fallon. You took one life, but God has made you responsible for another—mine."

Fallon's face was very pale now. He took a step back, turned and walked towards the hoist without a word. As he drew abreast of a buttress, some slight noise caused him to look to his left and he saw Anna da Costa hiding behind it.

He drew her out gently, but in spite of that fact, she cried out in fear. Fallon said softly, "It's all right. I promise you."

Father da Costa hurried forward and pulled her away from him. "Leave her alone."

Anna started to weep softly as he held her in his arms. Fallon stood looking at them, a slight frown on his face. "Perhaps she's heard more than was good for her."

Father da Costa held Anna away from him a little and looked down at her. "Is that so?"

She nodded, whispering, "I was in the church." She turned reaching out her hands, feeling her way to Fallon. "What kind of man are you?"

One hand found his face as he stood there as if turned to stone. She drew back hastily, as if stung, and da Costa put a protective arm about her again.

"Leave us!" she whispered hoarsely to Fallon. "I'll say nothing of what I heard to anyone, I promise, only go away and don't come back. Please!" There was a passionate entreaty in her voice.

Father da Costa held her close again and Fallon said, "Does she mean it?"

"She said, didn't she?" Father da Costa told him. "We take your guilt on our souls, Fallon. Now get out of here."

Fallon showed no emotion at all. He turned and walked to the hoist. As he opened the gate, da Costa called, "Two of us now, Fallon. Two lives to be responsible for. Are you up to that?"

Fallon stood there for a long moment, a hand on the open gate. Finally, he said softly, "It will be all right. I gave you my word. My own life on it, if you like."

He stepped into the hoist and closed the gate. There was the gentle whirring of the electric motor, a dull echo from below as the cage reached the ground floor.

Anna looked up. "He's gone?" she whispered.

Father da Costa nodded. "It's all right now."

"He was in the church earlier," she said. "He told me what was wrong with the organ. Isn't that the strangest thing?"

"The organ?" Da Costa stared down at her in bewilderment and then sighed. He shook his head and turned her gently round. "Come on, now, I'll take you home. You'll catch your death."

They stood at the cage, waiting for the gate to come up after he had pressed the button. Anna said slowly, "What are we going to do, Uncle Michael?"

"About Martin Fallon?" He put an arm about her shoulder. "For the moment, nothing. What he told me in the church spilled over from the confessional box because of my anger and impatience so that what you overheard was still strictly part of that original confession. I'm afraid I can't look at it in any other way." He sighed. "I'm sorry, Anna. I know this must be an intolerable burden for you, but I must ask you to give me your promise not to speak of this to anyone."

"But I already have," she said. "To him."

A strange thing to say, and it troubled him deeply. The cage arrived, and they moved inside and made the quick descent to the church.

Alone in his study, he did a thing he seldom did so early in the day and poured himself a glass of whisky. He sipped it slowly and stood, one hand on the marble mantelpiece and stared down into the flames of the small coal fire.

"And what do we do now, Michael?" he asked himself softly.

It was an old habit, this carrying on a conversation with his

inner self. A relic of three years of solitary confinement in a
Chinese prison cell in North Korea. Useful in any situation
where he needed to be as objective as possible about some close
personal problem.

But then, in a sense, this wasn't his problem, it was Fallon's,
he saw that suddenly with startling clarity. His own situation
was such that his hands were tied. There was little that he could
do or say. The next move would have to be Fallon's.

There was a knock at the door and Anna appeared. "Superintendent Miller to see you, Uncle Michael."

Miller moved into the room, hat in hand. "There you are,
Superintendent," da Costa said. "Have you met my niece?"

He made a formal introduction. Anna was remarkably controlled. In fact she showed no nervousness at all, which surprised
him.

"I'll leave you to it." She hesitated, the door half-open.
"You'll be going out, then?"

"Not just yet," Father da Costa told her.

Miller frowned. "But I don't understand, Father, I thought . . ."

"A moment, please, Superintendent," Father da Costa said
and glanced at Anna. She went out, closing the door softly and
he turned to Miller. "You were saying?"

"Our agreement was that you were to come down to the
Department to look at some photos," Miller said.

"I know, Superintendent, but that won't be possible now."

"May I ask why not, Father?" Miller demanded.

Father da Costa had given considerable thought to his answer,
yet in the end could manage nothing more original than, "I'm
afraid I wouldn't be able to help you, that's all."

Miller was genuinely puzzled and showed it. "Let's start
again, Father. Perhaps you didn't understand me properly. All
I want you to do is to come down to the Department to look at
some photos, in the hope that you might recognize our friend
of this morning."

"I know all that," Father da Costa told him.

"And you still refuse to come?"

442

"There wouldn't be any point."

"Why not?"

"Because I can't help you."

For a moment, Miller genuinely thought he was going out of his mind. This couldn't be happening. It just didn't make any kind of sense, and then he was struck by a sudden dreadful suspicion.

"Has Meehan been getting at you in some way?"

"Meehan?" Father da Costa said, his genuine bewilderment so perfectly obvious that Miller immediately dropped the whole idea.

"I could have you brought in formally, Father, as a material witness."

"You can take a horse to water but you can't make him drink, Superintendent."

"I can have a damn good try," Miller told him grimly. He walked to the door and opened it. "Don't make me take you in formally, sir. I'd rather not but I will if I have to."

"Superintendent Miller," Father da Costa said softly, "men of a harsher disposition than you have tried to make me speak in circumstances where it was not appropriate. They did not succeed and neither will you, I can assure you. No power on earth can make me speak on this matter if I do not wish to."

"We'll see about that, sir. I'll give you some time to think this matter over, then I'll be back." He was about to walk out when a sudden wild thought struck him and he turned, slowly, "Have you seen him again, sir, since this morning? Have you been threatened? Is your life in any kind of danger?"

"Goodbye, Superintendent," Father da Costa said.

The front door banged. Father da Costa turned to finish his whisky, and Anna moved silently into the room. She put a hand on his arm.

"He'll go to Monsignor O'Halloran."

"The bishop being at present in Rome, that would seem the obvious thing to do," he said.

"Hadn't you better get there first?"

"I suppose so." He emptied his glass and put it on the mantelpiece. "What about you?"

"I want to do some more organ practice. I'll be all right."

She pushed him out into the hall and reached for his coat from the stand with unerring aim. "What would I do without you?" he said.

She smiled cheerfully. "Goodness knows. Hurry back."

He went out, and she closed the door after him. When she turned, the smile had completely disappeared. She went back into his study, sat down by the fire and buried her face in her hands.

Nick Miller had been a policeman for almost a quarter of a century. Twenty-five years of working a three-shift system. Of being disliked by his neighbors, of being able to spend only one weekend in seven at home with his family and the consequent effect upon his relationship with his son and daughter.

He had little formal education but he was a shrewd, clever man with the ability to cut through to the heart of things, and this, coupled with an extensive knowledge of human nature gained from a thousand long, hard Saturday nights on the town, had made him a good policeman.

He had no conscious thought or even desire to help society. His job was in the main to catch thieves, and society consisted of the civilians who sometimes got mixed up in the constant state of guerrilla warfare which existed between the police and the criminal. If anything, he preferred the criminal. At least you knew where you were with him.

But Dandy Jack Meehan was different. One corruption was all corruption, he'd read that somewhere, and if it applied to any human being, it applied to Meehan.

Miller loathed him with the kind of obsessive hate that was in the end self-destructive. To be precise, ten years of his life had gone to Dandy Jack without the slightest hint of success. Meehan had to be behind the Krasko killing, that was a fact of life. The rivalry between the two men had been common knowledge for at least two years.

For the first time in God knows how long he'd had a chance and now, the priest . . .

When he got into the rear of the car he was shaking with anger, and on a sudden impulse he leaned across and told his driver to take him to the headquarters of Meehan's funeral business. Then he sat back and tried to light his pipe with trembling fingers.

5

Dandy Jack

Paul's Square was a green lung in the heart of the city, an acre of grass and flower-beds and willow trees with a fountain in the center surrounded on all four sides by Georgian terrace houses, most of which were used as offices by barristers, solicitors or doctors and beautifully preserved.

There was a general atmosphere of quiet dignity and Meehan's funeral business fitted in perfectly. Three houses on the north side had been converted to provide every possible facility from a flower shop to a Chapel of Rest. A mews entrance to one side gave access to a car park and garage area at the rear surrounded by high walls where business could be handled as quietly and unobtrusively as possible. The facility had other uses on occasion.

When the big Bentley hearse turned into the car park shortly after one o'clock, Meehan was sitting up front with the chauffeur and Billy. He wore his usual double-breasted melton overcoat and Homburg hat, and a black tie, for he had been officiating personally at a funeral that morning.

The chauffeur came round to open the door, and Meehan got out followed by his brother. "Thanks, Donner," he said.

A small grey whippet was drinking from a dish at the rear entrance. Billy called, "Here, Tommy!" It turned, hurled itself across the yard and jumped into his arms.

Billy fondled its ears and it licked his face frantically. "Now then, you little bastard," he said with genuine affection.

"I've told you before," Meehan said. "He'll ruin your coat. Hairs all over the bloody place."

As he moved towards the rear entrance, Varley came out of the garage and stood waiting for him, cap in hand. A muscle twitched nervously in his right cheek, his forehead was beaded with sweat. He seemed almost on the point of collapse.

Meehan paused, hands in pockets, and looked him over calmly. "You look awful, Charlie. You been a bad lad or something?"

"Not me, Mr. Meehan," Varley said. "It's that sod, Fallon. He . . ."

"Not here, Charlie," Meehan said softly. "I always like to hear bad news in private."

He nodded to Donner, who opened the rear door and stood to one side. Meehan went into what was usually referred to as the receiving room. It was empty except for a coffin on a trolley in the center.

He put a cigarette in his mouth and bent down to read the brass nameplate on the coffin.

"When's this for?"

Donner moved to his side, a lighter ready in his hand. "Three-thirty, Mr. Meehan."

He spoke with an Australian accent and had a slightly twisted mouth, the scar still plain where a harelip had been cured by plastic surgery. It gave him a curiously repellent appearance, modified to a certain extent by the hand-tailored, dark uniform suit he wore.

"Is it a cremation?"

Donner shook his head. "A burial, Mr. Meehan."

Meehan nodded. "All right, you and Bonati better handle it. I've an idea I'm going to be busy."

He turned, one arm on the coffin. Billy leaned against the wall, fondling the whippet. Varley waited in the center of the room, cap in hand, the expression on his face that of a condemned man waiting for the trap to open beneath his feet at any moment and plunge him into eternity.

"All right, Charlie," Meehan said. "Tell me the worst."

Varley told him, the words falling over themselves in his eagerness to get them out. When he had finished, there was a lengthy silence. Meehan had shown no emotion at all.

"So he's coming here at two o'clock?"

"That's what he said, Mr. Meehan."

"And the van? You took it to the wrecker's yard like I told you?"

"Saw it go into the crusher myself, just like you said."

Varley waited for his sentence, face damp with sweat. Meehan smiled suddenly and patted him on the cheek. "You did well, Charlie. Not your fault things went wrong. Leave it to me. I'll handle it."

Relief seemed to ooze out of Varley like dirty water. He said weakly, "Thanks, Mr. Meehan. I did my best. Honest I did. You know me."

"You have something to eat," Meehan said. "Then get back to the car wash. If I need you, I'll send for you."

Varley went out. The door closed. Billy giggled as he fondled the whippet's ears. "I told you he was trouble. We could have handled it ourselves only you wouldn't listen."

Meehan grabbed him by the long white hair, the boy cried out in pain, dropping the dog. "Do you want me to get nasty, Billy?" he said softly. "Is that what you want?"

"I didn't mean any harm, Jack," the boy whined.

Meehan shoved him away. "Then be a good boy. Tell Bonati I want him, then take one of the cars and go and get Fat Albert."

Billy's tongue flicked nervously between his lips. "Albert?" he whispered. "For God's sake, Jack, you know I can't stand being anywhere near that big creep. He frightens me to death."

"That's good," Meehan said. "I'll remember that next time you step out of line. We'll call Albert in to take you in hand." He laughed harshly. "Would you like that?"

Billy's eyes were wide with fear. "No, please, Jack," he whispered. "Not Albert."

"Be a good lad, then." Meehan patted his face and opened the door. "On your way."

Billy went out and Meehan turned to Donner with a sigh. "I don't know what I'm going to do with him, Frank. I don't, really."

"He's young, Mr. Meehan."

"All he can think about is birds," Meehan said. "Dirty little tarts in miniskirts showing all they've got." He shivered in genuine disgust. "I even found him having it off with the cleaning woman one afternoon. Fifty-five if she was a day—and on my bed."

Donner kept a diplomatic silence and Meehan opened an inner door and led the way through into the Chapel of Rest. The atmosphere was cool and fresh thanks to air-conditioning, and scented with flowers. Taped organ music provided a suitably devotional background.

There were half-a-dozen cubicles on either side. Meehan took off his hat and stepped into the first one. There were flowers everywhere and an oak coffin stood on a draped trolley.

"Who's this?"

"That young girl. The student who went through the windscreen of the sports car," Donner told him.

"Oh, yes," Meehan said. "I did her myself."

He lifted the face cloth. The girl was perhaps eighteen or nineteen, eyes closed, lips slightly parted, the face so skillfully made up that she might only have been sleeping.

"You did a good job there, Mr. Meehan," Donner said.

Meehan nodded complacently. "I've got to agree with you there, Frank. You know something. There was no flesh left on her left cheek when she came to me. That girl's face was mincemeat, I'm telling you."

"You're an artist, Mr. Meehan," Donner said, genuine admiration in his voice. "A real artist. It's the only word for it."

"It's nice of you to say so, Frank. I really appreciate that." Meehan switched off the light and led the way out. "I always try to do my best, of course, but a case like that—a young girl. Well, you got to think of the parents."

"Too true, Mr. Meehan."

They moved out of the chapel area into the front hall, the original Georgian features still beautifully preserved, blue and white Wedgwood plaques on the walls. There was a glass door leading to the reception office on the right. As they approached, they could hear voices and someone appeared to be crying.

The door opened and a very old woman appeared, sobbing heavily. She wore a headscarf and a shabby woollen overcoat bursting at the seams. She had a carrier bag over one arm and clutched a worn leather purse in her left hand. Her face was swollen with weeping.

Henry Ainsley, the reception clerk, moved out after her. He was a tall, thin man with hollow cheeks and sly, furtive eyes. He wore a neat, clerical-grey suit and sober tie, and his hands were soft.

"I'm sorry, madam," he was saying sharply, "but that's the way it is. Anyway, you can leave everything in our hands from now on."

"That's the way what is?" Meehan said, advancing on them. He put his hands on the old lady's shoulders. "We can't have this, love. What's up?"

"It's all right, Mr. Meehan. The old lady was just a bit upset. She's just lost her husband," Ainsley said.

Meehan ignored him and drew the old lady into the office. He put her in a chair by the desk. "Now then, love, you tell me all about it."

He took her hand and she held on tight. "Ninety, he was. I thought he'd last forever and then I found him at the bottom of the stairs when I got back from chapel, Sunday night." Tears streamed down her face. "He was that strong, even at that age. I couldn't believe it."

"I know, love, and now you're come here to bury him?"

She nodded. "I don't have much, but I didn't want him to have a state funeral. I wanted it done right. I thought I could manage nicely with the insurance money, and then this gentleman here, he told me I'd need seventy pound."

"Now look, Mr. Meehan, it was like this," Ainsley cut in.

Meehan turned and glanced at him bleakly. Ainsley faltered into silence. Meehan said, "You paid cash, love?"

"Oh, yes," she said. "I called at the insurance office on the way and they paid me out on the policy. Fifty pounds, I thought it would be enough."

"And the other twenty?"

"I had twenty-five pounds in the Post Office."

"I see." Meehan straightened. "Show me the file," he said.

Ainsley stumbled to the desk and picked up a small sheaf of papers which shook a little as he held them out. Meehan leafed through them. He smiled delightedly and put a hand on the old woman's shoulders.

"I've got good news for you, love. There's been a mistake."

"A mistake?" she said.

He took out his wallet and extracted twenty-five pounds. "Mr. Ainsley was forgetting about the special rate we've been offering to old-age pensioners this autumn."

She looked at the money, a dazed expression on her face. "Special rate. Here, it won't be a state funeral, will it? I wouldn't want that."

Meehan helped her to her feet. "Not on your life. Private. The best. I guarantee it. Now let's go and see about your flowers."

"Flowers?" she said. "Oh, that would be nice. He loved flowers, did my Bill."

"All included, love." Meehan glanced over his shoulder at Donner. "Keep him here. I'll be back."

A door had been cut through the opposite wall giving access

to the flower shop next door. When Meehan ushered the old lady in, they were immediately approached by a tall, willowy young man with shoulder-length dark hair and a beautiful mouth.

"Yes, Mr. Meehan. Can I be of service?" He spoke with a slight lisp.

Meehan patted his cheek. "You certainly can, Rupert. Help this good lady choose a bunch of flowers. Best in the shop and a wreath. On the firm, of course."

Rupert accepted the situation without the slightest question. "Certainly, Mr. Meehan."

"And Rupert, see one of the lads runs her home afterwards." He turned to the old lady. "All right, love?"

She reached up and kissed his cheek. "You're a good man. A wonderful man. God bless you."

"He does, my love," Dandy Jack Meehan told her. "Every day of my life." And he walked out.

"Death is something you've got to have some respect for," Meehan said. "I mean, this old lady. According to the form she's filled in, she's eighty-three. I mean, that's a wonderful thing."

He was sitting in the swing chair in front of the desk. Henry Ainsley stood in front of him, Donner was by the door.

Ainsley stirred uneasily and forced a smile. "Yes, I see what you mean, Mr. Meehan."

"Do you, Henry? I wonder."

There was a knock at the door, and a small, dapper man in belted continental raincoat entered. He looked like a Southern Italian, but spoke with a South Yorkshire accent.

"You wanted me, Mr. Meehan?"

"That's it, Bonati. Come in." Meehan returned to Ainsley. "Yes, I really wonder about you, Henry. Now the way I see it, this was an insurance job. She's strictly working-class. The policy pays fifty, and you price the job at seventy, and the old dear coughs up because she can't stand the thought of her Bill having a state funeral." He shook his head. "You gave her a receipt for fifty, which she's too tired and old to notice, and you enter fifty in the cash book."

Ainsley was shaking like a leaf. "Please, Mr. Meehan, please listen. I've had certain difficulties lately."

Meehan stood up. "Has he been brought in, her husband?"

Ainsley nodded. "This morning. He's in number three. He hadn't been prepared yet."

"Bring him along," Meehan told Donner, and walked out.

He went into cubicle number three in the Chapel of Rest and switched on the light. The others followed him in. The old man was lying in an open coffin with a sheet over him, and Meehan pulled it away. He was quite naked; he had obviously been a remarkably powerful man in his day, with the shoulders and chest of a heavyweight wrestler.

Meehan looked at him in awe. "He was a bull, this one, and no mistake. Look at the dick on him." He turned to Ainsley. "Think of the women he pleasured. Think of that old lady. By God, I can see why she loved him. He was a man, this old lad."

His knees came up savagely. Henry Ainsley grabbed for his privates too late and he pitched forward with a choked cry.

"Take him up to the coffin room," Meehan told Donner. "I'll join you in five minutes."

When Henry Ainsley regained his senses, he was lying flat on his back, arms outstretched, Donner standing on one hand, Bonati on the other.

The door opened and Meehan entered. He stood looking down at him for a moment, then nodded. "All right, pick him up."

The room was used to store coffins, which weren't actually made on the premises, but there were a couple of workbenches and a selection of carpenter's tools on a rack on the wall.

"Please, Mr. Meehan," Ainsley begged him.

Meehan nodded to Donner, and Bonati dragged Ainsley back across one of the workbenches, arms outstretched, palms uppermost.

Meehan stood over him. "I'm going to teach you a lesson, Henry. Not because you tried to fiddle me out of twenty quid. That's one thing that's definitely not allowed, but it's more than that. You see, I'm thinking of that old girl. She's never had a thing in her life. All she ever got was screwed into the ground."

His eyes were smoking now and there was a slightly dreamy quality to his voice. "She reminded me of my old mum, I don't know why. But I know one thing. She's earned some respect just like her old fella's earned something better than a state funeral."

"You've got it wrong, Mr. Meehan," Ainsley gabbled.

"No, Henry, you're the one who got it wrong."

Meehan selected two brad-awls from the rack on the wall. He tested the point of one on his thumb, then drove it through the center of Ainsley's right palm, pinning his hand to the bench. When he repeated the process with the other hand, Ainsley fainted.

Meehan turned to Donner. "Five minutes, then release him and tell him if he isn't in the office on time in the morning, I'll have his balls."

"All right, Mr. Meehan," Donner said. "What about Fallon?"

"I'll be in the preparation room. I've got some embalming to do. When Fallon comes, keep him in the office till I've had a chance to get up to the flat, then bring him up. And I want Albert up there as soon as he comes in."

"Kid-glove treatment, Mr. Meehan?"

"What else, Frank? What else?"

Meehan smiled, patted the unconscious Ainsley on the cheek and walked out.

The preparation room was on the other side of the Chapel of Rest. When Meehan went in he closed the door. He liked to be alone on such occasions. It aided concentration and made the whole thing somehow much more personal.

A body waited for him on the table in the center of the room covered with a sheet. Beside it on a trolley the tools of his trade were laid out neatly on a white cloth. Scalpels, scissors, forceps, surgical needles of various sizes, artery tubes, a large rubber bulb syringe and a glass jar containing a couple of gallons of embalming fluid. On a shelf underneath was an assortment of cosmetics, make-up creams and face powders, all made to order.

He pulled away the sheet and folded it neatly. The body was that of a woman of forty—handsome, dark-haired. He remembered the case. A history of heart trouble. She'd died in mid-sentence while discussing plans for Christmas with her husband.

There was still that look of faint surprise on her face that many people show in death: jaw dropped, mouth gaping as if in amazement that this should be happening to her of all people.

Meehan took a long curved needle and skillfully passed a thread from behind the lower lip, up through the nasal septum and down again, so that when he tightened the thread and tied it off, the jaw was raised.

The eyeballs had fallen into their sockets. He compensated for that by inserting a circle of cotton wool under each eyelid before closing it. He put cotton wool between the lips and gums and in the cheeks to give a fuller, more natural appearance.

All this he did with total absorption, whistling softly between his teeth, a frown of concentration on his face. His anger at Ainsley had disappeared totally. Even Fallon had ceased to exist. He smeared a little cream on the cold lips with one finger, stood back and nodded in satisfaction. He was now ready to start the embalming process.

The body weighed nine and a half stones, which meant that he needed about eleven pints of fluid of the mixture he habitually used. Formaldehyde, glycerine, borax with a little phenol added and some sodium citrate as an anticoagulant.

It was a simple enough case, with little likelihood of complications, so he decided to start with the axillary artery as usual. He extended the left arm at right angles to the body, the elbow supported on a wooden block, reached for a scalpel and made his first incision halfway between the mid-point of the collarbone and the bend of the elbow.

Perhaps an hour later, as he tied off the last stitch, he became aware of some sort of disturbance outside. Voices were raised in anger and then the door flew open. Meehan glanced over his shoulder. Miller was standing there. Billy tried to squeeze past him.

"I tried to stop him, Jack."

"Make some tea," Meehan told him. "I'm thirsty. And close that door. You'll ruin the temperature in here. How many times have I told you?"

Billy retired, the door closing softly behind him, and Meehan turned back to the body. He reached for a jar of foundation cream and started to rub some into the face of the dead woman with infinite gentleness, ignoring Miller completely.

Miller lit a cigarette, the match rasping in the silence. Without turning round, Meehan said, "Not in here. In here we show a little respect."

"Is that a fact?" Miller replied, but he still dropped the cigarette on the floor and stepped on it.

He approached the table. Meehan was now applying a medium red cream rouge to the woman's cheekbones, his fingers bringing her back to life by the minute.

Miller watched for a moment in fascinated horror. "You really like your work, don't you, Jack?"

"What do you want?" Meehan asked calmly.

"You."

"Nothing new in that, is there?" Meehan replied. "I mean, anybody falls over and breaks a leg in this town you come to me."

"All right," Miller said. "So we'll go through the motions. Jan Krasko went up to the cemetery this morning to put flowers on his mother's grave. He's been doing that for just over a year now—every Thursday without fail."

"So the bastard has a heart after all. Why tell me?"

"At approximately ten past eleven somebody put a bullet through his skull. A real pro job. Nice and public, so everyone would get the message."

"And what message would that be?"

"Toe the Meehan line or else."

Meehan dusted the face with powder calmly. "I had a funeral this morning," he said. "Old Marcus the draper. At ten past eleven I was sitting in St. Saviour's listening to the vicar say his piece. Ask Billy—he was with me. Along with around a couple of hundred other people, including the mayor. He had a lot of friends had old Mr. Marcus, but then he was a gentleman. Not many of his kind left these days."

He brightened the eyebrows and lashes with Vaseline and colored the lips. The effect was truly remarkable. The woman seemed only to sleep.

Miller said, "I don't care where you were. It was your killing."

Meehan turned to face him, wiping his hands on a towel. "Prove it," he said flatly.

All the frustration of the long years, all the anger, welled up in Miller, threatening to choke him. He pulled at his tie, wrenching open his collar.

"I'll get you for this, Meehan," he said. "I'll lay it on you, if it's the last thing I do. This time you've gone too far."

Meehan's eyes became somehow luminous, his entire personality assumed a new dimension, power seemed to emanate from him like electricity.

"You—touch me?" He laughed coldly, turned and gestured to the woman. "Look at her, Miller. She was dead. I've given her life again. And you think you can touch me?"

Miller took an involuntary step back and Meehan cried, "Go on, get the hell out of it!"

And Miller went as if all the devils in hell had been snapping at his heels.

It was suddenly very quiet in the preparation room. Meehan stood there, chest heaving, and then reached for the tin of vanishing cream and turned to the woman.

"I gave you life again," he whispered. "Life."

He started to rub the cream firmly into the body.

6

Face to Face

It was still raining when Fallon crossed Paul's Square and went up the steps to the main entrance. When he tried the office it was empty and then Rupert appeared, having noticed him arrive through the glass door of the flower shop.

"Can I help you, sir?"

"Fallon's the name. Meehan's expecting me."

"Oh yes, sir." Rupert was exquisitely polite. "If you'd like to wait in the office I'll just see where he is."

He went out and Fallon lit a cigarette and waited. It was a good ten minutes before Rupert reappeared.

"I'll take you up now, sir," he said, and with a flashing smile led the way out into the hall.

"And where would up be?" Fallon asked him.

"Mr. Meehan's had the attics of the three houses knocked together into a penthouse suite for his personal use. Beautiful."

They reached a small lift and as Rupert opened the door Fallon said, "Is this the only way?"

"There's the back stairs."

"Then the back stairs it is."

Rupert's ready smile slipped a little. "Now don't start to play games, ducky. It'll only get Mr. Meehan annoyed, which means I'll end up having one hell of a night and to be perfectly frank, I'm not in the mood."

"I'd have thought you'd have enjoyed every golden moment," Fallon said and kicked him very hard on the right shin.

Rupert cried out and went down on one knee and Fallon took the Ceska out of his right-hand pocket. He had removed the silencer, but it was still a deadly-looking item in every way. Rupert went white, but he was game to the last.

"He'll crucify you for this. Nobody mixes it with Jack Meehan and passes the post first."

Fallon put the Ceska back in his pocket. "The stairs," he said softly.

"All right." Rupert leaned down to rub his shin. "It's your funeral, ducky."

The stairway started beside the entrance to the Chapel of Rest. They climbed three flights, Rupert leading the way. There was a green baize door at the top, and he paused a few steps below. "That leads directly into the kitchen."

Fallon nodded. "You'd better go back to minding the shop then, hadn't you?"

Rupert needed no second bidding and went back down the stairs quickly. Fallon tried the door which opened to his touch. As Rupert had said, a kitchen was on the other side. The far door stood ajar and he could hear voices.

He crossed to it on tiptoe and looked into a superbly furnished lounge with broad dormer windows at either end. Meehan was sitting in a leather club chair, a book in one hand, a glass of whisky in the other. Billy, holding the whippet, stood in front of an Adam fireplace in which a log fire was burning brightly. Donner and Bonati waited on either side of the lift.

"What's keeping him, for Christ's sake?" Billy demanded.

The whippet jumped from his arms and darted across to the kitchen door. It stood there, barking, and Fallon moved into the lounge and crouched down to fondle its ears, his right hand still in his coat pocket.

460

Meehan dropped the book on the table and slapped a hand against his thigh. "Didn't I tell you he was a hard-nosed bastard?" he said to Billy.

The telephone rang. He picked it up, listened for a moment and smiled. "It's all right, sweetheart, you get back to work. I can handle it." He replaced the receiver. "That was Rupert. He worries about me."

"That's nice," Fallon said.

He leaned against the wall beside the kitchen door, hands in pockets. Donner and Bonati moved in quietly and stood behind the big leather couch facing him. Meehan sipped a little of his whisky and held up the book. It was *The City of God* by St. Augustine.

"Read this one, have you, Fallon?"

"A long time ago." Fallon reached for a cigarette with his left hand.

"It's good stuff," Meehan said. "He knew what he was talking about. God and the Devil, good and evil. They all exist. And sex." He emptied his glass and belched. "He really puts the record straight there. I mean, women just pump a man dry, like I keep trying to tell my little brother here, only he won't listen. Anything in a skirt, he goes for. You ever see a dog after a bitch in heat with it hanging half out? Well, that's our Billy twenty-four hours a day."

He poured himself another whisky, and Fallon waited. They all waited. Meehan stared into space. "No, these dirty little tarts are no good to anybody and the boys are no better. I mean, what's happened to all the nice clean-cut lads of sixteen or seventeen you used to see around? These days, most of them look like birds from the rear."

Fallon said nothing. There was a further silence and Meehan reached for the whisky bottle again. "Albert!" he called. "Why don't you join us?"

The bedroom door opened, there was a pause and a man entered the room who was so large that he had to duck his head to come through the door. He was a walking anachronism.

Neanderthal man in a baggy grey suit and he must have weighed at least twenty stone. His head was completely bald and his arms were so long that his hands almost reached his knees.

He shambled into the room, his little pig eyes fixed on Fallon. Billy moved out of the way nervously and Albert sank into a chair on the other side of Meehan, next to the fire.

Meehan said, "All right, Fallon. You cocked it up."

"You wanted Krasko dead. He's on a slab in the mortuary right now," Fallon said.

"And the priest who saw you in action? This Father da Costa?"

"No problem."

"He can identify you, can't he? Varley says he was close enough to count the wrinkles on your face."

"True enough," Fallon said. "But it doesn't matter. I've shut his mouth."

"You mean you've knocked him off?" Billy demanded.

"No need." Fallon turned to Meehan. "Are you a Catholic?"

Meehan nodded, frowning. "What's that got to do with it?"

"When did you last go to confession?"

"How in the hell do I know? It's so long ago I forgot."

"I went today," Fallon said. "That's where I've been. I waited my turn at da Costa's one o'clock confession. When I went in, I told him I'd shot Krasko."

Billy Meehan said quickly, "But that's crazy. He'd seen you do it himself, hadn't he?"

"But he didn't know it was me in that confessional box—not until he looked through the grille and recognized me—and that was after I'd confessed."

"So what, for Christ's sake?" Billy demanded.

But his brother was already waving him down, his face serious. "I get it," he said. "Of course. Anything said to a priest at confession's got to be kept a secret. I mean, they guarantee that, don't they?"

"Exactly," Fallon said.

"It's the biggest load of cobblers I've ever heard," Billy said.

"He's alive, isn't he? And he knows. What guarantees do you have that he won't suddenly decide to shoot his mouth off?"

"Let's just say it isn't likely," Fallon said. "And even if he did, it wouldn't matter. I'm being shipped out from Hull on Sunday night—or have you forgotten?"

Meehan said, "I don't know. Maybe Billy has a point."

"Billy couldn't find his way to the men's room unless you took him by the hand," Fallon told him flatly.

There was a dead silence. Meehan gazed at him impassively and Albert picked a steel and brass poker out of the fireplace and bent it into a horseshoe shape between his great hands, his eyes never leaving Fallon's face.

Meehan chuckled unexpectedly. "That's good—that's very good. I like that."

He got up, walked to a desk in the corner, unlocked it and took out a large envelope. He returned to his chair and dropped the envelope on the coffee table.

"There's fifteen hundred quid in there," he said. "You get another two grand on board ship Sunday night plus a passport. That clears the account."

"That's very civil of you," Fallon said.

"Only one thing," Meehan told him. "The priest goes."

Fallon shook his head. "Not a chance."

"What's wrong with you, then?" Meehan jeered. "Worried, are you? Afraid the Almighty might strike you down? They told me you were big stuff over there, Fallon, running round Belfast, shooting soldiers and blowing up kids. But a priest is different, is that it?"

Fallon said, in what was little more than a whisper, "Nothing happens to the priest. That's the way I want it. That's the way it's going to be."

"The way *you* want it?" Meehan said and the anger was beginning to break through now.

Albert tossed the poker into the fireplace and stood up. He spoke in a rough, hoarse voice. "Which arm shall I break first, Mr. Meehan? His left or his right?"

Fallon pulled out the Ceska and fired instantly. The bullet splintered Albert's right kneecap and he went back over the chair. He lay there cursing, clutching his knee with both hands, blood pumping between his fingers.

For a moment nobody moved, and then Meehan laughed out loud. "Didn't I tell you he was beautiful?" he said to Billy.

Fallon picked up the envelope and stowed it away in his raincoat. He backed into the kitchen without a word, kicked the door shut as Meehan called out to him, and started down the stairs.

In the lounge, Meehan grabbed his coat and made for the lift. "Come on, Billy!"

As he got the door open, Donner called, "What about Albert?"

"Call that Pakistani doctor. The one who was struck off. He'll fix him up."

As the lift dropped to the ground floor Billy said, "Look, what are we up to?"

"Just follow me and do as you're bleeding well told," Meehan said.

He ran along the corridor, through the hall and out of the front door. Fallon had reached the other side of the road and was taking one of the paths that led across the green center of the square.

Meehan called to him and ran across the road, ignoring the traffic. The Irishman glanced over his shoulder but kept on walking. He had reached the fountain before Meehan and Billy caught up with him.

He turned to face them, his right hand in his pocket and Meehan put up a hand defensively. "I just want to talk."

He dropped on to a bench seat, slightly breathless, and took out a handkerchief to wipe his face. Billy arrived a moment later, just as the rain increased suddenly from a steady drizzle into a solid downpour.

He said, "This is crazy. My bloody suit's going to be ruined."

His brother ignored him and grinned up at Fallon disarmingly. "You're hell on wheels, aren't you, Fallon? There isn't a tearaway in town who wouldn't run from Fat Albert, but you." He laughed uproariously. "You put him on sticks for six months."

"He shouldn't have joined," Fallon said.

"Too bloody true, but to hell with Albert. You were right, Fallon, about the priest, I mean."

Fallon showed no emotion at all, simply stood there watching him.

Meehan laughed. "Scout's honor. I won't lay a glove on him."

"I see," Fallon said. "A change of heart?"

"Exactly, but it still leaves us with a problem. What to do with you till that boat leaves Sunday. I think maybe you should go back to the farm."

"No chance," Fallon said.

"Somehow I thought you might say that," Meehan smiled good-humoredly. "Still, we've got to find you something." He turned to Billy. "What about Jenny? Jenny Fox. Couldn't she put him up?"

"I suppose so," Billy said sullenly.

"A nice kid," Meehan told Fallon. "She's worked for me in the past. I helped her out when she was having a kid. She owes me a favor."

"She's a whore," Billy said.

"So what?" Meehan shrugged. "A nice, safe house and not too far away. Billy can run you up there."

He smiled genially—even the eyes smiled—but Fallon wasn't taken in for a moment. On the other hand, the sober truth was that he did need somewhere to stay.

"All right," he said.

Meehan put his arm around Fallon's shoulders. "You couldn't do better. She cooks like a dream, that girl, and when it comes to dropping her pants, she's a little firecracker, I can tell you."

They went back across the square and followed the mews round to the car park at the rear. The whippet was crouched at the entrance, shivering in the rain. When Billy appeared, it ran to heel and followed him into the garage. When he drove out in a scarlet Scimitar, it was sitting in the rear.

Fallon slipped into the passenger seat and Meehan closed the door. "I'd stick pretty close to home if I were you. No sense in running any needless risks at this stage, is there?"

Fallon didn't say a word, and Billy drove away. The door to the reception room opened and Donner came out. "I've run for that quack, Mr. Meehan. What happened to Fallon?"

"Billy's taking him up to Jenny Fox's place," Meehan said. "I want you to go over to the car wash and get hold of Varley. I want him outside Jenny's place within half an hour. If Fallon leaves, he follows and phones in whenever he can."

"I don't follow, Mr. Meehan," Donner was obviously mystified.

"Just till we sort things out, Frank," Meehan told him. "Then we drop both of them. Him *and* the priest."

Donner grinned, as a great light dawned. "That's more like it."

"I thought you'd approve." Meehan smiled, opened the door and went inside.

Jenny Fox was a small, rather hippy girl of nineteen with good breasts, high cheekbones and almond-shaped eyes. Her straight black hair hung shoulder-length in a dark curtain, and the only flaw in the general picture was the fact that she had too much make-up on.

She came downstairs wearing a simple white blouse, black pleated miniskirt and high-heeled shoes. She walked with a general and total movement of the whole body that most men found more than a little disturbing.

Billy Meehan waited for her at the bottom of the stairs, and when she was close enough, he slipped a hand up her skirt. She stiffened slightly, and he shook his head, a sly, nasty smile on his face.

"Tights again, Jenny. I told you I wanted you to wear stockings."

"I'm sorry, Billy." There was fear in her eyes. "I didn't know you'd be coming today."

"You'd better watch it, hadn't you, or you'll be getting one of my specials." She shivered slightly and he withdrew his hand. "What about Fallon? Did he say anything?"

"Asked me if I had a razor he could borrow. Who is he?"

"None of your business. He shouldn't go out, but if he does, give Jack a ring straight away. And try to find out where he's going."

"All right, Billy." She opened the front door for him.

He moved in close behind her, his arms about her waist. She could feel his hardness pressed against her buttocks and the hatred, the loathing rose like bile in her throat, threatening to choke her. He said softly, "Another thing. Get him into bed. I want to see what makes him tick."

"And what if he won't play?" she said.

"Stocking tops and suspenders. That's what blokes of his age go for. You'll manage." He slapped her bottom and went out. She closed the door, leaning against it for a moment, struggling for breath. Strange how he always left her with that feeling of suffocation.

She went upstairs, moved along the corridor and knocked softly on Fallon's door. When she went in, he was standing in front of the washbasin in the corner by the window, drying his hands.

"I'll see if I can find you that razor now," she said.

He hung the towel neatly over the nail and shook his head. "It'll do later. I'm going out for a while."

She was gripped by a sudden feeling of panic. "Is that wise?" she said. "I mean, where are you going?"

Fallon smiled as he pulled on his trenchcoat. He ran a finger down her nose in a strangely intimate gesture that brought a lump to her throat.

"Girl dear, do what you have to, which I presume means ringing Jack Meehan to say I'm taking a walk, but I'm damned if I'll say where to."

"Will you be in for supper?"

"I wouldn't miss it for all the tea in China." He smiled and was gone.

It was an old-fashioned phrase. One her grandmother had used frequently. She hadn't heard it in years. Strange how it made her want to cry.

When Miller went into the Forensic Department at police headquarters, he found Fitzgerald in the side laboratory with Johnson, the ballistics specialist. Fitzgerald looked excited and Johnson seemed reasonably complacent.

Miller said, "I hear you've got something for me."

Johnson was a slow, cautious Scot. "That just could be, Superintendent." He picked up a reasonably misshapen piece of lead with a pair of tweezers. "This is what did all the damage. They found it in the gravel about three yards from the body."

"Half an hour after you left, sir," Fitzgerald put in.

"Any hope of making a weapon identification?" Miller demanded.

"Oh, I've pretty well decided that now." There was a copy of *Small Arms of the World* beside Johnson. He flipped through it quickly, found the page he was searching for and pushed it across to Miller. "There you are."

There was a photo of the Ceska in the top right-hand corner. "I've never even heard of the damn thing," Miller said. "How can you be sure?"

"Well, I've some more tests to run, but it's pretty definite. You see there are four factors which are constant in the same make of weapon. Groove and land marks on the bullet, their number and width, their direction, which means are they twisting to the right or left, and the rate of that twist. Once I have those facts, I simply turn to a little item entitled *Atlas of Arms*, and thanks to the two German gentlemen who so painstakingly put the whole thing together, it's possible to trace the weapon which fits without too much difficulty."

Miller turned to Fitzgerald. "Get this information to CRO at Scotland Yard straightaway. This Ceska's an out-of-the-way gun. If they feed that into the computer, it might throw out a name. Somebody who's used one before. You never know. I'll see you back in my office."

Fitzgerald went out quickly and Miller turned to Johnson. "Anything else, let me know at once." He went back to his office where he found a file on his desk containing a résumé of Father da Costa's career. Considering the limited amount of time Fitzgerald had had, it was really very comprehensive.

He came in as Miller finished reading the file and closed it. "I told you he was quite a man, sir."

"You don't know the half of it," Miller said and proceeded to tell him what had happened at the presbytery.

Fitzgerald was dumbfounded. "But it doesn't make any kind of sense."

"You don't think he's been got at?"

"By Meehan?" Fitzgerald laughed out loud. "Father da Costa isn't the kind of man who can be got at by anybody. He's the sort who's always spoken up honestly. Said exactly how he felt, even when the person who was hurt most was himself. Look at his record. He's a brilliant scholar. Two doctorates, one in languages, the other in philosophy, and where's it got him? A dying parish in the heart of a rather unpleasant industrial city. A church that's literally falling down."

"All right, I'm convinced," Miller said. "So he speaks up loud and clear when everyone else has the good sense to keep their mouths shut." He opened the file again. "And he's certainly no physical coward. During the war he dropped into Yugoslavia by parachute three times and twice into Albania. DSO in 1944. Wounded twice." He shrugged impatiently. "There's got to be an explanation. There must be. It doesn't make any kind of sense that he should refuse to come in like this."

"But did he actually refuse?"

469

Miller frowned, trying to remember exactly what the priest had said. "No, come to think of it, he didn't. He said there was no point to coming in, as he wouldn't be able to help."

"That's a strange way of putting it," Fitzgerald said.

"You're telling me. There was an even choicer item. When I told him I could always get a warrant, he said that no power on earth could make him speak on this matter if he didn't want to."

Fitzgerald had turned quite pale. He stood up and leaned across the desk. "He said that? You're sure?"

"He certainly did." Miller frowned. "Does it mean something?"

Fitzgerald turned away and moved across the room to the window. "I can only think of one circumstance in which a priest would speak in such a way."

"And what would that be?"

"If the information he had at his disposal had been obtained as part of confession."

Miller stared at him. "But that isn't possible. I mean, he actually saw this character up there at the cemetery. It wouldn't apply."

"It could," Fitzgerald said, "if the man simply went into the box and confessed. Da Costa wouldn't see his face, remember—not then."

"And you're trying to tell me that once the bloke has spilled his guts, da Costa would be hooked?"

"Certainly he would."

"But that's crazy."

"Not to a Catholic, it isn't. That's the whole point of confession. That what passed between the priest and individual involved, no matter how vile, must be utterly confidential." He shrugged. "Just as effective as a bullet, sir." Fitzgerald hesitated. "When we were at the cemetery, didn't he tell you he was in a hurry to leave because he had to hear confession at one o'clock?"

Miller was out of his chair and already reaching for his raincoat. "You can come with me," he said. "He might listen to you."

"What about the autopsy?" Fitzgerald reminded him. "I thought you wanted to attend personally."

Miller glanced at his watch. "There's an hour yet. Plenty of time."

The lifts were all busy and he went down the stairs two at a time, heart pounding with excitement. Fitzgerald had to be right—it was the only explanation that fitted. But how to handle this situation? That was something else again.

When Fallon turned down the narrow street beside Holy Name, Varley was no more than thirty yards in the rear. Fallon had been aware of his presence within two minutes of leaving Jenny's place—not that it mattered. He entered the church and Varley made for the phone-box on the corner of the street and was speaking to Meehan within a few moments.

"Mr. Meehan? It's me. He's gone into a church in Rockingham Street. The Church of the Holy Name."

"I'll be there in five minutes," Meehan said and slammed down the receiver.

He arrived in the scarlet Scimitar, with Billy at the wheel, to find Varley standing on the street corner, miserable in the rain. He came to meet them as they got out.

"He's still in there, Mr. Meehan. I haven't been in myself."

"Good lad," Meehan said and glanced up at the church. "Bloody place looks as if it might fall down at any moment."

"They serve good soup," Varley said. "To dossers. They use the crypt as a day refuge. I've been in. The priest, he's Father da Costa, and his niece, run it between them. She's a blind girl. A real smasher. Plays the organ here."

Meehan nodded. "All right, you wait in a doorway. When he comes out, follow him again. Come on, Billy."

He moved into the porch and opened the door gently. They passed inside and he closed it again quickly.

471

The girl was playing the organ, he could see the back of her head beyond the green baize curtain. The priest knelt at the altar rail in prayer. Fallon sat at one end of a pew halfway along the aisle.

There was a small chapel to St. Martin de Porres on the right. Not a single candle flickered in front of his image, leaving the chapel in semi-darkness. Meehan pulled Billy after him into the concealing shadows and sat down in the corner.

"What in the hell are we supposed to be doing?" Billy whispered.

"Just shut up and listen."

At that moment, Father da Costa stood up and crossed himself. As he turned he saw Fallon.

"There's nothing for you here, you know that," he said sternly.

Anna stopped playing. She swung her legs over the seat as Fallon advanced along the aisle and Billy whistled softly. "Christ, did you see those legs?"

"Shut up!" Jack hissed.

"I told you I'd see to things, and I have done," Fallon said as he reached the altar rail. "I just wanted you to know that."

"What am I supposed to do, thank you?" Father da Costa said.

The street door banged open, candles flickered in the wind as it closed again and to Jack Meehan's utter astonishment, Miller and Fitzgerald walked up the aisle towards the altar.

"Ah, there you are, Father," Miller called. "I'd like a word with you."

"My God," Billy Meehan whispered in panic. "We've got to get out of here."

"Like hell we do," Meehan said and his hand gripped Billy's right knee like a vise. "Just sit still and listen. This could be very interesting."

7

Prelude and Fugue

Fallon recognized Miller for what he was instantly and waited, shoulders hunched, hands in the pockets of his trenchcoat, feet apart, ready to make whatever move was necessary. There was an elemental force to the man that was almost tangible. Father da Costa could feel it in the very air and the thought of what might happen here filled him with horror.

He moved forwards quickly to place himself between Fallon and the two policemen as they approached. Anna paused uncertainly a yard or two on the other side of the altar rail.

Miller stopped, hat in hand, Fitzgerald a pace or two behind him. There was a slight awkward silence, and then da Costa said, "I think you've met my niece, Superintendent. He has Inspector Fitzgerald with him, my dear."

"Miss da Costa," Miller said formally, and turned to Fallon.

Father da Costa said, "And this is Mr. Fallon."

"Superintendent," Fallon said easily.

He waited, a slight, fixed smile on his mouth, and Miller, looking into that white, intense face, those dark eyes, was aware of a strange, irrational coldness as if somewhere, someone had

walked over his grave, which didn't make any kind of sense—
and then a sudden, wild thought struck him and he took an
involuntary step backwards. There was a silence. Everyone
waited. Rain drummed against a window.

It was Anna who broke the spell by taking a blind step towards
the altar rail and stumbling. Fallon jumped to catch her.

"Are you all right, Miss da Costa?" he said easily.

"Thank you, Mr. Fallon. How stupid of me." Her slight
laugh sounded very convincing as she looked in Miller's general
direction. "I've been having trouble with the organ. I'm afraid
that, like the church, it's past its best. Mr. Fallon has kindly
agreed to give us the benefit of his expert advice."

"Is that so?" Miller said.

She turned to Father da Costa. "Do you mind if we start,
Uncle? I know Mr. Fallon's time is limited."

"We'll go into the sacristy, if that's all right with you, Superintendent," Father da Costa said. "Or up to the house if you
prefer."

"Actually, I'd rather like to hang on here for a few minutes,"
Miller told him. "I'm a pianist myself, but I've always been
rather partial to a bit of organ music. If Mr. Fallon has no
objection."

Fallon gave him an easy smile. "Sure and there's nothing like
an audience, Superintendent, for bringing out the best in all of
us," and he took Anna by the arm and led her up through the
choir stalls.

From the darkness at the rear of the little chapel to St. Martin
de Porres, Meehan watched, fascinated. Billy whispered, "I said
he was a nutter, didn't I? So how in the hell is he going to talk
his way out of this one?"

"With his fingers, Billy, with his fingers," Meehan said. "I'd
put a grand on it." There was sincere admiration in his voice
when he added, "You know something? I'm enjoying every
bleeding minute of this. It's always nice to see a real pro in
action." He sighed. "There aren't many of us left."

* * *

Fallon took off his trenchcoat and draped it over the back of a convenient choir stall. He sat down and adjusted the stool so that he could reach the pedals easily. Anna stood at his right hand.

"Have you tried leaving the trumpet in, as I suggested?" he asked.

She nodded. "It made quite a difference."

"Good. I'll play something pretty solid and we'll see what else we can find wrong. What about the Bach Prelude and Fugue in D Major?"

"I only have it in Braille."

"That's all right. I know it by heart." He turned and looked down at Father da Costa and the two policemen on the other side of the altar rail. "If you're interested, this is reputed to have been Albert Schweitzer's favorite piece."

No one said a word. They stood there, waiting, and Fallon swung around to face the organ. It had been a long time—a hell of a long time and yet, quite suddenly and in some strange, incomprehensible way, it was only yesterday.

He prepared the swell organ, hands moving expertly—all stops except the vox humana and the celeste and on the Great Organ, diapasons and a four-foot principal.

He looked up at Anna gravely. "As regards the Pedal Organ, I'd be disinclined to use any reed stops on this instrument. Only the sixteen-foot Diapason and the Bourdon and maybe a thirty-two-foot stop to give a good, solid tone. What do you think?"

She could not see the corner of his mouth lifted in a slight, sardonic smile and yet something of that smile was in his voice. She put a hand on his shoulder and said clearly, "An interesting beginning, anyway."

To her horror, he said very softly, "Why did you interfere?"

"Isn't that obvious?" she answered in a low voice. "For Superintendent Miller and his inspector's sake. Now play."

"God forgive you, but you're a terrible liar," Fallon told her, and started.

He opened with a rising scale, not too fast, allowing each

note to be heard, heeling and toeing with his left foot in a clear, bold, loud statement, playing with such astonishing power that Miller's wild surmise died on the instant for it was a masterly performance by any standard.

Father da Costa stood at the altar rail as if turned to stone, caught by the brilliance of Fallon's playing as he answered the opening statement with the chords of both hands on the sparkling Great Organ. He repeated, feet, then hands again, manual answering pedals until his left toe sounded the long four bar bottom A and his hands traced the brilliant passages announced by the pedals.

Miller tapped Father da Costa on the shoulder and whispered in his ear, "Brilliant, but I'm running out of time, Father. Can we have our chat now?"

Father da Costa nodded reluctantly and led the way across to the sacristy. Fitzgerald was the last in and the door banged behind him in a sudden gust of wind.

Fallon stopped playing. "Have they gone?" he asked softly.

Anna da Costa stared blindly down at him, a kind of awe on her face, and reached out to touch his cheek. "Who are you?" she whispered. "What are you?"

"A hell of a question to ask any man," he said and, turning back to the organ, he moved into the opening passage again.

The music could be heard in the sacristy, muted yet throbbing through the old walls with a strange power. Father da Costa sat on the edge of the table.

"Cigarette, sir?" Fitzgerald produced an old, silver case. Father da Costa took one, and the light that followed.

Miller observed him closely—the massive shoulders, that weathered, used-up face, the tangled grey beard—and suddenly realized with something close to annoyance that he actually liked the man. It was precisely for this reason that he decided to be as formal as possible.

"Well, Superintendent?" Father da Costa said.

"Have you changed your mind, sir, since we last spoke?"

"Not in the slightest."

Miller fought hard to control his anger, and Fitzgerald moved in smoothly. "Have you been coerced in any way since this morning, sir, or threatened?"

"Not at all, Inspector," Father da Costa assured him with complete honesty.

"Does the name Meehan mean anything to you, sir?"

Father da Costa shook his head, frowning slightly, "No, I don't think so. Should it?"

Miller nodded to Fitzgerald, who opened the briefcase he was carrying and produced a photo, which he passed to the priest. "Jack Meehan," he said. "Dandy Jack, to his friends. That one was taken in London on the steps of West End Central police station after he was released for lack of evidence in an East End shooting last year."

Meehan, wearing his usual double-breasted overcoat, smiled out at the world hugely, waving his hat in his right hand, his left arm encircling the shoulders of a well-known model girl.

"The girl is strictly for publicity purposes," Fitzgerald said. "In sexual matters his tastes run elsewhere. What you read on the sheet pinned to the back is all we have on him officially."

Father da Costa read it with interest. Jack Meehan was forty-eight. He had joined the Royal Navy in 1943, at eighteen, serving on minesweepers until 1945, when he had been discharged with ignominy and sentenced to a year's imprisonment for breaking a Petty Officer's jaw in a brawl. In 1948 he had served six months on a minor smuggling charge, and in 1954 a charge of conspiracy to rob the mails had been dropped for lack of evidence. Since then, he had been questioned by the police on over forty occasions in connection with indictable offences.

"You don't seem to be having much success," Father da Costa said, with a slight smile.

"There's nothing funny about Jack Meehan," Miller said. "In twenty-five years in the police force he's the nastiest thing I've ever come across. Remember the Kray brothers and the Richardson torture gang? Meehan's worse than the whole damn

477

lot of them put together. He has an undertaking business here in the city, but behind that façade of respectability he heads an organization that controls drug-pushing, prostitution, gambling and protection in most of the big cities in the north of England."

"And you can't stop him? I find that surprising."

"Rule by terror, Father. The Krays got away with it for years. Meehan makes them look like beginners. He's had men shot on many occasions—usually the kind of shotgun blast in the legs that doesn't kill, simply cripples. He likes them around as an advertisement."

"You know this for a fact?"

"And couldn't prove it. Just as I couldn't prove he was behind the worst case of organized child prostitution we ever had or that he disciplined one man by crucifying him with six-inch nails and another by making him eat his own excreta."

For the briefest of moments, Father da Costa found himself back in the camp in North Korea—the first one where the softening up was mainly physical—lying half-dead in the latrine while a Chinese boot ground his face into a pile of human ordure. The guard had tried to make him eat, too, and he had refused, mainly because he thought he was dying anyway.

He pulled himself back to the present with an effort. "And you think Meehan is behind the killing of Krasko this morning?"

"He has to be," Miller told him. "Krasko was, to put it politely, a business rival in every sense of the word. Meehan tried to take him under his wing, and he refused. In Meehan's terms, he wouldn't see reason."

"And a killer was brought in to execute him publicly?"

"To encourage the others," Miller said. "In a sense, the very fact that Meehan dares to do such a thing is a measure of just how sick he is. He knows that *I* know he's behind the whole thing. But he wants me to know—wants everyone to know. He thinks nothing can touch him."

Father da Costa looked down at the photo, frowning, and Fitzgerald said, "We could get him this time, Father, with your help."

Father da Costa shook his head, his face grave. "I'm sorry, Inspector. I really am."

Miller said in a harsh voice, "Father da Costa, the only inference we can draw from your strange conduct is that you are aware of the identity of the man we are seeking. That you are in fact protecting him. Inspector Fitzgerald here, himself a Catholic, has suggested a possible explanation to me. That your knowledge is somehow bound up with the secrets of the confessional, if that is the term. Is there any truth in that supposition?"

"Believe me, Superintendent, if I could help you I would," Father da Costa told him.

"You still refuse?"

"I'm afraid so."

Miller glanced at his watch. "All right, Father, I have an appointment in twenty minutes and I'd like you to come with me. No threats—no coercion. Just a simple request."

"I see," Father da Costa said. "May I be permitted to ask where we are going?"

"To attend the postmortem of Janos Krasko at the city mortuary."

"I see," Father da Costa said. "Tell me, Superintendent, is this supposed to be a challenge?"

"That's up to you, Father."

Father da Costa stood up, suddenly weary. His will to resist was at a new low. He was sick of the whole wretched business. Strangely enough the only thing of which he was aware with any clarity was the sound of the organ, muted and far away.

"I have evening Mass, Superintendent, and supper at the refuge afterwards. I can't be long."

"An hour at the most, sir, I'll have you brought back by car, but we really will have to leave now."

Father da Costa opened the sacristy door and led the way back into the church. He paused at the altar, "Anna?" he called.

Fallon stopped playing and the girl turned to face him. "I'm just going out, my dear, with Superintendent Miller."

"What about Mass?" she said.

"I won't be long. As for the organ," he added, "perhaps Mr. Fallon would come back after Mass? We could discuss it then."

"Glad to, Father," Fallon called cheerfully.

Father da Costa, Miller and Inspector Fitzgerald walked down the aisle, past the chapel of St. Martin de Porres, where Jack Meehan and his brother still sat in the shadows, and out of the front door.

It banged in the wind. There was silence. Fallon said softly, "Well now, at a rough estimate, I'd say you've just saved my neck. I think he suspected something, the good Superintendent Miller."

"But not now," she said. "Not after such playing. You were brilliant."

He chuckled softly. "That might have been true once, as I'll admit with becoming modesty, but not any more. My hands aren't what they were, for one thing."

"Brilliant," she said. "There's no other word for it."

She was genuinely moved and for the moment it was as if she had forgotten that other darker side. She groped for his hands, a smile on her face.

"As for your hands—what nonsense." She took them in hers, still smiling, and then the smile was wiped clean. "Your fingers?" she whispered, feeling at them. "What happened?"

"Oh, those." He pulled his hands free and examined the ugly, misshapen finger-ends. "Some unfriends of mine pulled out my nails. A small matter on which we didn't quite see eye to eye."

He stood up and pulled on his coat. She sat there, horror on her face and reached out a hand as if to touch him, pawing at space. He helped her to her feet and placed her coat about her shoulders.

"I don't understand," she said.

"And please God, you never should," he told her softly. "Come on now and I'll take you home."

They went down the altar steps and out through the sacristy.

The door closed behind them. There was a moment of silence and then Billy Meehan stood up.

"Thank God for that. Can we kindly get the hell out of here now?"

"You can, not me," Meehan told him. "Find Fallon and stick to him like glue."

"But I thought that was Varley's job?"

"So now I'm putting you on to it. Tell Varley to wait outside."

"And what about you?" Billy said sullenly.

"Oh, I'll wait here for the priest to come back. Time we had a word." He sighed and stretched his arms. "I like it here. Nice and peaceful in the dark with all those candles flickering away there. Gives a fella time to think." Billy hesitated, as if trying to find some suitable reply, and Meehan said irritably, "Go on, piss off out of it, for Christ's sake. I'll see you later."

He leaned back, arms folded, and closed his eyes, and Billy left by the front entrance to do as he was told.

It was raining hard in the cemetery. As they moved along the path to the presbytery, Fallon slipped her arm in his.

"Sometimes I think it's never going to stop," she said. "It's been like this for days."

"I know," he said.

They reached the front door, she opened it and paused in the porch while Fallon stood at the bottom of the steps looking up at her.

"Nothing seems to make sense to me any longer," she said. "I don't understand you or what's happened today or any part of it—not after hearing you play. It doesn't make sense. It doesn't fit."

He smiled up at her gently. "Go in now, girl dear, out of the cold. Stay safe in your own small world."

"Not now," she said. "How can I? You've made me an accessory now, isn't that what they call it? I could have spoken up, but I didn't."

It was the most terrible thing she could have told him. "Then why didn't you?" he asked hoarsely.

"I gave my uncle my word, had you forgotten? And I would not hurt him for worlds."

Fallon moved back into the rain very softly. She called from the porch. "Mr. Fallon, are you there?"

He didn't reply. She stood there for a moment longer, uncertainty on her face, then went in and closed the door. Fallon turned and moved back along the path.

Billy had been watching them from the shelter of a large Victorian mausoleum, or rather, he had been watching Anna. She was different from the girls he was used to. Quiet, ladylike, and yet she had an excellent figure. There was plenty of warmth beneath that cool exterior, he was certain of that, and the fact of her blindness made his stomach churn, exciting some perversity inside him; he got an almost instant erection.

Fallon paused, hands cupped to light a cigarette, and Billy drew back out of sight.

Fallon said, "All right, Billy, I'm ready to go home now. Since you're here, you can drive me back to Jenny's place."

Billy hesitated, then stepped reluctantly into the open. "Think you're bleeding smart, don't you?"

"To be smarter than you doesn't take much, sonny," Fallon told him. "And another thing. If I catch you hanging around here again, I'll be very annoyed."

"Why don't you go stuff yourself," Billy told him furiously.

He turned and walked rapidly towards the gate. Fallon was smiling as he went after him.

The city mortuary was built like a fort and encircled by twenty-foot walls of red brick to keep out prying eyes. When Miller's car reached the main entrance the driver got out and spoke into a voice box on the wall. He climbed back behind the wheel. A moment later the great steel gate slid back automatically and they passed into an inner courtyard.

"Here we are, Father," Miller said. "The most modern mortuary in Europe, or so they say."

He and Fitzgerald got out first, and Father da Costa followed them. The inner building was all concrete and glass. Functional, but rather beautiful in its own way. They went up a concrete ramp to the rear entrance and a technician in white overalls opened the door for them.

"Good morning, Superintendent," he said. "Professor Lawlor said he'd meet you in the dressing-room. He's very anxious to get started."

There was the constant low hum of the air-conditioning plant as they followed him along a maze of narrow corridors. Miller glanced over his shoulder at Father da Costa and said casually, "They boast the purest air in the city up here. If you can breathe it at all, that is."

It was the kind of remark that didn't seem to require an answer, and Father da Costa made no attempt to make one. The technician opened a door, ushered them inside and left.

There were several washbasins, a shower in the corner, white hospital overalls and robes hanging on pegs on one wall. Underneath was a row of white rubber boots in various sizes. Miller and Fitzgerald removed their raincoats and the Superintendent took down a couple of white robes and passed one to Father da Costa.

"Here, put this on. You don't need to bother about boots."

Father da Costa did as he was told, and then the door opened and Professor Lawlor entered. "Come on, Nick," he said. "You're holding me up." And then he saw the priest and his eyes widened in surprise. "Hello, Father."

"I'd like Father da Costa to observe, if you've no objection," Miller said.

Professor Lawlor was wearing white overalls and boots and long pale-green rubber gloves, which he pulled at impatiently. "As long as he doesn't get in the way. But do let's get on with it. I've got a lecture at the medical school at five."

483

He led the way out and they followed along a short corridor and through a rubber swing door into the post mortem room. It was lit by fluorescent lighting so bright that it almost hurt the eyes and there was a row of half-a-dozen stainless-steel operating tables.

Janos Krasko lay on his back on the one nearest the door, head raised on a wooden block. He was quite naked. Two technicians stood ready beside a trolley on which an assortment of surgical instruments was laid out neatly. The greatest surprise for Father daCosta were the closed circuit television cameras, one set close up to the operating table, the other waiting nearby on a movable trolley.

"As you can see, Father, science marches on," Miller said. "These days, in a case like this, everything's videotaped and in color."

"Is that necessary?" Father da Costa asked him.

"It certainly is. Especially when you get the kind of defence council who hasn't much to go on and tries bringing in his own expert witness. In other words, some other eminent pathologist with his own particular theory about what happened."

One of the technicians was fastening a throat mike around Lawlor's throat and Miller nodded. "The medical profession are great on opinions, Father, I've learned that the hard way."

Lawlor smiled frostily. "Don't get bitter in your old age, Nick. Have you witnessed a postmortem before, Father?"

"Not in your terms, Professor."

"I see. Well, if you feel sick, you know where the dressing-room is and please stand well back—all of you." He turned and addressed the camera men and technicians. "Right, gentlemen, let's get started."

It should have been like something out of a nightmare. That it wasn't was probably due to Lawlor as much as anything else. That and the general atmosphere of clinical efficiency.

He was really quite brilliant. More than competent in every department. An artist with a knife who kept up a running commentary in that dry, precise voice of his during the entire proceedings.

"Everything he says is recorded," Miller whispered. "To go with the video."

Father da Costa watched, fascinated, as Lawlor drew a scalpel around the skull. He grasped the hair firmly and pulled the entire face forward, eyeballs and all, like a crumpled rubber mask.

He nodded to the technicians who handed him a small electric saw and switched on. Lawlor began to cut round the top of the skull very carefully.

"They call it a de Soutter," Miller whispered again. "Works on a vibratory principle. A circular saw would cut too quickly."

There was very little smell, everything being drawn up by extractor fans in the ceiling above the table. Lawlor switched off the saw and handed it to the technician. He lifted off the neat skullcap of bone and placed it on the table, then carefully removed the brain and put it in a rather commonplace red, plastic basin which one of the technicians held ready.

The technician carried it across to the sink, and Lawlor weighed it carefully. He said to Miller, "I'll leave my examination of this until I've finished going through the motions on the rest of him. All right?"

"Fine," Miller said.

Lawlor returned to the corpse, picked up a large scalpel and opened the entire body from throat to belly. There was virtually no blood, only a deep layer of yellow fat, red meat underneath. He opened the body up like an old overcoat, working fast and efficiently, never stopping for a moment.

Father da Costa said, "Is this necessary? The wound was in the head. We know that."

"The Coroner will demand a report that is complete in every detail," Miller told him. "That's what the law says he's entitled to and that's what he expects. It's not as cruel as you think. We had a case the other year. An old man found dead at his home. Apparent heart failure. When Lawlor opened him up he was able to confirm that, and if he'd stopped at the heart that would have been the end of the matter."

"There was more?"

"Fractured vertebrae somewhere in the neck area. I forget the details, but it meant that the old boy had been roughly handled by someone, which led us to a character who'd been making a nuisance of himself preying on old people. The sort who knocks on the door, insists he was told to clean the drains and demands ten quid."

"What happened to him?"

"The court accepted a plea of manslaughter. Gave him five years so he's due out soon. A crazy world, Father."

"And what would you have done with him?"

"I'd have hung him," Miller said simply. "You see, for me, it's a state of war now. A question of survival. Liberal principles are all very fine as long as they leave you with something to have principles about."

Which made sense in its own way and it was hard to argue. Father da Costa moved to one side as the technicians carried the various organs across to the sink in more plastic basins. Each item was weighed, then passed to Lawlor who sliced it quickly into sections on a wooden block with a large knife. Heart, lungs, liver, kidneys, intestines—they all received the same treatment with astonishing speed and the camera on the trolley recorded everything at his side.

Finally he was finished and put down his knife. "That's it," he said to Miller. "Nothing worth mentioning. I'll go to town on the brain after I've had a cigarette." He smiled at da Costa,

"Well, what did you think?"

"An extraordinary experience," Father da Costa said. "Disquieting more than anything else."

"To find that man is just so much raw meat?" Professor Lawlor said.

"Is that what you think?"

"See for yourself."

Lawlor crossed to the operating table, and Father da Costa went with him. The body was open to the view and quite empty. Gutted. Nothing but space from inside the rib cage and down into the penis.

"Remember that poem of Eliot's, 'The Hollow Men'? Well, this is what he was getting at or so it's always seemed to me."

"And you think that's all there is?"

"Don't you?" Lawlor demanded.

One of the technicians replaced the skullcap of bone and pulled the scalp back into place. Amazing how easily the face settled into position again. Quite remarkable.

Father da Costa said, "A superb piece of engineering, the human body. Infinitely functional. There seems to be no task that a man cannot cope with if he so desires. Wouldn't you agree, Professor?"

"I suppose so."

"Sometimes I find the mystery of it quite terrifying. I mean, is this all that's left in the end of an Einstein, let's say, or a Picasso? A gutted body, a few scraps of raw meat swilling about in the bottom of a plastic bucket?"

"Ah, no you don't." Lawlor grinned tiredly. "No metaphysics, if you please, Father, I've got other things to do." He turned to Miller. "Have you seen enough?"

"I think so," Miller said.

"Good, then get this Devil's Advocate out of here and leave me in peace to finish. It will be the morning before you get the full report now." He grinned at Father da Costa again. "I won't shake hands for obvious reasons, but any time you're passing just drop in. There's always someone here."

He laughed at his own joke, was still laughing when they went back to the dressing-room. One of the technicians went with them to make sure that the robes they had worn went straight into the dirty-laundry basket. So there was no opportunity to talk.

Miller led the way back outside, feeling tired and depressed.

He had lost, he knew that already. The trouble was he didn't really know what to do next, except to take the kind of official action he'd been hoping to avoid.

It was still raining when they went out into the courtyard. When they reached the car, Fitzgerald opened the door and Father da Costa climbed in. Miller followed him. Fitzgerald sat in the front with the driver.

As they moved out into the city traffic, Miller said, "I wanted you to see the reality of it, and it hasn't made the slightest difference, has it?"

Father da Costa said, "When I was twenty years of age, I dropped into the Cretan mountains by parachute, dressed as a peasant. All very romantic. Action by night—that sort of thing. When I arrived at the local village inn I was arrested at gunpoint by a German undercover agent. A member of the Feldgendarmerie."

Miller was interested in spite of himself. "You'd been betrayed?"

"Something like that. He wasn't a bad sort. Told me he was sorry, but that he'd have to hold me till the Gestapo got there. We had a drink together. I managed to hit him on the head with a wine bottle."

Father da Costa stared back into the past and Miller said gently, "What happened?"

"He shot me in the left lung and I choked him to death with my bare hands." Father da Costa held them up. "I've prayed for him every day of my life since."

They turned into the street at the side of the church and Miller said wearily, "All right, I get the picture." The car pulled in at the curb and there was a new formality in his voice when he said, "In legal terms, your attitude in this matter makes you an accessory after the fact. You understand that?"

"Perfectly," da Costa told him.

"All right," Miller said. "This is what I intend to do. I shall approach your superior in a final effort to make you see sense."

"Monsignor O'Halloran is the man you want. I tried to see

him myself earlier, but he's out of town. He'll be back in the morning—but it won't do you any good."

"Then I'll apply to the Director of Public Prosecutions for a warrant for your arrest."

Father da Costa nodded soberly. "You must do what you think is right. I see that, Superintendent." He opened the door and got out. "I'll pray for you."

"Pray for me!" Miller ground his teeth together as the car moved away. "Have you ever heard the like?"

"I know, sir," Fitzgerald said. "He's quite a man, isn't he?"

It was cold in the church and damp as Father da Costa opened the door and moved inside. Not long till Mass. He felt tired—wretchedly tired. It had been an awful day—the worst he could remember in a great many years—since the Chinese prison camp at Chong Sam. If only Fallon and Miller—all of them—would simply fade away, cease to exist.

He dipped his fingers in the Holy Water and on his right a match flared in the darkness of the little side chapel of St. Martin de Porres as someone lit a candle, illuminating a familiar face.

There was a slight pause and then the Devil moved out of the darkness and Father da Costa girded up his loins to meet him.

8

The Devil and All His Works

"What do you want here, Mr. Meehan?" Father da Costa said.

"You know who I am?"

"Oh, yes," Father da Costa told him. "I was taught to recognize the Devil from a very early age."

Meehan stared at him for a moment in genuine amazement. Then he laughed harshly, his head thrown back, and the sound echoed up into the rafters.

"That's good. I like that." Father da Costa said nothing and Meehan shrugged and turned to look down towards the altar. "I used to come here when I was a kid. I was an acolyte." He turned and there was a challenge in his voice. "You don't believe me?"

"Shouldn't I?"

Meehan nodded toward the altar. "I've stood up there many a time when it was my turn to serve at Mass. Scarlet cassock, white cotta. My old lady used to launder them every week. She loved seeing me up there. Father O'Malley was the priest in those days."

"I've heard of him," Father da Costa said.

"Tough as old boots," Meehan was warming to his theme

now—enjoying himself. "I remember one Saturday evening, a couple of drunken Micks came in just before Mass and started turning things upside down. Duffed them up proper, he did. Straight out on their ear. Said they'd desecrated God's house and all that stuff." He shook his head. "A real old sod, he was. He once caught me with a packet of fags I'd nicked from a shop round the corner. Didn't call the law. Just took a stick to me in the sacristy." He chuckled. "Kept me honest for a fortnight that, Father. Straight up."

Father da Costa said quietly, "What do you want here, Mr. Meehan?"

Meehan made a sweeping gesture with one arm that took in the whole church. "Not what it was, I can tell you. Used to be beautiful, a real picture, but now . . ." He shrugged. "Ready to fall down any time. This restoration fund of yours? I hear you've not been getting very far."

Father da Costa saw it all. "And you'd like to help, is that it?"

"That's it, Father, that's it exactly."

The door opened behind them, they both turned and saw an old lady with a shopping bag enter. As she genuflected, Father da Costa said, "We can't talk here. Come with me."

They went up in the hoist to the top of the tower. It was still raining as he led the way out along the catwalk, but the mist had lifted and the view of the city was remarkable. In the far distance, perhaps four or five miles away, it was even possible to see the edge of the moors smudging the grey sky.

Meehan was genuinely delighted. "Heh, I was up here once when I was a kid. Inside the belfry. It was different then." He leaned over the rail and pointed to where the bulldozers were excavating in the brickfield. "We used to live there. Thirteen, Khyber Street."

He turned to Father da Costa who made no reply. Meehan said softly, "This arrangement between you and Fallon? You going to stick to it?"

Father da Costa said, "What arrangement would that be?"

"Come off it," Meehan replied impatiently. "This confession thing. I know all about it. He told me."

"Then, as a Catholic yourself, you must know that there is nothing I can say. The secrets of the confessional are absolute."

Meehan laughed harshly. "I know. He's got brains, that Fallon. He shut you up good, didn't he?"

A small, hot spark of anger moved in Father da Costa, and he breathed deeply to control it. "If you say so."

Meehan chuckled. "Never mind, Father, I always pay my debts. How much?" His gesture took in the church, the scaffolding, everything. "To put all this right?"

"Fifteen thousand pounds," Father da Costa told him. "For essential preliminary work. More would be needed later."

"Easy," Meehan said. "With my help you could pick that up inside two or three months."

"Might I ask how?"

Meehan lit a cigarette. "For a start, there's the clubs. Dozens of them all over the north. They'll all put the old collecting-box round if I give the word."

"And you actually imagine that I could take it?"

Meehan looked genuinely bewildered. "It's only money, isn't it? Pieces of paper. A medium of exchange, that's what the bright boys call it. Isn't that what you need?"

"In case you've forgotten, Mr. Meehan, Christ drove the money-lenders *out* of the temple. He didn't ask them for a contribution to the cause."

Meehan frowned. "I don't get it."

"Then let me put it this way. My religion teaches me that reconciliation with God is always possible. That no human being, however degraded or evil, is beyond God's mercy. I had always believed that until now."

Meehan's face was pale with fury. He grabbed da Costa's arm and pushed him towards the rail, pointing down at the brickfield.

"Thirteen, Khyber Street. A back-to-back rabbit hutch. One room downstairs, two up. One stinking lavatory to every four houses. My old man cleared off when I was a kid—he had sense. My old lady—she kept us going by cleaning when she could get it. When she couldn't, there were always ten-bob quickies behind the boozer on a Saturday night. A bloody whore, that's all she was."

"Who found time to clean and iron your cassock and cotta each week?" Father da Costa said. "Who fed you and washed you and sent you to this church?"

"To hell with that," Meehan said wildly. "All she ever got—all anybody from Khyber Street ever got—was screwed into the ground, but not me. Not Jack Meehan. I'm up here now. I'm on top of the world, where nobody can touch me."

Father da Costa felt no pity, only a terrible disgust. He said calmly, "I believe you to be the most evil and perverted creature it has ever been my misfortune to meet. If I could, I would hand you over to the proper authorities gladly. Tell them everything, but for reasons well known to you, this is impossible."

Meehan seemed to be more in control of himself again. He said, with a sneer, "That's good, that is. Me, you wouldn't touch with a ten-foot pole, but Fallon, he's different, isn't he? I mean, he only murders women and children."

For a moment, Father da Costa had to fight for breath. When he spoke, it was with difficulty, "What are you talking about?"

"Don't say he hasn't told you," Meehan jeered. "Nothing about Belfast or Londonderry or that bus full of schoolkids he blew up?" He leaned forward, a strange intent look on his face and then he smiled softly. "You don't like that, do you? Fell for his Irish charm. Did you fancy him, then? I've heard some of you priests . . ."

There was a hand at his throat, a hand of iron, and he was back against the cage of the hoist, fighting for his very life, the priest's eyes sparking fire. Meehan tried to bring up a knee and found only a thigh turned expertly to block it. Father da Costa shook him like a rat, then opened the door and threw him inside.

The cage door slammed as Meehan picked himself up. "I'll have you for this," he said hoarsely. "You're dead meat."

"My God, Mr. Meehan," Father da Costa said softly through the bars of the cage, "is a God of Love. But he is also a God of Wrath. I leave you in his hands."

He pressed the button, and the cage started to descend.

As Meehan emerged from the church porch, a sudden flurry of wind dashed rain in his face. He turned up his collar and paused to light a cigarette. It was beginning to get dark and as he went down the steps he noticed a number of men waiting by a side door, sheltering against the wall from the rain. Human derelicts, most of them, in tattered coats and broken boots.

He moved across the street, and Varley came out of the doorway of the old warehouse on the corner. "I waited, Mr. Meehan, like Billy said."

"What happened to Fallon?"

"Went off in the car with Billy."

Meehan frowned, but for the moment, that could wait and he turned his attention to the queue again. "What are they all waiting for? This bleeding soup kitchen to open?"

"That's right, Mr. Meehan. In the crypt."

Meehan stared across at the queue for a while and then smiled suddenly. He opened his wallet and extracted a bundle of one-pound notes.

"I make it twenty-two in that queue, Charlie. You give them a quid apiece with my compliments and tell them the pub on the corner's just opened."

Varley, mystified, crossed the street to distribute his largesse. Within seconds, the queue was breaking up, several of the men touching their caps to Meehan, who nodded cheerfully as they shuffled past. When Varley came back, there was no one left outside the door.

"He's going to have a lot of bleeding soup on his hands tonight," Meehan said, grinning.

"I don't know about that, Mr. Meehan," Varley pointed out. "They'll only come back when they've spent up."

"And by then they'll have a skinful, won't they, so they might give him a little trouble. In fact, I think we'll make sure they do. Get hold of that bouncer from the Kit Kat Club. The Irishman, O'Hara."

"Big Mick, Mr. Meehan?" Varley stirred uneasily. "I'm not too happy about that. He's a terrible man when he gets going."

Meehan knocked off his cap and grabbed him by the hair. "You tell him to be outside that door with one of his mates at opening time. Nobody goes in for the first hour. Nobody. He waits for at least a dozen drunks to back him, then he goes in and smashes the place up. If he does it right, it's worth twenty-five quid. If the priest breaks an arm, accidental like, it's worth fifty."

Varley scrambled for his cap in the gutter. "Is that all, Mr. Meehan?" he said fearfully.

"It'll do for starters." Meehan was chuckling to himself as he walked away.

Father da Costa could count on only three acolytes for evening Mass. The parish was dying, that was the trouble. As the houses came down, the people moved away to the new estates, leaving only the office blocks. It was a hopeless task, he had known that when they sent him to Holy Name. His superiors had known. A hopeless task to teach him humility, wasn't that what the bishop had said? A little humility for a man who had been arrogant enough to think he could change the world. Remake the Church in his own image.

Two of the boys were West Indians, the other English of Hungarian parents. All a product of the few slum streets still remaining. They stood in the corner waiting for him, whispering together, occasionally laughing, newly washed, hair combed, bright in their scarlet cassocks and white cottas. Had Jack Meehan looked like that once?

The memory was like a sword in the heart. The fact of his own violence, the killing rage. The violence that had been so often his undoing through the years. The men he had killed in the war—that was one thing, but after . . . The Chinese soldier in Korea machine-gunning a column of refugees. He had picked up a rifle and shot the man through the head at two hundred yards. Expertly, skillfully, the old soldier temporarily in control. Had he been wrong? Had it really been wrong when so many lives had been saved? And that Portuguese captain in Mozambique stringing up guerrillas by their ankles. He had beaten the man half to death, the incident that had finally sent him home in disgrace.

"The days when bishops rode into battle with a mace in one hand are over, my friend." The Bishop's voice echoed faintly. "Your task is to save souls."

Violence for violence. That was Meehan's way. Sick and disgusted, Father da Costa took off the violet stole he had worn for confession and put on a green one, crossing it under his girdle to represent Christ's passion and death. As he put on an old rose-colored cope, the outer door opened and Anna came in, her stick in one hand, a raincoat over her.

He moved to take the raincoat, holding her shoulders briefly. "Are you all right?"

She turned at once, concern on her face. "What is it? You're upset. Has anything happened?"

"I had an unpleasant interview with the man Meehan," he replied in a low voice. "He said certain things concerning Fallon. Things which could explain a great deal. I'll tell you later."

She frowned slightly, but he led her to the door and opened it, pushing her through into the church. He waited for a few moments to give her time to reach the organ, then nodded to the boys. They formed into their tiny procession, one of them opening the door, and as the organ started to play, they moved into the church.

It was a place of shadows, candlelight and darkness alternating, cold and damp. There were perhaps fifteen people in the congregation, no more. He had never felt so dispirited, so close to the final edge of things, not since Korea, and then he looked across at the figure of the Virgin. She seemed to float there in the candlelight, so calm, so serene, and the slight half-smile on the parted lips seemed somehow for him alone.

"*Asperges me*," he intoned, and moved down the aisle, one of the West Indian boys carrying the bucket of holy water in front of him, Father da Costa sprinkling the heads of his congregation as he passed, symbolically washing them clean.

"And who will cleanse me?" he asked himself desperately. "Who?"

In the faded rose cope, hands together, he commenced the Mass. "I confess to Almighty God, and to you, my brothers and sisters, that I have sinned through my own fault." Here, he struck his breast once as ritual required. "In my thoughts and in my words, in what I have done, and in what I have failed to do."

The voices of the congregation swelled up in unison behind him. There were tears on his face, the first in many years, and he struck his breast again.

"Lord, have mercy on me," he whispered. "Help me. Show me what to do."

9

The Executioner

The wind howled through the city like a living thing, driving rain before it, clearing the streets, rattling old window frames, tapping at the glass like some invisible presence.

When Billy Meehan went into Jenny Fox's bedroom, she was standing in front of the mirror combing her hair. She was wearing the black pleated miniskirt, dark stockings, patent-leather high-heeled shoes and a white blouse. She looked extremely attractive.

As she turned, Billy closed the door and said softly, "Nice, very nice. He's still in his room, isn't he?"

"He said he was going out again, though."

"We'll have to change his mind, then, won't we?" Billy went and sat on the bed. "Come here."

She fought to control the instant panic that threatened to choke her, the disgust that made her flesh crawl as she moved towards him.

He slipped his hands under her skirt, fondling the warm flesh at the top of the stockings. "That's a good girl. He'll like that. They always do." He stared up at her, that strange, dreamy look in his

498

eyes again. "You muck this up for me, you'll be in trouble. I mean, I'd have to punch you and you wouldn't like that, would you?"

Her heart thudded painfully. "Please, Billy! Please!"

"Then do it right. I want to see what makes this guy tick."

He pushed her away, got up and moved to a small picture on the wall. He removed it carefully. There was a tiny peephole underneath, skillfully placed, and he peered through.

After a few moments, he turned and nodded. "Just taken his shirt off. Now you get in there and remember—I'll be watching."

His mouth was slack, and his hands trembled a little. She turned, choking back her disgust, opened the door and slipped outside.

Fallon was standing at the washbasin, stripped to the waist, lather on his face, when she knocked on the door and came in. He turned to greet her, a bone-handled cut-throat razor in one hand.

She leaned against the door. "Sorry about the razor. It was all I could find."

"That's all right." He smiled. "My father had one of these. Wouldn't use anything else till the day he died."

A line of ugly, puckered scars cut across his abdomen down into the left hip. Her eyes widened. "What happened?"

He glanced down. "Oh, that—a machine-gun burst. One of those times I should have moved faster than I did."

"Were you in the army?"

"In a manner of speaking."

He turned back to the mirror to finish shaving. She moved across and stood beside him. He smiled sideways, crookedly, stretching his mouth for the razor.

"You look nice enough to eat. Going somewhere?"

There was that warmth again, that prickling behind her eyes. She suddenly realized, with a sense of wonder, just how much she had come to like this strange, small man, and in the same moment she remembered Billy watching her every move on the other side of that damned wall.

She smiled archly and ran a finger down his bare arm. "I thought I might stay in tonight. What about you?"

Fallon's eyes flickered toward her once, something close to amusement in them. "Girl dear, you don't know what you'd be getting into. And me twice your age."

"I've got a bottle of Irish whiskey in."

"God save us and isn't that enough to tempt the Devil himself?"

He continued his shaving and she moved across to the bed and sat down. It wasn't going right—it wasn't going right at all and at the thought of Billy's anger, she turned cold inside. She summoned up all her resources and tried again.

"Mind if I have a cigarette?"

There was a packet on the bedside table and a box of matches. She took one, lit it and leaned back on the bed, a pillow behind her shoulders.

"Have you really got to go out?"

She raised one knee so that the skirt slid back provocatively exposing bare flesh at the top of dark stockings, sheer black nylon briefs.

Fallon sighed heavily, put down the razor and picked up a towel. He wiped the foam from his face as he crossed to the bed and stood looking down at her.

"You'll catch cold." He smiled softly and pulled down her skirt. "If you're not careful. And I'm still going out, but I'll have a glass with you before I do, so be off now and open the bottle."

He pulled her up from the bed and pushed her firmly across the room. She turned at the door, fear in her eyes. "Please?" she said fiercely. "Please?"

He frowned slightly and then a brief, sad smile touched his mouth. He kissed her gently on the lips and shook his head. "Not me, girl dear, not me in the whole wide world. You need a man. . . . I'm just a corpse walking."

It was such a terrible remark, so dreadful in its implication, that for the moment it drove every other thought from her mind. She stared up at him, eyes wide, and he opened the door and pushed her outside.

Fear possessed her now, such fear as she had never known. She couldn't face what awaited her in her bedroom. If she could only get downstairs—but it was already too late, for as she tiptoed past, the door opened and Billy pulled her so violently into the bedroom that she stumbled. She lost a shoe and went sprawling across the bed.

She turned fearfully and found him already unbuckling his belt. "You cocked it up, didn't you?" he said softly. "And after all I've done for you."

"Please, Billy. Please don't," she said. "I'll do anything."

"You can say that again. You're going to get one of my specials, just to keep you in line, and maybe next time I tell you to do something, you'll bloody well make sure it gets done." He started to unfasten his trousers. "Go on, turn over." She was almost choking and shook her head dumbly. His face was like a mirror breaking, madness staring at her from those pale eyes, and he struck her heavily across the face.

"You do as you're bloody well told, you bitch."

He grabbed her by the hair, forcing her round until she sprawled across the edge of the bed, face down. His other hand tore at her briefs, pulling them down. And then, as she felt his hardness, as he forced himself between her buttocks like some animal, she screamed at the top of her voice, head arched back in agony.

The door opened so violently that it splintered against the wall and Fallon stood there, one side of his face still lathered, the cut-throat razor open in his right hand.

Billy turned from the girl, mouthing incoherently, clutching at his trousers, and as he stood up Fallon took two quick paces into the room and kicked him in the privates. Billy went down like a stone and lay there twitching, knees drawn up to his chest in fetal position.

The girl adjusted her clothes as best she could and got up, every last shred of decency stripped from her, tears pouring down her face. Fallon wiped lather from his cheek mechanically with the back of his hand; his eyes were very dark.

She could hardly speak for sobbing. "He made me go into your room tonight. He was watching."

She gestured towards the wall and Fallon crossed to the peephole. He turned slowly. "Does this kind of thing happen often?"

"He likes to watch."

"And you? What about you?"

"I'm a whore," she said and suddenly it erupted from her. All the disgust, the self-hate, born of years of degradation. "Have you any idea what that means? He started me early, his brother."

"Jack Meehan?"

"Who else? I was thirteen. Just right for a certain kind of client, and from then on it's been downhill all the way."

"You could leave?"

"Where would I go to?" She had regained some of her composure now. "It takes money. And I have a three-year-old daughter to think of."

"Here—in this place?"

She shook her head. "I board her out with a woman. A nice woman in a decent part of town, but Billy knows where she is."

At that moment he stirred and pushed himself up on one elbow. There were tears in his eyes and his mouth was flecked with foam.

"You've had it," he said faintly. "When my brother hears about this you're a dead man."

He started to zip up his trousers and Fallon crouched down beside him. "My grandfather," he began in a conversational tone, "kept a farm back home in Ireland. Sheep mostly. And every year, he'd geld a few to improve the flavor of the mutton or make the wool grow more—something like that. Do you know what 'geld' means, Billy boy?"

"Like hell I do. You're crackers," Billy said angrily. "Like all the bloody Irish."

"It means he cut off their balls with a pair of sheep shears."

An expression of frozen horror appeared on the boy's face and Fallon said softly, "Touch this girl in any way from now on," he held up the cut-throat razor, "and I will attend to you personally. My word on it."

The boy scrambled away from him and pushed himself up against the wall, clutching at his trousers. "You're mad," he whispered. "Raving mad."

"That's it, Billy," Fallon said. "Capable of anything and don't you forget it."

The boy ducked out through the open door, his feet thundered on the stairs. The front door banged.

Fallon turned, a hand to his cheek. "Could I finish my shaving now, do you suppose?"

She ran forward, gripping his arms fiercely. "Please don't go out. Please don't leave me."

"I must," he said. "He won't be back, not as long as I'm staying here."

"And afterwards?"

"We'll think of something."

She turned away and he grabbed her hand quickly. "I'll be an hour, no more, I promise, and then we can have that glass of whiskey. How's that?"

She turned, peering at him uncertainly. The tears had streaked her make-up, making her somehow seem very young. "You mean it?"

"On the word of an Irish gentleman."

She flung her arms about his neck in delight. "Oh, I'll be good to you. I really will."

He put a finger on her mouth. "There's no need. No need at all." He patted her cheek. "I'll be back, I promise. Only do one thing for me."

"What's that?"

"Wash your face, for God's sake."

He closed the door gently as he went out and she moved across to the washbasin and looked into the mirror. He was right. She looked terrible and yet for the first time in years, the eyes were smiling. Smiling through that streaked whore's mask. She picked up some soap and started to wash her face thoroughly.

Father da Costa couldn't understand it. The refuge had been open for just over an hour without a single customer. In all the months he had been operating from the old crypt he had never known such a thing.

It wasn't much of a place, but the stone walls had been neatly whitewashed, there was a coke fire in the stove, benches and trestle tables. Anna sat behind one of them, knitting a sweater. The soup was in front of her in a heat-retaining container, plates piled beside it. There were several loaves of yesterday's bread supplied free by arrangements with a local bakery.

Father da Costa put more coke on the stove and stirred it impatiently with the poker. Anna stopped knitting. "What do you think has happened?"

"God knows," he said. "I'm sure I don't." He walked to the door and went out to the porch. The street was apparently deserted. The rain had declined into a light drizzle. He went back inside.

The Irishman, O'Hara, the one Varley had referred to as Big Mick, moved out of the entrance to a small yard halfway up the street and stood under a lamp. He was a tall, broad-shouldered man, six-foot-three at least, with curling, black hair and a perpetual smile. The man who moved out of the shadows to join him was two or three inches shorter and had a broken nose.

It was at this moment that Fallon turned into the end of the

504

street. He approached silently, pausing in the darkness to take stock of the situation when he saw O'Hara and his friend. When the Irishman started speaking, Fallon moved into a convenient doorway and listened.

"Sure, and I think the reverend gentleman's just about ready for it, Daniel," O'Hara said. "How many have we got in there now?"

Daniel snapped his fingers and several shadowy figures emerged from the darkness. He counted them quickly. "I make it eight," he said. "That's ten including us."

"Nine," O'Hara said. "You stay outside and watch the door, just in case. They all know what to do?"

"I've seen to that," Daniel said. "For a quid apiece they'll take the place apart."

O'Hara turned to address the shadowy group. "Remember one thing. Da Costa—he's mine."

Daniel said. "Doesn't that worry you, Mick? I mean you being an Irishman and so on. After all, he's a priest."

"I've a terrible confession to make, Daniel." O'Hara put a hand on his shoulder. "Some Irishmen are Protestants and I'm one of them." He turned to the others. "Come on, lads," he said and crossed the road.

They went in through the door and Daniel waited by the railings, his ear cocked for the first sound of a disturbance from inside. There was a slight, polite cough from behind and when he turned, Fallon was standing a yard or two away, hands in pockets.

"Where in hell did you spring from?" Daniel demanded.

"Never mind that," Fallon said. "What's going on in there?"

Daniel knew trouble when he saw it, but completely miscalculated his man. "You little squirt," he said contemptuously. "Get the hell out of it."

He moved in fast, his hands reaching out to destroy, but they only fastened on thin air as his feet were kicked expertly from beneath him.

He thudded against the wet pavement and scrambled to his

feet, mouthing obscenities. Fallon seized his right wrist with both hands, twisting it up and around. Daniel gave a cry of agony as the muscle started to give. Still keeping that terrible hold in position, Fallon ran him headfirst into the railings.

Daniel pulled himself up off his knees, blood on his face, one hand out in supplication. "No more, for Christ's sake."

"All right," Fallon said. "Answer, then. What's the game?"

"They're supposed to turn the place over."

"Who for?" Daniel hesitated, and Fallon kicked his feet from under him. "Who for?"

"Jack Meehan," Daniel gabbled.

Fallon pulled him to his feet and stood back. "Next time, you get a bullet in the kneecap. That's a promise. Now get out of it."

Daniel turned and staggered into the darkness.

At the first sudden noisy rush, Father da Costa knew he was in trouble. As he moved forward, a bench went over and then another. Hands pawed at him, someone pulled his cassock. He was aware of Anna crying out in alarm and turning, saw O'Hara grab her from behind, arms about her waist.

"Now then, darlin', what about a little kiss?" he demanded.

She pulled away from him in a panic, hands reaching out blindly and cannoned into the trestle table, knocking it over, soup spilling out across the floor, plates clattering.

As Father da Costa fought to get towards her, O'Hara laughed out loud. "Now look what you've done."

A soft, quiet voice called from the doorway, cutting through the noise.

"Mickeen O'Hara. Is it you I see?"

The room went quiet. Everyone waited. O'Hara turned, an expression of disbelief on his face that seemed to say this couldn't be happening. The expression was quickly replaced by one that was a mixture of awe and fear.

"God in heaven," he whispered. "Is that you, Martin?"

Fallon went towards him, hands in pockets and everyone waited. He said softly, "Tell them to clean the place up, Mick, like a good boy, then wait for me outside."

O'Hara did as he was told without hesitation and moved towards the door. The other men righted the tables and benches; one of them got a bucket and mop and started on the floor.

Father da Costa had moved to comfort Anna and Fallon joined them. "I'm sorry about that, Father," he said. "It won't happen again."

"Meehan?" Father da Costa asked.

Fallon nodded. "Were you expecting something like this?"

"He came to see me earlier this evening. You might say we didn't get on too well." He hesitated. "The big Irishman. He knew you."

"Little friend of all the world, that's me," Fallon smiled. "Good night to you," he said and turned to the door.

Father da Costa reached him as he opened it and put a hand on his arm. "We must talk, Fallon. You owe me that."

"All right," Fallon said. "When?"

"I'll be busy in the morning, but I don't have a lunchtime confession tomorrow. Will one o'clock suit you? At the presbytery."

"I'll be there."

Fallon went out, closing the door behind him and crossed the street to where O'Hara waited nervously under the lamp. As Fallon approached he turned to face him.

"Before God, if I'd known you were mixed up in this, Martin, I wouldn't have come within a mile of it. I thought you were dead by now—we all did."

"All right," Fallon said. "How much was Meehan paying you?"

"Twenty-five quid. Fifty if the priest got a broken arm."

"How much in advance?"

"Not a sou."

Fallon opened his wallet, took out two ten-pound notes and

handed them to him. "Traveling money—for old times' sake. I don't think it's going to be too healthy for you round here. Not when Jack Meehan finds out you've let him down."

"God bless you, Martin, I'll be out of it this very night." He started to turn away, then hesitated. "Does it bother you anymore, Martin, what happened back there?"

"Every minute of every hour of every day of my life," Fallon said with deep conviction. He turned and walked away up the side street.

From the shelter of the porch, Father da Costa saw O'Hara cross the main road. He made for the pub on the corner and went in at the bar entrance, and Father da Costa went after him.

It was quiet in the saloon bar, which was why O'Hara had chosen it. He was still badly shaken, and he ordered a large whisky, which he swallowed at once. As he asked for another, the door opened and Father da Costa entered.

O'Hara tried to brazen it out. "So there you are, Father," he said. "Will you have a drink with me?"

"I'd sooner drink with the Devil." Father da Costa dragged him across to a nearby booth and sat opposite him. "Where did you know Fallon?" he demanded. "Before tonight, I mean?"

O'Hara stared at him in blank astonishment, glass half-raised to his lips. "Fallon?" he said. "I don't know anyone called Fallon."

"Martin Fallon, you fool," Father da Costa said impatiently. "Haven't I just seen you talking together outside the church?"

"Oh, you mean Martin," O'Hara said. "Fallon—is that what he's calling himself now?"

"What can you tell me about him?"

"Why should I tell you anything?"

"Because I'll ring for the police and put you in charge for assault if you don't. Detective Superintendent Miller is a personal friend. He'll be happy to oblige, I'm sure."

"All right, Father, you can call off the dogs." O'Hara, mellowed by two large whiskies, went to the bar for a third and returned. "What do you want to know for?"

"Does that matter?"

"It does to me. Martin Fallon, as you call him, is probably the best man I ever knew in my life. A hero."

"To whom?"

"To the Irish people."

"Oh, I see. Well, I don't mean him any harm, I can assure you of that."

"You give me your word on it?"

"Of course."

"All right, I won't tell you his name, his real name. It doesn't matter anyway. He was a lieutenant in the Provisional IRA. They used to call him the Executioner in Derry. I've never known the likes of him with a gun in his hand. He'd have killed the Pope if he'd thought it would advance the cause. And brains." He shook his head. "A university man, Father, would you believe it? Trinity College, no less. There were days when it all poured out of him. Poetry—books. That sort of thing—and he played the piano like an angel." O'Hara hesitated, fingering a cigarette, frowning into the past. "And then there were other times."

"What do you mean?" Father da Costa asked him.

"Oh, he used to change completely. Go right inside himself. No emotion, no response. Nothing. Cold and dark." O'Hara shivered and stuck the cigarette into the corner of his mouth. "When he was like that, he scared the hell out of everybody, including me, I can tell you."

"You were with him long?"

"Only for a time. They never really trusted me. I'm a Prod, you see, so I got out."

"And Fallon?"

"He laid this ambush for a Saracen armoured car, somewhere in Armagh. Mined the road. Someone had got the time wrong. They got a school bus instead with a dozen kids on board. Five killed, the rest crippled. You know how it is. It finished Martin. I think he'd been worrying about the way things were going for a while. All the killing and so on. The business with the bus was the final straw, you might say."

"I can see that it would be," Father da Costa said without irony.

"I thought he was dead," O'Hara said. "Last I heard, the IRA had an execution squad out after him. Me, I'm no account. Nobody worries about me, but for someone like Martin, it's different. He knows too much. For a man like him, there's only one way out of the movement and that's in a coffin."

He got to his feet, face flushed. "Well, Father, I'll be leaving you now. This town and I are parting company."

He walked to the door and Father da Costa went with him. As rain drifted across the street, O'Hara buttoned up his coat and said cheerfully, "Have you ever wondered what it's all about, Father? Life, I mean?"

"Constantly," Father da Costa told him.

"That's honest, anyway. See you in hell, Father."

He moved off along the pavement, whistling, and Father da Costa went back across the road to the Holy Name. When he went back into the crypt, everything was in good order again. The men had gone and Anna waited patiently on one of the bench seats.

"I'm sorry I had to leave you," he said, "but I wanted to speak to the man who knew Fallon. The one who started all the trouble. He went into the pub on the corner."

"What did you find out?"

He hesitated, then told her. When he was finished, there was pain in her face. She said slowly, "Then he isn't what he seemed at first."

"He killed Krasko," Father da Costa reminded her. "Murdered him in cold blood. There was nothing romantic about that."

"You're right, of course." She groped for her coat and stood up. "What are you going to do now?"

"What on earth do you expect me to do?" he said half-angrily. "Save his soul?"

"It's a thought," she said, slipping her hand into his arm. They went out together.

There was an old warehouse at the rear of Meehan's premises in Paul's Square and a fire escape gave easy access to its flat roof.

Fallon crouched behind a low wall as he screwed the silencer on to the barrel of the Ceska and peered across through the rain. The two dormer windows at the rear of Meehan's penthouse were no more than twenty yards away and the curtains weren't drawn. He had seen Meehan several times pacing backwards and forwards, a glass in his hand. On one occasion, Rupert had joined him, putting an arm about his neck, but Meehan had shoved him away and angrily from the look of it.

It was a difficult shot at that distance for a handgun, but not impossible. Fallon crouched down, holding the Ceska ready in both hands, aiming at the left-hand window. Meehan appeared briefly and paused, raising a glass to his lips. Fallon fired the silenced pistol once.

In the penthouse, a mirror on the wall shattered and Meehan dropped to the floor. Rupert, who was lying on the couch watching television, turned quickly. His eyes widened.

"My God, look at the window. Somebody took a shot at you."

Meehan looked up at the bullet hole, the spider's web of cracks, then across at the mirror. He got up slowly.

Rupert joined him. "You want to know something, ducky? You're getting to be too damn dangerous to know."

Meehan shoved him away angrily. "Get me a drink, damn you. I've got to think this thing out."

A couple of minutes later the phone rang. When he picked up the receiver, he got a call-box signal and then the line cleared as a coin went in the other end.

"That you, Meehan?" Fallon said. "You know who this is?"

"You bastard," Meehan said. "What are you trying to do?"

"This time I missed because I meant to," Fallon said. "Remember that, and tell your goons to stay away from Holy Name—and that includes you."

He put down the receiver and Meehan did the same. He turned, his face white with fury, and Rupert handed him a drink. "You don't look too good, ducky, bad news?"

"Fallon," Meehan said between his teeth. "It was that bastard Fallon, and he missed because he wanted to."

"Never mind, ducky," Rupert said. "After all, you've always got me."

"That's right," Meehan said. "So I have. I was forgetting," and he hit him in the stomach with his clenched fist.

It was late when Fallon got back, much later than he had intended, and there was no sign of Jenny. He took off his shoes and went up the stairs and along the landing to his room quietly.

He undressed, got into bed and lit a cigarette. He was tired. It had certainly been one hell of a day. There was a slight, timid knock on the door. It opened and Jenny came in.

She wore a dark-blue nylon nightdress, her hair was tied back with a ribbon and her face was scrubbed clean. She said, "Jack Meehan was on the phone about half an hour ago. He says he wants to see you in the morning."

"Did he say where?"

"No, he just said to tell you it couldn't be more public so you've nothing to worry about. He'll send a car at seven-thirty."

Fallon frowned. "A bit early for him, isn't it?"

"I wouldn't know." She hesitated. "I waited. You said an hour. You didn't come."

"I'm sorry," he said. "It couldn't be helped, believe me."

"I did," she said. "You were the first man in years who didn't treat me like something you'd scrape off your shoe."

She started to cry. Wordless, he pulled back the covers and held out a hand. She stumbled across the room and got in beside him.

He switched off the lamp. She lay there, her face against his chest, sobbing, his arms about her. He held her close, stroking her hair with his other hand and after a while, she slept.

10

Exhumation

The car that called to pick Fallon up the following morning at seven-thirty was a black funeral limousine. Varley was at the wheel dressed in a neat blue serge suit and peaked cap. There were no other passengers.

Fallon climbed into the rear and closed the door. He reached across and slid back the glass window between the driver's compartment and the rest of the car.

"All right," he said, as Varley moved into gear and drove away. "Where are we going?"

"The Catholic cemetery." Fallon, in the act of lighting his first cigarette of the day, started, and Varley said soothingly, "Nothing to worry about, Mr. Fallon. Honest. It's just that Mr. Meehan has an exhumation first thing this morning."

"An exhumation?" Fallon said.

"That's right. They don't come along very often and Mr. Meehan always likes to see to a thing like that personally. He's very particular about his funeral work."

"I can believe that," Fallon said. "What's so special about this case?"

"Nothing, really. I suppose he thought you might find it interesting. The man they're digging up is a German. Died about eighteen months ago. His wife couldn't afford to take him back to Germany then, but now she's come into a bit of money, and wants to bury him in Hamburg." He swung the car out into the main road and added cheerfully, "It's a fascinating game, the funeral business, Mr. Fallon. Always something new happening."

"I just bet there is," Fallon said.

They reached the cemetery in ten minutes, and Varley turned in through the gate and went up the drive, past the chapel and the superintendent's office, following a narrow track.

The grave they were seeking was on top of the hill, covered by a canvas awning. At least a dozen people were grouped around it and there was a truck and a couple of cars. Meehan was standing beside one of them talking to a grey-haired man in rubber boots and an oilskin mac. Meehan wore a Homburg hat and his usual melton overcoat and Donner stood beside him holding an umbrella over his head.

As Fallon got out and splashed through the heavy rain towards them, Meehan turned and smiled. "Ah, there you are. This is Mr. Adams, the Public Health Inspector. Mr. Fallon is a colleague of mine."

Adams shook hands and turned back to Meehan. "I'll see how they're getting on, Mr. Meehan."

He moved away and Fallon said, "All right, what game are we playing now?"

"No games," Meehan said. "This is strictly business and I've a funeral afterwards so I'm busy all morning, but we obviously need to talk. We can do it in the car on the way. For the moment, just stick close to me and pretend to be a member of the firm. This is a privileged occasion. The cemetery superintendent wouldn't be too pleased if he thought an outsider had sneaked in."

He moved towards the grave, Donner keeping pace with the

umbrella, and Fallon followed. The smell was terrible—like nothing he had ever smelt before and when he peered down into the open grave, he saw that it had been sprinkled with lime.

"Two feet of water down there, Mr. Meehan," the Public Health Inspector called. "No drainage. Too much clay. Means the coffin's going to be in a bad state. Probably come to pieces."

"All in the game," Meehan said. "Better have the other one ready."

He nodded, and two of the gravediggers standing by lifted a large oak coffin out of the back of the truck and put it down near the grave. When they opened it, Fallon saw that it was zinc-lined.

"The old coffin drops inside and we close the lid," Meehan said. "Nothing to it. The lid has to be welded into place, mind you, in front of the Public Health Inspector, but that's what the law says if you want to fly a corpse from one country to another."

Just then there was a sudden flurry of movement, and as they turned, the half-dozen men grouped around the grave heaved up the coffin. Webbing bands had been passed underneath, which to a certain extent held things together, but as the coffin came into view, the end broke away and a couple of decayed feet poked through minus their toes.

The smell was even worse now as the unfortunate gravediggers lurched towards the new coffin clutching the old. Meehan seemed to enjoy the whole thing hugely and moved in close, barking orders.

"Watch it, now! Watch it! A little bit more to the left. That's it."

The old coffin dropped into the new, the lid was closed. He turned triumphantly to Fallon. "I told you there was nothing to it, didn't I? Now let's get moving. I've got a cremation at nine-thirty."

The gravediggers seemed badly shaken. One of them lit a cigarette, hands trembling, and said to Fallon in a Dublin accent, "Is it a fact that they're flying him to Germany this afternoon?"

"So I understand," Fallon said.

515

The old man made a wry face. "Sure and I hope the pilot remembers to wind the windows down."

Which at least sent Fallon to the car laughing helplessly to himself.

Donner drove and Meehan and Fallon sat in the back seat. Meehan opened a cupboard in the bottom half of the partition between the driver's compartment and the rear and took out a Thermos flask of Cognac. He half-filled a cup with coffee, topped it up with Cognac and leaned back.

"Last night. That was very silly. Not what I'd call a friendly gesture at all. What did you have to go and do a thing like that for?"

"You said the priest would be left alone," Fallon told him, "then sent O'Hara to the crypt to smash it up. Lucky I turned up when I did. As for O'Hara—he and I are old comrades in a manner of speaking. He's cleared off, by the way. You won't be seeing him around here any more."

"You have been busy." Meehan poured more Cognac into his coffee. "I do admit I got just a little bit annoyed with Father da Costa. On the other hand, he wasn't very nice when I spoke to him yesterday evening, and all I did was offer to help him raise the money to stop that church of his from falling down!"

"And you thought he'd accept?" Fallon laughed out loud. "You've got to be joking."

Meehan shrugged. "I still say that bullet was an unfriendly act."

"Just like Billy playing Peeping Tom at Jenny Fox's place," Fallon said. "When are you going to do something about that worm, anyway! He isn't fit to be out without his keeper."

Meehan's face darkened. "He's my brother," he said. "He has his faults, but we all have those. Anyone hurts him, they hurt me, too."

Fallon lit a cigarette and Meehan smiled expansively. "You don't really know me, do you, Fallon? I mean, the other side of me, for instance? The funeral game."

"You take it seriously."

It was a statement of fact, not a question, and Meehan nodded soberly. "You've got to have some respect for death. It's a serious business. Too many people are too off-hand about it these days. Now me, I like to see things done right."

"I can imagine."

Meehan smiled. "That's why I thought it might be a good idea to get together like this morning. You could find it very interesting. Who knows, you might even see some future in the business."

He put a hand on Fallon's knee and Fallon eased away. Meehan wasn't in the least embarrassed. "Anyway, we'll start you off with a cremation," he said. "See what you make of that."

He poured another coffee, topped it up with more Cognac and leaned back with a contended sigh.

When the car turned in through the gate of Pine Trees Crematorium, Fallon was surprised to see Meehan's name in gold leaf on the notice-board. He was one of half-a-dozen directors.

"I have a fifty-one percent holding in this place," Meehan said. "The most modern crematorium in the north of England. You should see the gardens in spring and summer. Costs us a bomb, but it's worth it. People come from all over."

The superintendent's house and the office were just inside the gate. They drove on and came to a superb, colonnaded building. Meehan tapped on the glass and Donner braked to a halt.

Meehan wound down the window. "This is what they call a columbarium," he said. "Some people like to store the ashes in an urn and keep it on display. There are niches in all the walls, most of them full. We try to discourage it these days."

"And what would you recommend?" Fallon demanded, irony in his voice.

"Strewing," Meehan said seriously. "Scattering the ashes on

the grass and brushing them in. We come out of the earth, we go back to it. I'll show you if you like, after the funeral."

Fallon couldn't think of a single thing to say. The man took himself so seriously. It was really quite incredible. He sat back and waited for what was to come.

The chapel and the crematorium were in the center of the estate, several hundred yards from the main gate, for obvious reasons. There were some cars parked there already, and a hearse waited with a coffin in the back, Bonati at the wheel.

Meehan said. "We usually bring the hearse on ahead of the rest of the party if the relations agree. You can't have a cortege following the coffin these days, not with present-day traffic. The procession gets split wide open."

A moment later, a limousine turned out of the drive followed by three more. Billy was sitting up front, beside the driver. Meehan got out of the car and approached, hat in hand, to greet the mourners.

It was quite a performance, and Fallon watched, fascinated, as Meehan moved from one group to the next, his face grave, full of concern. He was particularly good with the older ladies.

The coffin was carried into the chapel and the mourners followed it. Meehan joined on at the end and pulled at Fallon's sleeve. "You might as well go in. See the lot."

The service was painfully brief, almost as synthetic as the taped religious music with its heavenly choir background. Fallon was relieved when the proceedings came to an end and some curtains were closed by an automatic device, hiding the coffin from view.

"They pull it through into the funeral room on a movable belt," Meehan whispered. "I'll take you round there when they've all moved off."

He did a further stint with the relatives when they got outside. A pat on the back where it was needed, an old lady's hand held for an instant. It was really quite masterly. Finally, he managed to edge away and nodded to Fallon. They moved round to the rear of the building, he opened a door and led the way in.

There were four enormous cylindrical furnaces. Two were roaring away, another was silent. The fourth was being raked out by a man in a white coat.

Meehan nodded familiarly. "Arthur's all we need in here," he said. "Everything's fully automatic. Here, I'll show you."

The coffin Fallon had last seen in the chapel stood waiting on a trolley. "Rubber doors in the wall," Meehan explained. "It comes straight through on the rollers and finishes on the trolley."

He pushed it across to the cold oven and opened the door. The coffin was at exactly the right height and moved easily on the trolley rollers when he pushed it inside. He closed the door and flicked a red switch. There was an immediate roar and through the glass peephole, Fallon could see flames streak into life inside.

"That's all it needs," Meehan said. "These ovens operate by radiant heat and they're the last word in efficiency. An hour from beginning to end and you don't need to worry about pre-heating. The moment it reaches around a thousand degrees centigrade, that coffin will go up like a torch."

Fallon peered through the glass and saw the coffin suddenly burst into flames. He caught a glimpse of a head, hair flaming, and looked away hurriedly.

Meehan was standing beside the oven where Arthur was busily at work with his rake. "Have a look at this. This is what you're left with."

All that remained was a calcined bony skeleton in pieces. As Arthur pushed at it with the rake, it broke into fragments falling through the bars into the large tin box below which already contained a fair amount of ash.

Meehan pulled it out, picked it up and carried it across to a contraption on a bench by the wall. "This is the pulverizer," he said, emptying the contents of the tin box into the top. He clamped down the lid. "Just watch. Two minutes is all it takes."

He flicked a switch and the machine got to work, making a terrible grinding noise. When Meehan was satisfied, he switched off and unscrewed a metal urn on the underside and showed it to Fallon, who saw that it was about three-quarters full of powdery grey ash.

"You notice there's a label already on the urn?" Meehan said. "That's very important. We do everything in strict rotation. No possibility of a mistake." He pulled open a drawer in a nearby desk and took out a white card edged in black. "And the next-of-kin get one of these with the plot number on. What we call a Rest-in-Peace card. Now come outside and I'll show you the final step."

It was still raining as they moved along the path at the back of the building between cypress trees. They came out into a lawned area, criss-crossed by box hedges. The edges of the paths were lined with numbered plates.

A gardener was working away beside a wheelbarrow hoeing a flower-bed. Meehan called to him: "More work for the undertaker, Fred. Better note it down in your little black book."

The gardener produced a notebook into which he entered the particulars typed on the urn label. "Number five hundred and thirty-seven, Mr. Meehan," he said when he'd finished.

"All right, Fred, get it down," Meehan told him.

The gardener moved to the plate with the correct number and strewed the ashes across the damp grass. Then he got a besom and brushed them in.

Meehan turned to Fallon. "That's it. The whole story. Ashes to ashes. A Rest-in-Peace card with the right number on it is all that's left."

They walked back towards the chapel. Meehen said, "I'd rather be buried myself. It's more fitting, but you've got to give people what they want."

They went round to the front of the chapel. Billy and Bonati had gone, but Donner was still there and Varley had arrived in the other limousine. The crematorium superintendent appeared, wanting a word with Meehan, and Fallon was for the moment left alone.

The stench of that open grave was still in his nostrils. Just inside the main door to the chapel was a toilet, and he went inside and bathed his face and hands in cold water.

A pane of glass in the small window above the basin was missing, and rain drifted through. The open grave, the toeless feet protruding from the rotting coffin had been a hell of a start to the day and now this. A man came down to so little in the end. A handful of ashes.

When he went outside, Meehan was waiting for him. "Well, that's it," he said. "Do you want to see another one?"

"Not if I can help it."

Meehan chuckled. "I've got two more this morning, but never mind. Varley can take you back to Jenny's place." He grinned broadly. "Not worth going out on a day like this unless you have to. I'd stay in if I were you. I mean, it could get interesting. She's a real little firecracker when she gets going, is our Jenny."

"I know," Fallon said. "You told me."

He got into the rear seat of the limousine and Varley drove away. Instead of going down to the main gate, he followed a track that was barely wide enough for the car and round to the right through trees.

"I hope you don't mind, Mr. Fallon, but it saves a good mile and a half this way."

They came to a five-barred gate. He got out, opened it, drove through and got out to close the gate again. The main road was fifty yards farther on at the end of the track.

As they moved down towards the center of the city, Fallon said, "You can drop me anywhere here, Charlie."

"But you can't do that, Mr. Fallon. You know you can't," Varley groaned. "You know what Mr. Meehan said. I've got to take you back to Jenny's place."

"Well, you tell Mr. Meehan, with my compliments, that he can do the other thing."

They were moving along Rockingham Street now, and as they came to the Holy Name, Fallon leaned over suddenly and switched off the ignition. As the car coasted to a halt, he opened the door, jumped out and crossed the road. Varley watched him go into the side entrance of the church, then drove rapidly away to report.

11

The Gospel According to Fallon

The Right Reverend Monsignor Canon O'Halloran, administrator of the pro-cathedral, was standing at his study window when Miller and Fitzgerald were shown in. He turned to greet them, moving towards his desk, leaning heavily on a stick, his left leg dragging.

"Good morning, gentlemen, or is it? Sometimes I think this damned rain is never going to stop."

He spoke with a Belfast accent. Miller liked him at once and for no better reason than the fact that in spite of his white hair, he looked as if he'd once been a useful heavyweight fighter and his nose had been broken in a couple of places.

Miller said, "I'm Detective Superintendent Miller, sir. I believe you know Inspector Fitzgerald."

"I do indeed. One of our Knights of St. Columba stalwarts." Monsignor O'Halloran eased himself into the chair behind the desk. "The bishop is in Rome, I'm afraid, so you'll have to make do with me."

"You got my letter, sir?"

"Oh yes, it was delivered by hand last night."

"I thought that might save time." Miller hesitated and said carefully, "I did ask that Father da Costa should be present."

"He's waiting in the next room." Monsignor O'Halloran methodically filled his pipe from an old pouch. "I thought I'd hear what the prosecution had to say first."

Miller said, "You've got my letter. It says it all there."

"And what do you expect me to do?"

"Make Father da Costa see reason. He must help us in this matter. He must identify this man."

"If your supposition is correct, the Pope himself couldn't do that, Superintendent," Monsignor O'Halloran said calmly. "The secret nature of the confessional is absolute."

"In a case like this?" Miller said angrily. "That's ridiculous, and you know it."

Inspector Fitzgerald put a restraining hand on his arm, but Monsignor O'Halloran wasn't in the least put out. He said mildly, "To a Protestant or a Jew, or indeed to anyone outside the Catholic religion, the whole idea of confession must seem absurd. An anachronism that has no place in this modern world. Wouldn't you agree, Superintendent?"

"When I consider this present situation then I must say I do," Miller told him.

"The Church has always believed confession to be good for the soul. Sin is a terrible burden and through the medium of confession people are able to relieve themselves of that burden and start again."

Miller stirred impatiently, but O'Halloran continued in the same calm voice. He was extraordinarily persuasive. "For a confession to be any good as therapy, it has to be told to someone, which is where the priest comes in. Only as God's intermediary, of course, and one can only expect people to unburden themselves when they know that what they say is absolutely private and will never be revealed on any account."

"But this is murder we're talking about, Monsignor," Miller said. "Murder and corruption of a kind that would horrify you."

"I doubt that." Monsignor O'Halloran laughed shortly and

put another match to his pipe. "It's a strange thing, but in spite of the fact that most people believe priests to be somehow cut off from the real world, I come face to face with more human wickedness in a week than the average man does in a lifetime."

"Very interesting," Miller said, "but I fail to see the relevance."

"Very well, Superintendent. Try this. During the last war, I was in a German prisoner-of-war camp where escape plans were constantly being frustrated because somebody was keeping the German authorities informed of every move that was made." He heaved himself up out of his seat and hobbled to the window. "I knew who it was, knew for months. The man involved told me at confession."

"And you did nothing?" Miller was genuinely shocked.

"Oh, I tried to reason with him privately, but there was nothing else I could do. No possibility of my even hinting to the others what was going on." He turned, a weary smile on his face. "You think it easy carrying that kind of burden, Superintendent? Let me tell you something. I hear confessions at the cathedral regularly. Not a week passes that someone doesn't tell me something for which they could be criminally liable at law."

Miller stood up. "So you can't help us, then?"

"I didn't say that. I'll talk to him. Hear what he has to say. Would you wait outside for a few minutes?"

"Certainly, but I'd like to see him again in your presence before we leave."

"As you wish."

They went out, and Monsignor O'Halloran pressed a button on the intercom on his desk. "I'll see Father da Costa now."

It was a bad business and he felt unaccountably depressed in a personal sense. He stared out at the rainswept garden wondering what on earth he was going to say to da Costa, and then the door clicked open behind him.

He turned slowly as da Costa crossed to the desk. "Michael, what on earth am I going to do with you?"

"I'm sorry, Monsignor," Father da Costa said formally, "but this situation was not of my choosing."

"They never are," Monsignor O'Halloran said wryly as he sat down. "Is it true what they suppose? Is this business connected in some way with the confessional?"

"Yes," Father da Costa said simply.

"I thought so. The Superintendent was right, of course. As he said in his letter, it was the only explanation that made any kind of sense." He sighed heavily and shook his head. "I would imagine he intends to take this thing further. Are you prepared for that?"

"Of course," Father da Costa answered calmly.

"Then we'd better get it over with," Monsignor O'Halloran pressed the button on the intercom again. "Send in Superintendent Miller and Inspector Fitzgerald." He chuckled. "It has a certain black humor, this whole business. You must admit."

"Has it, Monsignor?"

"But of course. They sent you to Holy Name as a punishment, didn't they? To teach you a little humility and here you are, up to your ears in scandal again." He smiled wryly. "I can see the expression on the Bishop's face now."

The door opened and Miller and Fitzgerald were ushered in again. Miller nodded to da Costa. "Good morning, Father."

Monsignor O'Halloran pushed himself up on to his feet again, conscious that somehow the situation demanded it. He said, "I've discussed this matter with Father da Costa, Superintendent. To be perfectly frank, there doesn't seem to be a great deal I can do."

"I see, sir." Miller turned to Father da Costa, "I'll ask you again, Father, and for the last time. Are you prepared to help us?"

"I'm sorry, Superintendent," Father da Costa told him.

"So am I, Father." Miller was chillingly formal now. "I've discussed the situation with my chief constable and this is what I've decided to do. A report on this whole affair and your part in it goes to the Director of Public Prosecutions today, to take what action he thinks fit."

"And where do you think that will get you?" Monsignor O'Halloran asked him.

"I should think there's an excellent chance that they'll issue a warrant for the arrest of Father da Costa on a charge of being an accessory after the fact of murder."

Monsignor O'Halloran looked grave, and yet he shook his head slowly. "You're wasting your time, Superintendent. They won't play. They'll never issue such a warrant."

"We'll see, sir." Miller turned and went out, followed by Fitzgerald.

Monsignor O'Halloran sighed heavily and sat down. "So there we are. Now we wait."

"I'm sorry, Monsignor," Father da Costa said.

"I know, Michael, I know." O'Halloran looked up at him. "Is there anything I can do for you? Anything at all?"

"Will you hear my confession, Monsignor?"

"Of course."

Father da Costa moved round to the side of the desk and knelt down.

When Fallon went into the Church, Anna was playing the organ. It was obviously a practice session, hymns in the main— nothing complicated. He sat in the front pew listening, until after a while she abruptly stopped playing.

He walked up the steps between the choir stalls. "The curse of the church organist's life, hymns," he said.

She swung around to face him. "You're early. Uncle Michael said one o'clock."

"I'd nothing else to do."

She stood up. "Would you like to play?"

"Not at the moment."

"All right," she said. "Then you can take me for a walk. I could do with some air."

Her trenchcoat was in the sacristy. He helped her on with it. It was raining heavily when they went outside, but she didn't seem concerned.

"Where would you like to go?" he asked her.

"Oh, this will do fine. I like churchyards. I find them very restful."

She took his arm and they followed the path between the old Victorian monuments and gravestones. The searching wind chased leaves amongst the stones so that they seemed like living things crawling along the path in front of them.

They paused beside an old marble mausoleum for Fallon to light a cigarette, and at that precise moment Billy Meehan and Varley appeared at the side gate. They saw Fallon and the girl and ducked back out of sight.

"See, he's still here," Varley said. "Thank God for that."

"You go back to Paul's Square and wait for Jack," Billy said. "Tell him where I am. I'll keep watch here."

Varley moved away and Billy slipped in through the gate and worked his way towards Fallon and Anna, using the monuments for cover.

Anna said, "I'd like to thank you for what you did last night."

"It was nothing."

"One of the men involved was an old friend of yours. O'Hara, wasn't that his name?"

Fallon said quickly, "No, you've got it wrong."

"I don't think so," she insisted. "Uncle Michael spoke to him after you'd left, in the pub across the road. He told him a great deal about you. Belfast, Londonderry—the IRA."

"The bastard," Fallon said bitterly. "He always had a big mouth, that one. Somebody will be closing his eyes with pennies one of these fine days if he isn't careful."

"I don't think he meant any harm. Uncle Michael's impression was that he thought a great deal about you." She hesitated, then said carefully, "Things happen in war sometimes that nobody intends."

Fallon cut in on her sharply. "I never go back to anything in

528

thought or deed. It doesn't pay." They turned into another path and he looked up at the rain. "God, is it never going to stop? What a world. Even the bloody sky won't stop weeping."

"You have a bitter view of life, Mr. Fallon."

"I speak as I find and as far as I am concerned, life is one hell of a name for the world as it is."

"And is there nothing, then?" she demanded. "Not one single solitary thing worth having in this world of yours?"

"Only you," he said.

They were close to the presbytery now and Billy Meehan observed them closely with the aid of a pair of binoculars from behind a mausoleum.

Anna stopped walking and turned to face Fallon. "What did you say?"

"You've no business here." He made a sweeping gesture with one arm encompassing the whole cemetery. "This place belongs to the dead, and you're still alive."

"And you?"

There was a long pause, after which he said calmly, "No, it's different for me. I'm a dead man walking. Have been for a long time now."

She was to remember that remark always as one of the most terrible things she had ever heard in her life.

She stared up at him, those calm, blind eyes fixed on some point in space, and then she reached up for his head and kissed him hard, her mouth opening in a deliberately provocative gesture.

She pulled away. "Did you feel that?" she demanded fiercely. "Did I break through?"

"I think you could say that," he said in some amazement.

"Good," she said. "I'm going in now. I want to change, and then I have lunch to get ready. You'd better play the organ or something until my uncle gets back."

"All right," Fallon said and turned away.

He had only taken a few steps when she called, "Oh, and Fallon?" When he turned she was standing in the porch, the

529

door half-open. "Think of me. Remember me. Concentrate on that. I exist. I'm real."

She went in and closed the door and Fallon turned and walked away quickly.

It was only when he was out of sight that Billy moved from the shelter of the mausoleum holding his binoculars in one hand. *Fallon and the priest's niece.* Now that was interesting.

He was about to turn away, when a movement at one of the presbytery windows caught his eye. He went back into cover and raised the binoculars.

Anna was standing at the window and as he watched, she started to unbutton her blouse. His mouth went dry, a hand seemed to squeeze his insides and when she unzipped her skirt and stepped out of it, his hands, clutching the binoculars, started to shake.

The bitch, he thought, and she's Fallon's woman. Fallon's. The ache between his thighs was almost unbearable and he turned and hurried away.

Fallon had been playing the organ for just over an hour when he paused for breath. It had been a long time and his hands were aching, but it was good to get down to it again.

He turned and found Father da Costa sitting in the front pew watching him, arms folded. "How long have you been there?" Fallon got up and started down the steps between the choir stalls.

"Half an hour, maybe more," Father da Costa said. "You're brilliant, you know that, don't you?"

"Used to be."

"Before you took up the gun for dear old mother Ireland and that glorious cause?"

Fallon went very still. When he spoke, it was almost in a whisper. "That's of no interest to you."

"It's of every interest," Father da Costa told him. "To me, in particular, for obvious reasons. Good God, man, how could you do what you've done and you with so much music in you?"

"Sir Philip Sidney was reputed to be the most perfect of all knights of the court of Elizabeth Tudor," Fallon said. "He composed music and wrote poetry like an angel. In his lighter moments, he and Sir Walter Raleigh herded Irishmen together into convenient spots and butchered them like cattle."

"All right," Father da Costa said. "Point taken. But is that how you see yourself? As a soldier?"

"My father was." Fallon sat back on the altar rail. "He was a sergeant in the Parachute Regiment. Killed at Arnhem fighting for the English. There's irony for you."

"And what happened to you?"

"My grandfather raised me. He had a hill farm in the Sperrins. Sheep mostly—a few horses. I ran happily enough, wild and barefooted, till the age of seven when the new schoolmaster, who was also organist of the church, discovered I had perfect pitch. Life was never the same after that."

"And you went to Trinity College?"

Fallon frowned slightly. "Who told you that?"

"Your friend O'Hara. Did you take a degree?"

There was sudden real humor in Fallon's eyes. "Would you believe me, now, Father, if I told you the farm boy became a doctor of music, no less?"

"Why not?" da Costa replied calmly. "Beethoven's mother was a cook, but never mind that. The other? How did that start?"

"Time and chance. I went to stay with a cousin of mine in Belfast one weekend in August 1969. He lived in the Falls Road. You may remember what happened."

Father da Costa nodded gravely. "I think so."

"An Orange mob led by B specials swarmed in bent on burning every Catholic house in the area to the ground. They were stopped by a handful of IRA men who took to the streets to defend the area."

"And you became involved."

"Somebody gave me a rifle, let's put it that way, and I discovered a strange thing. What I aimed at, I hit."

"You were a natural shot."

"Exactly." Fallon's face was dark and suddenly he took the Ceska out of his pocket. "When I hold this, when my finger's on the trigger, a strange thing happens. It becomes an extension, an extension of me personally. Does that make sense?"

"Oh, yes," Father da Costa said. "But of the most horrible kind. So you continued to kill."

"To fight," Fallon said, his face stony, and he slipped the Ceska back inside his pocket. "As a soldier of the Irish Republican Army."

"And it became easier? Each time it became easier."

Fallon straightened slowly. His eyes were very dark. He made no reply.

Father da Costa said, "I've just come from a final showdown with Superintendent Miller. Would you be interested to know what he intends?"

"All right, tell me."

"He's laying the facts before the Director of Public Prosecutions and asking him for a warrant charging me with being an accessory after the fact to murder."

"He'll never make it stick."

"And what if he succeeds? Would it cause you the slightest concern?"

"Probably not."

"Good, honesty at last. There's hope for you yet. And your cause, Fallon. Irish unity or freedom or hatred of the bloody English or whatever it was. Was it worth it? The shooting and bombings. People dead, people crippled?"

Fallon's face was very white now, the eyes jet black, expressionless. "I enjoyed every golden moment," he said calmly.

"And the children?" Father da Costa demanded. "Was it worth that?"

"That was an accident," Fallon said hoarsely.

"It always is, but at least there was some semblance of reason to it, however mistaken. But Krasko was plain, cold-blooded murder."

Fallon laughed softly. "All right, Father, you want answers.

I'll try and give you some." He walked to the altar rail and put a foot on it, leaning an elbow on his knee, chin in hand. "There's a poem by Ezra Pound I used to like. 'Some quick to arm,' it says, and then later, 'walked eye-deep in hell, believing in old men's lies.' Well, that was my cause at the final end of things. Old men's lies. And for that, I personally killed over thirty people, assisted at the end of God knows how many more."

"All right, so you were mistaken. In the end, violence in that sort of situation gains you nothing. I could have told you that before you started. But Krasko," Father da Costa shook his head. "That, I don't understand."

"Look, we live in different worlds," Fallon told him. "People like Meehan—they're renegades. So am I. I engage in a combat that's nothing to do with you and the rest of the bloody civilians. We inhabit our own world. Krasko was a whoremaster, a pimp, a drug pusher."

"Whom you murdered," Father da Costa repeated inexorably.

"I fought for my cause, Father," Fallon said. "Killed for it, even when I ceased to believe it worth a single human life. That was murder. But now? Now, I only kill pigs."

The disgust, the self-loathing were clear in every word he spoke. Father da Costa said with genuine compassion, "The world can't be innocent with Man in it."

"And what in the hell is that pearl of wisdom supposed to mean?" Fallon demanded.

"Perhaps I can explain best by telling you a story," Father da Costa said. "I spent several years in a Chinese Communist prison camp after being captured in Korea. What they called a special indoctrination center."

Fallon could not help but be interested. "Brainwashing?" he said.

"That's right. From their point of view, I was a special target, the Catholic Church's attitude to Communism being what it is. They have an extraordinarily simple technique and yet it works so often. The original concept is Pavlovian. A question of inducing guilt or rather of magnifying the guilt that is in all of us.

533

Shall I tell you the first thing my instructor asked me? Whether I had a servant at the mission to clean my room and make my bed. When I admitted that I had, he expressed surprise, produced a Bible and read to me that passage in which Our Lord speaks of serving others. Yet here was I allowing one of those I had come to help to serve me. Amazing how guilty that one small point made me feel."

"And you fell for that?"

"A man can fall for almost anything when he's half-starved and kept in solitary confinement. And they were clever, make no mistake about that. To use the appropriate Marxian terminology, each man has his thesis and his antithesis. For a priest, his thesis is everything he believes in. Everything he and his vocation stand for."

"And his antithesis?"

"His darker side. The side which is present in all of us. Fear, hate, violence, aggression, the desires of the flesh. This is the side they work on, inducing guilt feelings to such a degree in an attempt to force a complete breakdown. Only after that can they start their own particular brand of reeducation."

"What did they try on you?"

"With me it was sex," Father da Costa smiled. "A path they frequently follow where Catholic priests are concerned, celibacy being a state they find quite unintelligible."

"What did they do?"

"Half starved me, left me on my own in a damp cell for three months, then put me to bed between two young women who were presumably willing to give their all for the cause, just like you." He laughed. "It was rather childish, really. The idea was, I suppose, that I should be racked with guilt because I experienced an erection, whereas I took it to be a chemical reaction perfectly understandable in the circumstances. It seemed to me that would be God's view also."

"So, no sin in you then. Driven snow. Is that it?"

"Not at all. I am a very violent man, Mr. Fallon. There was

a time in my life when I enjoyed killing. Perhaps if they'd worked on that they would have got somewhere. It was to escape that side of myself that I entered the Church. It was, still is, my greatest weakness, but at least I acknowledge its existence." He paused and then said deliberately, "Do you?"

"Any man can know about things," Fallon said. "It's knowing the significance of things that's important."

He paused, and Father da Costa said, "Go on."

"What do you want me to do, drain the cup?" Fallon demanded. "The gospel according to Fallon? All right, if that's what you want."

He mounted the steps leading up to the pulpit and stood at the lectern. "I never realized you had such a good view. What do you want me to say?"

"Anything you like."

"All right. We are fundamentally alone. Nothing lasts. There is no purpose to any of it."

"You are wrong," Father da Costa said. "You leave out God."

"God?" Fallon cried. "What kind of God allows a world where children can be happily singing one minute"—his voice failed for a moment—"and blown into strips of bloody flesh the next? Can you honestly tell me you still believe in a God after what they did to you in Korea? Are you telling me you never faltered, not once?"

"Strength comes from adversity always," Father da Costa told him. "I crouched in the darkness in my own filth for six months once, on the end of a chain. There was one day, one moment, when I might have done anything. And then the stone rolled aside and I smelled the grave, saw him walk out on his own two feet and I knew, Fallon! I knew!"

"Well, all I can say is, that if he exists, your God, I wish to hell you could get him to make up his mind. He's big on how and when. Not so hot on why."

"Have you learned nothing, then?" Father da Costa demanded.

"Oh, yes," Fallon said. "I've learned to kill with a smile, Father, that's very important. But the biggest lesson of all, I learned too late."

"And what might that be?"

"That nothing is worth dying for."

It was suddenly very quiet, only the endless rain drifting against the windows. Fallon came down the steps of the pulpit buckling the belt of his trenchcoat. He paused beside Father da Costa.

"And the real trouble is, Father, that nothing's worth living for either."

He walked away down the aisle, his footsteps echoing. The door banged, the candles flickered. Father da Costa knelt down at the altar rail, folded his hands and prayed as he had seldom prayed before.

After a while, a door clicked open and a familiar voice said, "Uncle Michael? Are you there?"

He turned to find Anna standing outside the sacristy door. "Over here," he called.

She moved towards him and he went to meet her, reaching for her outstretched hands. He took her across to the front pew and they sat down. And as usual she sensed his mood.

"What is it?" she said, her face full of concern. "Where's Mr. Fallon?"

"Gone," he said. "We had quite a chat. I think I understand him more now."

"He's dead inside," she said. "Everything frozen."

"And racked by self-hate. He hates himself so he hates all of life. He has no feeling left, not in any normal sense. In fact it is my judgment that the man is probably seeking death. One possible reason for him to continue to lead the life he does."

"But I don't understand," she said.

"He puts his whole life on the scales, gave himself for a cause he believed was an honorable one—gave everything he had. A dangerous thing to do, because if anything goes wrong, if you find that in the final analysis your cause is as worthless as a bent farthing, you're left with nothing."

"He told me he was a dead man walking," she said.

"I think that's how he sees himself."

She put a hand on his arm. "But what can you do?" she said. "What can anyone do?"

"Help him find himself. Save his soul, perhaps. I don't really know. But I must do something. I must!"

He got up, walked across to the altar rail, knelt down and started to pray.

12

More Work for the Undertaker

Fallon was in the kitchen having tea with Jenny when the door-
bell rang. She went to answer it. When she came back, Jack
Meehan and Billy followed her into the room.

"All right, sweetheart," Meehan told her. "Make yourself
scarce. This is business."

She gave Fallon a brief troubled look, hesitated, then went
out. "She's taken a shine to you, I can see that," Meehan
commented.

He sat on the edge of the table and poured himself a cup of
tea. Billy leaned against the wall by the door, hands in his
pockets, watching Fallon sullenly.

"She's a nice kid," Fallon said, "but you haven't come here
to discuss Jenny."

Meehan sighed. "You've been a naughty boy again, Fallon.
I told you when I left you this morning to come back here and
keep under cover and what did you do at the first opportunity?
Gave poor old Varley the slip again, and that isn't nice because
he knows how annoyed I get and he has a weak heart."

"Make your point."

"All right. You went to see that bloody priest again."

538

"Like hell he did," Billy put in from the doorway. "He was with that da Costa bird in the churchyard."

"The blind girl?" Meehan said.

"That's right. She kissed him."

Meehan shook his head sorrowfully. "Leading the poor girl on like that and you leaving the country after tomorrow."

"She's a right whore," Billy said viciously. "Undressing at the bloody window, she was. Anybody could have seen her."

"That's hardly likely," Fallon said. "Not with a twenty-foot wall round the churchyard. I thought I told you to stay away from there."

"What's wrong?" Billy jeered. "Frightened I'll queer your pitch? Want to keep it all for yourself?"

Fallon stood up slowly and the look on his face would have frightened the Devil himself. "Go near that girl again, harm her in any way, and I'll kill you," he said simply and his voice was the merest whisper.

Jack Meehan turned and slapped his brother across the face backhanded. "You randy little pig," he said. "Sex, that's all you can think about. As if I don't have enough troubles. Go on, get out of it!"

Billy got the door open and glared at Fallon, his face white with passion. "You wait, you bastard. I'll fix you, you see if I don't. You and your posh bird."

"I said get out of it!" Meehan roared and Billy did just that, slamming the door behind him.

Meehan turned to Fallon, "I'll see he doesn't step out of line, don't you worry."

Fallon put a cigarette between his lips and lit it with a taper from the kitchen fire. "And you?" he said. "Who keeps you in line?"

Meehan laughed delightedly. "Nothing ever throws you, does it? I mean, when Miller walked into church yesterday and found you talking to the priest, I was worried, I can tell you. But when you sat down at that organ." He shook his head and chuckled. "That was truly beautiful."

There was a slight frown on Fallon's face. "You were there?"

"Oh yes, I was there all right." Meehan lit a cigarette. "There's one thing I don't understand."

"And what would that be?"

"You could have put a bullet in my head last night instead of into that mirror. Why didn't you? I mean, if da Costa is so important to you and you think I'm some sort of threat to him, it would have been the logical thing to do."

"And what would have happened to my passport and passage on that boat out of Hull on Sunday night?"

Meehan chuckled. "You don't miss a trick, do you? We're a lot alike, Fallon, you and me."

"I'd rather be the Devil himself," Fallon told him with deep conviction.

Meehan's face darkened. "Coming the superior bit again, are we? My life for Ireland. The gallant rebel, gun in hand?" There was anger in his voice now. "Don't give me that crap, Fallon. You enjoyed it for its own sake, running around in a trenchcoat with a gun in your pocket like something out of an old movie. You enjoyed the killing. Shall I tell you how I know? Because you're too bloody good at it not to have done."

Fallon sat there staring at him, his face very white, and then, by some mysterious alchemy, the Ceska was in his hand.

Meehan laughed harshly. "You need me, Fallon, remember? Without me there's no passport and no passage out of Hull on Sunday, so put it away, like a good boy."

He walked to the door and opened it. Fallon shifted his aim slightly, following him, and Meehan turned to face him. "All right, then, let's see you pull that trigger."

Fallon held the gun steady. Meehan stood there waiting, hands in the pockets of his trenchcoat. After a while he turned slowly and went out, closing the door behind him.

For a moment or so longer Fallon held the Ceska out in front of him, staring into space, and then, very slowly, he lowered it, resting his hand on the table, his finger still on the trigger.

He was still sitting there when Jenny came in. "They've gone," she said.

Fallon made no reply and she looked down at the gun with distaste. "What did you need that thing for? What happened?"

"Nothing much," he said. "He held up a mirror, that's all, but there was nothing there that I hadn't seen before." He pushed back his hair and stood up. "I think I'll get a couple of hours' sleep."

He moved to the door. Diffidently she said, "Would you like me to come up?"

It was as if he hadn't heard her. He went out quietly, trapped in some dark world of his own. She sat down at the table and buried her face in her hands.

When Fitzgerald went into Miller's office, the Superintendent was standing by the window reading a carbon copy of a letter.

He offered it to Fitzgerald. "That's what we sent to the Director of Public Prosecutions."

Fitzgerald read it quickly. "That seems to sum up the situation pretty adequately to me, sir," he said as he handed the letter back. "When can we expect a decision?"

"That's the trouble, they'll probably take a couple of days. Unofficially, I've already spoken to the man who'll be handling it by telephone."

"And what did he think, sir?"

"If you really want to know, he wasn't too bloody hopeful." Miller's frustration was a tangible thing. "Anything to do with religion, you know what people are like. That's the English for you."

"I see, sir," Fitzgerald said slowly.

It was only then that Miller noticed that the Inspector was holding something in his right hand. "What have you got there?"

Fitzgerald steeled himself, "Bad news, I'm afraid, sir. From CRO about the Ceska."

Miller sat down wearily. "All right, tell me the worst."

"According to the computer, the last time a Ceska was used to kill someone in this country was in June 1952, sir. A Polish ex-serviceman shot his wife and her lover to death. They hanged him three months later."

"Marvellous," Miller said bitterly. "That's all I needed."

"Of course they're circulating arms dealers in the London area for us," Fitzgerald said. "It will take time, but something could come out of that line of enquiry."

"I know," Miller said bitterly. "Pigs might also fly." He pulled on his raincoat. "Do you know what the unique feature of this case is?"

"I don't think so, sir."

"Then I'll tell you. There's nothing to solve. We already know who's behind the killing. Jack Meehan, and if that damned priest would only open his mouth I could have his head on a platter."

Miller turned angrily and walked out, banging the door so hard that the glass panel cracked.

Fallon had only taken off his shoes and jacket and had lain on the top of the bed. He awakened to find the room in darkness. He had been covered with an eiderdown which meant that Jenny must have been in. It was just after eight when he checked his watch. He pulled on his shoes hurriedly, grabbed his jacket and went downstairs.

Jenny was doing some ironing when he went into the kitchen. She glanced up. "I looked in about three hours ago, but you were asleep."

"You should have wakened me," he said, and took down his raincoat from behind the door.

"Jack Meehan said you weren't to go out."

"I know." He transferred the Ceska to the pocket of his raincoat and fastened the belt.

"It's that girl, isn't it?" she said. "You're worried about her." He frowned slightly and she rested the iron. "Oh, I was listening outside the door. I heard most of what went on. What's she like?"

"She's blind," Fallon said. "That means she's vulnerable."

"And you're worried about Billy? You think he might try to pay you off for what happened last night by getting at her?"

"Something like that."

"I don't blame you." She started to iron a crisp white blouse. "Let me tell you about him so you know what you're up against. At twelve, most boys are lucky if they've learnt how to make love to their hand, but not our Billy. At that age, he was having it off with grown women. Whores mostly, working for Jack Meehan, and Billy was Jack's brother, so they didn't like to say no." She shook her head. "He never looked back. By the time he was fifteen he was a dirty, sadistic little pervert. It was downhill all the way after that." She rested the iron again. "So if I were you, I'd worry all right where he's concerned."

"Thanks," he said. "Don't wait up for me."

The door banged and he was gone. She stood there for a moment, staring into space sadly and then she returned to her ironing.

Anna da Costa was about to get into the bath when she heard the phone ringing. She put on a robe and went downstairs, arriving in the hall as her uncle replaced the receiver.

"What is it?" she asked.

"The Infirmary. The old Italian lady I visited the other day. She's had a relapse. They expect her to die some time tonight. I'll have to go."

She took down his coat from the hall stand and held it out for him. He opened the front door and they moved out into the porch. The rain was pouring down.

"I'll walk," he said. "It's not worth taking the van. Will you be all right?"

"Don't worry about me," she said. "How long will you be?"

"God knows, probably several hours. Don't wait up for me."

He plunged into the rain and hurried down the path passing a magnificent Victorian mausoleum, the pride of the cemetery with its bronze doors and marble porch. Billy Meehan dropped back into the shadows of the porch quickly, but when the priest had gone past, he moved forward again.

He had heard the exchange at the door and a cold finger of excitement moved in his belly. He had already had intercourse twice that night with a prostitute, not that it had been any good. He didn't seem to be able to get any satisfaction any more. He'd intended going home and then he'd remembered Anna—Anna at the window undressing.

He'd only been lurking in the shadows of that proch for ten minutes, but he was already bitterly cold and rain drifted in on the wind. He thought of Fallon, the humiliation of the previous night, and his face contorted.

"The bastard," he said softly. "The little Mick bastard. I'll show him."

He produced a half-bottle of Scotch from his pocket and took a long pull.

Father da Costa hurried into the church. He took a Host out of the ciborium and hung it in a silver pyx around his neck. He also took holy oils with him to anoint the dying woman's ears, nose, mouth, hands and feet and went out quietly.

The church was still and quiet, only the images floating in candlelight, the drift of rain against the window. It was perhaps five minutes after Father da Costa's departure that the door creaked open eerily and Fallon entered.

He looked about him to make sure that no one was there, then hurried down the aisle, went inside the cage and pressed the button to ascend. He didn't go right up to the tower, stopping the cage on the other side of the canvas sheet covering the hole in the roof of the nave.

It only sloped slightly and he walked across the sheeting lead and paused at the low retaining wall, sheltering in the angle of the buttress with the tower.

From here, his view of the presbytery was excellent and two tall concrete lampposts in the street to the left towered above the cemetery walls, throwing a band of light across the front of the house.

There was a light in one of the bedroom windows and he could see right inside the room. A wardrobe, a painting on the wall, the end of a bed and then Anna suddenly appeared wrapped in a large white towel.

From the look of things she had obviously just got out of the bath. She didn't bother to draw the curtains, probably secure in the knowledge that she was cut off from the street by twenty-foot-high walls. Or perhaps it was something to do with her blindness.

As Fallon watched she started to dry herself off. Strange how few women looked at their best in the altogether, he told himself, but she was more than passable. The black hair almost reached the pointed breasts, and a narrow waist swelled to hips that were perhaps a trifle too large for some tastes.

She pulled on a pair of hold-up stockings, black bra and panties, and a green silk dress with a pleated skirt, then started to brush her hair, perhaps the most womanly of actions. Fallon felt strangely sad, no desire in him at all, certainly not for anything physical. Just the sudden, terrible knowledge that he was looking at something he could never have on top of this earth and there was no one to blame but himself. She tied her hair back with a black ribbon and moved out of sight. A second later, the light went off.

Fallon shivered as the wind drove rain in his face and turned up his collar. It was very quiet, only the occasional sound of a car muted in the distance, and then, quite clearly, he heard the crunch of a foot in the gravel on the path below.

As he peered down, a figure moved out of the shadows into the light, the white shoulder-length hair identifying him at once. *Billy Meehan.* As Fallon leaned forward, the boy mounted the steps to the front door and tried the handle. It opened to his touch and he passed inside.

Fallon turned and scrambled down across the roof of the

hoist. He jumped inside the cage, closed the gate and pressed the button to descend, his heart racing.

The sight of Anna at the window had excited Billy Meehan to a state where he could no longer contain himself. The ache between his legs was unbearable, and the half-bottle of whisky which he had consumed had destroyed completely any last vestige of self-control.

He moved into the porch and tried the door and when it opened to his touch, he almost choked with excitement. He tiptoed inside, closing it behind him, and pushed the bolt home.

He could hear someone singing softly from a room at the end of the passage. He approached quietly and peered in through the partly opened door.

Anna was sitting at one end of a Victorian sofa, a small table at her elbow. On it was a large, open sewing box; she was sewing a button on a shirt. As he watched, she reached into the box, fumbled for a pair of scissors, then cut the thread.

Billy took off his overcoat, dropped it to the floor and moved towards her, shaking with excitement. She was aware first of the coat's dropping and then of the faint sound of his approach. She frowned, her face towards him.

"Who is it? Is anyone there?"

Billy paused momentarily. He approached on tiptoe, and as she half-turned, clutching the shirt to her, a needle in one hand, he circled behind her.

"Who is it?" she demanded, fear in her voice.

He slipped a hand up her skirt from the rear, cupping it between her thighs, and giggled. "That's nice. You like that, don't you? Most girls like what I do to them."

She gave a cry, pulling away and facing him at the same moment. He reached his hand forward and inside the neck of her dress, feeling for a breast.

Anna's face was a mask of horror. "No, please—in the name of God! Who is it?"

"Fallon!" he said. "It's me, Fallon!"

"Liar!" she screamed. "Liar!" She lashed out and caught him across the face.

Billy slapped her back-handed. "I'll teach you, you bitch. I'll make you crawl."

He knocked her across the sofa, then tore at her pants, forced her thighs apart brutally, crushed his mouth on hers. Through the unbelievable horror of it, the nameless digust, she was aware of his hand between his legs fumbling with the zip of his trousers and then the hardness pushing against her.

She screamed, he slapped her again, forcing her head back across the end of the sofa and her right hand, grabbing at the table for support, fastened upon the scissors. She was almost unconscious by then so that as the darkness flooded over her, she was not aware of her hand swinging convulsively, driving the scissors up under the ribs with all the force of which she was capable, piercing the heart and killing him instantly.

Having found the front door barred, Fallon had had to gain entry by breaking a kitchen window. He arrived in the sitting-room to discover Billy Meehan sprawled across the unconscious girl and hurled himself on him. Not until he dragged him away did he see the handle of the scissors protruding beneath the ribs.

He picked her up in his arms and carried her upstairs. The first room he tried was obviously her uncle's; the second was hers, and he laid her on the bed and covered her with an eiderdown.

He sat there holding her hand; after a while her eyelids flickered. She started violently and tried to pull her hands away.

Fallon said soothingly, "There, now, it's me—Martin Fallon. You're all right now. You've nothing to worry about."

She gave a great shuddering sigh. "Thank God! Thank God! What happened?"

"Can't you remember?"

"Only this dreadful man. He said he was you, and then he tried to . . . he tried to . . ." She shuddered. "Oh, God, the feel of his hands. It was horrible. Horrible. I fainted, I think."

"That's right," Fallon said calmly. "Then I arrived and he ran away."

She turned her face to him, those blind eyes focusing to one side. "Did you see who it was?" she asked.

"I'm afraid not."

"Was it . . ." She hesitated. "Do you think Meehan was behind it?"

"I should imagine so."

She closed her eyes and when Fallon gently took her hand, she pulled it away convulsively. It was as if for the moment she could not bear the touch of a man—any man.

He steeled himself for the obvious question. "Did he have his way with you?"

"No, I don't think so."

"Would you like me to get you a doctor?"

"For God's sake, no, not that. The very idea that anyone should know fills me with horror."

"And your uncle?"

"He's attending a dying woman at the infirmary. He could be hours."

Fallon stood up. "All right—stay here and rest. I'll bring you a brandy."

She closed her eyes again. The lids were pale, translucent. She seemed very vulnerable and Fallon went down the stairs full of controlled, ice-cold anger.

He dropped to one knee beside Billy Meehan, took out a handkerchief, wrapped it around the handle of the scissors and pulled them out. There was very little blood and obviously most of the bleeding was internal.

He cleaned the scissors, then went to the door and picked up the boy's overcoat. Some car keys fell to the floor. He picked them up mechanically, then draped the coat across the body.

As he looked down at it, he was conscious only of disgust

and loathing. The world was well rid of Billy Meehan. His ending had been richly deserved, but could Anna da Costa live with the knowledge that she had killed him? And even if the verdict of the court was as it should be—even if she were exonerated, the whole world would know. At the thought of the shame, the humiliation for that gentle creature, Fallon's anger was so great that he kicked the corpse in the side.

And in the same moment, a thought came to him that was so incredible it almost took his breath away. What if she didn't have to know, now or ever? What if Billy Meehan vanished utterly and completely from the face of the earth as if he had never existed? There was a way. It could be done. In any event, he owed it to her to try.

The keys which had fallen from the overcoat pocket indicated the presence of Billy's car somewhere in the vicinity, and if it was the red Scimitar, it should be easy enough to find. Fallon let himself out the front door, hurried through the cemetery to the side gate.

The Scimitar was parked at the curb only a few yards away. He unlocked the tailgate and when he opened it, Tommy, the grey whippet, barked once, then nuzzled his hand. The presence of the dog was unfortunate, but couldn't be helped. Fallon closed the tailgate and hurried back to the presbytery.

He pulled off the overcoat and went through the boy's pockets systematically, emptying them of everything they held. He removed a gold medallion on a chain around the neck, a signet ring and a wrist-watch and put them in his pocket, then he wrapped the body in the overcoat, heaved it over his shoulder and went out.

He paused at the gate to make sure that the coast was clear, but the street was silent and deserted. He crossed to the Scimitar quickly, heaved up the tailgate with one hand and dumped the body inside. The whippet started to whine almost immediately and he closed the tailgate quickly and went back to the presbytery.

He washed the scissors thoroughly in hot water in the

kitchen, went back to the sitting-room and replaced them in the sewing box. Then he poured a little brandy in a glass and took it upstairs.

She was already half asleep, but sat up to drink the brandy. Fallon said, "What about your uncle? Do you want him to know what happened?"

"Yes—yes, I think so. It's right that he should know."

"All right," Fallon said, and he tucked the quilt around her. "Go to sleep now. I'll be downstairs. You've nothing to worry about. I'll wait till your uncle comes back."

"He might be hours," she said sleepily.

"That's all right."

He walked to the door. "I'm sorry to be such a nuisance," she whispered.

"I brought you to this," he said. "If it hadn't been for me, none of this would have happened."

"It's pointless to talk like that," she said. "There's a purpose to everything under heaven—a reason—even for my blindness. We can't always see it because we're such little people, but it's there."

He was strangely comforted by her words, God knows why. "Go to sleep now," he said softly, and closed the door.

Time, now, was the critical factor and he quietly let himself out the front door and hurried through the churchyard to the Scimitar.

Strangely enough, the whippet gave him no trouble during the drive. It crouched in the rear beside the body, whining only occasionally, although when he put a hand on it, it trembled.

He approached Pine Trees Crematorium by the back lane Varley had used that morning, getting out of the car to open the five-barred gate that led into the estate. He followed the same narrow track down through the cypress trees, cutting the engine for the last hundred yards which was slightly down-hill. Not that it mattered, for as he remembered it, the super-intendent's house and the main gate were a good quarter of a mile from the crematorium itself, so noise was really no problem.

He left the Scimitar at the side of the chapel and gained access by reaching in through the broken pane in the lavatory which he had noticed during his visit that morning and unfastening the window itself.

The chapel door had a Yale lock so it opened easily enough from the inside. He returned to the Scimitar. There was a torch in the glove compartment which he slipped into his pocket, then he raised the tailgate and heaved the body over his shoulder. The whippet tried to follow, but he managed to shove it back inside with his free hand and closed the tailgate again.

He gained access to the furnace room by sliding the body along the rollers of the movable belt and crawling through after it himself, following the route the coffin had taken that morning.

The furnaces were cold and dark. He opened the door of the first one and shoved the body inside. Next he produced the various items he had taken from Billy Meehan's pockets and examined them in the light of the torch. Those things which would burn, he placed on top of his body. The ring, the watch and the medal he put back in his pocket. Then he closed the oven door and pressed the switch.

He could hear the muted rumble of the gas jets as they roared into life and peered inside. What was it Meehan had said? An hour at the most. He lit a cigarette, opened the back door and went outside.

The sound of the furnace in operation was barely discernible outside the building. Not at all when he moved a few yards away. He went back inside to see what was happening. The gauge was just coming up to the thousand degrees centigrade mark and as he peered through the observation panel in the door, the wallet he had left on the body's chest burst into flames. The clothing was already smouldering, there was a sudden bright flash, and the whole body started to burn.

He lit another cigarette, went and stood at the back door, and waited.

* * *

At the end of the specified period he switched off. There was part of the skull, the pelvic girdle and some of the limbs clearly visible, and much of this crumbled into even smaller pieces at the first touch of the rake.

He filled the tin box, found a handbrush and shovel, carefully swept up every trace of ash that he could see, then closed the furnace door and left it exactly as he had found it. Certainly all heat would be dissipated again before the morning.

He found an empty urn, screwed it on the bottom of the pulveriser then poured in the contents of the tin box. He clamped down the lid and switched on. While he was waiting, he opened the desk drawer and helped himself to a blank Rest-in-Peace card.

When he switched off about two minutes later and unscrewed the urn, all that was left of Billy Meehan was about five pounds of grey ash.

He walked along the path to the point Meehan had taken him to that morning until he came across a gardener's wheelbarrow and various tools, indicating where the man had stopped work that afternoon.

Fallon checked the number plate and strewed the ashes carefully. Then he took a besom from the wheelbarrow and worked them well in. When he was satisfied, he replaced the besom exactly as he had found it, turned and walked away.

It was when he reached the Scimitar that he ran into his first snag. As he opened the door to get behind the wheel, the whippet slipped through his legs and scampered away.

Fallon went after it fast. It went round the corner of the chapel and followed the path he had just used. When he reached the place where he had strewn the ashes, the whippet was crouching in the wet grass, whining very softly.

Fallon picked him up and fondled his ears, talking softly to him as he walked back. When he got behind the wheel this time, he held on to the animal until he had closed the door. He put it in the rear seat and drove away quickly.

It was only after he had closed the five-barred gate behind him and turned into the main road again that he allowed that iron composure of his to give a little. He gave a long, shuddering sigh, a partial release of tension, and when he lit a cigarette his hands were trembling.

It had worked and there was a kind of elation in that. For a while it had seemed that Billy Meehan might prove to be just as malignant an influence in death as he had been in life, but not now. He had ceased to exist, had been wiped clean off the face of the earth, and Fallon felt not even a twinge of compunction.

As far as he was concerned, Billy Meehan had been from under a stone, not fit to wipe Anna da Costa's shoes. Let be.

When he reached Paul's Square, he turned into the mews entrance cautiously, but luck was with him to the very end. The yard was deserted. He ran the Scimitar into the garage, left both the keys and the whippet inside and walked rapidly away.

When he got back to the presbytery, there was no sign of Father da Costa. Fallon went upstairs on tiptoe and peered into Anna's bedroom. She was sleeping soundly so he closed her door and went back downstairs.

He went into the sitting room and checked the carpet carefully, but there was no sign of blood. So that was very much that. He went to the sideboard and poured himself a large whisky. As he was adding a dash of soda, the front door opened.

Fallon turned round as Father da Costa entered the room. The priest stopped short in amazement. "Fallon, what are you doing here?" And then he turned very pale and said, "Oh, dear God! Anna!"

He turned and moved to the stairs, and Fallon went after him. "She's all right. She's sleeping."

Father da Costa turned slowly. "What happened?"

"There was an intruder," Fallon said. "I arrived in time to chase him away."

"One of Meehan's men?"

Fallon shrugged. "Maybe—I didn't get a good look at him."

Father da Costa paced up and down the hall, fingers intertwined so tightly that the knuckles turned white. "Oh, my God!" he said. "When will it all end?"

"I'm leaving on Sunday night," Fallon told him. "They've arranged passage for me on a ship out of Hull."

"And you think that will finish it?" Father da Costa shook his head. "You're a fool, Fallon. Jack Meehan will never feel safe while I am still in the land of the living. Trust, honor, truth, the sanctity of the given word. None of these exist for him personally so why should he believe that they have a meaning for someone else?"

"All right," Fallon said. "It's my fault. What do you want me to do?"

"There's only one thing you can do," Father da Costa said. "Set me free in the only way possible."

"And spend my life in a maximum security cell?" Fallon shook his head. "I'm not that kind of hero."

He walked to the front door and Father da Costa said, "She *is* all right?"

Fallon nodded soberly. "A good night's rest is all she needs. She's a much stronger person than you realize. In every way."

He turned to go out and Father da Costa said, "That you arrived when you did was most fortuitous."

"All right," Fallon said. "So I was watching the house."

Father da Costa shook his head sadly. "You see, my friend, good deeds in spite of yourself. You are a lost man."

"Go to hell!" Fallon said. He plunged out into the rain and walked rapidly away.

13

The Church
Militant

Father da Costa was packing his vestment into a small suitcase when Anna went into the study. It was a grey morning, that eternal rain still tapping at the window. She was a little paler than usual, but otherwise seemed quite composed. Her hair was tied back with a black ribbon, and she wore a neat grey skirt and sweater.

Father da Costa took both her hands and led her to the fire. "Are you all right?"

"I'm fine," she said. "Truly I am. Are you going out?"

"I'm afraid I have to. One of the nuns at the convent school of Our Lady of Pity died yesterday. Sister Marie Gabrielle. They've asked me to officiate." He hesitated. "I don't like leaving you."

"Nonsense," she said. "I'll be all right. Sister Claire will be bringing up the children from the junior school for choir practice at ten-thirty. I have a private lesson after that until twelve."

"Fine," he said. "I'll be back by then."

He picked up his case and she took his arm, and they went through to the hall together. "You'll need your raincoat."

He shook his head. "The umbrella will be enough." He opened the door and hesitated. "I've been thinking, Anna. Perhaps you should go away for a while. Just until this thing is settled one way or the other."

"No!" she said firmly.

He put down his case and took her by the shoulders standing there in the half-open doorway. "I've never felt so helpless. So confused. After what happened last night, I thought of speaking to Miller."

"But you can't do that," she said quickly—too quickly. "Not without involving Fallon."

He gazed at her searchingly. "You like him, don't you?"

"It's not the word I would choose," she said calmly. "I feel for him. He has been marked by life. No, used by life in an unfair way. Spoiled utterly." There was a sudden passion in her voice. "No one could have the music in him that man has and have no soul. God could not be so inhuman."

"The greatest gift God gave to man was free will, my dear. Good and evil. Each man has a free choice in the matter."

"All right," she said fiercely. "I only know one thing with any certainty. When I needed help last night, more than I have ever needed in my life before, it was Fallon who saved me."

"I know," Father da Costa told her. "He was watching the house."

Her entire expression changed, color touched those pale cheeks. "And you don't care what happens to him?"

"Oh, I care," Father da Costa said gravely. "More than you perhaps understand. I see a man of genius brought down to the level of the gutter. I see a human being—a fine human being—committing, for his own dark reasons, a kind of personal suicide."

"Then help him," she said.

"To help himself?" Father da Costa shook his head sadly. "That only works in books. Seldom in life. Whoever he is, this man who calls himself Martin Fallon, one thing is certain. He hates himself for what he has done, for what he has become. He is devoured by self-loathing."

By now she looked completely bewildered. "I don't understand this—not any of it."

"He is a man who seeks Death at every turn, Anna. Who would welcome him with open arms. Oh yes, I care what happens to Martin Fallon—care passionately. The tragedy is that he does not."

He turned and, leaving her there in the porch, hurried away through the churchyard, head down against the rain, not bothering to raise his umbrella. When he moved into the side porch to unlock the sacristy door, Fallon was sitting on the small bench leaning against the corner, head on his chest, hands in the pockets of his trenchcoat.

Father da Costa shook him by the shoulder and Fallon raised his head and opened his eyes instantly. He badly needed a shave and the skin of his face seemed to have tightened over the cheekbones and the eyes were vacant.

"A long night," Father da Costa said gently.

"Time to think," Fallon said in a strange, dead voice. "About a lot of things."

"Any conclusions?"

"Oh yes." Fallon stood up and moved out into the rain. "The right place for me, a cemetery." He turned to face da Costa, a slight smile on his lips. "You see, Father, I've finally realized one very important thing."

"And what's that?" Father da Costa asked him.

"That I can't live with myself anymore."

He turned and walked away very quickly and Father da Costa moved out into the rain, one hand extended as if he would pull him back.

"Fallon," he called hoarsely.

A few rooks lifted out of the tree on the other side of the churchyard, fluttering in the wild like a handful of dirty black rags, calling angrily. As they settled again, Fallon turned the corner of the church and was gone.

*　*　*

When Anna closed the front door of the presbytery and went down the steps, she was instantly aware of the organ. She stood quite still, looking across the cemetery towards the church, head slightly turned as she listened. The playing, of course, was quite unmistakable. The heart quickened inside her, she hurried along the path as fast as she dared, tip-tapping with her stick.

When she opened the sacristy door, the music seemed to fill the church. He was playing the *Pavane for a Dead Infanta*, infinitely moving, touching the very heart of things, the deep places of life, brilliant technique and emotion combining in a way she would never have thought possible.

He finished on a dying fall and sat, shoulders hunched, for a long moment as the last echoes died away. When he swung round on the stool, she was standing at the altar rail.

"I've never heard such playing," she told him.

He went down through the choir stalls and stood on the other side of the rail from her. "Good funeral music."

His words touched the heart of her like a cold finger. "You mustn't speak like that." She forced a smile. "Did you want to see me?"

"Let's say I hoped you'd come."

"Here I am, then."

"I want you to give your uncle a message. Tell him I'm sorry, more sorry than I can say, but I intend to put things right. You'll have nothing more to worry about, either of you. He has my word on that."

"But how?" she said. "I don't understand."

"My affair," Fallon told her calmly. "I started it, I'll finish it. Goodbye, Anna da Costa. You won't see me again."

"I never have," she said sadly, and put a hand on his arm as he went by. "Isn't that a terrible thing?"

He backed away slowly and delicately, making not the slightest sound. Her face changed. She put out a hand uncertainly. "Mr. Fallon?" she said softly. "Are you there?"

Fallon moved quickly towards the door. It creaked when he

opened it and as he turned to look at her for the last time, she called, "Martin, come back!" and there was terrible desperation in her voice.

Fallon went out, the door closed with a sigh, and Anna da Costa, tears streaming down her face, fell on her knees at the altar rail.

The Little Sisters of Pity were not only teachers. They also had an excellent record in medical missionary work overseas, which was where Father da Costa had first met Sister Marie Gabrielle in 1951, in Korea. A fierce little Frenchwoman who was probably the kindest, most loving person he had met in his entire life. Four years in a communist prison camp had ruined her health, but that indomitable spirit, that all-embracing love, had not been touched in the slightest.

Some of the nuns, being human, were crying as they sang the offertory: *"Domine Jesu Christe, Rex Gloriae, libera animas omnium fidelium . . ."*

The voices rose sweetly to the rafters of the tiny convent chapel as Father de Costa prayed for the repose of Sister Marie Gabrielle's soul, for all sinners everywhere whose actions only cut them off from the infinite blessing of God's love. For Anna, that she might come to no harm. For Martin Fallon, that he might face what must be done. And for Dandy Jack Meehan . . .

But here, a terrible thing happened, for his throat went dry and he seemed to choke on the very name.

Once the Mass was over and the absolutions given, the nuns carried the coffin out through the rain to the small private cemetery in a corner between the inner and outer walls of the convent.

At the gravesite Father da Costa sprinkled the grave and the coffin with holy water and incensed them and after he had prayed, some of the nuns lit candles, with some difficulty because of the rain, to symbolize Sister Marie Gabrielle's soul, with God now and shining still, and they sang together, very sweetly, the Twenty-third Psalm which had been her favorite.

Father da Costa remembered her, for a moment, during those last days, the broken body racked with pain. Oh God, he thought, why is it the good who suffer? People like Sister Marie Gabrielle?"

And then there was Anna. So gentle, so loving, and at the thought of what had taken place the night before, black rage filled his heart.

Try as he might, the only thought that would come to mind as he looked down into the open grave was that Meehan's firm had probably made the coffin.

Jenny Fox had taken two sleeping pills the previous night and overslept. It was after eleven when she awakened and she put on her dressing-gown and went downstairs. She went into the kitchen and found Fallon sitting at the table, the bottle of Irish whiskey in front of him, a half-filled tumbler at his elbow. He had taken the Ceska to pieces and was putting it carefully together again. The silencer was also on the table next to the whiskey bottle.

"You're starting early," she commented.

"A long time since I had a drink," he said. "A real drink. Now I've had four. I had some thinking to do."

He emptied his glass in a single swallow, rammed the magazine into the butt of the Ceska and screwed the silencer on the end of the barrel.

Jenny said wearily, "Did you come to any conclusions?"

"Oh yes, I think you could say that." He poured himself another whiskey and tossed it down. "I've decided to start a 'Jack Meehan must go' campaign. A sort of one man crusade, if you like."

"You must be crazy," she said. "You wouldn't stand a chance."

"He'll be sending for me some time today, Jenny. He has to because he's shipping me out from Hull tomorrow night, so we've got things to discuss."

He squinted along the barrel of the gun and Jenny whispered, "What are you going to do?"

"I'm going to kill the bastard," he said simply. "You know what Shakespeare said. A good deed in a naughty world."

He was drunk, she realized that, but in his own peculiar way. "Don't be a fool," she said desperately. "Kill him and there'll be no passage out of Hull for you. What happens then?"

"I couldn't really care less."

He flung up his arm and fired. There was a dull thud, and a small china dog on the top shelf above the refrigerator shattered into fragments.

"Well now," he said. "If I can hit that at this range after half a bottle of whiskey, I don't see how I can very well miss Dandy Jack."

He stood up and picked up the bottle of whiskey. Jenny said, "Martin, listen to me for God's sake."

He walked past her to the door. "I didn't go to bed last night so I will now. Wake me if Meehan calls, but whatever happens, don't let me sleep past five o'clock. I've got things to do."

He went out, and she stood there listening as he mounted the stairs. She heard the door of his bedroom open and close, and only then did she move, going down on her hands and knees wearily to pick up the shattered fragments of the china dog.

The Bull and Bell yard was not far from Paul's Square, a dirty and sunless cobbled alley named after the public house which had stood there for two hundred years or more. Beside the entrance to the snug stood several overflowing dustbins and cardboard boxes and packing cases thrown together in an untidy heap.

The Bull and Bell itself did most of its trade in the evening, which was why Jack Meehan preferred to patronize it in the afternoon. For one thing it meant that he could have the snug to himself, which was handy for business of a certain kind.

He sat on a stool, a tankard of beer at his elbow, finishing a roast beef sandwich and reading the *Financial Times*. Donner was sitting in the window seat playing solitaire.

Meehan emptied his tankard and pushed it across the bar. "Same again, Harry."

Harry was a large, hefty young man who, in spite of his white apron, had the physique of a professional Rugby player. He had long dark sideburns and a cold, rather dangerous looking face.

As he filled the tankard and pushed it across, the door opened and Rupert and Bonati came in. Rupert was wearing a sort of caped, ankle-length highwayman's coat in large checks.

He shook himself vigorously and unbuttoned his coat. "When's it going to stop, that's what I'd like to know."

Meehan drank some more beer and belched. He said, "What in the hell do you want? Who's minding the shop?"

Rupert slid gracefully on to the stool next to him and put a hand on his thigh. "I do have to eat some time, ducky. I mean, I need to keep my strength up, don't I?"

"All right, Harry." Meehan said, "Give him his Bloody Mary."

Rupert said, "By the way, does anyone know where Billy is?"

"I haven't seen him since last night," Meehan told him. "Who wants him, anyway?"

"The superintendent of Pine Trees phoned into the office just before I left."

"And what did he want?"

"It seems they found Billy's whippet wandering about up there. Soaked to the skin and trembling like a leaf apparently. Wanted to know what to do with him."

Meehan frowned. "What in the hell would it be doing up there?"

Donner said, "Last I saw it, was about half past eight this morning when I went into the garage. It was inside the Scimitar. I figured Billy had forgotten about it when he came in last night, so I let it out. I mean, he's done that before when he's been pissed or something. Left Tommy in the car, I mean."

"He still hadn't come in when I came out this morning," Meehan said, "and if he left his car in the garage, that means he went to one of the city center clubs. Probably still in bed with some whore, the dirty little bastard." He turned to Bonati. "You'd better go up to Pine Trees and get it. Take it back home and give it something to eat."

"All right, Mr. Meehan," Bonati said, and went out.

Meehan swallowed some more beer. "Inconsiderate little swine. I'll kick his arse for him when I see him."

"He's young, Mr. Meehan," Harry said. "He'll learn."

He picked up a bucket of slops, moved from behind the bar, and opened the door and went out into the yard. As he emptied the bucket across the cobbles, Father da Costa entered the yard. He was wearing his cassock and held the umbrella over his head against the rain.

Harry looked him over in some amazement, and Father da Costa said politely, "I'm looking for Mr. Meehan—Mr. Jack Meehan. They told me at his office that I might find him here."

"Inside," Harry said.

He moved into the snug and Father da Costa followed, pausing just inside the door to put down his umbrella.

It was Rupert who saw him first in the mirror behind the bar. "Good God Almighty!" he said.

There was a long silence, and Meehan turned on his stool very slowly. "And what in the hell are you doing here? Rattling the box for Christmas or something? Will a quid get rid of you?"

He took out his wallet ostentatiously and Father da Costa said quietly, "I was hoping we might have a few words in private."

He stood there with the umbrella in his hand, the skirts of his cassock soaking wet from the long grass of the convent cemetery, mud on his shoes, grey beard tangled, waiting for some sort of response.

Meehan laughed out loud. "God, but I wish you could see yourself. You look bloody ridiculous. Men in skirts." He shook his head. "It'll never catch on."

Father da Costa said patiently, "I don't expect it will. Now can we talk?"

Meehan indicated Donner and Rupert with a wave of the hand. "There's nothing you can say to me that these two can't hear."

"Very well," Father da Costa said. "It's simple enough. I want you to stay away from Holy Name and I don't want any repetition of what happened at the presbytery last night."

Meehan frowned. "What in the hell are you talking about?"

"All right, Mr. Meehan," Father da Costa said wearily. "Last night, someone broke into the presbytery when I was out, and attacked my niece. If Fallon hadn't arrived at the right moment and chased the man away, anything might have happened to her. On the other hand, I suppose you'll now tell me that you know nothing about it."

"No, I bloody well don't," Meehan shouted.

Father da Costa struggled to contain his anger. "You're lying," he said simply.

Meehan's face was suffused with blood, the eyes bulging. "Who in the hell do you think you are?" he demanded hoarsely.

"It's my final warning," Father da Costa said. "When we last spoke I told you my God was a God of Wrath as well as of Love. You'd do well to remember that."

Meehan's face was purple with rage and he turned to the barman in fury. "Get him out of here!"

Harry lifted the bar flap and moved out. "Right, on your way, mate."

"I'll go when I'm ready," Father da Costa told him.

Harry's right hand fastened on his collar, the other on his belt and they went through the door on the run to a chorus of laughter from Donner and Rupert. They crowded to the door to see the fun, and Meehan joined them.

Father da Costa was on his hands and knees in the rain in a puddle of water. "What's up, ducky?" Rupert called. "Have you pissed yourself or something?"

It was a stupid remark, childish in its vulgarity. And yet it was some sort of final straw that set black rage boiling inside Father da Costa, so that when Harry dragged him to his feet, an arm about his throat, he reacted as he had been taught to react thirty years earlier in that hard, brutal school of guerrilla warfare and action by night.

Harry was grinning widely. "We don't like fancy sods like you coming round here annoying the customers."

He didn't get a chance to say anything else. Father da Costa's right elbow swung back into his ribs, and he pivoted on one foot as Harry reeled back, gasping.

"You should never let anyone get that close. They haven't been teaching you properly."

Harry sprang forward, his right fist swinging in a tremendous punch. Father da Costa swayed to one side, grabbed for the wrist with both hands, twisted it round and up, locking the arm and ran headfirst into the stack of packing cases.

As Father da Costa turned, Donner came in fast and received a kick under the right kneecap, perfectly delivered, that doubled him over in pain and Father da Costa followed with a knee in the face that lifted him back against the wall.

Rupert gave a cry of dismay and in his haste to regain the safety of the snug, slipped on the top step, bringing Meehan down with him. As Meehan started to get up, Father da Costa punched him in the face, a good, solid right hand that carried all his rage, all his frustrations with it. Bone crunched. Meehan's nose flattened beneath Father da Costa's knuckles, and he fell back into the snug with a groan, blood gushing from his nostrils.

Rupert scrambled behind the bar on his hands and knees, and Father da Costa stood over Meehan, the killing rage still on him, his fists clenched. And then, as he looked down at his hands and saw the blood on them, an expression of horror appeared on his face.

He backed slowly out into the yard. Harry lay on his face amongst the packing cases. Donner was being sick against the wall. Father da Costa looked once again in horror at the blood on his hands, turned and fled.

* * *

When he went into his study at the presbytery, Anna was sitting by the fire knitting. She turned her face towards him. "You're late. I was worried."

He was still extremely agitated and had to force himself to sound calm. "I'm sorry. Something came up."

She put down her knitting and stood up. "After you'd gone, when I went down to the church to get ready for choir practice, Fallon was playing the organ."

He frowned. "Did he say anything? Did you speak with him?"

"He gave me a message for you," she told him. "He said to tell you that it had all been his fault and he was sorry."

"Was there anything else?"

"Yes, he said that there was no need to worry from now on. That he'd started it, so he'd finish it. And he told me we wouldn't be seeing him again. What did he mean? Do you think he intends to give himself up?"

"God knows," Father da Costa forced a smile and put a hand on her shoulder, a gesture of reassurance. "I'm just going down to the church. Something I have to do. I won't be long."

He left her there and hurried down through the cemetery, entering the church by way of the sacristy. He dropped on his knees at the altar rail, hands clenched together and looked up at Christ on the cross.

"Forgive me," he pleaded. "Heavenly Father, forgive me."

He bowed his head and wept, for in his heart, he knew there was not one single particle of regret for what he had done to Jack Meehan. Worse than that, much worse, was the still, small voice that kept telling him that by wiping Meehan off the face of the earth he would be doing mankind a favor.

Meehan came out of the bathroom at the penthouse, wearing a silk kimono and holding an ice-bag to his face. The doctor had been and gone, the bleeding had stopped, but his nose was an ugly, swollen, bruised hump of flesh that would never look the same again. Donner, Bonati and Rupert waited dutifully by the door. Donner's mouth was badly bruised and his lower lip was twice its usual size.

Meehan tossed the ice-bag across the room. "No bloody good at all, that thing. Somebody get me a drink."

Rupert hurried to the drinks trolley and poured a large brandy. He carried it across to Meehan, who was standing at the window, staring out in the square, frowning slightly.

He turned, suddenly and mysteriously his old self again.

He said to Donner, "Frank, what was the name of that old kid who was so good with explosives?"

"Ellerman, Mr. Meehan, is he the one you're thinking of?"

"That's him. He isn't inside, is he?"

"Not that I know of."

"Good, then I want him here within the next hour. You go get him, and you can tell him there's a couple of centuries in it for him."

He swallowed some more of his brandy and turned to Rupert. "And you, sweetheart—I've got just the job for you. You can go and see Jenny for me. We're going to need her, too, for what I have in mind."

Rupert said, "Do you think she'll play? She can be an awkward bitch, when she feels like it."

"Not this time," Meehan chuckled. "I'll give you a proposition to put to her that she can't refuse."

He laughed again as if it was a particularly good joke and Rupert glanced uncertainly at Donner. Donner said carefully, "What's it all about, Mr. Meehan?"

"I've had enough," Meehan said. "That's what it's all about. The priest, Fallon, the whole bit. I'm going to clean the slate once and for all. Take them both out this very night, and here's how we're going to do it."

Harvey Ellerman was fifty years of age and looked ten years older, which came of having spent twenty-two years of his life behind bars if he added his various sentences together.

He was a small diffident individual who habitually wore a

567

tweed cap and brown raincoat and seemed crushed by life, yet this small, anxious-looking man was reputed to know more about explosives than any man in the north of England. In the end, his own genius had proved his undoing. Such was the uniqueness of his approach to the task in hand that it was as if he had signed his own name each time he did a job, and for some years the police had arrested him with monotonous regularity the moment he put a foot wrong.

He came out of the lift into the penthouse, followed by Donner, holding a cheap fiber suitcase in one hand that was bound together by a cheap leather strap. Meehan went to meet him, hand extended, and Ellerman put the suitcase down.

"Great to see you, Harvey," Meehan said. "Hope you'll be able to help. Did Frank explain what I'm after?"

"He did, Mr. Meehan, in a manner of speaking," Ellerman hesitated. "You won't want me personally on this thing, Mr. Meehan? There's no question of that?"

"Of course not," Meehan told him.

Ellerman looked relieved. "It's just that I've retired from active participation in anything, Mr. Meehan," he said. "You know how it is?"

"Too true, I do, Harvey. You were too bloody good for them." He picked up Ellerman's suitcase and put it down on the table. "Okay, let's see what you've got."

Ellerman unfastened the strap and opened the suitcase. It contained a varied assortment of explosives carefully packed in tins, a selection of fuses and detonators, neat coils of wire and a rack of tools.

"Frank told me you wanted something similar to the sort of thing the IRA have been using in Ireland."

"Not just similar, Harvey. I want it to be exactly the same. When the forensic boys get to examine what's left of this bomb I don't want there to be the slightest doubt in their minds where it's come from."

"All right, Mr. Meehan," Ellerman said in his flat, colorless voice. "Just as you say." He produced a tin from the case. "We'll use this, then. A Waverley biscuit tin. Made in Belfast. Packed with plastic gelignite. Say twenty pounds. That should do the trick."

"What about a fuse?"

Ellerman held up a long, slim, dark pencil. "They've been using a lot of these things lately. Chemical fuse of Russian manufacture. Virtually foolproof. Once you break the cap seal you've got twenty minutes."

"Just the job," Meehan rubbed his hands together. "You'd better get started, then."

He turned and walked across to the window, whistling happily.

14

Grimsdyke

Fallon came awake to find Jenny shaking him by the shoulder. "Wake up!" she kept saying insistently. "Wake up!"

There was a slight persistent throbbing ache behind his right eye, but otherwise he felt strangely light-headed. He sat up, swinging his legs to the floor, and ran his hands over his stubbled chin.

"What time is it?" he asked her.

"About four. Your friend, Father da Costa, was on the phone. He wants to see you."

Fallon straightened slowly and looked at her, a slight, puzzled frown on his face. "When was this?"

"About ten minutes ago. I wanted to come and get you, but he said there wasn't time."

"And where does he want to see me? At Holy Name?"

She shook her head. "No, he said he was taking his niece into the country. He thought it would be safer for her. A little place called Grimsdyke. It's about twenty miles from here in the marshes. He wants you to meet him there as soon as possible."

"I see," Fallon said. "Do you know where this place is?"

She nodded. "I used to go there for picnics when I was a

570

kid. I've never been to this place he's going to, Mill House, he called it, but he told me how to get there."

Fallon nodded slowly. "And you'd take me?"

"If you like. We could go in my car. It wouldn't take much more than half an hour."

He stared at her, the eyes very dark, no expression there at all. She glanced away nervously, unable to meet his gaze, and flushed angrily. "Look, it's no skin off my nose. Do you want to go or don't you?"

He knew she was lying, yet it didn't seem to matter because for some strange reason he knew beyond any shadow of a doubt that she was leading him in the right direction.

"All right," he said. "Fine. Just give me a couple of minutes to get cleaned up. I'll meet you downstairs."

As soon as she had gone he took the Ceska from his jacket pocket, ejected the magazine, reloaded carefully with eight rounds and slipped it into the right-hand pocket of his trenchcoat.

He moved across to the window, dropped to one knee and raised the carpet to disclose a Browning automatic he had used at his first meeting with Kristou in London. Underneath it was a large buff envelope containing the best part of two thousand pounds in ten-pound notes, the bulk of the money he had received from Meehan. He slipped the envelope into his breast pocket and checked the Browning quickly.

He found a roll of surgical tape in the cabinet over the washbasin and cut off a couple of lengths, using the razor Jenny had loaned him, then taped the Browning to the inside of his left leg just above the anklebone, covering it with his sock.

He buttoned his trenchcoat as he went downstairs. Jenny was waiting in the hall, dressed in a real plastic mac. She gave him a tight smile as she pulled on her gloves. "Ready to go, then?"

He opened the front door, but stopped her with a hand on her shoulder as she was about to step outside. "There isn't anything else, is there? Anything you've forgotten to tell me?"

She flushed, and the anger was in her voice again. "Would I be likely to do a thing like that?"

"That's all right, then." He smiled calmly. "We'd better get going."

He closed the door and followed her down the steps to the Mini-Cooper parked at the bottom.

The marsh at Grimsdyke on the river estuary was a wild, lonely place of sea-creeks and mud flats and great, pale barriers of reeds higher than a man's head. Since the beginning of history men had come here for one purpose or another, Roman, Saxon, Dane, Norman, but now it was a place of ghosts. An alien world inhabited mainly by the birds, curlew and redshank and brent geese coming south from Siberia for the winter on the mud flats.

They passed through the village, a pleasant enough little place. Thirty or forty houses, a garage and pub, and then they were out on the other side. It was raining quite hard, and wind driving it in off the sea and across the marshes in great clouds.

"Half a mile beyond the village on the right." Jenny glanced at Fallon briefly. "That's what the man said."

"This looks like it," Fallon told her.

She turned the Cooper off the main road and followed a track no wider than a farm cart that was little more than a raised causeway of grass. On either side miles of rough marsh grass and reeds marched into the heavy rain, and a thin sea mist was drifting before the wind.

Fallon lowered the window on his side and took a deep breath of the pungent salt air. "Quite a place.'

"I used to love coming here when I was a kid," she said. "It was like nowhere else on earth. A different world after the city."

The closer they got to the estuary, the more the mist seemed to close in on them and then they topped a rise and saw what was very obviously the mill sticking up above a clump of trees about a hundred yards to the south of them.

Fallon put a hand on her arm, and she braked to a halt. "Now what?"

"We'll walk from here."

"Is that necessary?"

"If I've learned anything in life it's never to take anything for granted."

She shrugged, but got out of the car without further argument. Fallon left the track and forced his way through a fir plantation towards the mill, dimly seen through the trees.

He crouched under a bush, pulling Jenny down beside him and examined the place carefully. There was a three-storeyed stone tower, roof open to the sky. At one end there was an extension made of wood, which looked like a barn and seemed to be in a better state of repair than the rest of the building. A thin trickle of smoke drifted up from an iron chimney.

At the other side there was an immense water-wheel and it was moving round now with an unearthly creaking and groaning, forced by the rushing waters of the flooded stream.

"No sign of his Mini van," Fallon said softly.

"He'll have it inside that barn, won't he?" Jenny replied, and then added impatiently. "For goodness sake, make your mind up. Are we going on or aren't we? I'm getting wet."

She seemed angry and yet the fingers on her left hand trembled slightly. He said, "You go. Give me a call if everything is all right."

She glanced at him with a certain surprise in her eyes, then shrugged, stood up and walked out into the open. He watched her go, all the way to the barn. She turned to look at him once, then opened the big double door and went in.

She reappeared a moment later and called, "It's all right. Everything's fine. Come on."

Fallon hesitated for a moment and then shrugged and walked out into the clearing, a slight, fixed smile on his face. When he was four or five yards from the door, Jenny said, "They're here," then went back inside.

He followed her in without hesitation. The place smelled of

old hay and mice. There was a decrepit cart in one corner and a large loft ran round three sides of the building with round glassless windows letting in light. A fire was burning in an old iron stove in the corner.

There was no sign of Father da Costa or Anna, not that Fallon had really expected there to be. Only Jenny, standing alone beside a small iron cot bed against the far wall on which a little fair-haired girl was apparently sleeping, covered by a blanket.

"I'm sorry, Martin," she said. There was genuine distress in her face now. "I didn't have any choice."

"Up here Fallon," a voice called.

Fallon looked up and saw Donner on the edge of the loft holding an Armalite rifle. Rupert was standing beside him clutching a sawn-off shotgun and Harry, the barman from the Bull and Bell, appeared in the loft at the other side of the building, some sort of revolver in his hand.

Donner raised the Armalite a little. "They tell me that a bullet from one of these things goes in at the front and out at the back and takes a sizeable piece of you with it on the way, so I'd advise you to stay very still."

"Oh, I will," Fallon assured him without irony. And he raised his hands.

Harry came down the ladder from the loft first. He looked terrible. His left eye was completely closed and one side of his face was very badly bruised. He stood a yard or two away, covering Fallon with his revolver while Rupert followed him down the ladder. When they were both in position, Donner lowered the Armalite and joined them.

"Never trust a woman, ducky," Rupert said with a mocking smile. "I'd have thought you'd have learnt that. Unreliable bitches, the lot of them. Ruled by the moon. Now me, for instance . . ."

Donner kicked him in the leg. "Shut up and search him. He'll probably have the shooter in his right-hand pocket."

Rupert found the Ceska at once and the buff envelope containing the money. Donner looked inside and whistled softly. "How much?" he demanded.

"Two thousand," Fallon said.

Donner grinned. "That must be what they meant by an unexpected bonus."

He put the envelope in his inside pocket and Rupert started to run his hands over Fallon's body. "Lovely," he breathed. "I could really go for you, ducky." He patted Fallon's cheek.

Fallon sent him staggering back with a stiff right arm. "Put a hand on me again, and I'll break your neck."

Rupert's eyes glittered and he picked up the sawn-off shotgun and thumbed back the hammer. "My, my, aren't we butch?" he said softly. "But I can soon fix that."

Donner kicked him in the backside. "You bloody stupid little bitch," he cried. "What are you trying to do? Ruin everything at this stage?" He shoved him violently away. "Go on and make some tea. It's all you're fit for."

Rupert moved over to the stove sullenly, still clutching his shotgun, and Donner took a pair of regulation police handcuffs from his pocket. He snapped them around Fallon's wrists, locked them and slipped the key into his breast pocket.

"You can have it the hard way, or you can have it easy," he said. "It's all one to me. Understand?"

"I always try to," Fallon said.

"Right, go and sit down by the bird, where I can keep an eye on both of you."

Fallon moved across to the cot and sat down beside it, his back against the wall. He looked at the child. Her eyes were closed, the breathing easy.

"The daughter you told me about?" he said. "Is she all right?"

She nodded. "They gave her a sedative, that's all." Her eyes were bright with tears. "I'm sorry, Martin, I didn't have any choice. I collected her after lunch like I do every Saturday, and took her to the playground in the local park. That's where Rupert and that creep Harry picked us up."

575

"And they threatened you?"

"They said they'd hang on to Sally. That I could have her back if I managed to get you out here." She put a hand on his arm. "What else could I do? I was terrified. You don't know Jack Meehan like I do. He's capable of anything—just like Billy."

"Billy will never bother you again," Fallon said. "I killed him last night."

She stared at him, eyes wide. "You what?"

"Just as I intend to kill Dandy Jack," Fallon said calmly. "There's a packet of cigarettes in my left-hand jacket pocket, by the way. Light me one, will you, like a good girl?"

She seemed stunned by the enormity of what he had said but did as she was told. She put a cigarette in his mouth and as she struck a match, Donner joined them. He was carrying a tartan bag in one hand and squatted down in front of Fallon and unzipped it. One by one he produced three bottles of Irish whiskey and placed them on the ground.

"Jameson," Fallon said. "My favorite. How did you guess?"

"And all for you," Donner told him. "All three bottles."

"I must say it sounds like an interesting idea," Fallon said. "Tell me more."

"Why not?" Donner said. "Actually, it's very good. I think you'll like it. You see, we have three problems, Fallon. The priest and his niece, because they know more than what's good for them."

"And me?" Fallon said.

"Exactly." Donner helped himself to a cigarette. "Anyway, Mr. Meehan had this rather nice idea. It's beautifully simple. We get rid of da Costa and his niece and put the blame on you."

"I see," said Fallon. "And just how do you propose to do that?"

"You were a big man with a bomb in your hand over there in Ulster, weren't you? So it would make sense if you used the same method when you wanted to knock someone off over here."

"My God," Jenny said.

Donner ignored her and he was obviously enjoying himself. He said, "Evening Mass at Holy Name is at six o'clock. When it's over, Mr. Meehan and Bonati will pick up Father da Costa and his niece and take 'em up that tower, together with about twenty pounds of plastic gelignite and a chemical fuse packed in a Waverley biscuit tin. When that little lot goes up, they go with it and the church comes down."

"I see," Fallon said. "And me—what about me?"

"That's easy. Bonati drives out here in da Costa's Mini van. You get three bottles of Irish whiskey poured down your throat, we put you behind the wheel and send you for a drive. There's a hill called Cullen's Bend about three miles from here. A terrible place for accidents."

"And you think that will wrap things up?" Fallon asked him.

"As neat as a Christmas parcel. When they check what's left of that van they'll find bomb-making equipment and a few sticks of gelignite from the same batch the church bomb was manufactured from, not to mention the gun that was used to kill Krasko. The forensic boys will have a field day and let's face it—the Special Branch and Intelligence have been after you for years. They'll be delighted."

"Miller won't buy it for a second," Fallon said. "He knows Meehan was behind the Krasko killing."

"Perhaps he does, but there won't be a thing he can do about it."

Jenny said in a whisper, "It's murder. Cold-blooded murder. You can't do it."

"Shut your mouth!" Donner said.

She backed away fearfully and then she noticed an extraordinary thing. Fallon's eyes seemed to have changed color slightly, the dark flecked with light, and when he looked up at her there was a power in him that was almost physical, a new authority.

Somehow it was as if he had been asleep and was now awake. He glanced across at the other two. Harry was examining the old cart, his back to them, and Rupert stood beside the stove, fingering the shotgun.

"That's it, then?" he said softly.

Donner shook his head in mock sorrow. "You should have stayed back home in the bogs, Fallon. You're out of your league."

"So it would appear," Fallon said.

Donner leaned across to help himself to another cigarette. Fallon got both hands to the butt of the Browning he had taped so carefully to the inside of his leg above the ankle, tore it free and shot Donner through the heart at point blank range.

The force of the shot lifted Donner off his feet, slamming him back against the ground, and in the same instant Fallon shot Harry in the back before he could turn, the bullet shattering his spine, driving him head first into the cart.

And as Jenny screamed, Fallon knocked her sideways, on his feet now, the Browning arcing towards Rupert as he turned in alarm, already too late, still clutching the shotgun in both hands.

His mouth opened in a soundless scream as Fallon's third bullet caught him squarely in the forehead. Blood and brains sprayed across the grey stones as the skull disintegrated and Rupert was knocked back against the wall, his finger tightening convulsively on the trigger of the shotgun in death, discharging both barrels.

Jenny sprawled protectively across the child, still deep in her drugged sleep. There was silence. She looked up fearfully and saw that Fallon was standing quite still, legs apart, perfectly balanced, the Browning held out in front of him in both hands. His face was very white, wiped clean of all expression, the eyes dark.

His right sleeve was torn and blood dripped to the floor. She got to her feet unsteadily. "You're hurt."

He didn't seem to hear her, but walked to the cart where Harry sprawled on his face and stirred him with his foot. Then he crossed to Rupert.

Jenny moved to join him. "Is he dead?" she whispered, and then she saw the back of the skull and turned away, stomach heaving, clutching at the wall to steady herself.

When she turned again, Fallon was on his knees beside Donner, fumbling in the dead man's breast pocket. He found the key he was looking for and stood up.

"Get me out of these things."

The stench of that butcher's shop filled her nostrils, seeped into her very brain, and when she walked towards him, dazed and frightened, she stumbled and almost fell down.

He grabbed her by one arm and held her up. "Steady, girl. Don't let go now. I need you."

"I'm fine," she said. "Really I am."

She unlocked the handcuffs. Fallon threw them to one side, dropped to one knee again and took the buff envelope from Donner's inside pocket.

As he stood up, Jenny said wearily, "You'd better let me have a look at that arm."

"All right," Fallon said.

He took off his jacket and sat on the edge of the bed, smoking a cigarette while she did what she could for him.

The arm was a mess. Three or four nasty wounds where steel buckshot had ripped into the flesh. She bandaged it as best she could, with the handkerchief from Donner's breast pocket. Fallon picked up one of the bottles of Jameson, pulled the cork with his teeth and took a long swallow.

When she was finished, she sat on the bed beside him and looked around the barn. "How long did it take? Two, maybe three seconds?" She shivered. "What kind of man are you, Martin?"

Fallon pulled on his jacket awkwardly. "You heard Donner, didn't you? A little Mick out of his league, who should have stayed back home in the bogs."

"He was wrong, wasn't he?"

"Where I come from, he wouldn't have lasted a day," Fallon said dispassionately. "What time is it?"

She glanced at her watch. "Five-thirty."

"Good." He stood up and reached for his trenchcoat. "Evening Mass at Holy Name starts at six and finishes around seven. You take me there—now."

She helped him on with the trenchcoat. "The boat," she said. "The one you were supposed to leave on from Hull? I heard the name. Donner and Rupert were talking. You could still go."

"Without a passport?"

He turned, trying to belt his coat, awkwardly because of his wounded arm, and she did it for him.

"Money talks," she said. "And you've got plenty in that envelope."

She stood very close, her hands around his waist, looking up at him. Fallon said calmly, "And you'd like to come with me, I suppose?"

She shook her head. "You couldn't be more wrong. It's too late for me to change now. It was too late the day I started. It's you I'm thinking of. You're the only man I've ever known who gave me more than a quick tumble and the back of his hand."

Fallon stared at her somberly for a long moment and then said quietly, "Bring the child."

He walked to the door. Jenny picked up her daughter, wrapped her in a blanket and followed. When she went outside, he was standing, hands in pockets, staring up into the rain where brent geese passed overhead in a V formation.

He said quietly, "They're free and I'm not, Jenny. Can you understand that?"

When he took his right hand out of his pocket, blood dripped from the fingers. She said, "You need a doctor."

"I need Dandy Jack Meehan and no one else," he said. "Now let's get out of here." And he turned and led the way back along the track to the car.

580

15

The Wrath of God

Meehan was feeling pleased with himself, in spite of his broken nose, as he and Bonati walked past the town hall. Pleased and excited. His Homburg was set at a jaunty angle, the collar of his double-breasted melton overcoat was turned up against the wind, and he carried a canvas holdall containing the bomb in his right hand.

"I know one thing," he said to Bonati as they crossed the road. "I'd like to know where our Billy is right now. I'll have the backside off him for this when I see him."

"You know what it's like for these young lads when they get with a bird, Mr. Meehan," Bonati said soothingly. "He'll turn up."

"Bloody little tarts," Meehan said in disgust. "All that lad ever thinks of is his cock-end."

He turned the corner into Rockingham Street and received his first shock when he heard the organ playing at Holy Name and voices raised in song.

He dodged into a doorway out of the rain and said to Bonati, "What in the hell goes on here. Evening Mass starts at six. I only make it ten to."

581

"Search me, Mr. Meehan."

They crossed the street, heads down in a flurry of rain, and paused at the notice board. Bonati peered up, reading it aloud. "Evening Mass, six o'clock, Saturdays, five-thirty."

Meehan swore softly. "A bloody good job we were early. Come on, let's get inside."

It was cold in the church and damp, and the smell of the candles was very distinctive. There were only a dozen people in the congregation. Father da Costa was up at the altar praying and on the other side of the green baize curtain, Meehan could see Anna da Costa's head as she played the organ.

He and Bonati sat down at one side, partially hidden by a pillar, and he put the canvas holdall between his feet. It was really quite pleasant sitting there in the half-darkness, Meehan decided, with the candles flickering and the organ playing. The four acolytes in their scarlet cassocks and white cottas reminded him nostalgically of his youth. Strangest thing of all, he found that he could remember some of the responses.

"I confess to Almighty God, and to you, my brothers and sisters," said Father da Costa, "that I have sinned through my own fault."

He struck his breast, and Meehan joined in enthusiastically, asking blessed Mary ever Virgin, all the angels and saints and the rest of the congregation to pray for him to the Lord our God.

As they all stood for the next hymn it suddenly struck him, with something like surprise, that he was thoroughly enjoying himself.

As the Cooper went over a humped-back bridge, Fallon, who had been sitting with his head forward on his chest, sat up with a start.

"Are you all right?" Jenny asked him anxiously.

He touched his right arm gingerly. The shock effects were wearing off now and it was beginning to hurt like hell. He winced and Jenny noticed at once.

"I think I should take you straight to the Infirmary."

He ignored the remark and turned to look at the child who lay on the back seat, still in her drugged sleep, wrapped in the blanket in which Jenny had carried from the mill.

"She's a nice kid," he said.

The road was dangerous now in the heavy rain as darkness fell and needed all her attention, yet there was something in his voice that caused her to glance wearily at him.

He lit a cigarette one-handed and leaned back against the seat. "I'd like you to know something," he said. "What Donner said back there about me being bomb-happy wasn't true. Those kids in that school bus—it was an accident. They walked into an ambush we'd laid for a Saracen armored car. It was a mistake."

He hammered his clenched fist against his right knee in a kind of frenzy.

"I know," Jenny told him. "I understand."

"That's good, that's marvellous," he said. "Because I never have."

The agony in his voice was more than she could bear and she concentrated on the road, tears in her eyes.

As the congregation moved out, Anna continued to play and Father da Costa went into the sacristy with the acolytes. He took off his cope as the boys got out of their cassocks and into their street clothes. He saw them out of the side door, bidding each one of them good night.

Anna was still playing, something more powerful now, which meant that the last of the congregation had left. She always seemed to sense that moment. It was Bach again from the sound of it. The piece Fallon had played. She stopped abruptly. Father da Costa paused in the act of pulling off his alb, but she did not start playing again. He frowned, opened the sacristy door and went into the church.

Anna was standing at the altar rail and Jack Meehan was holding her firmly by the arm. Father da Costa took an angry step forward and Bonati moved from behind a pillar holding a Luger in his left hand.

It stopped Father da Costa dead in his tracks and Meehan smiled. "That's better. Now we're all going to take a little ride in the cage up to the catwalk. There's only room for two at a time so we'll have to split up. I'll stick with the girl, you go with Bonati, Father, and remember one thing. Anything you try that's the slightest bit out of turn will be reflected in the girl's treatment, so keep your hands to yourself and don't try any rough stuff."

"All right, Meehan," Father da Costa said. "What do you want with me?"

"All in good time." Meehan pushed Anna across to the hoist, opened the cage door and followed her inside. As they started to rise he looked out at Father da Costa. "Remember what I told you," he said. "So don't try anything funny."

Father da Costa waited, the black, killing rage in him again and he fought to control it. What on earth did the man want? What was it all about? When the hoist descended again, he rushed inside eagerly and Bonati followed him and pressed the button.

When it jolted to a halt, Father da Costa opened the gate at once and stepped out. Meehan had switched the light on and the boards of the catwalk, wet with rain, glistened in the darkness.

Anna was standing, one hand on the rail, complete uncertainty on her face. Father da Costa took a step towards her and Meehan produced a Browning from his pocket. "Stay where you are!" He nodded to Bonati. "Tie his wrists together."

There was little that Father da Costa could do except comply and he put his arms behind him. Bonati lashed his wrists together quickly with a piece of thin twine.

"Now the girl," Meehan said.

Anna didn't say a word as Bonati repeated the performance. As he finished, her uncle moved to join her. "Are you all right?" he asked her in a low voice.

"I think so," she said. "What's going to happen to us?"

"I'm afraid you'll have to address that question to Mr. Meehan personally," he said. "I'm sure I don't know."

Meehan unzipped the holdall, slipped his hand inside and broke the detonating cap on the chemical fuse, then he zipped the bag up again and put it down casually at the side of the catwalk in the shadows.

"All right, Father, I'll tell you what I'm going to do with you. I'm going to leave you and your niece up here on your own for fifteen minutes to meditate. When I return, I hope to find you in a more reasonable frame of mind. If not, then . . ."

"But I don't understand," Father da Costa interrupted. "What on earth are you hoping to accomplish?"

At that moment, the organ in the church below broke into the opening bars of the Bach Prelude and Fugue in D major.

The astonishment on Meehan's face was something to see. "It's Fallon," he whispered.

"It can't be," Bonati said.

"Then who the hell am I listening to—a ghost playing?" Meehan's anger overflowed like white-hot lava. "Go and get him," he raved. "Bring the bastard up here. Tell him the girl gets it first if he doesn't come."

Bonati hurriedly stepped into the cage, closed the gate and started down. When he was halfway there, the organ stopped playing. The cage juddered to a halt. It was suddenly very quiet. He cocked the Luger, kicked the gate open and stepped out.

When the Cooper turned into Rockingham Street and pulled up opposite Holy Name, Fallon was leaning in the corner, eyes closed. At first Jenny thought he was unconscious, or at the very least asleep, but when she touched him gently he opened his eyes at once and smiled at her.

"Where are we?"

"Holy Name," she said.

He took a deep breath and straightened up. "Good girl." He put a hand inside his coat and produced the buff envelope and passed it across to her. "There's nearly two thousand pounds in there. The money I received from Jack Meehan on account, and hard earned. I won't need it where I'm going. Go off somewhere. Somewhere you've never even heard of. Take the kid with you and try again."

The envelope was slippery with blood as she examined it in the light from the instrument panel. "Oh my God," she said, and then she switched on the interior light and turned to look at him. "Oh, Martin," she said in horror. "There's blood all over you."

"It doesn't matter," he said, and he opened the car door.

She got out on her side. "He'll kill you," she said desperately. "You don't know him like I do. You don't stand a chance. Let me get the police. Let Mr. Miller handle him."

"God save us, but I've never asked a policeman for help in my life." A slight, ironic smile touched Fallon's mouth fleetingly. "Too late to start now." He patted her face gently. "You're a nice girl, Jenny. A lovely girl. It didn't touch you, any of it. Always believe that. Now get the hell out of it and God bless you."

He turned and crossed the road to Holy Name. Jenny got into the Cooper and started the engine. He was going to his death, she was convinced of that, and the compulsion to save him was something that she was unable to deny.

Suddenly, resolute, she drove round the corner, stopped at the first telephone-box she came to and dialed nine-nine-nine. When they put her through to the main switchboard at police headquarters, she asked for Detective Superintendent Miller.

There were still lights at the windows, but it was the absence of music that Fallon found puzzling until, gazing up at the noticeboard, he made the same discovery that Jack Meehan had about the time of evening Mass on a Saturday.

Panic moved inside him. Oh my God, he thought. I'm too late.

The door went back against the wall with a crash that echoed throughout the silent building, but the church was empty. Only

the eternal ruby light of the sanctuary lamp, the flickering candles, the Virgin smiling sadly down at him, Christ high on his
cross down there by the altar.

He ran along the center aisle and reached the hoist. The
cage was not there. They were still on top and he was conscious
of a fierce joy. He pressed the button to bring the cage down,
but nothing happened. He pressed it again with the same result.
Which meant that the cage was standing open up there.

He hammered his clenched fist against the wall in despair.
There had to be a way to bring Meehan down. There had to
be.

And there was, of course, and it was so beautifully simple
that he laughed out loud, his voice echoing up the nave as he
turned and moved towards the altar rail and went up through
the choir stalls.

He sat down on the organ stool, switched on and pulled out
an assortment of stops feverishly. There was blood on the keys,
but that didn't matter and he moved into the opening of the
Bach Prelude and Fugue in D Major. The glorious music
echoed between the walls as he gave it everything he had, ignoring the pain in his right hand and arm.

"Come on, you bastard!" he shouted aloud. "Let's be having
you."

He stopped playing and was immediately aware of the slight
clanging the cage made on its descent. He got up and went
down the steps through the choir stalls, drawing the Ceska from
his pocket and screwing the silencer into place with difficulty,
arriving at the correct vantage point as the cage reached ground
level.

Fallon flattened himself against the wall and waited, the Ceska
ready. The cage door was kicked open and Bonati stepped out,
clutching the Luger. Fallon shot him through the hand and
Bonati dropped the Luger with a sharp cry and turned to face
him.

"Meehan," Fallon said. "Is he up there?"

Bonati was shaking like a leaf in a storm, frightened out of his wits. He tried to speak, but could only manage to nod his head vigorously.

"All right." Fallon smiled, and Bonati saw that face again, a face to frighten the Devil. "Go home and change your ways."

Bonati needed no second bidding and ran up the aisle clutching his wrist. The door banged behind him, the candles fluttered. It was quiet again. Fallon moved into the cage and pressed the button to ascend.

On the catwalk, Meehan, Anna and Father da Costa waited, the rain falling in silver strands through the yellow light. The cage jerked to a halt, the door swung open. It was dark in there.

Meehan raised his Browning slightly. "Bonati?"

Fallon drifted out of the darkness, a pale ghost. "Hello, you bastard."

Meehan started to take aim and Father da Costa ducked low in spite of his bound hands and shouldered him to the rail, tripping him deftly so that Meehan fell heavily. The Browning skidded along the catwalk and Fallon kicked it into space.

He leaned against the rail for support, suddenly strangely tired, his arm really hurting now, and gestured with the Ceska. "All right, untie him."

Meehan did as he was told reluctantly and the moment he was free, Father da Costa untied Anna. He turned to Fallon, concern in his voice. "Are you all right?"

Fallon kept all his attention on Meehan. "The bomb? Have you set the fuse?"

"Get stuffed," Meehan told him.

"Bomb?" Father da Costa demanded.

"Yes," Fallon said. "Did he have a bag with him?"

"Over there," Father da Costa pointed to where the canvas holdall stood in the shadows.

"All right," Fallon said. "You'd better get Anna out of here fast and I mean out. If that thing goes off, it will bring the whole church down like a house of cards."

Father da Costa didn't even hesitate. He grabbed Anna by the arm and guided her towards the hoist, but she pulled free and turned towards Fallon. "Martin!" she cried, and caught at his trenchcoat. "We can't go without you."

"The cage only takes two at a time," he said. "Be sensible."

There was blood on her hand from his sleeve, and she held it close to her face as if trying to see it. "Oh my God," she whispered.

Father da Costa put an arm around her shoulders and said to Fallon, "You're hurt."

"You're running out of time," Fallon said patiently.

Father da Costa pushed Anna inside the cage and followed her in. As he pressed the button to descend he called through the bars. "I'll be back, Martin. Wait for me."

His voice was swallowed up by darkness and Fallon turned to Meehan and smiled. "You and me, Jack, at the final end of things. Isn't that something? We can go to hell together."

"You're mad," Meehan said. "I'm not waiting here to die. I'm going to get rid of this thing."

He moved towards the holdall, and Fallon raised the Ceska threateningly. "I've had experience, remember? At this stage it'll go up at the slightest touch." He chuckled. "I'll tell you what we'll do. We'll leave it with God. If the cage gets back in time, we leave. If not . . ."

"You raving bloody lunatic." Meehan was shouting now.

Fallon said calmly, "By the way, I've just remembered I've got something for you." He produced a crumpled white card with a black border and held it out.

Meehan said, "What in hell is that supposed to be?"

"A Rest-in-Peace card, isn't that what you call them? It's for Billy. Plot number five hundred and eighty-two at Pine Trees."

Meehan seemed stunned. "You're lying."

Fallon shook his head. "I killed him last night because he tried to rape Anna da Costa. I took him up to the crematorium and put him through the whole process, just like you showed me. Last I saw of your brother, he was five pounds of grey ash scattered across damp grass."

Meehan seemed to break into a thousand pieces. "Billy!" he screamed and went for Fallon, head down.

Fallon pulled the trigger of the Ceska. There was a dull click and then Meehan was on him, smashing him back against the guard rail. It splintered, sagged, then gave way and Fallon went over the edge into space. He hit the canvas tarpaulin stretched over the hole in the roof and went straight through.

Meehan turned and reached for the holdall. As he picked it up and turned to throw it out into the darkness, it exploded.

As Father da Costa and Anna went out of the door into the street, two police cars arrived at speed. Miller scrambled out of the first one and hurried towards them. As he put a foot on the first step leading up to the porch, the bomb exploded.

The effect was extraordinary, for the whole church started to fall in, almost in slow motion, first the tower, the steel scaffolding crumpling around it, and then the roof.

Miller grabbed Anna's other arm, and he and Father da Costa ran her down into the safety of the street between them. As they reached the cars, a scaffolding pole rebounded from the wall of the warehouse above their heads and everyone ducked.

Father da Costa was first on his feet and stood, fists clenched, gazing up at the church. As the dust cleared, he saw that most of the walls and the rear entrance porch were still standing.

A young constable came forward from one of the police cars holding a spot lamp, and Father da Costa simply took it from him and turned to Miller. "I'm going back in."

He started forward, and Miller grabbed him by the arm. "You must be crazy."

"Fallon was in there," Father da Costa said. "He saved us, don't you understand? He might still be alive. I must know."

"Fallon?" Miller said in astonishment. "My God, so it was Fallon all the time."

Father da Costa hurried up the steps to the porch and pushed open the door. The scene inside was incredible. Holy Name was finished; at the end of things at last, but the worst damage was by the tower or what was left of it.

Father da Costa went up the central aisle, flashing the spot before him. The area in front of the altar where the tower and roof had come down together was a mountain of bricks and mortar.

The spot picked out something inside. It could have been a face, he wasn't sure. There seemed to be a tunnel of sorts. He got down on his hands and knees and started to crawl through, holding the spot before him.

He found Fallon at the end of the tunnel, only his head and shoulders exposed. The figure of Christ on the cross, the large one which had stood by the altar, had fallen across him protectingly, at least for the moment.

Father da Costa crouched beside him, and the great cross sagged under the weight it was holding. Dust descended on his head.

"Martin?" he said. "Can you hear me?"

There was a scraping sound behind him as Miller arrived. "For God's sake, Father," he said. "We must get out of here. The whole damn lot might come down at any moment."

Father da Costa ignored him. "Martin?"

Fallon opened his eyes. "Did you get Anna out?"

"I did, Martin."

"That's all right, then. I'm sorry. Sorry for everything."

The cross sagged a little more, stones and rubble cascaded over Father da Costa's back, and he leaned across Fallon to protect him.

"Martin," he said. "Can you hear me?" Fallon opened his eyes. "I want you to make an act of contrition. Say after me: 'My God, Who are infinitely good in Thyself . . .'"

"Oh my God," Martin Fallon said, and died.

There was a long silence. Even that mass of rubble and debris seemed to have stopped moving. For some strange reason Miller suddenly felt as if he didn't belong, as if he had no right to be there. He turned and started to crawl out.

Behind him, Father Michael da Costa got down on his knees, head bowed beneath that frail roof, and started to pray for the soul of the man who had called himself Martin Fallon.